I0676493

Splice

The Perigalacticon Series Book 2

Sara Judson Brown

Copyrobot Publishing

ISBN (ebook) 978-0-578-36863-4

ISBN (print) 978-0-578-36862-7

Cover design by: Original Syn
Edited by Rebecca Hodgkins Editing
Printed in the United States of America

To all my early readers who enthusiastically embraced my characters and kept asking me when the next book was coming out. And to my family for their understanding and support when I was lost in thought, daydreaming about the universe in my head.

CONTENTS

ONE

JEREMIAH BRINK

The people had become violent savages upon the land—murdering and making war wherever they went—so the gods saw fit to put a heavy weight upon their backs. If the burden could be made great enough, the load might temper the beast. The people repented and bowed under the yoke. They cried out to the universe and all of creation, "Cursed are we and we will serve until the gods see fit to release us from our labors."

- Ancient Andarrian Text

"I am the Reverend Jeremiah Brink and I have a special message for you."

The reverberation of an enormous fart shredded the quiet evening. The sound was so loud that Montressador Sean Chapman jumped and skidded on the footpath, his hand instinctively reaching for the hilt of his sword. One moment he'd been walking through Palladium Beta's Capital City Park enjoying the songs of crickets and nightjars, and the next...

Well, Sean wasn't sure what this moment was, but he knew for certain the sound he heard had not been a cricket.

A burst of laughter came from behind the hedge-row. Sean arched one dark brow and listened. A symphony of burps, interspersed with giggles and more sounds of hysterics, continued its nocturnal assault from the other side of the thick foliage. Sean released the grip on his sword. Whatever the joke was, he didn't seem to be the subject or the punchline. He crept silently around the hedge that ran alongside the path.

A group of students—Sean guessed, from the jackets and caps with school insignias—huddled in the light of a park transport shelter and stared intently at one of the digital information screens. The grotesque noises coming from the display continued and took on the well-known melody of *The Vicar's Wife*, a popular university drinking song. The oom-pah-pah chorus sent the group into more howls of laughter.

Sean stood a short distance behind the students, arms crossed, and gathered all the authority his office could muster before loudly clearing his throat. "Ahem."

A tall angular boy in the back of the group glanced over his shoulder then turned wide-eyed and stared openly at the swordsman. The boy's throat bobbed in a hard swallow. He nudged a female student with shocking pink hair who locked eyes with Montressador Chapman and swore loudly just as the information screen repeated its opening line and the symphony began again. *"I am the Reverend Jeremiah Brink and I have a special message for you."*

Word spread through hurried whispers and jabs. One by one the students turned, and Sean caught them in his gaze. When the last of the group faced him, he spoke.

"Which one of you is responsible for this...night music?" A loud belch from the screen hung in the air along with Sean's question.

The students shuffled nervously and parted a fraction. A teenager, wearing an oversized jacket and cap standing closest to the display, glanced around helplessly at his companions and stepped forward.

"Montressador Chapman..." The student lifted his chin. His expression of angst changed to resigned acceptance. "I did it. I hacked into the program." The tune of *The Vicar's Wife* played from the screen on the wall behind.

Sean kept his eyes firmly on the young man's face as the song sped merrily to its lusty chorus. He did his best to restrain the mirth building at the corners of his mouth. "Why?"

The boy frowned then burst with anger. "Brink had a lot of nerve putting up his display so close to your museum. We had to do something!" The other students muttered and nodded in agreement.

Sean held up a hand for silence. "First—the National Museum is not *my* museum. Second—Reverend Brink had permission from the Park Conservancy to put up the display, and, regardless of your personal feelings, you had no right to tamper with the reverend's message."

The students protested en masse, coming to the aid of their friend. Sean silenced their objections with a sharp gesture.

"Fix it!"

The boy's countenance fell at the command. "I...I can't. I deleted the original and I can't hack into the existing program without uploading a new one."

Sean sighed and scratched his beard in thought. Shutting down the display screen would be impossible without access to the power source. It looked like the reverend would be farting and burping till morning.

"I should report you all to the Park Conservancy." He paused to let the thought sink in. The students shuffled their feet and glanced at each other with contrite faces. "Go home."

The group scattered like a flock of birds. Sean listened to the sound of their running feet then looked back to the digital display. He would ask his assistant, Josephine, to report the vandalism to the conservancy in the morning.

The screen continued its loop. Jeremiah Brink's silver-haired image appeared. *"I am the Reverend Jeremiah Brink and I have a special message for you."* Sean watched as the image of the reverend dropped his trousers, mooning the viewer and blowing a loud fart. The mirth Sean had held in check finally had nowhere else to go. He threw his head back and laughed.

TWO

TRADITION

Sean left the flatulent Reverend Brink and continued along the footpath. The detour at the transport shelter had taken longer than planned, so he picked up the pace to make up for lost time.

Lamps alongside the path illuminated his route through the trees like white squares on a chessboard. The night air breathed crisp and clear. In the distance, the icy towers of Palladium Beta glittered, framing the green expanse of the park. Andarria's capital city winked and smiled like a show girl, preening before an audience.

The only thing that shone on Sean was the large sword strapped to his side. The weapon served as a constant companion and a lethal reminder to all of his office. Instead of his uniform, he wore an open-collared work shirt and a pair of plain trousers for the evening jaunt. A dark, clipped beard accentuated his profile. He was a man in his prime with a confident stride that matched his responsibilities—old enough to have left impetuous youth, but still young enough to be reckless when it suited him.

Sean's thoughts returned to his earlier conversation with Agent Fionna Knox as he walked. Fionna had sounded anxious when she contacted him on the comm. She refused to explain and simply asked that he meet her at the National Museum.

"Odd place for a rendezvous," Sean had said, hoping to needle the ministry agent. Fionna offered him few opportunities these days. "Wouldn't you rather get a drink somewhere?"

The agent's brief pause before responding was the equivalent of an agitated sigh. "Montressador Chapman, please come as soon as you can. Use the back entrance of the East Wing of the Main Hall. Someone will let you in."

Sean frowned and drummed his fingers on the hilt of his sword. The Montressador's Hall was in the East Wing. The exhibit boasted an eon of Andarrian history. Priceless artifacts told the story of his predecessors. He hadn't visited the hall in several months. While Sean enjoyed walking the gallery, the visits always made him wonder how long it would be until the museum curator made him a permanent part of the exhibit.

Sean crossed the museum's wide east lawn and knocked on a rear service entrance. The squeal of the bolt came a second later and the door pushed open. White light spilled from the widening gap, brightening the smooth brown face of a girl with eyes the color of blue-green water.

Sean blinked in surprise and smiled. "Sydra, what

are you doing here so late?"

Clepsydra, the museum curator's thirteen-year-old daughter, grinned at Montressador Chapman. Black hair drifted down to her shoulders. The hem of her dress hung past her knees. The teenager finished pushing open the door and held it in place with one arm to allow passage inside, a light wand in the other.

"Father is busy with Agent Knox. He asked me to let you in."

Sean stepped through the doorway and into the radiance of the girl's light wand. "You are very brave. The museum can be spooky at night."

"I *wanted* to come. You haven't visited us in so long," Clepsydra said.

The girl turned and walked back down the aisle, almost bumping into the corner of the glass case that displayed the desiccated remains of Montressador Jabiru the Mute. She danced away from the exhibit with a yelp after a nervous glance at the wrapped figure inside. Sean chuckled. Clepsydra looked back and caught him smirking.

"I'm NOT scared!"

The teen punctuated the statement with a stamp of a foot, but her frown turned into a reluctant grin a second after her heel struck the floor.

Sean laughed and waved his hands in mock surrender. "Okay, okay! You're fearless! Sydra the Lionhearted!"

Clepsydra lifted her chin with a pleased expression. "That's better!" She continued down the middle of the aisle, light wand held high. "This way and try to keep up else I'll leave you in the dark with your dead friend."

"I could just turn on the gallery lights, you know. I do know how to operate a light switch," Sean said with a sly glance to the teen. He expected another playful riposte and was surprised to see a shade of worry pass over Sydra's expression before she answered.

"Father said the overhead lights would attract too much attention from the outside. He doesn't want people to worry."

The reply was given with indifference, but Sean noticed a slight quickening in the girl's steps as she weaved through the hall. He frowned and lengthened his stride.

Montressador Hall was a maze of galleries and smaller antechambers that branched off in all directions. The Montressador line—the King's Champion—dated back to Andarria's earliest records. Sean recognized many of the exhibits as they hurried through the hall—a painting of the Battle of Tilia; the dented armor of Impero the Red; and the chair where Fregoli the Paranoid was murdered by his valet, the gash in the back of the seat dark and ragged like an open wound. And then there were the official portraits. Long-ago Montressadors stared from gilded frames. The swords of the fallen heroes hung underneath each picture along with a brass plaque. Sean felt the eyes of the dead following him and he gripped the hilt of his sword as he passed.

Most of the champions honored in the hall served the Andarrian monarchy of their time, but the royal line was dead and buried for two millennia. Sean always thought it strange how the bones of the monarchy had crumbled to dust, much in the same way as the severed limbs of Montressador Jabiru, but inexplicably the tradition of the King's Champion lived on.

Clepsydra led Sean to a small forgotten alcove at one end of the great hall. The official seal of the Doge of Erna adorned the interior chamber door. Sean's curiosity twitched again. The events surrounding the Doge were already a riddle. If Fionna's mysterious message connected somehow...

Clepsydra pushed open the brass door, and gallery lights from the chamber flooded the alcove. Sean blinked and stepped inside. The round windowless room was small by gallery standards. A few modest displays decorated the walls. At the far end, two forensic technicians and their equipment sat idle in front of the Doge's portrait. Nearby, Mr. Gimirri, the museum's curator, stood with Agent Fionna Knox deep in conversation. Sean thought the curator looked even more agitated than usual in his formal blue cassock.

Fionna, Sean noted with some pleasure, was not dressed in the usual conservative jacket and trousers of a Ministry of Investigations agent. The black and silver brocade gown she wore hugged curves that Sean had wondered about but had never actually had the privilege of seeing. The agent's blond hair was pinned at the base of her neck in a delicate knot, nestled like a bird between her bare shoulders. Sean's mind wandered—emotions playing tug of war with deeper urges. Clearly, Fionna had been enjoying a night out on the town prior to coming to the museum. *But with whom?* Sean felt a twinge of discontentment—he refused to call it jealousy. Fionna turned to speak to Gimirri, and Sean saw the glint from the bio-vision glasses she sometimes wore. The glasses assisted Fionna in her investigations by reading bio-rhythms and helped her to interpret the emotions of interview subjects, but they were far from perfect. An ill-fated kiss loomed in Sean's memory. He instinctively stuffed all of his emotions into a locked drawer in his subconscious, kept for just such an occasion, and turned his attention to the Doge's portrait.

The floor-to-ceiling curtain that usually covered the enormous painting had been pulled to one side. The image of Montressador Livonia Syrovar, the Doge of Erna, looked down from her lofty perch and surveyed the room with dark eyes. Ash blond hair lay windswept across her shoulders and blended into the gray of her chain mail. A dark purple tunic covered the Doge's hips and flowed down to her knees. One hand rested lightly on the hilt of a sword. The opposite foot rested on a rock in a traditional warrior pose. Anyone viewing the painting would agree—the warrior was beautiful...and dangerous. Only one feature bothered Sean about the Doge's portrait. A slight twist in the line of the dark red mouth hinted at cruelty. This detail seemed unnecessary, more political commentary than artistic license. Sean's eyes widened at the two empty metal brackets underneath the portrait where Syrovar's sword should have been displayed.

"You took your time."

Sean turned and saw Fionna watching him through the yellow tint of her glasses. Twin strands of blond hair framed the agent's face and gently curled. Sean's pulse quickened briefly before he could master his emotions again. Her figure-hugging dress was just as intriguing from the front. Sean shrugged, careful to keep his eyes on the agent's face rather than let his gaze drift below the line of her chin.

"You said to come as soon as I could." Sean nodded toward the empty sword brackets. "What do you need me for anyway? You're the investigator. Doesn't sword theft fall under your job description?"

Fionna replied with a hint of a smile. "Mr. Gimirri requested your presence."

Sean looked to the curator, confused. Gimirri stepped forward and cleared his throat.

"Montressador Chapman, the Ministry of Investigations has requested access to the National Museum's visual archive and security systems; the right to use investigative equipment within the walls of the museum; and if need be, examine and possibly handle museum artifacts. As the current Montressador, you must give consent in person to the representative of the National Museum who will then grant the Ministry's requests. Do I have your consent?"

Sean's brows shot upward in genuine surprise. "You need my *permission?*"

"Yes."

"To begin an investigation into the theft of museum property?"

"Yes."

Sean blinked at the absurdity. "That's crazy."

Gimirri stiffened. "It's *tradition.*"

Sean nodded, suddenly grasping the situation. The hardest known substance in the universe, impervious to logic and nearly impossible to crack, was Andarrian Tradition. He eyed the prim curator for a moment and adjusted his sword belt.

"You called the Ministry when you discovered the theft?"

The curator smiled respectfully and gestured to Fionna. "Yes, but I assumed Agent Knox was aware we needed your consent before she could begin the investigation."

"The Ministry of Investigations doesn't specialize in ancient customs," Sean said. "Even I had no idea my responsibilities extended to the National Museum."

"Only regarding artifacts within Montressador Hall," Gimirri said. "I guess I can see why you were unaware. The last time we required permission from a Montressador was six hundred years ago."

Sean tilted his head inquisitively. "Did someone need to take a piss?"

The curator gave Sean a sour look. "Ah, your little jokes are so amusing. I never grow tired of them," Gimirri said with a sniff. "I assume we have your permission to begin the investigation?"

Sean waved his hands frantically, his patience finally cracking. "Yes! Yes! By all means!"

Gimirri nodded and handed Sean a piece of yellowed parchment and a feathered quill. Sean glanced at the plumage of the antique pen and rolled his eyes heavenward before signing.

Satisfied, the curator retrieved the document and quill without comment and turned to Fionna with a tight smile. "You may proceed, Agent Knox. I'll be in my office if you need me. Come along, Clepsydra." Gimirri and his daughter left the chamber, closing the brass door behind them.

Fionna stepped away to give a quick word to the techs who then hurried to unpack the equipment.

"Thank you," Fionna said to Sean when she returned. "I'm sorry you had to come down here. I would have told you Gimirri needed your signature, but I thought..."

"It's all right," Sean said, letting go of his irritation. The truth was had he known it was Gimirri and not Fionna that requested his presence, he probably would have found a way to delay even longer. "Have you been able to find out anything at all?"

"Not much. I've only been able to secure the scene and ask a few preliminary questions," Fionna said, checking notes on a digital pad. "Gimirri gave me a description of the sword and a picture."

Sean rattled off the details from memory. "Hunting sword with a twenty-seven-inch straight blade. Grip of carved tarpon horn. One-shot brass barreled pistol mounted on the right ricasso—trigger located below the clamshell languet. Raised grape leaf design on the guard representing the city of Erna. Leather scabbard with silver trim."

Fionna followed along in her notes and looked up impressed. "You have a head for details."

Sean grinned and gave a quick bow. "Montressador Chapman, at your service." Fionna chuckled. He lifted one shoulder in a half shrug. "I remember swords. Occupational hazard."

Fionna returned to her notes. "A cleaning crew discovered the sword was missing about nine this evening when they pulled back the curtain to dust, but before that the last time the sword was seen was two days ago during an evening tour." She scribbled a note with her stylus. "I'll talk to the rest of the museum staff tomorrow to see if anyone else saw the sword."

"The staff has strict instructions the curtain is not to be removed during the day, but that's not to say it wasn't."

Fionna looked up at the painting. "If the Doge's portrait hadn't been cloaked, the museum would have realized the sword was missing much sooner. I've never heard of a Montressador's official portrait being kept under a curtain."

"The Doge's portrait is cloaked because she disgraced the office," Sean said, glancing at the agent.

"You don't know the story?"

"Not really. Gimirri said Syrovar murdered a nobleman or something—"

"Ten."

Fionna looked at Sean, eyes wide.

"All in one night. Cut their heads off while they slept."

"Why?"

Sean shrugged. "Syrovar never said. Raved like a lunatic all through the trial. She was convicted and put to death."

Fionna frowned. "If she was a murderer, then why have her picture here at all?"

"However badly her life ended, Livonia Syrovar was still a Montressador and served faithfully as the leader of her city," Sean said, looking up at the portrait. "Her early career was very promising. Did you know Syrovar never served in the Royal Guard? After Montressador Glamorgon of the Vale died, King Haakon appointed Syrovar directly to the Montressador's office."

The agent's eyes brightened. "That's why people still refer to her as the Doge of Erna."

Sean nodded. "Syrovar had already proven herself defending Erna. From what I've read, she was seen as a loyal supporter of the throne without question right up until the night of the murders. Syrovar's behavior during the trial and her execution changed all that. People quickly forgot her achievements and now she's only remembered as a lunatic and a traitor." Sean sighed. "Even her title is a curse. Now, if you refer to someone as 'the Doge' you are implying a public fall from grace."

Fionna looked thoughtfully at Sean through her bio-vision glasses. "You feel sorry for her."

Sean continued to look at the Doge's portrait, still irritated by the artist's interpretation. On closer examination, the rock Syrovar's foot rested on held a vague resemblance to a skull. He frowned. "No. But I acknowledge Syrovar's achievements along with her failings out of respect for the office...more so than the artist who painted this picture did." *A life's work reduced to a single image on canvas.*

Sean stepped back to allow a tech carrying a metal tripod and a pair of chronoculars to pass. He pulled his thoughts away from the painting and looked at Fionna. "Back to more important matters. Who steals an antique sword and why?"

"I think we're dealing with the black market," Fionna said, flipping to a new screen on the digital pad. "There are swords all over the gallery. Nothing else was taken. The thief wanted *this* sword. Maybe for a private collector."

"A very *particular* private collector," Sean said, nodding in agreement. "How much do you know about black market antiquities?"

"Not much but I'm a quick study." Fionna's eyes skimmed Syrovar's portrait. "My hunch is the buyer is someone off-world. The sword would be too recognizable to keep on Andarria. I'll start sweeps at the shuttleports, but there's a good chance the thief is already long gone with as much as a two-day head start." Fionna made another note in the digital pad and shrugged. "Gimirri mentioned there's a group of Luctari protestors that have been in the park over the last few weeks. I'll talk to them and see if they saw anything. I'll need reinforcements to track the sword off world if it comes to that. Do you think Special Forces would help?"

"Possible. I'm not sure it falls into a time jumper's job description, but Special Forces would be the best equipped to track off-world," Sean said, drumming fingers on the hilt of his sword. "I'll send a message to Commander Garin. As long as there are no First Law violations or Cox's Conundrum, it should be a good training mission. I'll appeal to Garin's sense of national pride."

Fionna tucked the digital pad under an arm. "That reminds me. How's Anaya doing?"

"Very well. She'll be back on Andarria tomorrow. She's staying with me for a few days while she attends some lectures. She's hoping to be assigned to a mission soon."

Sean's younger sister Anaya, or Ann as she preferred to be called since her accident onboard the *Kairos*, lived off-world on the Colonies. Ann had recently begun attending lectures at the Academy on Andarria with the hopes of returning to active duty soon.

"Maybe you could put a bug in Commander Garin's ear and tell him to hurry up and assign Ann a mission." Sean shot Fionna a doubtful look. Fionna shrugged. "It couldn't hurt."

"If my sister found out I had used my influence to help get her an assignment, it would most definitely indeed *hurt*."

The technicians' investigation would take several hours, so Fionna walked with Sean back through Montressador's Hall to the rear service door. She held up a light wand and examined the portraits and swords that lined the walls as they passed. Sean's own weapon clanked at his side, echoing off the marble columns.

"I just realized something," Fionna said, pausing briefly to read a brass plaque on the wall. "A lot of the Montressadors name their swords."

"A lot of them wore fur capes and tights too," Sean said. "What's your point?"

"How come you haven't named your sword?"

Sean frowned, feeling the prickle of an old burr. "Because it's childish. A sword is a thing. It's a tool —not a person. It's my sword, my weapon, my blade. It's not a pet. It doesn't need a name."

"I thought it was tradition."

"No. It's not," Sean said, irritation growing. "They didn't *all* name them. When they did, it was usually because they won a significant battle, or after they killed their first dragon or something," he said, gesturing to the portrait of Eric the Hunchback. "Look, in case you haven't noticed, a Montressador hasn't led troops into battle for at least five hundred years and there's been a distinct shortage of dragons for the last thousand."

Fionna stopped and held the light wand up to see Sean's face. Her eyes narrowed from behind the bio-vision glasses.

Just because you can't think of a *good* name doesn't mean you shouldn't give it a name at all."

Sean gave Fionna a flat stare. He snatched the light wand from the agent's hand and continued through the gallery. Fionna's laughter bubbled behind him.

"Ha! I was right! You can't think of a name!"

Sean gritted his teeth and muttered, "Damn those glasses."

THREE

INELUCTABILIS

"ONE MINUTE, LIEUTENANT!" The portal master's voice boomed through the corridor.

Lieutenant Anaya Chapman stood trapped behind a wall of prep school students at the security entrance, a solitary figure in blue fatigues pushing through a mass of brown uniforms. She was almost through the scrum when the space between bodies closed again, trapping the satchel on her shoulder between two burly undergrads. Ann elbowed the taller of the two in the back.

"Hey, watch it!"

"Then make a hole, Day Tripper!" Ann glared up at him, leaned forward, and tugged.

Surprised, the undergrad took a step backward. Ann pulled through the breach, stumbled, and sprinted past the remaining students toward the portal steps. Hoots and hollers from the younger underclassmen urged her on.

"30 SECONDS TO CLOSURE!"

Ann gritted her teeth and ran past the portal

master's station, heart pounding. The clock on the wall ticked away the seconds. Once the portal closed, it wouldn't reopen again for eight hours and by then she would have missed a full day of lectures. Ann raced up the last few steps toward the shimmering blue oval, her braid bobbing along behind. *Just a few more feet...*

"MIND THE GAP!"

One...two...THREE!

Ann took three bounding steps then leapt toward the portal, timing the jump so both feet left the ground before intersecting with the gate. Any contact with the ground would mean the jump would fail...painfully. Ann felt her lead foot break the pool's surface. A tingling sensation, like a swarm of bees, covered and quickly spread as momentum carried her into the pool. Ann closed her eyes just before her head broke the surface. Other time jumpers told of the grandeur and beauty inside the portal, the very fabric of the universe itself, but majesty meant nothing if vertigo made you lose your breakfast. Ann's body stretched. The snatch and jerk of portal forces pulled her through a corkscrew of terror. No matter how many times she used the gate, Ann always felt like her stomach tried to crawl up and hide behind her rib cage.

An instant later, Ann's foot broke through the other side of the portal. She opened her eyes. A blue shimmer distorted her vision then cleared as she exited the gate. The ground met her feet. She took a few extra steps and slowed to a stop. Ann looked over a shoulder and blew out a breath. The iron doors of the gate advanced and closed over the blue oval with a clang. Laughter sounded from the portal master's station.

"You're cutting it mighty fine, Lieutenant!" Eddie, the academy's portal master, waved from the guard's walk. "Don't want to have to send out a search party for ya!"

"Not today, Eddie!" Ann waved with a grin and trotted down the walkway.

While the journey through the portal felt like only a few feet, Ann knew the jump had carried her ninety-seven million kilometers from her home on the Colonies to the capital city of Palladium Beta on the planet Andarria. The Weyl Gate was a natural connection between the two worlds, a remnant of an ancient time quake—or divine judgment—that allowed passage between the Colonies and Andarria. With her time jumper privileges restored, Ann could use the gate housed at the military prep school in Idlewild on the Colonies rather than take the fifteen-hour shuttle ride civilians used to reach Andarria. The gate, however, was not time travel, which meant Ann could still—she glanced at the clock on the academy's campanile—be late for class. Ann hitched up her knapsack and broke into a run.

***

"Come, come! All the way down to the front!"

Professor Huxley spread his arms and conducted the arriving students with quick-rolling hand gestures as he paced in front of the lectern.

"Form a tight group facing the podium. That's it! Plenty of room. Budge up a bit on this side if you please. Tall ones in the back." The white-haired professor kept his head bowed as he walked the dais, glancing up occasionally from under heavy brows to monitor the group's progress and direct students. "No, no, my dear. There will be no need to take notes. Please leave your notebook in one of the open seats."

Ann hurried down the steps into the lecture hall, past miles of empty rows, and dropped her satchel into an open aisle seat close to the front. Lines of nearly identical satchels took up the first three rows.

Ann pulled the keravnos implant from a pocket and deftly looped the black metal disc around an ear as she walked toward the dais. The disc chimed, sensing the power sources in the hall, and alerted a few nearby cadets. Ann ignored their curious stares and joined the group standing in front of the lectern. The implant sharpened the musical notes of the hall's electrical impulses already playing in her head and added layers of complex rhythms and harmonies from power sources beyond her current range of detection. Ann sighed. The familiar music, unnoticed by the other students around her, was a welcomed comfort. A year ago, a time-teleportation accident and the resulting time sickness had robbed Ann of memories along with the ability to sense power sources. With the help of the implant, she had almost regained full range of electroperception. Ann's memory slowly returned as well with only a few remaining gaps, so it came as a slight surprise

to Colonel Wick, the hospital administrator oversee-
ing her recovery, when she'd asked to attend lectures at the academy. And so, Ann, or Anaya as she
was still known by some on campus, returned to the
classroom as a full-fledged time jumper, a curiosity
dressed in blue among a sea of green cadets.

The cadets fidgeted with first-day nerves. Ann
shifted her attention away from the electrical
chorus in her head to Professor Huxley who continued to pace the dais in his rumpled suit. The
old academic's reputation for the dramatic, unusual
for a *Tempus Lex* professor, was known throughout
campus. Somehow Huxley always made Time Law
interesting. Or at least Ann had a vague sense he did.
Lieutenant *Anaya* Chapman had sat through Huxley's class before as a cadet, but gaps in *Ann's* memory kept those details hidden.

Professor Huxley finished his circuit of the dais
and leaned against the podium, shoulders rounded,
as he looked down at the group. Even in this relaxed
position, Huxley's frame towered over most of the
students. White hair covered his forehead almost
reaching the tips of the wiry brows that shaded his
bright gray eyes. While the top of the professor's
head was tidy, wisps of white hair in the back and
the sides showed signs of staging a coup.

Huxley surveyed the new crop of cadets. Satisfied,
he stepped forward, full lips stretching into a wel-
coming smile as he pulled a handheld device from a
pocket.

"Ineluctabilis. Who can state the First Law? Anyone?"

Without waiting for an answer, Huxley bent over the device in his hand to fiddle with the controls. With his chin tucked, the lines of the professor's face pulled his mouth into a permanent pout. The effect gave the impression of a rubber mask on the verge of slipping.

The students glanced at each other with apprehension. The question was unexpected due to its simplicity. *Who would answer?* From the corner of her eye, Ann saw the hand of a sacrificial lamb shoot into the air.

"Professor."

Huxley looked up.

A brave cadet on the opposite end spoke, "The First Law of Ineluctabilis states that Andarrians can not alter their own timeline."

The old professor nodded and paced the line of students, a slow swing in his step. "An excellent answer, but it's important to note, particularly in regard to the law, that you missed the word *knowingly*. Andarrians cannot knowingly alter their own timeline. Without that subtle difference, many of our finest time jumpers would be *serving* time rather than *fixing* it." Warm laughter swelled the ranks of cadets. Huxley continued. "Take for example the curious case of Woonsocket vs. the Republic..."

The group sipped the professor's words like honey from a spoon. Huxley's rich baritone and ambling delivery had the power to wrap audiences in a fog of heavy contentment, more suitable for telling bedtime stories than lecturing in a classroom, Ann thought. But woe to the student who could not think on her feet. *Quick's the word, sharp's the motion* ruled the time law professor's classroom.

Professor Huxley rounded his tangent and came full circle. "Woonsocket's defense hung on '*knowingly*.' Did he know?" The professor dismissed his own question with a shrug and turned back to the brave student in the front row. "Add knowingly and your answer is correct in legal terms, but there is a simpler way to state the First Law. Lieutenant Anaya Chapman?"

Ann stiffened as thirty pairs of eyes swiveled in her direction.

Huxley turned abruptly and retraced his easy steps back toward Ann.

"How would a seasoned time jumper, in non-legal terms, explain the First Law?"

Ann's face flushed. She swallowed before answering.

"We don't get do-overs."

Professor Huxley's bright gray eyes rested on her another second. It seemed to Ann that a sad smile touched the old professor's mouth before he nodded agreement.

"Yes, Lieutenant, that is correct." Huxley turned and addressed the group. "If you wake up late, you forget your girlfriend's birthday, you break your favorite coffee mug, you fail a class...this class perhaps...all of these things you can not knowingly alter. The First Law forbids it." Ann shifted self-consciously in place. "But you know this even though you've never taken a Tempus Lex class in your life. You know this because you are *Andarrian*. You have been taught the First Law since you were old enough for nursery rhymes. The First Law is for children, dipping their toes into the water for the first time. As time jumpers, you'll swim in much more dangerous currents. Today, I'm going to introduce you to the Second Law of Ineluctabilis."

Huxley raised the device in his hand and pressed a button.

A soft pop accompanied a noticeable change in air pressure as a shimmering arc appeared over the group.

A few cadets gasped in surprise. Ann's keravnos implant let out a low whistle causing the cadet next to her to jump. The cadet looked at Ann and then stared at the black disc blinking in her ear.

Ann scowled and resisted the urge to kick the student in the shins. "Eyes front, Cadet!" she said.

The chastised cadet blinked at Ann and stammered out a 'yes, ma'am' before turning his attention back to Professor Huxley.

The time law professor marshaled the students.

"Hold your position! Please stay as you are so as not to disrupt the *tempus memoria*."

Through the keravnos implant, Ann continued to sense the energy dome that now encircled the group. She kept her attention focused on the translucent bow echo that extended just beyond where Huxley stood.

The image of the lecture hall beyond the dome shimmered and melted away, leaving a snowy field and a sky of gun-metal gray. A pink smear of light glowed on the horizon. It was impossible for Ann to determine whether the light was from a sunrise or a sunset. A row of stout trees several stories high lined the edge of the field fifty yards to her right. Ann turned to take in the group's more immediate surroundings. The remains of dry brown stalks rustled and crunched under the students' shoes as they stood shifting from side to side on nervous feet. Wind gusted and blew ribbons of snow across the frozen field. The granules of snow and ice blowing against the stalks sounded like sand pouring onto a sheet of paper. Ann shivered even though she couldn't detect any change in temperature inside the now invisible dome.

Huxley waited for the students to adjust to their new surroundings. "The *tempus memoria* is a captured, recorded memory...one that I hope will help to illustrate today's lesson. While your senses tell you otherwise, I assure you we haven't left the lecture hall." The anxious shuffling of the students diminished.

"Very well then." The professor glanced at the device in his hand and resumed pacing. "The Second Law of Ineluctabilis states, *A point in time that is Ineluctabilis cannot be changed, but the events leading up to or away from that point can be altered to lessen the event's impact.*"

Ann's ears pricked to the sound of distant buzzing.

Huxley continued. "What does this mean? As time jumpers, you will sometimes encounter events so formidable they are unmoved by time's currents. Nothing short of a divine lever and fulcrum will dislodge these events from their resting place."

The buzzing grew louder, closer. Ann cocked her head to listen. Other students heard it too and searched for the source. Ann could hear the sound more clearly now, coming from behind the row of trees. Unease shifted inside her as the cadence became recognizable. Ann's pulse quickened. An engine—an air ship perhaps—straining against wind and gravity. The noise rose in pitch, faltered then began again as a low growl. Huxley continued to speak, unmoved by the drumming of the engine or the growing distraction of the students.

"These events will test your skills as a time jumper, they'll put you in great personal danger... and they will break your heart. For what you cannot change, you must accept." Huxley paused, giving a final glance to the device he held. The clamor of the engine was now deafening, and yet, while Huxley never raised his voice, his words were still perfectly audible. The old academic looked up from the device with weary sadness. "As difficult as the First Law may be to accept, the Second Law is the heavier burden. It's always easier to accept your own fate than the fate of others."

A flock of birds took flight seconds before the dying air ship burst through the treetops, shearing off the uppermost branches and sending splinters in all directions. Students cried out and raised their arms to cover their heads. Wood and debris showered the group. Ann raised her arms as a shield against a large chunk of wood coming towards her. A branch, with the thickness of a fireplace log, ghosted through the head of the student in front of her and continued through Ann's raised arm and shoulder without pause.

Ann looked back toward the air ship. Her insides twisted as the craft nosed downward as it passed, dipping one wing in a slow roll. The wing tip dug into the soil, carving a deeper furrow as the craft lost altitude with every second. Metal screamed against dirt. With a final teeth-grinding metal howl, the wing tore free of the fuselage. The wreckage cartwheeled, nose and tail trading places again and again, as the air ship shed the second wing and hunks of metal. The mass rolled across the field slowly losing momentum until catching on a wire fence line, unseen in the dim light. The ruin of the air ship hung on the fence and wheezed out a sigh. All that remained of the craft was a twisted metal ball. Smoke and the oily stench of fuel rose from a dozen or more small fires burning across the field and within the wreckage. The flames guttered and cast a spectral glow in the fading light. A dark shape slumped from the cockpit. Two other dark figures lay in nearby snow drifts.

The cadets stared at the wreckage in silence. Ann blew out a slow breath to loosen the tightness in her chest, but she could still hear the rumble of the engines and feel the throttle from a doomed time ship. *It's just a ghost from a memory.* The tightness eased, returning to the usual level of anxiety she'd grown accustomed to in the year since her accident. Ann felt the thud of her pulse slow. She wiped the cold sweat from her brow with the back of a shaky hand. The wind gusted again with the same sand on paper sound. A muffled sob escaped from a student in the front row.

Professor Huxley, who had moved to one side of the group, stepped forward again and faced the students.

"The man whose life was spared never set foot on the air ship." Huxley's gray eyes searched the faces of the cadets. "Had he boarded then he would have become beholden to the Second Law. The crash was *Ineluctabilis*, but his impending death was not. The time jumper whose case file this memory comes from was successful in preventing the man from boarding. The pilot and other passengers were not part of this mission."

Huxley clicked a button. The wreckage and field faded from view as the energy dome dissipated. The professor and students stood once more on the dais of the lecture hall.

Huxley gazed at his students with grandfatherly affection and continued in somber tones, "I am a time law professor, not a counselor. But I feel compelled to offer you this small grain of advice in regard to the Second Law. If you feel you cannot bear the burden of this responsibility, resign now. No one will think less of you. If you choose to stay and become a time jumper, hold your grief close to you. Close enough to feel the pain, but not enough to let it consume you. If you are fortunate and clever enough not to be killed in the line of duty, you may be a time jumper for many years. But...if there ever comes a day you can no longer feel grief...retire. You will have become too calloused to be any good to us. Class dismissed."

FOUR

A MATTER OF LAW

The students dispersed and exited quietly in singles and pairs. Their steps and muted whispers echoed off the walls of the lecture hall.

Ann hoisted her satchel to a shoulder, anxious to leave the dim hall. A little sunlight and fresh air would help chase the nagging doubts from her head.

"Lieutenant Chapman."

Ann looked up, grateful that her hands had stopped shaking only moments before. Professor Huxley strolled toward her from the dais.

"Anaya, it's good to see you in my classroom again...although I'm sorry for the circumstances. How are you?" The weight of the professor's words suggested more than a polite inquiry.

Ann searched for the right thing to say. Several possible answers flitted through the space of a few seconds. She hadn't told anyone the real reason behind her request to attend lectures. She'd simply allowed many of her acquaintances on campus to assume it was part of her memory therapy. If they had access to her medical file, however, they'd discover that no medical requirement existed. Ann defaulted to her standard answer.

"I'm fine. Doing well all considering, I guess."

Huxley nodded. "The Academy is quite good at helping time jumpers in your position. Sadly, you're not the first time jumper to return to the classroom after a traumatic injury."

Ann gave the professor a wry smile. "Am I the first time jumper to return to the classroom after being dead?"

Huxley chuckled in low rumbles, gray eyes brightening with a mischievous light. "Oh, come now. You know as well as I do that being dead and wrongly *presumed* dead are two entirely different things. You survived a horrific accident while test piloting a time ship. You were dematerialized by an exploding experimental time coil and safely rematerialized within your own timeline two weeks prior to the crash, millions of light years away. A *Day Tripper* would say you played hide and seek with death." Ann snorted a laugh, surprised by the professor's uncharacteristic use of time jumper slang for cadets. "But some of our veteran time jumpers would argue that the entire incident was fairly mundane for a random Tuesday afternoon. What do you say?"

"Well, first of all, it was a Thursday and I disagree with the phrase *safely rematerialized*."

Huxley's laughter joined Ann's. "Yes, that point could be debated at some length, but you are here." The professor gestured toward Ann with an outstretched palm, his expression once again one of genuine kindness, a look that endeared him to so many of his students. "Alive, at least by my initial observations, perhaps with a few frayed edges, but those will mend with time."

Ann felt her face flush, touched by Professor Huxley's concern.

The old professor continued to radiate warmth even as the lines around his eyes drew more serious. "I'm happy to see you, but disappointed you haven't come to visit me. I thought you might have some questions."

Ann's memory drew a blank. The sensation wasn't unfamiliar to her, especially in the year since the accident, but always unsettling.

"Sir? Did I have an appointment with you?"

"Most students are curious to hear the results of a First Law violation review."

Ann gulped cold fear. First Law violations were serious business. *Career-ending serious if found guilty.* Ann tried to speak, but the questions piled up in her mouth, all fighting to be first.

Huxley frowned at her confusion. "You didn't know I was asked to review your case, did you?" The lines in his face deepened, pulling his wiry brows lower. "Strange. Very strange, indeed." He turned and crossed to the other side of the lecture hall.

Ann pushed past her initial shock and blurted out, "Professor, I don't understand. No one told me I was under a First Law Review."

Professor Huxley walked to an ancient wooden table pushed up against the wall on one side of the lecture hall a few steps from the dais. Stacks of books covered the desk and teetered between order and chaos.

"After you were found alive on the Colonies, I was asked to review your accident for possible First Law violations." The professor pulled a leaf of papers from between the stacks. "I looked at the details and recommended that a full panel convene to investigate further." Huxley looked up, saw the look of distress on Ann's face, and gave a reassuring smile. "It's standard procedure to convene a First Law panel when an agent jumps their own timeline. An investigation is never proof of guilt," Huxley said, handing Ann the report. "There was also the question of whether you had tried to circumvent Cox's Conundrum by leaving Andarrian space."

Ann chewed her lip as she glanced through the report. The pieces began to fit. Cox's Conundrum was the unseen force that prevented Andarrians from time traveling within their own home world—another consequence of the time quake that separated Andarria from the rest of the universe. Leaving Andarrian space was the only way Ann could have accessed her own timeline. In the events leading up to the destruction of her ship, the *Kairos*, Ann had left Andarrian space when she attempted to realign the ship's time coils. The last-ditch effort ultimately failed, but the ship's one surviving time coil caused a secondary event that led to her time-teleportation accident. On the surface, an argument could be made that Ann had intentionally jumped her own timeline to escape death; however, the details of the case told a different story. Ann had been severely injured in the attempt to save the *Kairos* and had no control over the effects of the exploding time coil.

The anxiety that had taken up residence deep inside her gave a sharp twist. Ann had remembered during the investigation that a malfunctioning time coil had caused the crash, but in the months since the trial she'd sensed there was more. There'd been something else. Something before her crash that now lay just out of reach, hidden in the gaps of her memory. *A feeling...? A doubt...? What was it?* She'd hoped attending lectures at the academy, a place where she'd always felt safe, would've helped to fill in those missing pieces, but so far, her plan hadn't worked. The doubts persisted, twisting inside her and whispering in her ear whenever her thoughts returned to the *Kairos*.

"I only knew about the crash investigation. I was never told about the First Law panel," Ann said and handed the report back to Huxley.

"Because there never was one...officially. But I'm still surprised they never told you about my review." Huxley sighed. "My recommendation for a full panel was ignored. By then, the crash investigation was well underway. When your missing memory of the time coil was submitted as evidence and you were found not guilty of pilot error, I again asked that a First Law panel convene if only to formally accept the findings of the crash investigation and close the First Law inquiry. I was told that a full panel review was no longer necessary."

Doubt crowded Ann's mind again. "Professor, would I have been found guilty of violating the First Law had the panel convened?"

"No. Your memory of the time coil proved that you never had any intention of jumping your time-line. You had no choice in the matter. Had the panel convened, nothing more would have come of it, only a footnote in your personnel file."

Ann sighed and tried not to let her frustration show. "Sir, I still don't follow you. If the crash investigation proved I didn't violate the First Law, then why would a separate panel need to meet?"

"It's a matter of law. By not convening an official panel, the question of a First Law violation that was asked during the review process was never formally answered," Huxley said. "You can't un-ring a bell, Lieutenant. Where the law is concerned, this bell will continue to reverberate until such time as a for-mal First Law panel convenes."

Ann's eyes widened as the professor's words took on a new meaning. "Which means I could still be under a First Law investigation."

Huxley gave a grim nod. "As incredible as it sounds...yes."

Ann wrestled with the anxiety freely churning now in her gut. "But why would they refuse to close the inquiry?"

"I've been in many courtrooms. I've seen the prosecution pressured for a conviction regardless of whether or not the guilty party was sitting in the defense chair. I was in the gallery the day you gave your testimony. The easiest path to a conviction was to hang you for pilot error. The crash investigation committee wanted to convict based on the evidence they already had," Huxley said.

Ann's throat tightened. Her brother, Sean, and Agent Fionna Knox had both voiced similar concerns at the time. *Had the committee been right all along? Did I make a mistake? But if it wasn't pilot error and it wasn't a First Law violation, then what was it?*

"They had already concluded their investigation and were simply ticking off the boxes when they ordered you to testify," Huxley continued. "Testimony, I might add, that was destined to fail because at that time you had not completely regained your memory of the accident. They were counting on that fact, and you thwarted them at the last moment when you recovered the one piece of evidence that proved your innocence."

"When I remembered it was a faulty time coil that caused all the problems to begin with," Ann said.

Huxley nodded. "That same evidence also proved that you didn't violate any First Laws and yet they have not formally dismissed it."

"It doesn't make any sense," Ann said. "The time coil proves I didn't do anything wrong." *Or does it?*

"*The Kairos* was an expensive prototype," Huxley said, rubbing his chin. "The crash investigation committee might have been getting pressure from their superiors to blame you for someone else's mechanical failures."

Ann said sourly, "Well, it didn't work." Doubt whispered in her ear, *At least, not yet.*

Huxley smiled. "Yes, and now someone's feelings are hurt so they're keeping the First Law inquiry open out of spite. As ignoble as it seems, Andarrians aren't above base motivations."

Ann sighed and met the professor's eyes. "What should I do?"

"There's not much you can do, but the law is on your side," Huxley said. "I'll keep pushing to convene a First Law panel. That will settle the matter. Until then, don't do anything that a prosecutor might find useful."

FIVE

MIND THE GAP

The fresh air didn't help.

Ann left the lecture hall bowed under the weight of Professor Huxley's words. *How can I still be under investigation?* During the inquest, the crash investigation committee had acted as if they couldn't wait to find her guilty of the loss of the *Kairos*, but now shadows bided their time, continuing an investigation that at least according to the Professor, would bear no fruit. As Huxley pointed out, the fact she hadn't been formally charged with a First Law violation offered some reassurance. Whoever Ann's detractors were, they had yet to find the evidence they sought. A chill passed over her despite the warm sun on her shoulders. *What do they know that I can't remember?*

The walkway Ann followed emerged from the cloister of Tempus Law buildings and cut across the campus quadrangle. The green expanse was the heart of campus life at the Academy.

Groves of trees and ivy-covered buildings of brick and marble framed the quad. On one side, Ann could see the Great Hall, an enclosed amphitheater of metal and glass that also housed the Academy's administrative offices and time jumper headquarters. On the opposite end through the mid-morning haze, winked the twin domes of the National Museum. Beyond the museum were the Wilds of Palladium Beta's Capital City Park and the Montressador's Keep where Ann's brother, Sean, spent much of his day. From the ancient castle of kings to the Academy's Great Hall, Andarria's past, present, and future stretched like a ley line of power, cutting a swath through the center of its capital city.

Ann struck out toward the Great Hall, passing cadets in green fatigues and other time jumpers in blue along the way. She could talk to her brother at dinner, but unless Ann could get a clear communication signal, telling John about Huxley's revelation would have to wait until she was back home on the Colonies.

Siren's Cove, the rustic old tavern where Ann lived on the Colonies, had been her home ever since the accident with the *Kairos*. Captain John Galeas, the tavern owner, had found her and taken her in while her injuries healed. Over time, their relationship had turned passionate, but before Ann's true identity had been discovered.

John had run the tavern for several years while he worked as an undercover time jumper, infiltrating and tracking the movements of freighter pirates. After his wife died, he turned his back on the mission, his contacts on Andarria, and continued to live as one of the colonists. Ann's sudden arrival unbalanced everything. John's past came to light when Chohon-Lo and his band of Tyrhenian freighter pirates tried to recruit him to rejoin their group. John and Ann were almost killed when the tavern's winery burned to the ground during the final stand against Chohon-Lo and his men.

They now ran the tavern together, an imperfect but not unmanageable arrangement, while Ann worked toward full reinstatement as a time jumper. Her current schedule meant that she spent four days at the Academy on Andarria and three days at home at Siren's Cove. John had said he planned to return to active duty as a time jumper, but so far had not been assigned to any missions. From Ann's perspective, John seemed content to run the tavern, rebuild the winery, and enjoy his new life with her—a life blessedly free of freighter pirates.

Ann hurried past the campanile and the Weyl Gate pavilion. The crowds grew thicker, moving slower. Up ahead a steady drumbeat came from behind a group loosely gathered around a stand of shade trees. Ann dodged and weaved between green and blue fatigues until finally abandoning the walkway and trekking across the short grass. She scanned faces in the crowd, edging closer to the musicians.

Lieutenant Kel Stravage leaned against a tree trunk and took pulls from a water bottle as he watched the musicians sitting in the grass. Stravage stood just a breath under five foot ten in blue fatigues with short, curly brown hair and light golden-brown eyes. A gold time jumper pin shone from a top pocket. The usual two days of scruff shadowed his square jaw. The young man's blank expression made it impossible to determine if he enjoyed the music or not. Ann's own best guess would be that her friend was somewhere between a joyous reverie and a nanosecond short of a murderous rage. It was often said among the other time jumpers that Kel had no tell. He gave nothing away except when it suited him. Consequently, no one liked to play cards with Lieutenant Stravage.

The musicians were everything the cadets and time jumpers were not. Instead of neatly pressed fatigues, the Luctari's clothes were undisciplined, mismatched castoffs in a riot of clashing colors. Loose-fitting shirts and pants sat next to halter tops and woven skirts—at least among the musicians that were actually wearing clothes. The bare-chested look was not reserved solely for men. Some of the Luctari had simply taken strips of cloth and tied them artfully around their bodies, wrangling a wayward breast or giving shelter to more intimate areas.

The instruments were as hodgepodge as the players, some cobbled together from everyday items. Drums were pounded by hand, sticks marked time on blocks of wood or metal, but an overturned bucket and spoon worked just as well. Bells, flutes, and all manner of real or improvised stringed instruments rounded out the ensemble.

The drummers finished their set to scattered applause. Ann closed the distance and stood next to Lieutenant Stravage.

"Hey, Stravage."

"Lieutenant Death Wish. When did you get here?"

Ann smirked at Kel's latest attempt to pin her with a nickname.

"Heh. Not one of your better ones. I thought Sieve for Brains had a more lyrical ring."Kel eyed Ann sideways, flicked a barely perceptible half-smile in response, and then turned his attention back to the musicians.

"We should go," Ann said. "We still need to find Sarolea."

Kel took another pull from the water bottle. "Relax. We've got time."

The drummers took up their instruments again and pounded out a new riff. Ann shifted impatiently.

"Oh, come on, Kel. It's not like you haven't heard them play before."

"Hang on a second!"

The drumming stopped. A Luctari woman stood, threw off the blanket from around her shoulders, and slowly...

...gracefully...

...stepped barefoot to the front of the group.

Ann arched a brow and settled in to watch. *This is new.*

The musicians took up a slow syncopated beat and the woman began to dance. The Luctari woman's dark hair was wrapped in a brightly colored turban. Delicate silver hoops graced her earlobes. A necklace of matching silver medallions shone from her throat.

Her modest breasts were covered by a wide strip of cloth held in place with a single leather strap that crossed from her right breast to the opposite shoulder. An acre of naked flesh lay exposed between the bandeau top and a low-slung skirt, accentuating a nip of waist and the full bloom of the dancer's hips.

The roll and swell of the dancer's movements were both angular and fluid. Sensual. The silver bells that hung from the Luctari's short skirt shivered with every quiver of her hips. Full lips parted into a knowing smile as smoky eyes drew in the onlookers, never lingering on any one person for long.

The cadence of the drums quickened and crashed upon the dancer until it seemed the motion of her hips created the rhythm. Then the music changed abruptly as a mournful flute took up the melody. Every muscle twitch, eyelid flutter, and sway moved in time with the music. The audience held their breath as the silver bells trembled, arms inflamed passions, and delicate fingers shaped worlds.

The dance ended with a coy smile and, unless Ann had imagined it, a surreptitious wink in Kel's direction. His sudden intake of breath was so slight that had Ann not been standing next to her friend she would not have thought it possible.

The audience erupted in cheers and thunderous applause. Sensing an encore, Ann palmed the side of the satchel bag slung over Kel's shoulder and felt for the outline of the data link pad in the outside pocket and the energy radiating from within. The keravnos implant in Ann's ear gave a soft whistle as she made an effort of will, captured the energy from the device, and then released it when her outstretched index finger touched the tip of Kel's earlobe. The shock was immediate.

"AGH! What did you do that for?" Kel jerked his head away and glowered at Ann.

Ann flashed a teasing smile. "So, you've given up chasing cadets? It's dancing girls now?"

"Shut up!" Kel frowned, rubbing his ear. "Let's go, Sparky."

The time jumpers pushed through the crowd as the musicians struck up another number. Kel glanced over a shoulder. His eyes found the Luctari girl briefly before turning and walking away.

"So, what does your brother think of them... the Luctari," Kel said, looking down at Ann. They emerged from the crowd and came out on the walkway that led to the Great Hall.

Ann considered her words before answering. The Luctari were free spirits and claimed to have thrown off the shackles of any tradition or laws that Andarrian society followed. More recently, the group's spiritual leader, the Reverend Jeremiah Brink, had expressed the belief and political bombshell that Andarrians should no longer enforce the laws of time travel and take their place as just one of the other races of the universe. Time travel was so ingrained in the culture and politics of Andarria that it seemed the Luctari's cause was a fool's errand. The Luctari were tolerated. Many Andarrians viewed them as a joke, but their growing popularity among younger generations had caused concern in some circles.

"Sean thinks the Luctari are harmless...just odd," Ann said.

Kel nodded without comment.

"So which scenario did Professor Huxley run for the first day of class? Earthquake? Volcano? Tsunami?"

Ann's stomach clenched with the memory. She swallowed before answering.

"Air ship crash," Ann said, forcing herself to meet Kel's eye.

Kel cringed. This time sincerity shaded his features as he looked at Ann.

"Ouch. Tough luck, Rewind."

Kel and Ann walked the rest of the way to the Great Hall. Crowds of time jumpers and cadets gathered in knots around the fountain at the foot of the amphitheater's stone steps. A large armillary sphere of weathered brass, a replica of a time navigational device, rose three stories from the center of the fountain's shallow reflecting pool. Blue sky and the sphere's intersecting rings mirrored in the water underneath.

Ann spotted Sarolea's wild blue hair—a short tangle of cobalt and faded denim—in a cluster of time jumpers sitting on stone blocks at the fountain's far edge.

Kel shouted to the group, "TIME!"

A cadet near the fringe of Sarolea's group turned

to Lieutenant Stravage perplexed and pointed toward the campanile clock.

"Twenty minutes!"

Ann snickered.

Kel fired back. "Not the assembly, you Bender! THE ARM!"

"Anaya!"

Lieutenant Sarolea Picquet returned Ann's wave. A puckish grin dimpled rounded cheeks and wrinkled the bridge of her upturned nose.

Sarolea checked the digital readout display attached to the metal brace on her left arm. The brace traveled the length of the young woman's bare arm from above the elbow to a jointed metal band that encircled her wrist. A network of straps crossed Sarolea's back and shoulders to secure the rig around her middle. Numbers raced on the screen, counting the milliseconds.

"Seven hours, fifty-two minutes and counting. Three minutes till a new record!" Sarolea's announcement came amid a backdrop of cheers from nearby onlookers.

It wasn't unusual to see time jumpers at the academy with missing bits and pieces, but in Sarolea's case, and to the consternation of the academy doctors, the arm was *nusquam esse*. Lieutenant Picquet's arm wasn't amputated, nor invisible, just occasionally not present. A time portal accident phased Sarolea's arm between nowhere and somewhere, which caused the limb to disappear and reappear at random intervals. Betting on when the limb would phase in and out had become a favorite activity of time jumpers on campus.

When the arm was in residence, it appeared perfectly normal in its cage of metal and electrical wiring. Fortunately for Sarolea when the arm phased out, death from severe blood loss didn't occur since the arm was still present inter-dimensionally. When the arm disappeared, curious observers (preferably with strong stomachs) could still see the slice of bone, muscles, and blood vessels in the stump all working smoothly as if under a thin pane of glass. As one of Sarolea's friends, Ann had the privilege of seeing the stump for free. Anyone else had to buy Sarolea a drink or offer something in trade for even a bare glimpse.

Ann sat on a stone block next to Sarolea.

"What do you think?" She held the brace out for Ann to see and flexed her arm. "Do I get to keep it this time?" Her eyes gleamed with hope and excitement.

"John and I say your arm sticks around or at least sets a new record," Ann grinned and flipped Sarolea a coin.

"You missed last call," she said, catching the coin in the air. "They closed the betting five minutes ago."

"Keep it for luck then. Sorry, we got held up," Ann said with a glance to Kel. He flicked a smile in acknowledgment of Ann's discretion. "So, if the arm stays this time, what will we do for excitement?"

"We could go back to playing cards," Kel said, hands in his pockets.

"No one else wins when you play, Stravage," Sarolea said. "At least betting on my arm..."

"Ghost arm," Kel muttered.

"...everyone has a fighting chance," Sarolea said, ignoring him.

"Everyone but me." Kel looked sideways at Sarolea. "I lost ten dories last week when it phased three times before lunch."

"I warned you," Ann said. "It does weird things during lightning storms."

Sarolea jerked a thumb in Ann's direction. "Should have listened to the Vego."

Ann gave Kel an I-told-you-so smirk.

Kel blinked at Sarolea. "What's the difference? It phased six times the week before all on sunny days."

Sarolea shrugged with a hopeless gesture. "It's predictably unpredictable."

"TIME!"

The shout came from across the fountain, giving the three friends a start. Sarolea glanced at the digital screen.

Kel barked out, "FORTY-FIVE SECONDS!"

Conversations hushed as the gathered cadets and time jumpers turned to watch, all eyes on Lieutenant Picquet's Ghost Arm.

"This is it!" Sarolea looked to Ann, eyes wide. "Anaya, are you getting anything?"

Ann shook her head and gave her friend's hand a squeeze. "Nothing yet." As a Vego, her electroperception allowed her to sense the energy through the keravnos implant when the arm was about to phase, but only by a few seconds.

Nervous anticipation settled on the group. Sarolea closed her eyes as the countdown chant began.

"THREE!"

"TWO!"

"ONE!"

Sarolea opened her eyes and lifted the braced arm in triumph. The crowd exploded in cheers. Sarolea accepted congratulations from the other time jumpers as she gazed at her arm in disbelief.

"The doctors said the phasing energies would disperse over time. Maybe...what if..."

"It's a new record," Kel snapped. "Don't worry about *maybe* or *what if*, just be happy."

Sarolea and Ann blinked at Kel in astonishment.

Kel frowned. "What?"

Ann found her voice first, "That was just so..."

"Sensitive!" Sarolea supplied the right descriptor.

Kel's frown deepened. "Shut up!" He eyed them both, flicked a smile, and turned to talk to some other time jumpers.

Ann and Sarolea's laughter bubbled over. Some days Ann's memories of before the accident felt as elusive as Sarolea's arm, but then there were moments when all the pieces fit. Kel and Sarolea were her friends. Ann knew from the first day back at the academy when Sarolea tackled her in a rib-breaking hug. Ann accepted their companionship, and the tangible memories came back a little at a time, slowly eroding the blank space inside her head.

Sarolea gasped for breath as their laughter receded. "Hey! You won!"

"I missed the cutoff," Ann said. "That coin was just for luck. It wasn't an official bet."

Sarolea grabbed her duffle bag and rummaged inside. "Piss the rules! You made the bet with me. You said my arm would set a new record, you were right, so you get a prize."

Lieutenant Picquet's duffle was a trove of mostly secondhand goods given in trade for a glimpse of her ghosted arm. The more unique or useful items she doled out generously to friends. After a few seconds of searching, Sarolea gave an exclamation of triumph and held up a dented metal water bottle and a used package of bootlaces.

"What's it gonna be? Bottle or bootlaces?"

Ann gave a moment of serious consideration before pointing to the water bottle.

"Good choice! It looks like hell, but it doesn't leak. I checked." Sarolea stowed the laces and zipped up the duffle just as Kel rejoined them.

"What else you got in there, Picquet? I need a new charger for my data link pad," Kel said.

Sarolea pulled a vapor stick from a top pocket and placed the tube between her lips. "Sorry. The store's closed." She inhaled water vapor and blew rings of strawberry-and-mint scented steam toward the fountain. "Ensign Thorn's birthday is this week, so she gets the next pick."

"Fine." Kel eyed Ann's water bottle. "I guess you have all the luck, Kitchen Girl."

Rage splashed Ann's insides and burned through

to the surface of her skin. She surged forward and stiff-armed Kel hard in the shoulder. He took a step back to catch his balance, stumbled over a stray satchel bag, and fell ass-first into the shallow reflecting pool. Ann was on him in an instant.

"Call me Sparky, Rewind, or even Death Wish, but you will NEVER call me Kitchen Girl again! Is that understood, Lieutenant?"

Kel looked up at Ann, his face blank with surprise. He held his already wet arms out at a ridiculous angle to try and keep them above the water. Everything below the waist submerged except for his bent knees. Truth be told, he did a fairly decent imitation of a scarecrow. And then to everyone's astonishment, Kel tossed his head back and broke into rolls of laughter.

Taken aback, Ann looked to Sarolea at a complete loss.

Sarolea crossed her arms and said between puffs, "I think you broke him."

Ann looked back at Kel who continued to convulse with laughter. Her fists unclenched. Kel's Kitchen Girl remark had been a jab at Ann serving tables at Siren's Cove. What he didn't know, because Ann had never told him or Sarolea, was that the last person to call her Kitchen Girl had on two separate occasions tried to break her neck. That man would never make that mistake again or do anything other than occupy a microscope slide in the morgue. Kel, however, was a friend and deserved a little more benefit of the doubt. A cold bucket of guilt doused

Ann's anger. She held out a hand and pulled him to his feet.

Kel stepped from the pool still chuckling, his pants sloshing water onto the paving stones. "I've been trying for weeks to get a rise out of you with all those dumb nicknames. I can't believe Kitchen Girl was the one that finally lit you up."

Ann's face burned, seeing the joke. "Just not that one, okay?" She gestured to Kel's sopping pants. "Sorry."

Kel shrugged, his emotional control returning. "I'm sorry you have anger management issues." He flicked Ann a smile.

Ann snorted a laugh.

Sarolea took another drag on the vapor stick and hitched up her duffle. "Well, that was fun. Come on. We gotta get going or we'll be sitting up against the rafters." She turned and began to walk up the steps to the Great Hall.

The keravnos implant trilled in Ann's ear as the sound of a trumpet crescendo crashed her senses.

"Sarolea!"

The warning came too late. The space around the Ghost Arm began to shimmer as swirls of energy and light encircled. The air folded and in a blink, the arm disappeared and with it the vapor stick Sarolea had been holding, leaving only the empty metal brace behind. The energy Ann sensed as a trumpet blast cut off as if a door had suddenly slammed shut. The brace's digital clock automatically reset to zero and began counting the seconds again.

Sarolea doubled over and made a face. "Damn it, that stings!" She looked down at where her arm had been a moment before. "*And* my last vapor stick!" She swore continuously for several seconds.

Ann picked up Sarolea's duffle bag and hoisted it to a shoulder. "Sorry I couldn't give you more warning."

"It doesn't matter," Sarolea said. She pulled a prosthetic hand from a side pocket of the bag. "Just means we won't have to go back to playing cards with Stravage yet."

Sarolea snapped the metal hand to the wrist joint of the arm brace and tested the movement of the fingers. She looked up to see a wide-eyed, first-year cadet staring at the empty mechanical brace. Sarolea offered the cadet a dark warning.

"Keep your arms and legs inside the time portal, Day Tripper."

The three jogged up the steps to the Great Hall and joined the queue of time jumpers shuffling through the main doors.

"When this is over, do you want to go to West End? I'll buy," Ann said.

Sarolea shook her head. "Can't. I'm making a cargo run with the *What Cheer.* The crew is meeting at the hangar right after. Stravage has pawn shop duty."

Kel ignored the quip. "Meeting with the AIR Commander."

Sarolea grinned and said more insistently, "Pawn shop duty."

Ann snickered. The Artifact Identification and Retrieval (AIR) unit took a fair amount of teasing from other time jumpers.

Kel turned his gaze to Ann. "I thought you said you were taking your flight test today."

Ann blushed. "Not yet. I wanted more time in the simulator first."

Ann saw Kel and Sarolea exchange glances and felt her temper flair again.

"I know. I know. I'll get it done!"

Ann could have said Huxley's airship lesson that morning had unnerved her, but she never would have admitted it even if it had been true. The truth was Ann had never scheduled the test date in the first place. Since the accident, flying had become a challenge. As a passenger she was fine, but the thought of climbing into the cockpit again left her cold. Unfortunately, as an independent operative, not having a pilot's license greatly reduced the number of missions she could be assigned. Hence, no assignment had come her way, not even a low-level mission. People were beginning to notice that Lieutenant Anaya Chapman was grounded. And eventually, no pilot's license would delay Ann's full reinstatement as a time jumper.

Sarolea rested a hand on Ann's shoulder. "Hey, I'll be back in a couple days if you want some company in the simulator."

Ann blew out a sigh. "Sure..."

Designed to hold the full complement of time jumpers and cadets, the Great Hall was ten times the largest lecture room on campus. The bowl-shaped amphitheater had three sections of seating that curved toward the stage that held the speaker's podium. Sarolea always grumbled if they had to sit too close to the top row, but there wasn't a bad seat in the house with monitor screens positioned throughout the hall. The trio received a few stares on account of Stravage's wet fatigues and Picquet's mechanical arm as they searched for and found three open seats in the middle section.

No sooner had they taken their seats when Ann's keravnos implant trilled again, the trumpet crescendo in her head barely perceptible over the round of applause as the speakers took the stage. The prosthetic hand automatically disengaged from the end of Sarolea's mechanical brace, a swirl of light, and the Ghost Arm popped into existence still holding the vapor stick.

Ann nudged Sarolea who quickly stowed the vapor stick and the rest of her gear just as Commander Garin began to address the assembled.

"Good day to all of you! There are several topics I'd like to bring to your attention, so we'll begin without delay. Item number one..."

At seventy-five years of age, Commander Vesto Garin still maintained a formidable strength much like a stout, old tree. Scars lined the trunk and the limbs creaked, but the tree remained standing facing down the worst gales as if they were merely summer showers. During his career, Garin had walked hand in hand with grief, losing friends and comrades, two wives and three siblings. He completed over two-thousand missions, and still found time to raise five sons and two daughters. As commander of the Time Jumpers, Garin had built a reputation for being quick with reprimands but generous with praise. It was said his gaze of flint and steel could force a confession from troublemakers faster than any threat of punishment. While not blessed with height, his bald head and distinct bearing made the commander easily recognizable even from a distance.

Commander Garin concluded his opening remarks and yielded the podium to a handful of speakers who offered reports ranging from promotions and commendations to staffing changes and general announcements regarding campus maintenance, including repainting of the faculty commissary.

"If the professors don't want people setting off fireworks in their dining hall, they should really post signs," Kel said.

Ann leaned over and looked at Kel, eyes wide. "That was you?"

Kel answered by sliding his gaze towards Ann and flicking another one of his half-smiles.

Commander Garin returned to the podium.

"Before I dismiss you, I have one more announcement. Effective immediately, I will be retiring from my post as commander of the time jumpers."

The assembled time jumpers reacted with disbelief, murmurs growing into shouts of dissent.

Sarolea snapped to attention. "Did he just say he

was going to retire?"

Kel nodded. "Effective immediately, the crazy bastard."

Sarolea groaned and slumped back against the seat.

Ann sighed. "Which means he's already done it."

Garin held up a hand and waited patiently for the audience to settle before continuing.

"I know this comes as a surprise. I've intentionally not spoken of it before now to avoid my exact retirement date from becoming a matter of speculation or a side wager that I know many of you are fond of participating in." Garin's disapproving expression shifted to one of wry amusement.

A chuckle rippled through the audience.

"While the news today may seem abrupt, I assure you my decision was made after considerable thought and planning. I'm leaving you in good hands." Garin gestured to a female officer who'd stepped onto the stage. "Commander Virginia Rectrix will serve in the post at least through the interim until a proper search for a permanent candidate can be conducted."

Ann's breath hitched in her throat as she watched Commander Rectrix acknowledge the audience's polite applause.

"Commander Rectrix is an exemplary officer," Garin said. "She's fair-minded and strong of character. My hope is you'll show her the same loyalty and respect you've shown me during my tenure."

Ann listened to Garin list Rectrix's qualifications

and tried not to choke.

Sarolea nudged Ann. "Anaya, wasn't Rectrix the head of your accident investigation committee?"

Ann nodded. Rectrix had seemed sympathetic toward her during the inquest, but that hadn't stopped the committee from initially ruling pilot error on flimsy evidence.

"I'm not one for careless displays of emotion," Garin said. "But I'd be remiss if I didn't say how proud I am of all of you. I've been honored to serve as your commander and before that, I had the privilege of serving with the most senior among you in the field. You gave everything I ever asked of you..." Garin's voice grew thick with emotion and trailed off. He quickly cleared his throat and continued.

"And so, it's with a note of sadness that I leave you today, but I'll carry with me the honor and many blessings you've given to me. Be well..." And then Garin ended his speech with the words he so often quoted, a phrase that every new cadet learned during their first hour of instruction of jumping through time portals and the old Timers still muttered in their sleep. "...and Mind the Gap."

The audience was on their feet in an explosion of cheers and stomping. Garin shook hands with Commander Rectrix, waved to the crowd, and exited the stage.

Huxley's warning played in Ann's head as Commander Rectrix stepped to the podium.

SIX

SIREN'S COVE

Siren's Cove hummed with the buzz of saws and the shouts of workmen coming from the broken shell of the winery. The burned timbers had been removed a month before, and now the sweet smell of freshly cut wood slowly replaced the haze of charcoal and smoke.

In the tavern next door, the summer afternoon breeze through the windows did little more than stir the scent of sawdust between the empty tables, while the spindle legs of upturned chairs cast shadows across the floor. A mini-bot, the size and color of a copper saucepan, droned through the air. Beetle wings blurred, flickering madly, until landing with the tinkle of metal feet on the front window-pane. The bot whistled, lowered itself, and began polishing the glass.

Captain John Galeas sat at the long wooden bar and scrolled through a report on a data link pad. He frowned as he bent over the screen. His free hand fingered the short stiff pigtail at the back of his head. A second mini-bot, slightly larger than its companion, made a slow circular sweep of the tavern's plank floor. As the bot trundled under the barstool, John automatically lifted his feet, resting his boots momentarily on the rungs until the bot passed.

The report gave a thorough account of the fight with Chohon-Lo and his men. Three months ago, Ann and John had barely survived the encounter with the Tyrhenian freighter pirates, which had resulted in the tavern's winery burning to the ground, but the question was, had any of the pirates managed to escape before the flames consumed the building?

John reached the last screen and set the data pad on the bar. Agent A.K. Max sat next to him with the usual woeful expression. The intelligence officer had waited patiently, sipping beer in silence. John looked to A.K. "How accurate are the identifications of the bodies?"

A.K. gave him a slow smile that lifted the curved white scar under his bottom lip.

"Reasonably accurate. Chohon-Lo was easy. They found him in the courtyard with a grappling hook still in him and a scoop of his skull missing." The agent gave John a sideways glance over the top of his pint glass. "You're welcome."

John smirked. A.K. had fired the sniper's rifle that had finally taken out the freighter pirate commander.

The agent continued. "Xebec, Zabra, Polacca, Razzia, and Vago were found under the collapsed wine tanks."

John nodded and reached for his beer. "What about Scrivani?"

"He was the only question mark. The med techs couldn't find enough of him."

John felt his nerves tighten and took a sip of beer. Scrivani had gone down. He was sure of it. No one had seen Scrivani get up again and yet... The syndicate's front man had an irritating habit of not dying.

John set his glass down. "What are the odds I need to keep looking over my shoulder?"

"The evidence says fifty-fifty. Science isn't an exact..." A.K. cringed, "...science. The heat from the fire could've destroyed the body completely or pan-fried enough of what was left to screw up the test results."

John gave the intelligence man a hard look. "You made me play my part for as long as I did because of Chohon-Lo and his crew. They still found me, and now you're telling me Scrivani could still be alive?"

"I can't give you guarantees, Galeas," A.K. said, meeting John's gaze. "Scrivani's either breathing or he's not. That's about as accurate as you can get with inconclusive, but if you're asking what my *instincts* tell me, you can relax. Siren's Cove hasn't been compromised. I would've told you and Ann to get off the Colonies instead of giving you the report if I thought otherwise."

A series of metallic squawks from underneath the barstools made both men look down. The sweeper bot nudged the agent's boots.

A.K. lifted his feet to allow the bot to pass. "Sorry,

Luff." The bot chirped and continued his circuit.

"Scrivani could have dragged himself out of the winery," John said. "There was time. That's how Chohon-Lo got out."

A.K. looked back at John and nodded. "We checked that theory. It's been three months, and no one has reported a silver-tongued jackass walking around with skin like a burnt rotisserie chicken. No sightings. No word of any kind. If Scrivani is walking on top of the dirt instead of under it, he's hiding."

John snorted into his beer glass as he downed the last swallow. "That's what I'm afraid of."

A.K. leaned forward. "If Scrivani's hiding he's in the darkest corner of the farthest outpost on the loneliest moon orbiting the deadest planet in the universe where no one's ever heard of Chohon-Lo, Tyrhenian pirates…" The agent loosed a mocking smile. "…or the great Captain John Galeas."

John chuckled and gestured to A.K.'s empty glass. The agent nodded and pushed the glass forward. John reached across the bar and pulled two more pints.

A.K. leaned back on the bar stool with a creak. "Seriously, John. We've had all our operatives listening and haven't heard so much as a limp rumor." He lifted his refilled glass. "If that doesn't convince you, take this for what it's worth. If Scrivani isn't dead, you hurt him bad."

"Bad enough so he won't come back this time?"

A.K.'s brows flew up to his brown sweep of hair. "I sure as hell wouldn't. You brought the whole winery down on him. With any luck, if Scrivani isn't dead, there isn't enough left of him to wipe his own ass."

The mini-bot finished cleaning the front window, flicked its wings, and soared lazily across the tavern, a slight roll toward its left side. The agent watched as the bot flew to the bar and landed next to Captain Galeas.

John crooked a smile and gave the bot an affectionate pat. "Port, the mirror is dusty."

The bot whistled and took flight, sailing behind the bar, and landing on the mirror.

A.K. studied John over the rim of his pint glass. "If I gave you Scrivani's head in a box tied with a big red bow, would you still sleep with a pistol next to you?"

"I've had good reasons," John said, sipping beer. "Should I read you the list?"

"I'm the reason why you had to make that list. I'm not telling you to break the habit. I'm just saying I think you can cross Scrivani off along with the rest of Chohon-Lo's crew. I'll let you know if I hear otherwise."

"Fair enough."

John pushed the data link pad across the bar and watched the agent return the device to an inside coat pocket. John narrowed his eyes.

"You could've sent the report over the comm. Why are you really here?"

A.K. pointed to his glass. "Free beer."

John grunted in disbelief. The agent responded with another slow smile. Never a good sign.

"Because I knew you'd have questions about

Scrivani and to sweet talk you into this." A.K. produced a black data stick from an unseen pocket and handed it to John. "Nothing fancy. A short jump and you're home before last call. All the details are in here."

John turned the stick between his fingers. His injuries from the night of the winery fire had healed. A broken back and a shattered leg sustained during the fall from a third-story window had required weeks of physical therapy and forced him to wear a clumsy leg brace for a time—an experience that was as humbling as it was exasperating. The debriefings after years of living as an undercover operative, a period of time during which John had grieved the death of his wife, had taken longer. The thought of a new assignment, even a small one, gave him pause. A.K. was asking him to put a mask back on that he'd only recently taken off.

"I haven't even told Ann yet that Colonel Wick cleared me for duty." John's mood brightened a shade, remembering that Ann was due home later that evening.

The agent shrugged. "Take a look. Think about it. Talk to Ann. I just need to know if you're onboard by tomorrow."

John's eyes darted to A.K. "Tomorrow?"

A crash like an avalanche of glass followed by a high-pitched shriek brought both men to their feet. The wailing sounded continuously as John tore around the end of the bar to the kitchen.

"MRS. BEAUMONT!"

John halted in the kitchen doorway. A week's worth of broken dishes covered the floor, and in the middle of the destruction Tosh, the kitchen boy, was on his knees. His arms wrapped around a stack of dinner plates that had tipped from the safety of the kitchen table and now rested precariously against his shoulder.

The high-pitched shrieking came from the mini-bot clutching the inside edge of the kitchen sink, its sensor dome fully dilated as the air-splitting siren continued. Mrs. Beaumont stood at the opposite end of the kitchen, face frozen in shock. The cook's hands gripped a heavy tray loaded with pies ready for the oven.

John saw another plate start a slow slide from the top of the stack. Tosh instinctively made a move to grab it. The stack rattled and shifted ominously on his shoulder.

"Tosh, don't move! JIB, BE QUIET!"

Tosh froze. Jib silenced the alarm. John cringed as the topmost plate finished its slide and crashed to the floor. He took two quick steps toward the boy and reached for the stack.

The kitchen's garden door flung open with a bang. Tosh jumped and sent the remaining plates toppling to the floor, each one shattering in turn. The wailing of Jib's alarm began anew.

John pressed his palm to his face and peered through fingers at Ann standing in the kitchen doorway. His heart warmed at the sight of her after four days apart, but Ann's timing couldn't have been more disastrous.

Mrs. Beaumont snapped, "Jib! ENOUGH!"

The mini-bot shut off the alarm and returned to scrubbing the sink.

Ann cringed, seeing the state of things. "The breeze caught the door when I opened it. Sorry!"

"You certainly know how to make an entrance, Buttercup," A.K. said to Ann. He turned to John and slapped him on the back. "Well, you're busy. I'll see you later." The agent left through the tavern, but not before John heard the start of a low chuckle.

Mrs. Beaumont sighed and rolled her eyes heavenward. "Tosh, get Luff."

Tosh sprinted to the Tavern.

"I'll grab a box for the big pieces." Ann dropped her satchel and headed to the pantry.

A chirp above John's head made him look up. The little bot had followed him from the tavern and now hung upside down from the door jam.

"False alarm, Port."

At least one mini-bot was functioning correctly, John thought. He would have to fine-tune Jib's threat sensor.

Port detached himself and flew back to the tavern. John watched the bot's lopsided flight path. He considered calling Port back and using the laser pistol hidden in the bot's secret compartment to blast the mountain of broken dishes into oblivion and save the trouble of sweeping, but decided it wasn't worth wasting the power cell.

John turned back to the kitchen and looked at his

cook. Anger edged his voice.

"Mrs. Beaumont…"

"It was an accident, Captain." The older woman slid the tray of pies into the oven.

John pointed in the direction of the tavern. "That boy has cost me a fortune in plates and glassware."

"He bumped the table as he was walking past. It could have happened to anyone."

"But it keeps happening to HIM!"

Mrs. Beaumont slammed the oven door shut and turned to John. Her short white hair glowed like a fire bolt in the light from the window. With a hushed voice, she returned fire.

"Would you have me take it out of the boy's pay?"

John clamped his mouth shut. Mrs. Beaumont, John's cook of ten years, always knew how to back him into a corner. With the boy's mother sick and the family's finances tight, John knew how much Tosh depended on the job.

"You put me in charge so you could focus on your recovery and repairs to the winery," Mrs. Beaumont said. "I hired the best I could find to fill in for Ann when she's away. The boy has potential, he just needs time."

John grumbled, "Fine. Just keep him away from my plates!"

Mrs. Beaumont eyed him in disbelief, hands on her hips. "A kitchen boy who can't touch plates? Brilliant!"

Ann returned from the pantry with a box and started tossing the largest of the broken pieces inside. Tosh reappeared carrying Luff under one arm. The boy set the mini-bot down to sweep. Luff scanned the field of debris, let out an irritated squawk, and trundled forward sucking up the scattered shards. Tosh joined Ann picking up the larger pieces.

John sighed and turned his attention to stowing the surviving stacks of plates still sitting on the kitchen table.

"I'll do that," Mrs. Beaumont said, patting Ann on the shoulder and squatting down to pick up another piece of plate. "You're back early. I didn't think Dr. Brainard was due to pick you up in Idlewild until later tonight."

Ann stood and brushed off her fatigues. "My last lecture was canceled. I ran into Mike and he gave me a ride into town."

John smiled to himself as he lifted a stack of dishes to the cabinet. The beer man's delivery routes were well known and more reliable than any transport in town.

Mrs. Beaumont scrutinized a chipped plate and set it aside. "How's your brother? Has he and Agent Knox found any leads on that stolen sword yet?"

"It's only been five days since the theft," John said as he lifted the last of the plates to the shelf and closed the cabinet door. "You can't expect miracles."

"I'm just *curious*." Mrs. Beaumont shot John an irritated glance before looking back to Ann. "The whole town's been reading about it on the news network. It's all folks talk about."

Ann picked up her satchel and put a water bottle in the cooler. "Sean's doing all right." A faint smile drifted across her mouth. "He's been spending a lot of time with Fionna the last few days, but I don't think they've found many leads yet."

"It's a disgrace!" The older woman frowned and tossed another piece of broken plate into the box. "Why would anyone steal from the museum?" Ann opened her mouth to answer, but Mrs. Beaumont, who'd been surveying the remaining debris, stood with a sigh. "That's all for today, Tosh. I think Luff can handle the rest."

"I'm sorry about the plates. I didn't mean..." Tosh blushed until his freckles disappeared.

The cook gave the boy a gentle smile. "It's all right. Accidents happen in the kitchen. You should ask Captain Galeas about accidents sometime." Mrs. Beaumont's smile curled into a smirk. "He has a story about a beer barrel you should hear." John scowled from across the kitchen. "Why don't you come back in the morning? I have some errands you can run for me. Give my best to your mother."

Mrs. Beaumont closed the kitchen door behind Tosh. She turned and looked at Ann in her blue fatigues.

"You should go change...and take the Captain with you," the cook said, hoisting the box of broken dishes to a hip. "It'll do wonders for his mood." She gave them both a knowing grin before slipping through the kitchen door.

Ann laughed and blushed. John snorted and muttered under his breath to hide a smile of his own.

John's hand rested on the curve of Ann's hip, her body an intriguing silhouette under the bed sheet as she curled next to him. He drank in the sight of her as if they'd been apart a year rather than a mere four days. Ann looked up at him with sleepy contentment. Her braid had come undone, and her hair lay soft about her face. Her hazel eyes sparkled like distant galaxies. John drew Ann closer and found her mouth eager for his. How his arms ached for her when they were apart and how sweet their reunion was when she returned.

His eyes strayed to the trail of clothing on the floor that led from the master bedroom door to the four-poster bed they now shared.

"Remind me to write a letter to the academy quartermaster."

Ann brushed the hair from John's forehead and found the pigtail at the back of his head. She looked at him perplexed. "Why?"

John's lips traced the line of Ann's neck to her ear as he whispered, "I need to thank him for designing the academy fatigues with a full-length front zipper."

Ann laughed. "I'll pass along your thanks. I'm sure the quartermaster will be pleased."

John chuckled and rolled to his back. Ann snuggled into his side, resting her head on his chest.

John kissed the top of her head. "I missed you." He could say that he loved her a thousand times a day and it still wouldn't come close to how he felt.

"I can tell."

John pinched Ann's bottom through the sheets and was pleased with the effect when she yelped and squirmed against his side.

"I missed you, too," Ann said with a sigh. "With all my heart."

Ann moved quickly, throwing a leg over John, and sat up straddling him in one deft maneuver. She paused, looked down at him with a coy smile, and continued the motion to roll out the other side of the bed.

John's eyes followed her with growing disappointment. "You're leaving?"

She smiled over a smooth bare shoulder. Her hair fell in dark auburn waves down her back. "If we don't head downstairs soon, Mrs. Beaumont will come looking for us."

John grunted. "She was the one who suggested we come up here in the first place." His thoughts turned to what an encounter of that nature would be like with the cook. He rolled out of bed grumbling and reached for his trousers.

"So what's the word on Commander Garin?" John asked, remembering the communications Ann had sent him while she was at headquarters. "Is he really gone?"

Ann scooped up her discarded clothes and tossed them into a laundry basket on the way to the closet. "Long gone. Walked off the stage after his speech and went home. I heard he already left for his family homestead on the Outer Banks. I'm sorry to see him go. Everyone is."

"Vesto Garin was a good commander. One of the best we've ever had."

"I wish he'd given us more time to get used to the idea."

"That was his way," John said, retrieving his shirt from the headboard. "I never met him personally, but I'm told from those who served with him that once he made up his mind about something there was no waiting around. Garin made things happen." John pulled on his shirt to discover all the buttons torn off. He arched a brow in Ann's direction as the memory tempted him again, but Ann was too busy lacing her blouse to notice. Her smooth bare legs encircled by a fringe of white linen made a pretty sight. *Pace yourself, lad.* John sighed, tossed the buttonless shirt in a corner, and grabbed a new shirt from the closet. "How's Commander Rectrix getting along? Not making any trouble, I hope?"

Ann tucked the tail of her blouse as she stepped into a long blue colony skirt. "It's only been a few days, but so far she's keeping a low profile. The cadets don't seem to care, and it's been business as usual for the time jumpers." Ann secured a wide leather belt around her waist. She took a seat at the dressing table and picked up a hairbrush. "Honestly, you wouldn't know anything has changed except the name plate on the commander's office door."

"Good. And Professor Huxley hasn't said anything else?"

"He's been busy with the start of the term. Huxley said he'd contact me when he knew something." Ann paused as she ran the brush through her hair. "Do you think I should be worried with what the professor said about me still being under investigation and Commander Rectrix taking over?"

John flopped into a cushioned armchair, one foot shod and the other still bare, and scanned the floor for the missing boot. "Has she done anything? Approached you in any way?"

"No. I guess I'm just not in a hurry to trust anyone who was on that committee," Ann said with a sigh.

John looked up and frowned at the bitter edge of Ann's words. "Of everyone on the crash investigation committee Rectrix seemed to be the most sympathetic toward you. Her appointment to the academy could be a coincidence."

Ann smirked at him in the dresser mirror. "Since when do time jumpers believe in coincidence?"

John replied with a lopsided grin of his own. "Lots of times, especially when we're the reason for them." He tugged thoughtfully at his pigtail. "Until we hear back from Huxley, or something happens to suggest otherwise, all we have is a conspiracy theory."

John found the missing boot under the bed and pulled it on. He slouched back into the armchair and watched Ann braid her hair, fingers flying expertly through the thick strands. He weighed the next question carefully before loosening his tongue.

"Did you talk to Colonel Wick about your flight test?"

Ann dropped her eyes from the mirror to the dresser as she fastened the end of her braid. "No."

John tried and failed to hold his exasperation in check.

"Ann…"

"I've been busy."

"It'll only get harder the longer you wait."

Ann stood and tossed the hairbrush into a dressing table drawer with a slam. "I *will* talk to him." She took a step toward the bedroom door.

John jumped up from his chair, blocking her path. Ann always managed to duck out of the conversation when the topic of the flight test came up, but this time he was ready. "Send Wick a message tonight. Tell him you need to see him the next time you're at headquarters." The muscles in John's shoulders tensed, ready for the confrontation he knew would follow when he spoke the next words. "Either you do it…or I will."

Ann's eyes flashed. Her face darkened. "I don't need a nanny."

John took an agitated swipe through his hair and tried to rein in his frustration. "You *need* to talk to someone."

Her next words came out clipped from between her teeth. "I told *you* about it."

"I'm not a counselor!" The volume of his voice rose against his will. John blew out an aggravated sigh and looked at Ann as she stood as stiff and straight as an iron mast. Her face was a storm ready to unleash. He hadn't wanted to start an argument.

For four days, he'd practiced what he'd planned to say if she'd once again returned home without speaking to Colonel Wick, but now the words left him, marooned on an island of helplessness. John took a deep breath and tried again.

"You've aced every written test. You've answered every question for every drill. You could sketch the controls of the cockpit down to the last detail right now if I asked you to. You should be able to fly blindfolded." Ann threw her hands up in exasperation and turned away, putting distance between them. John stood his ground and continued. "You told me, 'I get into the cockpit, John, and it all leaves me. I can't think. I can't breathe. And all I want is out.'" John took a breath to keep his voice steady. "Then you told me that the only button on the control panel you recognize is the one that blows the cockpit hatch."

Ann turned her head toward him a fraction, the only outward sign she'd heard him.

"Isn't that what you told me?"

Her shoulders rounded almost imperceptibly as if her body wanted to curl in on itself. Ann gripped the back of John's desk chair. When she spoke, her voice was small, the anger gone. "I'll get over it. I just need more time."

John took a step toward her. He knew, even before her recent confession, that she still carried trauma from her accident. The fear he felt for her bloomed in his chest. "This isn't something that goes away on its own. Colonel Wick can help you. Don't wait ten years. Don't make the mistake I made. I won't let you." John touched Ann's shoulder. He spoke near to a whisper, his voice ragged. "Ann...*please*..."

The last of the fight left her. Ann sunk into the chair and leaned against the desk. She rested her head on the heel of one hand. Ann's voice shook, but John was satisfied she meant it this time. "I'll message him tonight."

John pulled the armchair closer and took her hands in his. "Captain Shaw owes me a favor. He has a flight trainer with a dual seat. We could go flying tomorrow. If you got into trouble, I could take the controls."

Ann shook her head. "John, I...I don't want anyone with me. It's too..." John's heart twisted at the unspoken word. *Dangerous.* She blinked rapidly to keep the tears from spilling and took a deep breath. "It's just not a good idea. Not until I can get through the simulation. Sarolea said she would help me practice when the *What Cheer* got back." Ann frowned. "I thought she said she'd be back before I left to come home."

"The crew probably went for a post-mission drink that turned into an all-nighter," John said, squeezing her hands. "You'll see her as soon as she sleeps it off."

Ann nodded and they sat in silence for a moment. John poured her a glass of water from the jug on the bedside table. Ann sipped and looked across at John.

"Why was Agent Max here?"

John hesitated. It didn't seem like the best time to tell Ann about Scrivani, but there was no point in delay. Ann showed concern but took the news well.

"A.K. doesn't think we have anything to worry about," John said.

"What do *you* think?" Ann asked, leveling her gaze.

John tugged his pigtail. "I don't know. We'll take the usual precautions…"

Ann nodded, gathering strength. "…and if something changes, adapt."

John smiled at Ann quoting him. "There's more. While you were gone, Colonel Wick cleared me for duty. A.K. has a job for me. That's the real reason why he came to see me."

Ann's face lit up with a bright smile. "That's wonderful! It's what you wanted, isn't it?"

"I haven't had a chance to review the mission files yet, but he says it's only a short jump." John met Ann's eyes. "Going on missions will mean we'll have less time together. It'll make things harder for us…and for Mrs. Beaumont. She'll have to keep Siren's Cove running when we're both gone."

The question was an old one. What to do with Siren's Cove when they both returned to duty? John had mentioned the possibility of selling the tavern before, but Ann had resisted. Truth be told, John had no desire to sell either, but he would choose Ann over the tavern if it came to it.

Ann nodded. "We knew this was coming. Mike and Arnold said they can help out behind the bar, and Mrs. Beaumont's working on lining up other staff who can fill in on short notice." Ann waved her hand as she took another sip. "We'll find a way to make it work."

John sighed and allowed himself a weary grin. All the women in his life had fallen in love with the old tavern. Why would Ann be any different?

Ann set her glass down and picked up an open envelope lying on the desk.

"What's this?" She pulled the stiff, cream-colored card from inside and flipped it over. Formal black calligraphy swirled.

John cringed. "I forgot. It came yesterday addressed to both of us."

Ann's eyes danced as she read the invitation. She laughed in surprise. "Ambassador Mirina Canopus has invited us to her wedding." Ann arched a brow. "Odd. I thought she'd sooner invite a barrel of eels than have us there."

John smirked. "Speak for yourself. I've never met her."

Ann laughed. "Neither have I. I just naturally assume she hates me."

"We don't have to go. Nobody would expect you to."

Ann pursed her mouth in thought. "No, we should go..." Ann tossed the invitation back onto the desk, stood and stretched. "Vincent is still a friend, and I would like to try and keep it that way despite Mirina."

John looked at Ann in her long colony skirt and peasant blouse. The wide leather belt nipped her slender waist. So different from the fatigues she wore while at headquarters. It was how she looked when he first fell in love with her. John stood and drew Ann to him again. She smiled up at him, eyes bright.

"Enough already," John said. "I only have you for three days. I plan to make the most of it."

SEVEN

POLITICS

"Doesn't it get tiring having that big thing s-trapped to your thigh all the time?"

Sean blinked and covered his shock with a polite smile. "I beg your pardon?"

The foreign diplomat, a stout man in saffron-colored robes whose name Sean couldn't remember, wore a pewter e-polyglot clipped to an ear. The Andarrian Ambassador standing next to his brightly attired guest winced.

"Your *sword*, Montressador Chapman." Ambassador Aldebaran gestured to Sean's blade. "Minister Meritxell was wondering about some of the traditions of your office. For example, I explained to him that the King's Champion must wear his sword or keep it within arm's reach at all times."

Diplomatic functions were usually dry affairs, but the Ambassador and Minister Meritxell offered a reprieve from polite small talk with Madame DuCeaux and her daughter, Ismena. The young socialite had eyed Sean in his black and silver dress uniform like a bag of candy since he arrived at Hautwesel Hall but conversing with her properly was impossible given the close attention of the mother.

"Ah, yes of course, Ambassador." Sean turned to address Meritxell. "Anatomically speaking, it's more accurate to say the sword is strapped to my hip." Aldebaran paled slightly at Sean's use of the word *anatomically*. "And to answer your question, Minister, the first five years are the hardest and then you get used to it."

Meritxell listened to the translation in his ear from the e-polyglot and nodded before looking back to Sean. "But in an age of ion pistols...isn't a sword..." The Minister cast his eyes about for a moment. "What is the saying...? Bringing a sharp object to a battle against superior fire power?"

Sean felt his diplomacy begin to slip. "That's true. But there are the ladies to consider."

Meritxell listened to the translation. "The ladies? How's that?"

"It's been my experience that women prefer *swordplay*," Sean said and flashed a wicked grin.

It took a few seconds for the e-polyglot to translate. Meritxell reacted, his face quizzical. Ambassador Aldebaran coughed into a fist, squeaked something about priceless tapestries, and quickly ushered his confused guest to the other end of the crowded ballroom. Sean turned his attention back to the DuCeauxs, but mother and daughter had left to join a group of dignitaries. *Perhaps another time*, Sean thought.

"I see you're still doing your part for foreign relations."

Sean looked over a shoulder. Commander Vincent Lazar stood behind him, grinning and looking like a recruitment poster for Andarrian Forces in his dress uniform. His blond wavy hair glinted with the same shade of gold as the buttons on his blue jacket.

Sean gripped Vincent's hand in a firm handshake. "I was hoping to improve relations closer to home, but Miss Ismena left with Madame DuCeaux when I wasn't looking."

"Another socialite?" Vincent frowned. "Are you sure that's wise?"

Sean shot his friend a questioning look.

"If you don't mind me saying so...she has a reputation with the tabloids," Vincent said with a confidential tone. "The only ones to benefit would be the gossip pages. I thought after the last time you might want to be more careful."

Sean leveled his eyes at his friend. "You. Cad."

Vincent drew back in surprise.

"*Madame* DuCeaux is a perfectly respectable woman," Sean said, a wry grin curling his mouth. "You force me to defend her honor."

Vincent chuckled. "Pistols at dawn?" His face shone with amusement.

Sean's eyes flew open. "Pistols?" He pointed to his sword. "Are you insane? We'll settle this like men." He paused to straighten his jacket. "We'll sit around and drink until we can't remember what we were arguing about."

Vincent's reserve crumbled under a hearty belly

laugh.

Ambassador Mirina Canopus swept forward from a throng of guests, hands dramatically raised to her ears, and stepped to the commander's side.

"Vincent, darling, that laugh! I thought I heard the chandelier rattle!"

Mirina's effect on Vincent, Sean noted with a frown, was immediate. Commander Lazar mumbled an apology and cast his eyes downward before recovering. All the warmth and camaraderie a moment ago pulled behind a wall of formality. Vincent seemed diminished, somehow smaller than when Anaya was on his arm, Sean thought.

Mirina latched her eyes onto Sean. "Delightful to see you again, Montressador Chapman. It's been too long."

Ambassador Canopus stood out among the other dignitaries like a swan in a room full of undertakers. A great deal of credit was owed to her dressmaker. Her snow-white gown, belted in silver, left one shoulder bare with the gathered bodice fitted to her exact measurements. The long skirt, embroidered with green, purple, and gold feathers from the hem to the waist, flowed about Mirina with every step.

As to her natural beauty, while she was certainly pleasant enough to gaze upon with her hair the color of warm honey and high cheekbones, in Sean's opinion Mirina fell a degree short of being extraordinarily beautiful. Regardless, he'd observed that the ambassador dressed, spoke, and moved—every crafted little gesture—as if she were always the most beautiful woman in the room.

Mirina's tall and slender figure complemented Vincent's frame. Together, the commander and the ambassador made a well-matched pair, a fact Sean thought cynically that was not lost on Mirina.

"Ambassador..." Sean took her offered hand, catching the heavy floral scent of perfume as he gave a customary bow. Vincent's engagement ring sparkled on Mirina's hand. Her fingernails were perfect ovals the color of plums. "Yes, it has been too long," Sean said and looked up sideways at the commander. "Vincent, where has she been keeping you?"

Vincent gave an awkward laugh and looked uncertain.

Mirina joined in, although her laughter was rimmed with ice.

"Oh, Sean. You wound me. I do encourage him to see his friends, but lately, there is just so much to do."

"We have been awfully busy," Vincent said, turning to Mirina. "Perhaps after the wedding, we could..."

She looped an arm through his and dismissed him with a pat. "My poor darling! Of course, there will be plenty of time to socialize after the wedding." Mirina turned her attention back to Sean. "Speaking of which, I was so happy to receive your reply along with Anaya's that you would both be attending. How nice it will be to finally meet your sister."

Vincent's face colored at the mention of Anaya's name.

"A meeting for the ages, I'm sure," Sean replied, and tried to catch Vincent's eye.

"I'm absolutely parched," Mirina said, fanning her face. "Diplomacy is such a chatty business. I've been talking with dignitaries since we arrived." She turned to the commander and flashed a megawatt smile. "Vincent, would you mind finding me something cold to drink?"

"Of course, darling." Vincent chanced an apologetic look toward Sean before striding purposefully through the crowd.

No sooner had Vincent stepped away, than Mirina took Sean's arm and gently steered him across the room. Guests parted at their approach. Mirina smiled and nodded at the admiring faces as she walked.

Sean glanced over a shoulder toward the refreshment table. "You've done well bringing Vincent to heel so quickly. Now if you can just teach him not to pee on the furniture or dig in the garden."

Mirina laughed, and Sean sensed that her merriment was more for the benefit of the people watching them than for any true enjoyment of his company. Her crisp reply confirmed his suspicions.

"How is it your earthy humor only makes you all the more charming?"

Sean shrugged as they arrived at the hall's impressive marble fireplace, the grate empty due to the warm weather. "Years of study and practice." He leaned a shoulder against the mantel, one hand rested on the hilt of his sword. "I medaled in vulgarity at the academy."

The ambassador ignored the remark and pretended to admire the fireplace fresco. "I noticed you indicated two guests on your reply card." Mirina looked at Sean, eyes sparkling. "Don't be coy. Which one of the many beauties that chase after you will you be bringing to the wedding?"

As was so often when talking with Mirina, Sean felt a growing unease. He mentally adjusted his stance and prepared to counter.

"If I tell you now, I'll ruin the surprise," Sean said. "You'll just have to wait." The truth was Sean hadn't decided yet whom to invite, but he saw no reason to confide in the ambassador. The fact Mirina seemed so keen on knowing was reason enough in his mind not to tell her anything.

"I know someone who would make the perfect escort." Mirina fingered the strand of pearls around the hollow of her throat and turned her body a fraction to show a more flattering silhouette. "Beautiful. Intelligent. You would do well to have her on your arm."

Sean chuckled. "You're very kind, but your matchmaking won't be necessary." He pivoted with a quick change of subject before Mirina could riposte. "I've been meaning to thank you and Vincent for inviting Anaya to the wedding. It's very generous of you. She was pleasantly surprised to receive the invitation."

"Well, why not? You've both been good friends to Vincent for a long time. I want us all to be good friends and what better way to begin? It would be awkward if only you were invited. You are Vincent's friend and Anaya is your sister...."

"Who used to be engaged to Vincent."

Mirina tittered and danced away from Sean's cut. "Oh, poo. I'm above such pettiness. It's all in the past. I know that Vincent and your sister were engaged for a short time before her accident, but he made his choice. And by all accounts, your sister is happy with her bartender."

Sean frowned. "Bartender. You mean Captain Galeas? He wasn't awarded a Distinguished Service Medal for pulling pints."

"Forgive me." Mirina lowered her eyes in contrition. *A clever feint.* "Captain Galeas was very brave to work undercover tracking and capturing those pirates, but what has he done lately?" She leaned forward to a more intimate distance. "The fact is he runs a tavern...on the Colonies of all places...very successfully I'm told. Whatever he was in the past is not what he is now." Mirina straightened and gestured to the ballroom. A string quartet had started to play, and the elegant sounds of a minuet drifted through the crowd. "When I look around, I can't help but think I made the better match."

Sean smirked. It was all about image. He had long suspected that Mirina saw a political advantage to cultivating a public relationship with him even though she disapproved of him personally. That much was obvious. To have a good relationship with him meant she would also need to be on at least civil terms with Anaya.

But pride demanded Mirina also dispel the cloud that she'd been Vincent's second choice. After Anaya's accident, he'd left, convinced she was dead, and accepted a deep space assignment that kept him away and out of communication range for months. It was an act of cowardice that Sean knew his friend deeply regretted. It was only later when Vincent returned that Sean found out the assignment was to bring Ambassador Canopus home to Andarria.

What Mirina didn't know was that Sean remembered what Vincent had said after he discovered Anaya was alive. "What have I done? If I'd only known…" Had Vincent stayed, had Anaya been found sooner and not fallen in love with Captain Galeas, their story might have ended differently. Instead, Mirina had seduced Vincent during their long voyage home, and in his grief, he proposed.

Sean also suspected, although he'd never broach the subject, that Vincent felt trapped by a sense of duty to go through with the marriage. Sean hoped that Vincent could find happiness with Mirina, assuming his friend was too boneheaded to break off the engagement, but Sean had his doubts.

All these thoughts pressed on Sean's consciousness as he met Mirina's gaze. Ambassador Canopus used her influence to charm and to persuade, not for the good of the Republic, but for her own personal political gain. The most dangerous creature was a politician in a diplomat's clothes. Mirina could give lessons to the wolf.

Out of the corner of his eye, Sean saw Vincent returning through the crowd.

"Mirina..." Sean sighed. "You're a remarkable woman."

Vincent handed Mirina her drink just as an attendant in black and yellow livery approached.

"Montressador Chapman..."

Sean snatched a shrimp from the appetizer tray of a passing waiter and popped it into his mouth as he nodded to the attendant. To his displeasure, he realized too late the shrimp hadn't been properly shelled.

"Agent Knox is waiting in the vestibule," the attendant said. "She's requested to speak with you."

Sean's irritation turned to alarm.

"Please excuse us, Montressador, but we must be going," Mirina said, stirring her drink. "Undoubtedly, you have business with Agent Knox and there are still—"

Vincent's face brightened. "Fionna is here? I haven't seen her in ages. Surely, we have time for a quick hello?"

Mirina shot Vincent a look designed to retract a man's balls to his spine. Sean felt his own tighten up, but the commander had caught the full power of the ambassador's glare.

Vincent coughed into a fist. "But perhaps another time would be better..."

Mirina's charm returned as quickly as it left. "As I was saying, there are still some people I should speak to and you should meet, darling."

"Of course." Vincent turned to Sean with a pained expression. "Please give Fionna our regards."

Sean smiled and nodded, doing his best to hide the shrimp in his mouth. Mirina dragged Vincent off to diplomacy hell, leaving Sean alone with his invisible shrimp problem.

The attendant gestured toward the vestibule. "This way, Montressador."

Sean glanced around frantically as he followed. The blasted waiters with the napkins were never around when you needed one. Expelling the shrimp politely was impossible. Fionna had already eyed him from across the room. Seeing no other option, he swallowed the shrimp whole.

Sean coughed. "Agent Knox…" His voice cracked.

The shrimp had been cooked in a weird spice that tickled the back of his throat. For one terrifying second, Sean wondered if he might be allergic and pictured himself turning purple and foaming at the mouth in front of Fionna.

"Montressador Chapman…" Fionna smiled in greeting then grew concerned. "Are you…?"

Sean blinked back tears. *Damn eyes.* "I'm fine…" *Damn poisonous shrimp coated in ground-up steel wool.* "Let's talk on the balcony."

Sean grabbed a drink from a passing waiter and used the walk up the stairs to wash down the remains of the shrimp. He followed Fionna and wiped his eyes with his sleeve when she wasn't looking.

Fionna took a seat on a marble bench next to the balustrade overlooking the ballroom and opened her data pad. She wore the usual pea-green jacket she favored while on duty and dark gray slacks. Sean found himself thinking fondly of the figure-hugging, black and silver gown she'd worn at the museum. He shook his head to clear his thoughts and was grateful her golden bio-vision glasses rested on the top of her blond head. Sean's breath hitched in his throat when her violet eyes found his.

"The chronocular sweep at the museum picked up two spacetime distortions," Fionna began, clicking her stylus. "One faint and the other much stronger."

"Time travel?" Sean's thoughts raced back to him from their pleasant wanderings. Cox's Conundrum, a natural force of unexplained origins, prevented time travel on the Andarrian home world, but did allow for the manipulation of spacetime for instantaneous travel between two points like the Academy's Weyl Gate. Someone circumventing the Conundrum would bring the Republic to its knees.

Fionna glanced up. "No. The distortion was the wrong frequency for time jumping. The thief folded spacetime to gain access to the museum. Cox's Conundrum is still in play."

Sean let out a sigh. "That's a relief. I hadn't planned on dealing with total societal collapse today."

Fionna smirked. "Your schedule should be safe at least for today. Neither distortion had a time signature, so we're dealing with an unlicensed and therefore unknown traveler."

Sean nodded. Unknown travelers on the home

world were rare, but still a better option than a hiccup with Cox.

Fionna flipped to a new screen. "My blackmarket antiquities informant came up dry. No chatter on or off-world about the missing sword. The trail's gone cold..." Fionna tilted her head as she read the information on the screen. "Assuming there was a trail to follow at all. I'm beginning to doubt it was an antiquities theft."

Sean drummed his fingers on the hilt of his sword. "If the sword wasn't stolen for someone's personal art collection, why would someone want it?"

"I don't know." Fionna frowned. "That's why I wanted to talk to you. You know the sword's history. Can you think of any other motive? Who would be interested in a sword like that?"

Sean shrugged. "No one other than a private collector, a museum curator, or a Montressador would have any interest in it."

The corner of Fionna's mouth twitched as she checked off something on the screen with her stylus. "I'll add you to my list of suspects."

"Maybe we're overthinking this," Sean said. "If you take away its historical significance, a sword is only good for one thing." Fionna met Sean's gaze. "It's a weapon."

Fionna arched a brow in disbelief. "There are a lot easier ways to get a weapon than to break into the National Museum."

Sean grumbled and nodded. "And as I'm so often

reminded, swords aren't really in much demand these days."

"So what else could the sword represent?"

Sean sighed and mumbled to himself as he gazed over the balcony and watched the party still in full swing in the ballroom below. *"Why is a raven like a writing desk?"*

The quartet finished to polite scattered applause and began a new piece, older and drearier than the sprightly minuet. Visiting dignitaries and nobles filled the hall, drinking and conversing in groups or pairs. The perfect timbre of Mirina's party laugh floated through the air. Ambassador Canopus was easy to spot in her gleaming white gown conversing with Ambassador Aldebaran and Minister-What's-His-Name of the saffron-colored robes. Vincent stood nearby looking thoroughly miserable even from a distance. A thought struck Sean.

"Politics," Sean said, turning back to Fionna. "The sword was used to murder noblemen. It was, on some level, a political assassination."

Fionna blinked. "But you don't know the motive for sure. You said Montressador Syrovar was a raving lunatic by the time she was convicted, and no one knew why she did it."

"True. But I might know someone who could take an educated guess."

EIGHT

THE PADOME

Sean walked up the stone steps to the curved patina-covered door. His assistant, Josephine, had once again performed scheduling wizardry on short notice.

"Is this really necessary?" Fionna walked at his side. "You do realize the Ministry of Investigations has the largest database in the Republic?"

The cracked yellow plaster and old brick of the manse's facade looked ancient in Sean's eyes even in the heart of the capital's historic old town. The drone of air ships between the gleaming towers in the distant Financial District felt out of place and gave him a peculiar sensation of detachment as if he'd stepped into another world.

"If you had all the answers, you wouldn't have come to me asking for help in the first place," Sean said. The agent gave a serene smile and dipped her head in acknowledgment. Sean lifted the iron latch, half expecting it to crumble under the pressure of his hand, and pushed the door open. A puff of cold air crossed the threshold in greeting. He held the door open for Fionna to step through. "You wanted to know why else the sword would've been stolen. What it represents. The Ministry's database is only as good as the question it's being asked."

"And your experts know the right questions to ask? Better than the Ministry..." Fionna arched a pale brow. "...of *Investigations*?"

Sean crossed into the dimly lit stone interior and pushed the door shut behind them. The foyer smelled of cold stone and old books.

"You can't engineer intuition," he said as he continued down the hallway. The ring of his sword belt echoed off the walls with every step. "Sometimes experience is better for making connections. The Padome has advised Montressadors for a thousand years."

Historically, Montressadors had used the Padome to consult on matters of importance, but over the last two hundred years or so there hadn't been much use for the council. Like the office of the Montressador, the tradition lived on. As members died, new ones were appointed even though there wasn't much for them to do except hoard and catalog information while pursuing their own research. The position was mostly honorary, one last feather in the cap of a long scholarly career.

"I'm sure military strategy and protocol are very useful to your office," Fionna said, matching Sean's stride. "But I don't see how the Padome can help in this case."

Sean chuckled. "The council has experts in every

field of study. You'd be surprised what I need to know to do this job."

The hallway opened into a large chamber. Sabadell sat toward the middle of the head table with his nose in a book. A few chairs away snored Gregor, his bald pate looking like an enormous spotted pink egg resting on the table. Sean spied four other council members at the far end. As expected, the card game was in full swing.

Helda tapped her cards impatiently. "Lydian, it's your move."

"I played the eight," Lydian said, clenching his jaw.

"That was last round," Helda said, her white bouffant bristling. "Coloma played the five, Aural played the deuce, and I played the peg."

"Fine!" Lydian ground his teeth, shuffled his cards with crooked fingers, and slapped down a card as if swatting a fly.

"Aha!" Helda quickly played the next card to take the trick.

"Wait!" Lydian shouted. "I can play two cards. I have the raven. I want to play it!"

"You can't! I already played my knave."

"You didn't give me a chance!" Lydian's bark ended in a whine. "I said wait!"

"Cheater!" Helda banged her fist on the table. "CHEEEATER!"

Coloma and Aural threw their cards down in disgust while their two companions continued to trade insults.

Coloma sighed and looked at Aural from underneath a fringe of faded red hair. "I hate playing Rook with them."

"Rook?" Aural blinked through his thick spectacles. "I thought we were playing Double Folly."

Coloma shook her head and said dryly, "And that is why you always lose."

Sean crooked a smile and approached the table. As entertaining as Helda's and Lydian's squabbles were, Josephine had him on a tight schedule. Sean cleared his throat.

Sabadell glanced up from his book. The old gentleman's thin gray mustache twitched. "Montressador Chapman. Have you come to see Helda and Lydian murder each other, or do you need advice on your love life again?" Fionna stepped to Sean's side. Sabadell brightened and straightened in his chair. "Ah! You brought the lady with you this time."

Sean gave an awkward cough. "This is *Agent* Fionna Knox..."

"A pleasure to meet you," Sabadell squinted in Fionna's direction then looked back to Sean. "She is intelligent and lovely. I see no problem." He waved a hand dismissively and returned to his book. "Marry the woman. Make babies."

Fionna covered her mouth to hide a smile.

Sean flushed beneath his beard. He spoke loudly enough for the room to hear and was grateful when his voice didn't crack. "I believe Jo might have mentioned I called a *formal session*?" Sean gestured to his uniform.

Conversations stopped. Heads turned.

Sabadell locked eyes on Sean and hollered into the silence. "Darby!" A young steward appeared from an alcove in the back of the chamber and approached looking flustered. "A formal session? Is this true?"

The steward leaned over and whispered hurriedly in the old man's ear. Sabadell's face crumpled in anger as he slammed his book shut.

"Idiot!"

In an instant, the room was in motion. Robes were donned and playing cards swept from the table as council members took their seats.

Sabadell growled, "Someone wake up Gregor!"

Hearing his name Gregor jolted awake. "RATS!"

"Not rats, Gregor," Coloma said, taking a seat next to the octogenarian. "We're in session. Zip up your robe."

Darby ran to the front of the chamber carrying a ceremonial baton, his own robe flapping about his legs as he struggled to close it. The steward took his place next to Montressador Chapman and looked to Sabadell with the eyes of a frightened rabbit.

Sabadell roared, "GET ON WITH IT!"

The usual pomp filled the next few minutes with formal introductions given by Darby. Guest chairs were brought along with the traditional stand for the Montressador to remove his sword while addressing the council, but only after Sabadell threw a book at the hapless steward. Sean bore it all with dignity and patience except for the slight irritation he felt whenever Fionna pressed her lips together to hide a smile.

Sean noted the empty seats at the head table as he took his own chair. "Is this everyone?"

Sabadell made a rueful gesture. "The best we can do. Olinka and Maunder are traveling..."

"And Gasten and Yamal are dying," Helda snapped. "You might have more open seats to fill soon."

Sean's heart pained him to hear the news. "I'm sorry. I didn't know."

"A great honor you've given us. Dying members appointed to a dying council for a dying tradition." Lydian avoided Sean's eye and tugged at the hem of his sleeve.

Sean's heart twisted again. It always grieved him to appoint new members. He turned to Sabadell. "I'd like to be kept informed on Gasten and Yamal."

Sabadell nodded. "Of course. And we will update our colleagues on our session today. Now..." The old gentleman sighed. "How may we serve the realm?"

"The Ministry of Investigations needs your help finding a missing sword," Sean said, gesturing to Fionna.

Gregor leaned forward, eyes brightening, as he looked to Agent Knox. "The sword of Montressador Syrovar, the Doge of Erna?"

"How many missing swords are there, you dolt!" Lydian growled from the opposite end of the table.

The older man seemed to ignore Lydian's remark, but Sean saw the look Gregor threw as he settled back into his chair.

"The Ministry doesn't believe the sword was

stolen for its monetary value, but we don't know why else someone would want it," Fionna said, opening her data pad. "We need to know what could the sword symbolize that would make someone want it enough to steal it?"

Lydian scoffed. "It's the sword of a traitor. Of broken loyalty. Of upheaval, chaos, and murder."

"But to the right person it could also represent justice, the sword of a martyr, and revolution," Aural said. Thick spectacles magnified the councilman's eyes to the size of dinner plates.

Fionna frowned. "Revolution?"

"The murdered noblemen were all from families supportive of the King," Gregor said. "Syrovar didn't just murder the heads of those houses, she also murdered their heirs. The events of that night greatly weakened those families at least for a time. Three years later the king died, and the line of succession was challenged."

"The first of the Great Wars." Sean mentally kicked himself for not remembering his history lessons. "If Syrovar hadn't murdered the noblemen, the king's son might have had the support needed to keep his crown."

"So the question you should be asking is not what the sword symbolizes," Sabadell said. "But what do the *events* that Syrovar put into motion represent?"

Sean narrowed his eyes in thought. "Change...political change...for better or worse."

"Your point of view often depends on what side of history you're standing on," Coloma said, nodding in approval.

Fionna scratched a quick note with her stylus. "From what I've seen, everyone hates Syrovar."

"All except one," Aural said. "Your thief. Doubtful he or she would have gone through the trouble of stealing the sword if they felt otherwise."

Fionna scribbled a few more notes then stood to address the Padome. "Thank you for your time. This has been very helpful."

"It has?" Sean looked up confused before taking his feet. "We still don't have a suspect."

"Maybe not..." Fionna said, a faraway look in her eye. "But if Syrovar represents political change... who do we know that is unhappy with the way things are and who just happened to be protesting outside of the museum the night the sword was stolen?"

Sean's mouth spread into a grin. "The Luctari."

"Or someone who shares their point of view," Fionna said.

Lydian's chair scraped against the stone floor as he stood. "Glad you have your answers. It's time we got back to our card game. I'll see you at our next formal session, or if I'm dead then my replacement will."

"Lydian, we're still in session," Sabadell said with a disapproving tone.

"Take your seat, councilman." The authority in Sean's voice rang through the chamber. "I have one more request of the Padome before we adjourn." He held Lydian in his gaze until the councilman grudgingly returned to his seat. Sean turned his attention back to Sabadell. "I charge the council to uncover why Montressador Syrovar committed those murders."

Up and down the head table, council members blinked in surprise. A few exchanged glances with their neighbors. Gregor was the first to speak.

"Montressador Chapman, there are several theories, but none that offer concrete proof. It's a mystery that historians have never been able to solve."

From the corner of his eye, Sean saw Fionna looking at him with the same confused expression. Sean frowned. Why was everyone looking at him like he was the dumbest kid in the classroom? He whispered to Fionna, "It might be helpful."

Fionna continued to look doubtful and whispered back, "I'm not sure how. I don't see that it really applies in this case."

Sean ignored the agent and turned to address the Padome again. "I want to know why. Can it be done?"

"Most of the official histories were written years after Syrovar's execution," Coloma said. "Plenty of time for hearsay and innuendo to poison the truth. We would need to separate facts from rumor."

"All we have are rumors," Lydian grumbled.

"The rumors themselves may hold the breadcrumbs we need to follow," Aural replied.

Council members exchanged looks again, but this time it was as if a flame passed between them as a fever took hold. *A puzzle to solve.* Sean saw their growing interest and grinned in satisfaction.

Sean looked back to Sabadell and caught him smirking. The old gentleman had figured out his ruse.

"It will be the first time the Padome has attempted to research the issue as a group in modern history," Sabadell said. "But yes. We can do it and we'll make it a priority."

"I'll search the archive," Helda said. "It's possible a previous council member took it up as a personal research project."

"Good." Sean nodded as he buckled his sword belt. "I'll expect regular reports on your progress."

"Montressador, any in-depth investigation might be seen as an attempt to exonerate Syrovar, which will most likely cause certain inflexible people some level of distress," Sabadell cautioned. "Are you sure you want to dig up thunderbolts?"

"Yes, and I'll provide you with bigger shovels if needed," Sean said meeting the old gentleman's eye. "Let me know if you run into any trouble. Thank you for your time."

Sean bowed, officially ending the session, and walked out with Fionna.

NINE

A SHORT JUMP

John's boots landed in soft dirt.

He dropped into a defensive crouch, hand on the laser pistol strapped to his side, and blinked as he scanned the surroundings.

Sunlight.

Trees.

Birds.

Big ferns.

And most importantly...

Nothing trying to shoot at me or eat me.

A cool breeze brought the smell of vegetation, a whiff of animal dung, and...beer. John's ears pricked to music and laughter coming from somewhere nearby. A glance over a shoulder showed the top of a dirty canvas tent in a clearing a few yards behind.

John relaxed his shoulders and blew out a sigh. He stood, letting his long black coat sweep forward to cover his sidearm. The time beacon was programmed to make the drop in places devoid of activity where he could appear unnoticed. A nice feature, but sometimes it made for awkward landing areas.

Jokes were rampant about time jumpers appearing in broom closets, bathrooms, and dark alleys. All clichés, of course, but with every ridiculous tale came a nugget of truth. One of the most dangerous aspects of being a time jumper was landing and not knowing exactly where you might be. John heard of one unlucky time jumper whose defective beacon dropped her into the middle of a street riot. The rioters had been too busy looting and causing mayhem to notice the time jumper's sudden appearance...but neither did the runaway horse carriage that trampled her five seconds later.

John took a step toward the clearing and froze when he heard the unmistakable sound of a zipper and then the splatter of water pouring onto the ground. The mini-bot squirmed inside his coat. John gripped the bot with one hand and whispered, "*Hold still.*"

As the water continued to flow, John turned a fraction and saw a blue-skinned Leucothean relieving himself against a nearby tree. Thinking quickly, John pretended to zip his own trousers, turned, and walked past nonchalantly, making sure to give the Leucothean a wide berth as they were known to have a generous spray. John nodded to the outlander who gave a drunken salute in return as he continued to grunt and spray his foul water against the unfortunate tree.

John strolled from the tree line into the clearing where an outdoor market had been constructed. The merchants drew a heavy crowd. Tents of every size and color and smaller wooden stalls formed crisscrossing avenues. Food stalls sold their fare between weapons dealers and slave traders. Merchants hawked their goods to the people passing by. *Need repairs to your ship? Looking for a charter? Forged travel documents? Weapons or ammunition? Pick up or delivery and a meat pie or a whore while you wait.* John smirked. The black market fun fair had it all.

John headed toward the back of the largest tent where the sounds of merriment grew louder. He stepped between some old crates and looked around before opening his coat. Port's sensor dome peeked from the oversized cargo pocket sewn into the lining.

"Okay...let's do this fast. In and out and done," John said as the mini-bot crawled from the pocket onto the top of a wooden barrel. John opened the access door behind Port's sensor dome and adjusted the bot's receiver. "Take pictures. We're looking for illegal time devices but get shots of the vendors and customers too. Might be useful."

Port flexed his wings and chirped a reply.

John ran his tongue over a back molar as he worked and felt for the transmitter that Dr. Brainard implanted earlier that afternoon. The bitter taste of dental glue made his throat constrict. John remembered the doc's instructions. Drinking was fine as long as the liquid wasn't hot (might melt the glue). If eating was unavoidable, chew on the opposite side. A.K.'s advice was more direct, "If you swallow the transmitter, I'll take it out of your pay."

John muttered under his breath to test the microphone. "Can you hear me?"

Port blinked his sensor dome.

John snapped the access door shut and looked Port over one last time. The little bot had been his backup once before and proved invaluable, but this mission would challenge how well he could work independently. Port may have been a secondhand purchase held together with scrap metal and spare parts, but John had grown fond of the little bot and the thought of putting his friend in harm's way left a queasy feeling in his stomach.

"All right then." John sighed. "Keep close. Stay out of sight. I'll holler if I need you. Watch for trouble. We'll meet back here when we're done. Got it?" Port gave a whistle. John looked around. Seeing no one, he turned back to the mini-bot. "Get going."

Port buzzed his wings and took to the air. John watched the little bot's lopsided flight path as he soared up and over the top of the tent.

John stepped through the tent's rear entrance and into the boiling chaos inside. Every kind of drunken, black-hearted freighter pirate he could name—mercenaries, traders, smugglers, assassins, and grifters —from every quadrant and points unknown filled the long wooden tables and the spaces between. The strain of a drinking ballad, more shouted than sung, competed with the shrieks of laughter from the whores and working boys. The air itself felt thicker than blood and smelled of smoke and sweat.

John hesitated, but it took only a fraction of a second to slip back into the role he played for so many years. His face hardened as he took a step toward the bar.

A Maskelyne trader took a sucker punch to the jaw and fell backward. John shoved the unlucky trader aside and back toward his cohorts. A flash of steel and the Maskelyne fell to the ground.

Sorry, friend.

John pushed the guilt aside just as he pushed his way through the crowd. The rules were different here. Following the rules kept you alive...most of the time.

The one rule all the revelers respected was the wicked ion rifle the barkeep wore slung over a shoulder. John tossed a silver piece on the barrelhead. The barkeep nodded, pulled a cracked mug from a barrel of cloudy water, and drew a pint.

John took a sip of beer and tried not to make a face as he continued through the tent. The watered-down, bootlegged ale was hardly strong enough to kill the microbes in the bottom of the mug and certainly not worth the silver he just paid. He gulped more beer and made for the front entrance.

John muttered into his glass. "Leaving through the opposite entrance." He hoped Port could hear him through the blaring opening verse of *The Boy from Merope*. He left his half-finished mug on a nearby table.

"Disko!"

John winced at the name but kept walking. The tent was crowded. He probably heard it wrong. So many names sounded alike – *Frisko, Sisko…*

"Disko! HEY, DISKO!"

Damn it.

The old nickname hit John like a brick to the back of the head. He turned and peered through the haze. Hengen Vanamo and Little Sister waved from a table in a back corner of the tent.

What. Are. The odds?

More than ten years had passed since John last saw the Ulvilaen smuggler. In this business, long stretches between sightings usually meant retirement of a more permanent kind.

John muttered again to the mini-bot. "Belay that. I'll be in here a little longer."

Vanamo's face brightened as John drew closer. "Disko! Join us! Have a drink!" The smuggler's salt-and-pepper hair was longer, but he'd kept the same sculpted silver beard and lean athletic build John remembered.

The curly-haired youth sitting next to Vanamo stood at John's approach. John met the young man's eye and watched him slide from the table and disappear into the crowd.

Vanamo tipped the bottle in front of him and poured a fresh round of drinks. Stacks of pewter and copper rings decorated each of the smuggler's fingers and caught the light with every gesture. "I wasn't sure if that was you," he said, looking John over. "Too many years between us." Little Sister, Venla, stared at the table with sleepy eyes.

John grinned as he took a seat on the bench across

from them. "I should have kept walking."

John accepted the shot glass and the sweet smell of Esina filled his nose. The clear Ulvilaen liquor was strong but tasted too much like spice candy for John to develop a palate for it, not to mention it always made his ears itch after a few sips. But when you drank with Vanamo you took what was offered. Would be better than the watered-down piss they were serving as beer. John took a sip.

The smuggler laughed and flashed a set of perfect white teeth. "Heh! Heh! Then you would not enjoy the pleasure of our company and Little Sister would miss you." He lifted a shot glass to Venla's lips.

Hengen Vanamo and his twin sister were one and the same. Venla, the misshapen lump of flesh that sprouted from Hengen's shoulder, was the size of a doll's head. Little Sister did not speak, but ate, drank, slept, made faces, and most unnerving of all, watched you with dark eyes just as she watched John now. The parasitic twin caused whores to charge Hengen double, but to hear him tell the story the women always gave half the money back after he had satisfied *them*.

Venla's eyes widened with recognition when John sat down. He nodded in greeting, knowing Hengen would expect him to, and felt a twist of cold in his gut when the crooked mouth stretched into a macabre grin, showing a red tongue and scattered pebble teeth the color of the inside of an oyster's shell. As John watched, a fly landed and sipped from the corner of Venla's eye. John took a slug of Esina to suppress a shiver of disgust.

Hengen waved the fly away and poured John another drink. "Where have you been, Disko? I heard you left your crew after the big raids?"

"The Tyrhenians were hit hard," John said, cupping his glass. "We lost a lot of associates, so we split up. Had to lay low for a while."

Hengen nodded as he sipped. "I heard you went domestic?"

John shrugged. "For a while."

The smuggler leaned across the table, his face contorted into a sneer. "I heard you left for a woman?"

Fear drew a boney finger down John's spine. Hengen Vanamo, despite first impressions, could be dangerously unpredictable. The smuggler's sanity was tethered by the thinnest of gossamer threads. John forced a roguish grin.

"Which one?"

"Heh! Heh! Heh!" Hengen drew back with a belly laugh. Venla grinned, her twisted smile a dark mirror of her brother's.

John chuckled with them as he lifted his glass. "What about you?"

Hengen gave Venla another sip and wiped her mouth with a piece of cloth. "Always lots of women." John knew the smuggler well enough to know it was a statement of fact, not bravado. "After the raids, I went to the Taygeta system. Business was good..." Hengen waggled one hand. "But could have been better." His smile brightened. "Now I'm back!

Such excellent timing to run into you."

Just my excellent luck, John thought as he took another sip.

Hengen filled their glasses again. "What brings you here?"

"I'm looking for cargo to haul," John said. "Something easy to get started again."

Venla yawned.

"I need to build up a stake." John spoke directly to Venla, remembering Hengen became agitated if Little Sister wasn't included in the conversation. Venla responded with a slow blink.

Hengen rubbed his bearded chin. "Ah, your women are expensive?"

"Most are," John said, scratching the familiar prickle spreading along the back of one ear. "And domestic life doesn't pay enough. What's good here? Who needs cargo moved?"

Hengen thought and sipped. The rings on his fingers glowed in the dim light. Venla, no longer smiling, watched John without blinking. Black eyes burrowed into him until he thought Little Sister could see the hairs standing on the back of his neck.

"I would hire you myself, but sadly..." The smuggler sighed. "My cargo is already loaded, and I have plenty of crew." Hengen stroked Venla's cheek and under her chin with one ringed finger. Her mouth opened. Her eyes rolled back with pleasure. "But there is something here that might be of interest... Maybe not to your taste...but it would be a quick and easy score."

John left the beer tent a couple drinks later, ears burning and head buzzing from the Esina. He mumbled an update to Port and walked down the main thoroughfare.

The merchants turned a brisk trade. Crowds strolled the midway making it easy for anyone to observe the peddlers and their wares without drawing unwanted attention. John eyed the tents and wooden stalls on either side with casual interest as he looked for his mark. He passed a stall and saw a merchant showing an outlander a collection of time shifters. John turned away and stopped to linger at a small weapons dealer across the avenue.

"Get some pictures of the merchant in the yellow tent behind me," John muttered to the mini-bot. *"Looks like he might have Brakers. See what else he has."*

John glanced up and spotted Port sailing low over the tents farther down the midway and flying towards him. He picked up an ion pistol from the counter, tested its weight, and looked down the sight. "If I can see you, then a security drone can see you."

When he looked up again, Port had disappeared. John smiled to himself, returned the pistol, and kept walking.

The weathered green tent was exactly as Hengen described. John waited while the Grandk merchant finished giving a sales pitch to a Dramgoole raider on some lightweight armor. The raider grunted, shook his head, and walked away empty-handed.

The merchant threw his hands up in disgust. "Idiot. I hope you get all three of your cocks shot off!"

The Grandk turned and eyed John. The sour expression never changed as he leaned against the counter.

"You got a cock?"

John arched a brow. "Yes."

"You want armor?"

John scowled. "No!"

"Well, good luck keeping it." The merchant picked up the armor on the counter and tossed it in a bin behind him. "What do you want?"

The Grandk, like most of his kind, struggled and failed to reach five feet tall. His brown hair was short and combed straight. He wore a plain work shirt, open at the collar, and trousers stuffed into tall black boots. A leather belt encircled a thick waist. Large brown eyes stared out of a round pink face.

"I heard you got a new shipment," John said. The Grandk stared at him without comment. John returned the stare, perplexed by the merchant's reluctance. "In the *back* room?"

The merchant rolled his eyes and sighed. "Yes, I got a new *shipment*. Come on." He waved for John to follow. "I don't sell baked goods here. Why don't you just come out and ask me? 'Hey, Chabot. I'm tapped out. Can you hook me up?' You don't have to be coy."

John shot the merchant a dark look and growled, "Maybe next time." He was losing patience with this peddler.

Chabot led John through, past bins and racks of

merchandise, to the tent behind the stall. Stacks of shipping containers ten feet high divided the tent into sections and created narrow aisles. Two Grandk workmen with anti-gravity clamps lifted a container from a nearby stack and carried it down an aisle and out the back. John followed Chabot to one side of the tent to a worktable with a display case. Rows of colored vials glittered inside with labels under each written on slips of paper.

Chabot gestured to the case. "Here's what I got."

John read the names and picked up a blue vial. "This one. How much?"

"Sorry." Chabot took the vial out of John's hand. "Just sold out of that one. My crew is loading it now."

"What about the sample?"

The Grandk snorted a laugh. "The jar's empty. I just use it for display purposes." He returned the vial to the case. "I got a lot of good stuff here. Is there something else I can set you up with? I usually keep at least two containers on site. Orders bigger than five containers take up to 30-days."

A loud crash came from the back of the tent.

"HEY!" Chabot yelled over a shoulder. "YOU PROKS BREAK MY STUFF, AND I'LL BREAK YOUR EMPTY HEADS!"

A smaller crash answered from the back. Chabot gritted his teeth and turned to John.

"Look at the case. I'll be back in a minute." The merchant hurried down an aisle muttering Grandk curses.

John watched Chabot disappear around a wall of

containers in the back. He listened to the steady stream of vulgarities and edged over to the stack the workmen had pulled the container from. If he was lucky, the workmen might not have finished loading the shipment. John popped the latch of the next container in the stack and looked inside. Luck finally favored him with a kiss from her petulant mouth.

John grabbed a blue vial from inside the packing material and stowed it in a pocket just as he heard Chabot's footsteps coming back towards him through the tent.

"Sorry about that," the merchant said, rounding a stack of crates. "Did you make a decision?"

John jerked a thumb to the blue vial in the display case. "How fast can you get ten containers?"

John grinned as he headed for the exit. The information Chabot provided may not have been what A.K. sent him originally to find out, but he hoped it would be useful.

John stepped from the tent. A blow to his face knocked him flat. He drew his sidearm, but before he could even see to aim a boot the size of a shovel blade kicked the pistol from his hand.

Massive fists grabbed John's collar, hoisted him off the ground, and launched him backward through the air. He crashed into a refuse pile next to the tent, the sound of a gong reverberating through his skull. It took him a couple seconds to realize the gong was the sound of the back of his head when it struck the side of a metal trash barrel.

"WHERE IS SHE?"

John struggled to stand. "What? Who?" He blinked hard and tried to keep the ground from slipping out from under his feet.

"Puuttuva! She is gone. You took her!"

John looked up. His eyes focused on an assailant that looked like the offspring of a side of beef and a space freighter. Bulging muscles strained a sleeveless leather and fur doublet, a style favored by the Nyrkki raiders. The outlander's hair was twisted into short stiff pigtails and stuck straight out in all directions, giving the warrior the appearance of an electrocuted sea urchin from the neck up. Assuming there was a neck under all that muscle. All told, the raider stood a foot taller and tipped the scales at more than twice John's weight. From the Nyrkki's glassy eyes and slurred speech, John guessed the raider was also...drunk.

I'm a dead man.

Nyrkki raiders were known to have violent tempers when sober. Drunk Nyrkki were to be avoided at any cost. For a moment, John contemplated how much alcohol would be required to achieve a state of drunkenness in a Nyrkki of such size, a train of thought brought on by the concussion he was fairly certain he was nursing from hitting the barrel. Somewhere Luck laughed, and John's thoughts returned to his impending death.

John held up his hands in what he hoped was a non-threatening gesture and backed away from the raider. "You've got the wrong guy. I didn't take her. I don't know where she is."

"LIAR!" The Nyrkki pulled a truncheon as thick as a man's arm from a belt and advanced on John's position.

"I'll help you find her," John said. Anything to keep the outlander talking. "What does she look like?"

"Tell me where she is!" The Nyrkki took a swing with the truncheon. John dodged and heard the bat whistle past.

"Let's get a drink. Let's talk."

"GIVE HER BACK!"

The Nyrkki rushed forward in a sudden burst of speed. The ensuing collision rattled John's vertebrae and threw him back into the wall of a tent. John's back struck a tent pole that gave way as he tore through the canvas. Ripping cloth, groans of metal, shrieks and profanities followed as an entire section of the tent roof and all came crashing down.

John lay on his back stunned by the impact. Blinded and trapped by the canvas on top of him, he gasped for air in the tight space. Somewhere above, the Nyrkki raged and slammed the truncheon down on a collapsed section of the tent not far away.

John rolled over onto the tent's wet wooden floorboards. Water soaked through his trousers and shirt. He dragged himself forward using only his elbows and whispered through clenched teeth. "Port!"

Another blow from the truncheon crashed down. Closer.

"Port, I need you!"

John weighed options. If he could reach the edge of the canvas, he could run or turn and fight if necessary, but every move gave away his position. Go slow and risk getting beaten to death like a rat under a rug, or go fast, take a few hits, but hopefully make it out in one piece. Either way, it was going to cost him.

John took a deep breath and scrambled, head down. Blows rained all around him. Pain lashed across the back of one leg as the truncheon connected. John grunted. The canvas softened the blow, but just barely. He surged forward, taking shelter under a table. The Nyrkki howled with frustration above as John darted through a maze of overturned chairs and discarded objects that the raider then proceeded to smash. John could see the edge of the canvas just a few more feet in front of him. He put on another burst of speed and dove for daylight.

John threw off the canvas, gasping for air. He staggered to his feet and looked around. The fight had landed him in a bathhouse. Naked freighter pirates and whores fled through the opening torn in the side of the tent or took refuge behind large steaming tubs of water. The remaining pirates, recovered from their initial shock, locked eyes on John like so many ion pistols. A Leucothean raider in a nearby tub stood and took a swing at John's head. John blocked and punched the raider in the face. The pirate's nose cracked under his fist. The stunned raider fell, sloshing backward into the tub.

John turned. The Nyrkki had spotted him. The chaos from fleeing patrons and the debris in the tent hampered the raider's progress, but he was gaining fast. John reached up and toppled a large shelf of bath supplies on top of the raider. Scores of perfume bottles and soaps crashed to the floor. John ran for a side exit. Piles of clothing and personal belongings caught his eye. He scanned for weapons. *Please let there be an ion pistol.* Nothing. He grabbed two short wooden fighting staffs from a corner and ran from the tent.

"PORT!"

John scoured the sky between the tents for the mini-bot. *Where is he?* Behind him, the Nyrkki unleashed an undulating battle cry. John turned in time to see the raider rip through the side of the tent and stalk toward him. Liquid soap dripped from the Nyrkki's head and muscled arms and matted the fur on the doublet, his face red with fury.

Anger clenched John's jaw. He braced himself and held up the wooden fighting staffs... He did a double-take at the weapons in his hands. What he thought were fighting staffs were in actuality long-handled bath brushes.

"Bloody hell!" John ground teeth and growled, "Port! Where are you?"

He lunged forward and swung one heavy brush as hard as he could at the side of the Nyrkki's head. The square head of the wooden brush connected with a clap. The raider staggered backward, and John swung the other brush striking the Nyrkki again across the opposite side of the face. The raider checked himself and raised the truncheon for a killing blow to the head. John raised the two brushes and blocked, catching the bat between the crossed wooden handles. *That worked?* John's surprise was short-lived when the Nyrkki's fist crashed into his face. John's head snapped back from the force of the blow. He lurched on unsteady feet. He shook off the punch, raised both brush handles, and slammed them down on the Nyrkki's weapon hand. The wooden handles splintered on impact. The raider roared in pain, dropped the truncheon, and backed away clutching his wrist.

John pressed his advantage and unleashed a combination of quick punches, connecting with the raider's jaw and gut, driving him backward. The Nyrkki tried to block, but John was faster, ducking under and landing another punch to the raider's side.

The Nyrkki spun and came forward, fists flying. John dodged and blocked a few punches and landed more of his own. A fist whistled past, and he counted himself lucky until a left hook hammered his sternum. The force of the blow drove the air from his lungs. John doubled over, almost dropping to a knee, and tried to suck air. Another blow drove into the side of his head. Sparkles of light filled his vision.

John swung in desperation. The raider deflected the punch and grabbed his arm, pulling it up and backward over John's head and forcing him forward and down, until the muscles in the shoulder screamed.

Stupid! Stupid! Stup— "ARGH!"

John heard the crack as the joint wrenched from the socket. Pain strobed white-hot through his shoulder followed by a wave of nausea. He clenched his teeth over a moan. He couldn't lose consciousness. He couldn't go down.

The Nyrkki grabbed him in a chokehold and dragged him backward. John struggled. His injured arm dangled, useless.

"You *will* tell me where she is!"

John couldn't see where they were going. He kicked and clawed at the thick arm around his neck, but it made no difference.

Heat and the smell of cooking oil hung like a curtain of grease as they crossed the threshold into a merchant stall. John tried to steady his breathing. Panic would be no friend to him here. The raider turned. John's insides shrunk.

The cooktop stretched the length of the wall in the makeshift kitchen. Blue tongues of flame licked the black metal grates on top of the stove where a cook finished lowering a fry basket into a large pot. The sizzle and pop of meat frying made John break into a cold sweat.

The Nyrkki looked at the cook. "GET OUT!"

The cook made a quick assessment of the situation and ran for the exit.

The raider tightened his hold and pushed John forward.

"TELL ME NOW!"

John fought like a mad dog as the raider inched closer to the stove. Fear burned inside him as bright as a flame. With every spatter of grease, he imagined his own skin blackening on the hot metal burners. John kicked hard against the edge of the stove, driving the raider backward. The raider recovered and shoved forward again. John twisted, delivering a solid kick to the side of the pot on top of the stove. The pot slid across the length of the burners, slammed into the side wall, and tipped its contents over the open flame.

The oil ignited into a fireball that reached the ceiling and sent both John and the Nyrkki scrambling to the floor in a tangle of limbs.

John struggled to stand as the raider grappled underneath him. He threw a crushing elbow into the Nyrkki's crotch. The raider grunted and released his hold. John staggered, cradling his lifeless arm. He could feel the heat from the fire through the back of his coat. Acrid smoke burned his eyes and lungs as he stumbled to the door.

The muscles in John's injured shoulder screamed as he lurched across the alleyway, breathing hard.

"Damn it, Port! Where are you?"

He couldn't fight the Nyrkki and hope to win. His only chance was to hide until he could find Port and make it to their jump point. John pushed through the crowd that had gathered to watch the fire and moved as fast as he could to a nearby tent.

John lifted a back corner of canvas and slipped inside. Rows of shelving housed stacks of bins. The storage area was dark enough. Now if he could just find a corner to hide...

The canvas lifted again and the Nyrkki stepped inside, eyes glittering in the dim light. John turned to run. The raider grabbed the back of his coat and threw him against a wall of shelves. John raised his good arm to block as the raider cocked a fist. The blow hammered into the side of his face. John felt the transmitter in the back molar crack. He spit out the transmitter, blood, and what looked like a piece of tooth. The raider slammed another fist into John's gut, grabbed him again, and threw him into a stack of shelves across the aisle. The stack tipped over with a crash with John sprawled across the top. He heard a rumble and the other shelving unit crashed down. Heavy bins fell, popping open and showering merchandise everywhere.

John lay on his back heaving and soaked in sweat unable to move. Blood pooled in his mouth. The Nyrkki lifted the shelves and pushed them out of the way before turning fists on John with renewed fury.

"TELL! ME! WHERE! SHE! IS!"

The blows came again and again, but John felt only dull thuds and a ringing in his ears. His hands wandered through the pile of debris searching, desperate for something to fight back, or a shield from the torrent of the Nyrkki's fists. The beating would finish him, and he would die on top of a pile of illegal contraband in a tent city of thieves. John wondered vaguely if A.K. would find his body to take home to Ann at Siren's Cove.

John's fingers skimmed a familiar, smooth cylindrical object the length of his palm just out of reach.

His brain clicked. He looked up past the fist falls, past the Nyrkki's blurry figure above him, to the top of the merchant tent. The yellow hue of the canvas roof glowed under the bright sun.

Time shifters.

"Hey!" John croaked between punches. "HEY! I can't tell you anything if you kill me!"

The punching stopped. The Nyrkki looked down at John and blinked as if surprised to finally hear him speak. John lunged for the cylinder and released the safety. The Nyrkki grabbed hold of the device in his fist just as John pulled the trigger. A shock wave radiated outward and extended past the tent.

A bead of sweat trickled down the Nyrkki's nose and fell...

...towards John's bruised cheek...

...and hung in the air...

...as time...

...stopped.

Time shifters came in a wide range of devices. A Braker or Dead Man's Brake allowed a time jumper to pause time in an emergency for a few seconds or minutes as needed to give safe passage or expedite a getaway.

The cylinder in John's fist emitted a green flash. His eyes darted to the time shifter.

Oh, no.

A Rewinder, however, moved time backward forcing events and individuals within the affected area to replay in reverse, returning to a starting point predetermined by the length of time programmed into the device. As with all time shifters, there were risks of side effects, injury, and possible death.

"Bloody hell."

The curse pulled back into John's mouth. The Nyrkki's eyes grew wide as the bead of sweat reversed course from above John's cheek, gained speed, and rolled back up his nose and into his hairline.

The Nyrkki raised fists and the punching reversed. Each time the raider's fist pulled away, John could feel the force of the blows leave his body. All that remained was a peculiar echo of pain.

The combatants sprung apart. John flew to his feet as shelves righted themselves and bins refilled and settled into their proper places. He careened through the air to the opposite shelf. Blood and spit along with the broken transmitter and a sliver of tooth rushed up from a dark corner of the floor and darted into his mouth. John felt the tooth knit back together a second before the raider's fist left his cheek. The Nyrkki grabbed the back of his coat and threw him away from the wall of shelves before stalking backward out of the tent.

The pair hurried backward across the alleyway, pushing past the mob gawking at the blaze coming from the food merchant stall. As the flames folded back into the roof of the structure, the crowd thinned in reverse, some walking while others ran away from the shrinking fire.

John watched the crowds as they came into view. While he couldn't fight the physical effects of the Rewinder, his mind remained clear since he'd been the one to trigger the device. He considered the strong possibility that the Nyrkki also remained unaffected given the raider's close contact with the Rewinder right before the time distortion began. There was no way to know how long the time shift would last. He'd need to be ready to fight or flee at the exact moment the Rewinder wound down and time moved forward again.

John's path led to the merchant stall. He entered the kitchen and lay down with his back to the Nyrkki. He delivered an elbow to the raider's crotch and the struggle resumed.

The flames above the stove pulled from the ceiling, coalesced into a ball of fire, and shrunk to the burners on the stove top. Cooking oil flowed from the stove back into the overturned pot. The Nyrkki and John rose from the floor as the pot skidded back across the burners to meet the side of John's boot. The shoving match replayed in front of the stove; the cook returned to tend the fry pot; and the two combatants left the merchant stall, this time with John in the lead and the raider following behind with one arm around John's neck

The foes separated and the raider forced John's arm over and back. John hollered, blinded with pain, as the shoulder snapped back into place. John and the raider squared off. The impact of John's reverse punches absorbing back into his body took a greater toll than when the Nyrkki had struck him.

A bright green flash followed by a shock wave knocked John and the Nyrkki to the dirt. John pushed to his hands and knees, gasping for air and lightheaded from the Rewinder. *Cheap piece of junk.* He struggled to stand. Every muscle ached with the ghost of an injury.

The Nyrkki clamored to his feet a few yards away. John steadied himself and raised his fists. He didn't know how he would survive another encounter with the Nyrkki, but at least he had the use of both arms. The raider turned glassy eyes to John and snarled. The outlander clenched his fists and took a step forward. John braced for an attack. The Nyrkki stopped, the sneer turned to a pucker. The raider's face blanched as he dropped to all fours and puked before passing out in a pool of vomit.

John lowered his fists and looked down at the Nyrkki with a smirk.

"Yeah, I remember my first Rewind, too. Bender."

John spied a pair of anti-gravity clamps abandoned on a nearby stack of crates. A wicked thought tapped him on the shoulder.

"That should keep you from bothering me," John said and gave the Nyrkki a slap on the back. "Say 'Hi' to Puuttuva for me."

John left the raider vomiting upside down and spinning four feet above the ground, suspended by the anti-gravs attached to his boots.

"Heh! Heh! Heh!"

John turned toward the sound of the familiar belly laugh.

Hengen Vanamo and Little Sister watched from a

nearby merchant tent.

"You were always good in a fight, Disko," Hengen said, hands on hips. Venla stared wide-eyed with excitement. The smuggler tried to rein in his laughter as he walked forward and squatted down for a closer look at the Nyrkki. "Always tragic when a man falls in love with a whore." Hengen looked up with a wicked grin. "Broken-hearted, drunken men are so easily led, yes?" He gave the raider a push, increasing the rate of rotation, and let loose with another round of laughter. The Nyrkki moaned in misery.

Anger clenched John's jaw as he realized he was the butt of one of the smuggler's jokes.

"Pretty good joke, Vanamo," John said with a scowl as Hengen continued to chuckle. "I'll have to return the favor someday."

John turned to leave. He had to find Port and get home. He rotated his shoulder and stretched. He'd need to sleep for a week to shake off the hangover from the cheap Rewinder.

The snap and whine of a power cell charging froze John's feet to the ground. He chanced a look over a shoulder. Hengen stood a few feet away and held an ion pistol aimed at John's back.

The smuggler's face took on a dangerous sneer. "Where have you been, Disko? What happened to your old crew?"

John kept his hands in view and faced Hengen. "I told you. We split up."

"No. Not then. Now," the smuggler said, his tone impatient. "I heard Chohon-Lo and his crew went looking for you a few months ago." John's insides twisted. "They haven't been seen since. But now here you are, and they are not. Where are they?"

A screech from above made both men look up. A copper blur hurtled between them and crashed into the dirt. Port thrashed in a circle, one wing ripped away while the other flickered madly. Exposed electrical wires from the missing wing arced and cast blue sparks. A power cell popped, and Port's systems went dark. The mini-bot rolled on to its back and lay still.

Grief tugged at John's heart. He heard a hum and looked up in time to see a security drone hovering over a tent.

Hengen chuckled as he glanced down at Port then watched the drone dart away. "Someone will be missing their toy."

John heard a click and looked down. Port ejected an ion pistol into the air from his belly like a hot piece of toast. John made a grab for the pistol, the grip slipping easily into his palm. He cocked and dropped to one knee as Hengen turned and fired. John felt the heat from the laser bolt as the smuggler's shot flew past. He pulled the trigger. The laser bolt struck Hengen in the chest. The smuggler dropped his pistol and fell backward into the dirt.

John stood over Hengen, face grim, and kicked the pistol out of reach. "Sorry, friend."

Port staggered. John scooped up the mini-bot with one hand and tucked him under an arm, relieved the little faker had been playing dead.

SARA JUDSON BROWN

He looked down at the bot and smirked. "My hero."

Port responded with a rude noise.

Hengen groaned and laughed. John pointed his pistol at the smuggler.

"You bastard! That stings!" He pulled his shirt open and examined the laser burn on the dark gray ribs of a dielectric vest. Venla's eyes rolled as she snapped and bared pearly teeth.

John backed away, pistol still trained on Hengen. "No hard feelings?"

The smuggler's dark sneer returned. "It will be my turn to shoot you next time." Venla gave John a flat stare.

John gulped. This time Hengen wasn't joking. He took a few more paces backward until he reached the cover of the tree line then turned and ran for the jump point.

TEN

SPLICE

Back at Siren's Cove, John's boots had barely struck the floor when he felt Ann's arms around him steering him toward a chair. Mrs. Beaumont took one look at him and ran to the kitchen to get Dr. Brainard on the comm and make a pot of tea. The cook might have stopped to make the tea first. John wasn't entirely sure since he was already battling the early signs of a Rewinder Hangover. The fight with the Nyrkki raider and the aftereffects of the time shifter left every muscle in his body simultaneously cramping in waves of random agony.

Dr. Brainard arrived with his medical bag and was followed an hour later by a knock on the door. Agent A.K. Max showed up on time and in true intelligence officer fashion with no one able to deduce his exact mode of transportation. John wondered at times if A.K. carried a pocket-sized wormhole.

"You're welcome to stay, Mrs. Beaumont," A.K. said, taking a seat in front of the bookcase in the sitting room. "You don't have to leave on my account."

Mrs. Beaumont activated another cold pack and handed it to John. "I don't *need* to know."

John grabbed the cold pack and put it on his sore shoulder as he eased back into his leather chair. He'd shared some details of the jump with Ann, Mrs. Beaumont, and Dr. Brainard between spasms, but had saved the most important information for when A.K. arrived.

The cook continued. "It wouldn't be the first time I didn't know what went on under this roof, Agent Max, and I think I might prefer it that way."

John gritted his teeth against a convulsion of pain and tried to get his muscles to relax. Dr. Brainard raised a brow and looked up from the digital notepad in his lap where he monitored John's vital signs. The wire-rimmed glasses perched on the edge of his nose reflected the light from the screen. The doctor looked at John and pointed to the bottle sitting on the side table between them.

"Drink."

Dr. Brainard was John's oldest friend in Llewellyn. He saw to John's injuries even when he thought he ran with freighter pirates. After John's wife died, the doctor was the only one on the Colonies who knew the truth about John's undercover mission. He'd even conspired with Mrs. Beaumont on more than one occasion over the last ten years for John's own good and all because he'd made a promise to a dying woman to look after her husband. He'd been a better friend to John than he deserved...until today.

John slugged the elixir from the bottle and pulled

a face. By the taste of things, Dr. Brainard was trying to kill him with his Rewinder Hangover cure. The medicine tasted the way kerosene smelled.

"There are more cold packs in the pantry and tea in the pot," Mrs. Beaumont said, turning her attention to Ann.

Ann sat on the settee and ratcheted Port's new wing into place. The mini-bot hummed, content in Ann's lap. "Thank you, Mrs. Beaumont." Ann cast a look of concern in John's direction.

John gave her a tired but gentle smile. "I'm fine."

Ann paused in her work long enough to meet John's eye and express doubt. She looked up at the older woman.

"Please stay," Ann said. "At least for a little while longer. You made the tea. You should have another cup."

Mrs. Beaumont turned to the room with a sigh. "Well...all right then." The cook gave an appraising look to John before taking a seat next to Ann and refilling her cup.

John glowered. Another set of anxious eyes to peer at him. *Why not?*

"So..." A.K. leaned forward and poured himself a cup of tea. "You made it back..." The agent leaned against the back of the chair and eyed John's cold packs. "...mostly in one piece. What did you find?"

John gave the intelligence officer a dark look before handing off a data stick and the transmitter. "Port took pictures. The merchants had mostly low-grade stuff. Chronoculars and..." He cringed, overcome by another spasm of pain.

Dr. Brainard frowned. "Drink."

John took another pull from the bottle and waited for the pain and the aftertaste to subside before continuing. "A merchant with time shifters was passing off cheap Rewinders as Brakers. Nothing to send in a squadron for. His customers will kill him soon enough." He took a breath to steady himself as the last of the pain faded and allowed himself a satisfied smile. "But I also found this."

A.K. took the blue vial from John's hand and popped the cap. John was pleased to see the agent's normally reticent expression turn to one of surprise as he poured the milk-white crystals into his palm.

"A Grandk merchant named Chabot had crates of the stuff," John said. "He'd just met with his supplier, too. There was a large shipment heading out while I was there."

A.K. pinched a crystal between a thumb and index finger and gave John a questioning look. "Is this...?"

John nodded and took a drink in anticipation of another muscle spasm. "The doctor already confirmed it."

Mrs. Beaumont looked over the top of her teacup. "What is it?"

"It's called Splice, a highly addictive and illegal narcotic." Dr. Brainard set his notepad aside.

"I remember reading about it at the Academy." Ann inserted a fresh power cell into Port's access panel. The mini-bot chirped, buzzed his wings, and flew across the sitting room to roost on the bookcase. "Time jumpers used it as a phasing agent for a while. It's outdated technology. It was discontinued after they discovered side effects." She put the depleted power cells into the charger.

"More than that. It was just too damn complicated," John said and adjusted a cold pack. "They called it Splicing. A time jumper had to use the drug along with directional anchors and nanobots to help them get to where they were going. It was only good for short jumps and emergency retriev..." John shuddered as another wave contorted his muscles. "Damn!" He grunted and leaned forward to try and break the surge.

Dr. Brainard leaned over the table. "Drink!"

John looked up at the doctor and snapped, "I've already drunk half the bottle. My back teeth are about to float! How long am I supposed to drink this stuff?"

Dr. Brainard replied with perfect bedside manner. "Are you still in pain?"

John grumbled, upended the bottle taking several huge gulps, and wiped his mouth with the back of a hand. He set the empty bottle down hard on the table next to the doctor before continuing.

"Splice was already on the way out by the time they discovered the side effects." John stifled a belch with the back of a fist. "Now we use a Shepherd's Hook wormhole if we need to do a quick retrieval."

Dr. Brainard looked at John without comment and reached into the medical bag at his feet. "Now, Splice is primarily used as a recreational drug although banned on most worlds." The doctor pulled out a new bottle and set it down next to John. He gave John a pointed look and removed the empty bottle. "I thought the authorities had stamped it out, but from what Captain Galeas discovered it may be making a comeback."

John flashed a look that the doctor ignored. From the corner of his eye, he saw Ann hide a smile. It was Ann's last night at home before she went back to headquarters, and now he was going to be up all night with a Rewinder Hangover. He took an aggravated swipe through his hair.

"Not sure if you want to do anything about it or if anything can be done," John said, turning to A.K. "I know it wasn't part of my mission, but I thought you should know."

A.K. returned the crystals to the vial and replaced the stopper. "I'm not sure. It's out of our jurisdiction as long as it's not being used for time jumping." The agent pocketed the vial, transmitter, and data stick. "I can send out a bulletin. The proper authorities can take it from there."

Dr. Brainard shook his head dismayed. "Leave it to the bureaucrats and politicians to ban the drug because it was too dangerous for time jumping but allow people to continue to use it for recreational sport." He sighed and looked at the intelligence officer. "I'm sorry, Agent Max. It's not your fault. I know what this drug is capable of, and this particular variety is more potent."

"What do you mean?"

"The chemical properties of this sample seem to

be concentrated."

Ann frowned. "If the drug is more powerful, wouldn't that change how it would react if used for time jumping?"

"I wonder..." A.K. narrowed his eyes.

Dr. Brainard nodded. "I'm not sure, but I bet your superiors might want to find out."

John twisted open the cap and took a reluctant pull from the fresh bottle. "I think we also need to do something about Hengen Vanamo."

A.K. looked at John in surprise. "You saw him?"

John nodded and gave a rundown of his encounter with the smuggler. "Not sure what rumors he's heard or from whom."

"He's always been a wild card," the agent said with a shrug. "I'll put out some counter rumors. Plant some false sightings of Chohon-Lo and the others to throw him off the trail along with anyone else who might be asking questions."

Ann looked at John amused. "Why does he call you Disko?"

John grinned. "Disko is the name of the space freighter I was serving on when we first crossed paths."

The intelligence officer snorted a laugh. "You have to tell her the whole story, Galeas." A.K. leaned towards Ann. "When they first met, Vanamo was celebrating a big haul. Buying drinks for everyone in the bar. John got so drunk all he could remember was the name of his ship – Disko. That's all he could say."

The room broke into laughter.

"Good heavens!" Mrs. Beaumont looked wide-eyed. "I've seen you drunk, Captain, but never like that."

John gave a rueful grin. "Don't drink Dramgoole brandy." He took another sip ahead of the next spasm.

"Ah, yes. I am familiar with that apéritif." Dr. Brainard said, cleaning his spectacles. "The lesson, Captain, is to not have more than one. There may even be a warning printed on the bottle." The doctor paused and looked at John with sudden apprehension. "How many did you have?"

John thought. "I lost count after four." The expression on his face prompted another round of laughter.

A.K. stood and moved toward the door chuckling. "Nice job, Galeas. Thanks for the favor." He patted the vial in his pocket.

John eyed the intelligence man. "You didn't think I was going to find anything, did you?"

The agent raised his eyebrows in innocence. "I had no idea what you might find."

"The merchants only had low-level contraband," John said. "If I hadn't run into Vanamo, the job would've been a stroll. You didn't need me to recon for you. You could have gotten a Day Tripper to do it."

A.K. broke into a wide grin. "It's great to have you back!" The agent slipped out the door.

John shouted after him as the door shut. "I'm NOT ba—" Another shudder of pain cut off his words.

A chorus of shouts came from the four corners of the room.

"DRINK!"

John growled and took another slug.

ELEVEN

FLIGHT

Warning sirens scream. The horizon spins past the cockpit windows as the ground races upward, eating blue sky. The hatch! The hatch! Blow the hatch! *Forces slam the cockpit. Fire engulfs. Glass shatters and the world plunges into night.*

Silence.

The cockpit's running lights brightened, illuminating the simulator's cabin interior. Ann released the yoke and fell back against the jump seat shaking and soaked in a cold sweat underneath her fatigues. She gulped air until her fingers and the tip of her nose began to tingle. With every breath, the cockpit controls came more clearly into focus. The button that blew the hatch faded into the background becoming no more prominent than any of the other dials and switches that stretched across the control panel.

Ann looked down at her hands blistered raw from the fire... *No.* She caught herself. *Not this time.* That was another crash, a different ship. The ghost of the *Kairos* again. Ann flexed her fingers. The skin shone smooth and perfect in the glow of the cabin lights.

She steadied herself, balancing her panic on the edge of reason. The defective time coil had caused the accident with the *Kairos.* She was sure of it. But once again, a stray thought pressed in the back of her mind, *'What if...?'* Ann squeezed her eyes tight to try and finish the thought. She remembered the question had come before those last desperate minutes of trying to reroute power away from the time coil to save the *Kairos. What if...? What if what? What am I missing?*

Kel's voice broke over the comm. "Wow. Did you mean to do that?"

Ann tried to slow her breathing to avoid the embarrassment of hyperventilating on top of total failure. She'd worked in the simulator with Lieutenant Stravage for over an hour with the same result. Ann had hoped that forcing herself to repeat the flight drills over and over in a sort of masochistic immersion therapy would eventually make her immune to the panic ricocheting through her chest, or at least help to fill in the gaps in her memory surrounding the accident, but every scenario the simulator ran ended the same. *Crash. Fire. Death.* And she was no closer to remembering, 'What if...?'

Ann drew in and blew out a long slow breath. *One more time.* She triggered the comm. "Run that last one again."

Kel replied. "The part when you crashed on takeoff, or the part when you cocked up the landing?"

Ann ignored the remark and how her hands shook as they flew over the control panel. "I'm resetting."

"And then there's the one when you plummeted out of the sky for no reason…"

Ann settled back and grabbed the yoke, determined. "I'm ready."

"…took out a skyscraper and hundreds of simulated innocent bystanders. You should know…the simulants got a lawyer and are filing a lawsuit."

Ann frowned. "Not funny, Stravage. Let's go!" Kel's smart-ass remarks weren't going to get in her head.

"You've destroyed enough simulated airships for one day. Do you even know how many?"

"Come on, Kel." Ann gripped the yoke tighter.

"Fifteen."

Doubt padded in again on quiet feet. *What if…?* Ann shook off the feeling. "I'll let you pick which drill this time."

"Fif. Teen. You should take a break."

Ann snapped, "I don't *need* a break!" She blew out a breath and focused on the viewscreen that doubled as the cockpit windows. "Canyon run or cityscape?" Silence. "Kel!"

A familiar gravel voice came over the comm and filled the simulator cabin. "Stand down, Lieutenant. We've all seen enough."

That was it. Ann let go of the yoke, closed her eyes, and rested her head against the back of the seat. Shame covered her and exposed every secret and fear. A pilot that couldn't fly was as useful as a fish that couldn't swim.

She exited the simulator and climbed down the short ladder to the flight deck. Colonel Gideon Wick stood behind Kel who was seated at the control desk. The short heavyset hospital administrator wore a dark suit and bright blue striped tie pulled loosely to one side. The lines of Wick's face creased in serious thought as he watched Ann approach. Kel's face remained a blank slate. Ann gave her friend a look that should have doubled him over, but it was Kel so of course he didn't react.

Knowing the conversation that would follow, Ann grabbed her water bottle from the console panel and took a swig as a stall tactic. The dent in the side of the bottle made her think of Sarolea. If Sarolea had been at the control desk, she would have found a way to warn her that Wick was watching, but the tech specialist hadn't returned to headquarters. Stranger still, no one had seen or heard from the crew of the *What Cheer* since the day they left. Rumors floated that the crew's mission was extended, but Ann wondered how a cargo run originally scheduled for two days could get extended almost a week?

"I'm sorry to interrupt your session, Lieutenant, but after your message I wanted to observe your work in the simulator for myself," Wick said, the volume of his voice a notch below drill sergeant. "I ordered Lieutenant Stravage not to tell you I was watching. I didn't want my presence to affect your performance." The lines around his eyes crinkled. "I see now I needn't have worried."

Wick, in his role as hospital administrator, commanded teams of med techs and specialists of every 'ology' to care for the physical and mental well-being of time jumpers. It was Wick's team that helped Ann recover the missing memory that cleared her of pilot error during the crash investigation. He was also currently helping her meet the requirements for full reinstatement. More recently, it was the colonel's signature that approved John for active duty. Ann had every reason to trust Wick's guidance and judgment. He would give an honest assessment without hesitation. Ann slipped her keravnos implant into an ear. The electrical symphony of the simulator's flight deck sharpened into focus. Ann glanced in Wick's direction and prepared for the worst.

"What's the problem, Lieutenant?"

Ann tried to swallow the lump in her throat before answering. "I can't remember how to fly."

"Your written exams show that not to be the case." Wick leaned across the console in Ann's direction. "What's going on in your head?"

When Ann first contacted the colonel, she assumed they would have this conversation in the administrator's office. Ann looked at Kel. He stood to leave.

Wick placed a hand on Kel's shoulder. "Hold your position, Stravage." He looked at Ann. "Lieutenant Stravage watched your flight drills on the console viewscreen. I might have questions for him. I doubt anything you say at this point will come as a surprise to the Lieutenant." Kel sat back down with a glance to Ann that came close to an apology.

Ann's hand shook as she took another sip of water. She wasn't ready to tell Colonel Wick about her doubts, about 'What if,' yet. The crash investigation committee had originally tried to convict her for the loss of the *Kairos*. How would it look if she voiced her own doubts now?

She drew a deep breath before launching into a description of the panic attacks. The colonel listened quietly as she told him everything she'd told John.

"I start off fine and then I can't remember...I can't think..." Ann said. "...and then all I can think about is blowing the hatch."

Wick nodded. "You're reliving your last minutes on the *Kairos*. Interesting to note that you didn't choose to blow the hatch, and yet this is the memory you are experiencing during your panic attacks."

Ann's face burned. While trapped and injured in the wreckage she'd considered blowing the hatch before life support ran out—a decision that would've instantly ended her life. She knew no one thought less of her given the circumstances, but that moment of fear and desperation darkened Ann's thoughts whenever her mind wandered back to the crash.

"There was one bright spot in your drills," Wick said. "I watched you pull out of a steep dive."

Ann muttered, "I crashed seconds later."

"True. But before that your roll out of the dive was masterful. What did you do differently?"

Ann thought and shook her head. "I don't remember."

Wick frowned. "It could be you still have gaps in your memory." Ann chewed the inside of her lip. The colonel was closer to the truth than he imagined. "We could try more memory therapy to see if—"

"She closed her eyes."

Colonel Wick and Ann looked at Kel, surprised to hear him speak.

"Lieutenant Chapman closed her eyes during the dive a few seconds before she pulled up," Kel said, pointing to the monitor. "I watched her on the screen. Anaya doesn't have a memory problem she has a decision-making problem."

Ann's back stiffened. Her eyes widened as she looked at Kel.

Wick arched his black brows and stared at Lieutenant Stravage. "And how did you come to *that* conclusion?"

"I watched her. Every crash." Stravage's eyes flicked to Ann's. "All fifteen of them." Ann stared a hole through Kel and crossed her arms. Kel looked at Wick. "I could see her eyes on the viewscreen. In the seconds right before each crash, Lieutenant Chapman looked from side to side. She's looking at the controls. It's quick, but if you know what to look for you can see it. She's trying to make a decision, choosing between options. In my opinion, that proves she remembers.

"It's the same when you're playing cards. If a player knows the game, they look from side to side when trying to choose which card to play. Players that don't know the game and don't know what to do stare straight ahead." Kel shrugged. "Anaya knows how to fly she's just stuck in the decision part. When she closed her eyes during the dive, her subconscious took over and made a choice for her."

Wick looked at Stravage, doubtful. "And you know this from playing cards?"

"Yes."

Wick grunted in disbelief.

Kel flicked a smile. "Cadet Wallace's rate of blinking increases from an average of twelve blinks per minute to seventeen when he's got a hot hand, depending on alcohol consumption. There's a professor on campus who touches his tongue to the inside of a cheek when he's bluffing. I also know a commander whose body odor is altered slightly when she's ovulating."

Ann's mouth fell open as her eyes darted from Kel to Wick and back again.

Wick cut off Lieutenant Stravage with an impatient gesture. "What does *that* have to do with cards?"

"She plays more aggressively," Kel said. "Bigger bets and more bluffing. Changes the pace of the game."

Wick's skeptical expression changed to one of grudging respect. "Anything else?"

"I know the commissary worker lied to me at breakfast yesterday when he said they were out of bacon." Kel thought a moment then looked at Wick.

"I know you didn't want to wear that tie this morning because your wife picked it out."

Wick drew back as if he'd been slapped, eyes wide. "How can you possibly know that?"

Kel flicked another smile. "Okay, I guessed about the tie, but the bacon thing was obvious." Stravage looked at the front of Wick's shirt. "Your wife has good taste in ties."

Wick turned to Ann, incredulous. She shared the colonel's amazement. Ann knew Kel had a talent, but she had no idea to what degree.

"Lieutenant Stravage is the best card player at headquarters," Ann said with a gesture of surrender.

Wick turned back to Kel. "Who's your commanding officer?"

"Commander Kralik. I'm assigned to an AIR unit."

Wick blinked in surprise. "Why are you classifying objects and not working as an investigator?"

"My commander doesn't think I understand people," Kel said, without a trace of irony.

Wick stared at Kel a moment longer and mulled that nugget over before turning back to Ann. "I tend to agree with Lieutenant Stravage's unorthodox diagnosis. I suspect the trauma from your accident is causing anxiety and interfering with your ability to make decisions. It would explain why you aced the written exams and fail the simulator. The reaction time on a written test is different from the split-second reflexes needed in flight."

Ann nodded. "Okay...so what do I do? How can I fix this?"

"You've already taken the first step by recognizing the problem," Wick said, straightening his tie. "The second is more time with one of our counselors. Unfortunately, until this matter is resolved, you're grounded from flying. You may practice with the simulator but keep your feet on the ground and out of the cockpit. Being aware of the problem is sometimes enough to push through it. Someone from my counseling team will contact you." Wick gave a nod to Lieutenant Stravage and left the flight deck.

Ann felt a weight lift from her shoulders only to be replaced with another. With the immediate pressure of getting into the cockpit gone, she faced a new worry. Would she ever have the confidence to fly again?

The tri-chord tone that proceeded an official announcement sounded through the comm. Commander Rectrix's somber face filled the console view screen.

"Friends. A week ago, I stood before you for the first time. It's with a heavy heart I come to you today." Commander Rectrix took a breath. "Five days ago, the cargo ship *What Cheer* missed its delivery with outpost Eremitas. Per protocol a scout ship was sent and discovered the cargo ship adrift and abandoned."

Kel traded looks with Ann.

Commander Rectrix continued. "Our investigators found no sign of the crew. All escape pods were accounted for. The missing crew members are Captain Charles Bowditch, Lieutenant Commander Will

Solloway, Lieutenant Sarolea Picquet, Crewman Calvin Vaux, and Crewman Melita Thorn."

A gallery of pictures with names of the missing appeared on the screen. Ann's heart sunk to see Sarolea's smiling face.

"Rest assured we're doing everything we can to locate the crew and bring them home," Rectrix said. "The *What Cheer* is being brought back to headquarters for a thorough investigation. Updates will be given as new information becomes available. That is all."

The viewscreen winked out.

Kel muttered under his breath. "Damn."

Ann looked up and saw Kel's mouth slant with worry.

TWELVE

THE WHAT CHEER

Palladium Beta's National Mall stretched from the Wilds of the city park surrounding Montressador's Keep into the heart of the capital. Walking paths led visitors through the pedestrian mall, past the reflecting pool of *The Lost,* and wound through memorial gardens where splashing fountains called to the coins in the tourists' pockets. Monuments honored the heroes of the Republic or told the bright and glorious history of the realm from the Golden Age of the Monarchy and the Montressadors through the Great Wars to the Quake, Calamity and Judgement, and the Awakening that ushered in the new age of time jumping and the modern era.

Ann caught up with Sean and Agent Fionna Knox in Vespertine Square by the time jumper's monument. The statue depicted the Awakening—the moment Andarrians received the divine knowledge of Time. Ann's brother called the thirty-foot statue ridiculously oversized and dramatically preposterous, but the cafe with the red umbrellas in the monument's shadow across the square had according to the swordsman, "the best steak sandwiches on the mall."

"It's just the strangest thing. Where could they have gone?" Ann gave an update on the *What Cheer* between bites of sandwich. The rhythms and harmonies of nearby power sources drifted faintly through the keravnos implant tucked in her ear.

"Were they attacked and boarded? Any sign of a fight?" Sean took a huge bite of steak and bun.

Ann shook her head and sucked sauce from a finger. "No, and no other ships in the area that we know of friendly or otherwise. The crew made their first delivery on schedule to outpost Viator and were on the way to Eremitas. The scout ship found the *What Cheer* adrift and sent over a boarding party when the crew didn't respond to hails. No one was on board. There were half-eaten plates of food left on the table in the galley."

"Whatever happened must have taken them by surprise," Sean said.

"I would check for spacetime distortions," Fionna said. "I'm guessing the crew time jumped off the ship to a safe house and haven't been able to make contact yet."

"But what would make them leave in the first place?" Ann looked to Fionna and back to Sean. "Kel said they brought the *What Cheer* back to the hanger a couple days ago. The ship's in perfect condition. It's like the crew left in mid-flight and just disappeared."

"They'll strip the ship down to the bolts looking

for clues. The log might have some answers." Sean frowned in thought and then gave Ann a teasing glance. "I suppose it would be too much to hope Captain Galeas finds more time jumpers on his back stoop?"

Ann returned a tight smile. "I'm afraid so." Her own strange disappearance a year ago was solved when Fionna and Agent Evan Drake showed up at Siren's Cove and found her working in the kitchen. "That outcome was one in a quadrillion." Worry prickled the back of Ann's mind. Cargo runs were not considered high risk and yet anything was possible once a ship left Andarrian space.

Sean dipped his sandwich into the puddle of sauce on his plate. He turned to Fionna. "What about Syrovar's missing sword? Any luck?" He took another bite.

Fionna lowered her sandwich, chewing thoughtfully, and swallowed before answering. "I've been interviewing Luctari, but it's taking longer than I expected. I had to call in other agents to help. There were at least a hundred in the park that night and the size of their camp changes day to day. Trying to track everyone down has been a challenge. Not to mention some of the unorthodox interviews my investigators are reporting."

"What do you mean?" Ann took another bite.

"One of my agents said a Luctari girl insisted she was a Lynx and would only answer questions if he held a stick with a feather attached so she could chase it. And he hasn't been the only one. Yesterday,

I interviewed a naked man wearing a chicken mask."

Sean looked up from his plate, eyes wide with alarm. "Why were you wearing a chicken mask?"

Fionna snorted. Sean flashed a grin.

Ann rolled her eyes at her brother and looked back to Agent Knox. "Did the man think he was a chicken?"

"No. He just liked to be naked," Fionna said. "He never told me the reason for the mask and after a few Luctari interviews..." Fionna widened her eyes. "...you learn not to ask."

Laughter ran around the table.

Ann wiped her mouth with a napkin. "What about the people on the night tour? Weren't they the last ones to see the sword?"

Fionna nodded and chased a bite with a sip of beer. She set the bottle on the table. "There was a group of fifteen that night. Mostly students and tourists. I interviewed them myself along with the tour guide. As part of the tour, the guide removed the sword from its brackets on the wall and offered the group a closer look."

Sean perked up. "Did the guide mention if anyone seemed overly interested in the sword?"

Fionna shook her head. "I asked that same question and she said no. Some people took a quick look and then wandered the room while others spent more time admiring the sword. She did mention one of the students leaned in too close to a floor exhibit and had to be asked to step back. The guide told me that it's not an unusual occurrence, so it didn't cause any alarm at the time."

"Maybe the student is an art critic." Ann looked at Sean and munched a chip, elbow on the table. "Sounds like you two would get along great."

Sean flicked a smile in Ann's direction. "Heh. You're hilarious." Ann smirked. Sean turned back to Agent Knox. "With fifteen people on the tour that had to be difficult to keep track of everyone. Where'd you find the two spacetime distortions?"

"The stronger signal appeared directly in front of Syrovar's picture in the space behind the curtain. The other signal was towards the center of the room. Everyone on the tour group says they saw the sword hanging under the picture when the guide replaced the curtain, but it's possible the thief could have appeared behind the curtain without being seen after the tour left." Fionna shrugged. "I'm still working on background checks. Nothing unusual so far."

"The Padome is still researching why Syrovar murdered the nobles," Sean said. "From reading their latest report, it sounds like they've found lots of rabbit holes, but no solid theories."

"History lessons." Fionna cringed. "I'm sorry, Montressador. It will be interesting to see what the council uncovers from a purely academic perspective, but I still don't see how that information will help us find the sword."

Sean shrugged. "It's not supposed to." Fionna gave him an arched look. He flashed a clever smile. "I wanted to give the Padome something to do.

To make them feel needed and important and it worked. They have a purpose now, more than just a fancy title, and I don't think I've ever seen them happier."

Fionna eyed Sean. A smile scrolled across her face as she nodded approval. "Then it'll be worth the effort regardless of the outcome."

Ann munched another chip, happy to see her brother and Agent Knox getting on so well. For once Fionna's bio-vision glasses, the ones that made Sean so nervous, were nowhere in sight.

Sean popped the last bite of sandwich into his mouth, making a cheek bulge, and chewed as he looked across the table to Ann. "So, are we going to talk about whatever it is you don't want to talk about?" He swallowed and took a quick sip of beer before continuing. "Or are we going to not talk about it, and I'll keep pretending that I don't notice you're holding something back."

Ann paused in mid-chew to frown at her brother and saw Fionna slide a quizzical look in his direction.

Sean muttered sideways to Fionna without taking his eyes off Ann. "She's been like this since she was a teenager. Casual coaxing doesn't work. Best to confront head-on."

Ann swallowed and looked to Fionna. "And he's always been kind of an ass. We haven't found a cure for it yet."

Fionna laughed and took another sip of beer. Sean grinned and flipped a balled-up napkin at Ann's head. "Out with it."

Ann blocked the shot and glowered back. "Fine. Wick grounded me."

"What?" Sean's brows shot up in surprise. "Grounded? As in no flying?"

Ann explained her panic attacks in the simulator.

"I'm sorry," Sean said. "You never mentioned it before."

Ann stared at the remains of the sandwich on her plate. "It's not the easiest subject to work into casual conversation."

Ann was startled to find Fionna's hand resting suddenly on top of her own. She looked up and met the agent's eyes.

"You're still recovering from your injuries," Fionna said. "It's nothing to be ashamed of or feel guilty about. You should never be embarrassed to talk about it or to ask for help."

Ann's face warmed, touched by Fionna's concern. She gave the agent a weak smile. "Thanks." She reached for her beer and took a sip to cover her embarrassment.

"You've done well in your recovery the past few months. Great even," Sean said. "But the best time jumpers still need backup. Wick's team will help get you sorted out." He leaned back, took a sip of beer, and turned thoughtful. "Can you be assigned a mission that doesn't require being a pilot?"

The keravnos implant shrieked as a massive energy pulse rocked Ann's senses. She yelled, dropping her beer bottle. The glass shattered on the pavement. The entire brass section of the Royal Orchestra blared fortissimo in her head. Ann ripped the implant from her ear, but the shrieking continued.

"Anaya!"

The pulse cut out as suddenly as it began. Ann tried to catch a breath. Sean's hand grabbed her shoulder. Sean and Fionna's faces were blank with shock. Startled patrons stared at Ann from all around the cafe.

Sean blinked. "What the hell was that?"

Ann felt as if every hair on her head stood on end. She looked down at the half-moon disk in her hand. "I...don't know..."

A scream shattered the air.

"OH, MY GOD! HELP THEM! GET THEM DOWN!"

Ann leapt to her feet with Sean and Fionna and ran into the square toward the scream. More cries of despair joined the first, becoming a chorus.

A crowd gathered around the fountain at the base of the monument. Onlookers shielded their eyes and pointed toward the top of the statue. Sean and Fionna pushed the crowd back. Ann slowed her steps and looked up, searching for the cause of alarm.

The statue of a male and female time jumper towered over the square. The golden sphere of knowledge balanced on the fingertips of their upraised hands. The statues' faces gazed up in glorious rapture, while the sphere caught the rays of the noonday sun. Light danced in Ann's eyes. She squinted and raised a hand. She moved closer to the fountain at the statues' feet to stand in the monument's shadow. A cry went up from the crowd.

"LOOK OUT!"

A figure in blue crashed to the pavement at the fountain's edge, sending up a spray of water. Ann jumped backward, arms raised. The thud of the impact echoed in the pit of her stomach. The body landed face down, legs splayed out behind, while the shoulders and arms bowed forward headfirst into the fountain. Ann raced to the figure and stopped cold. Horror seized her by the throat. The male figure's broad back and arms floated half-submerged in the clear water, but where the head should have bobbed Ann saw only a clean slice of flesh and bone above the collar of the blue fatigues, a *What Cheer* crew patch stitched to a sleeve.

Ann recoiled. Her stomach rolled. She staggered back on jelly legs into the shadow of the monument and battled to keep her lunch from hitting the pavement next. Ann swallowed hard, hands on her knees. *It wasn't Sarolea. Not Sarolea! Get it together, Lieutenant!* She straightened and leaned against the statue with one hand. The body fell from somewhere. Ann looked up. The sight stole her breath. Three more figures dangled like puppets at the top of the monument. Ropes were tied to their feet, arms stretched to the pavement below. All wearing blue fatigues. All headless.

THIRTEEN

FOUR OUT OF FIVE

Four corpses lay side-by-side on a plastic sheet under the blue medical tent. The bodies' distended abdomens pushed against the front of their fatigues. Ann watched from the back of the tent as the forensic tech hovered with a medical tablet. The spotlights' glare turned the corpses into nothing more than inanimate objects and banished shadows to the fringes of the tent. The antiseptic of the tech's gown and the rot of death mingled with the cooking smells from the nearby cafe.

Ann's stomach tightened each time she read the names stitched on the pockets of the fatigues. *Solloway. Vaux. Thorn. Bowditch.* The one name she didn't see filled her with a mixture of fear and hope.

The tent flap opened. Ann saw Sean's hand move to rest on the hilt of his sword and then relax when Fionna Knox stepped inside.

"The barriers are up," Fionna said, face grim. She wore her bio-vision glasses. "The monument is secure. Can't remember the last time I had a vertical crime scene."

"At least it's not an anti-grav environment...or an airlock breach..." All eyes shifted to the tech as he continued to speak. "Or power cell explosion. Industrial metal shredder..." The tech nodded vigorously, eyes wide, as he worked the medical tablet. "That image will stay with you a few days..."

"Kegler." Fionna interrupted the tech's verbal stream of thought.

The tech glanced up at the agent then back to the medical tablet. "Sorry, Knox. You know death makes me chatty." Ann saw the left side of Kegler's face spasm, pulling the side of his mouth into a grimace as if hooked like a fish.

Fionna looked to Sean and Ann and answered the unspoken question. "This is Forensic Tech Roan Kegler."

Kegler nodded without looking up. His fingers flew across the tablet's screen. "Montressador Chapman and his here-today-gone-tomorrow-back-last-week-sister. We can shake hands later. You'll probably want me to wash up first anyway." Another spasm gripped the tech's face.

Ann hadn't paid much attention to the tech before, but now gave him a closer look. Everything about Kegler was long. Long black hair slicked back from his forehead and hung down to his collar. A long face and nose complemented a jutting chin. Lean arms with pale hands held the medical tablet as long fingers danced across the screen. Ann and her brother exchanged looks with Fionna.

"Kegler's the best." Fionna nodded. "I always request him on my cases."

Kegler barked a nervous laugh. "Lucky for me you do."

Fionna responded with a small smile. "What do you have for me so far?"

"Not yet. You can't rush the dead." The tech grimaced, fighting another spasm. "I need another minute." He moved to the next body, eyes never leaving the tablet.

Fionna looked to Ann and Sean. "I talked to some of the witnesses. They all said the bodies appeared out of nowhere above the monument and fell until the ropes they were tied to caught on the statue. I have techs with chronoculars looking for spacetime distortions. Anaya, you sensed something right before the screaming started. Do you know what it was?"

"An energy pulse," Ann said. "Massive. I still sensed it even after I pulled off my implant. It was the same type of energy I always sense when Sarolea Picquet's ghost arm pops in and out."

Fionna blinked. "Ghost arm?"

"Time portal accident," Sean said. "Sarolea's ghost arm doesn't stay in one place for long."

"I didn't recognize it right away because this pulse was huge by comparison," Ann said. "I've never sensed an energy source so large and then have it disappear so completely. It's there and then it's not." A flicker of anger found its way into her voice. "Why would anyone want to kill time jumpers?"

Sean nodded, grim. "And why cut off their heads?"

"Knox."

The three turned and saw Kegler waiting. His medical pad hung from a shoulder strap.

"The killer was kind enough to leave the uniforms on the victims," Kegler said, after the three approached the spotlighted area. "The names are a match."

"So, they *are* the missing crew," Fionna said, mouth tight.

"Without a doubt. Picquet is the only one still unaccounted for. Cause of death..." Kegler gave a dramatic pause. "Decapitation." Ann's mouth twisted into a frown. The tech gave a nervous laugh and looked at his feet. "I know that comes as no surprise, but I like to be thorough. Complete exsanguination followed immediately after. All the blood was drained from the victims."

"Not much of a surprise given the cause of death," Sean said.

"In this case, it is. I'm picking up traces of anticoagulants that made the process faster. There are also ligature marks around the victims' wrists and ankles," Kegler said, gesturing to the bodies. "The killer bound them and hung them by their feet before or immediately after taking their heads. Whoever killed them wanted them to bleed out quickly."

Fionna frowned and looked up at the tech. "Why would—?"

"I was getting to that." Kegler fought off a mild spasm so only a flicker passed over his features. "You better have a look for yourself."

He unhooked the medical pad from its strap, tapped the screen, and held it over the distended abdomen of Lieutenant Thorn.

Sean muttered a curse. Ann drew back in horror as a three-dimensional digital image of the terror-stricken face of Melita Thorn appeared on the tablet's screen, eyes wide as in her last moments in life.

Fionna took the medical pad from the tech's hands and moved down the row of corpses, watching the screen.

"They're all like that. The killer scooped them out like melons. Sewed their heads inside their abdomens." Kegler bent down and carefully unzipped the front of Lieutenant Thorn's fatigues with a gloved hand.

A jagged haphazard row of metal staples began just under the woman's bra line and ran a crooked trail over the rounded stomach, the skin taut against the stitching. Gaps in the row of staples puckered the flesh, creating dark openings in the incision. Ann shivered as she imagined the face inside.

"This is amateur work," Kegler said, pointing to the stitches. "The killer must have practiced enough to get the job done but only barely. Lieutenant Thorn was killed first. The killer's technique, what little of it there is, improved with each victim." He zipped up Thorn's fatigues and stood. "Scans show the heads are matched to the right bodies. I'll confirm when I extract them." Kegler looked at Knox. "If you want to put out an order on missing body parts, make it for organs and entrails."

Fionna handed back the medical tablet. "Any thoughts on a murder weapon?"

Kegler clipped the tablet to its shoulder strap. "The decapitations were clean cuts—no tearing or crushing of the soft tissue." The tech continued, his voice picking up speed, excitement growing as he spoke. "The heads were removed with a single slice. My first thought was industrial cutting equipment, but...no...laser cutters would leave burn marks. A water jet cutter is too slow, the tissue would tear. It was something thin...possibly a metal garrote like the Corday assassins use...or maybe..."

"Kegler." Fionna spoke firmly, but without reproach.

The tech stopped mid-stream and stared at his feet until the mania passed. He turned his head to look at Sean. "A sword." Sean frowned. Kegler cracked a smile and shrugged a shoulder. "Sorry, Montressador. A guy with a sword on his hip stands behind me, and I can't help but think about it, but yes. A sword or a scythe would fit the profile."

Fionna looked at Sean, a question in her eye. "You're my sword expert. Could a sword do this?"

"It's possible," Sean said and adjusted his sword belt. "A sharp enough blade with the right amount of force applied at the right angle. It's simple physics." He lifted a shoulder in a half shrug. "Given the right circumstances, you could make heads fly but it's not easy to do in a single slice."

"Would Syrovar's sword have been sharp enough?"

Sean gave the agent a startled look.

"You can't be serious," Ann said. "It has to be a coincidence."

"I'm not saying I believe the murder weapon is Syrovar's sword," Fionna said, looking at Ann. "I'm just asking my sword expert if a particular sword—in this case, the missing sword—would've been capable of this kind of damage. I have to be able to rule it out."

"Syrovar's sword is a museum piece," Sean said. "It hasn't been sharpened to fighting condition in years."

"Swords can be sharpened," Fionna said, narrowing her eyes.

"There are also laws of metallurgy to consider. The sword is old. The amount of brute force needed to slice through the muscles of the neck in a single slice—not to mention bone—would most likely have shattered the blade or snapped the handle." Sean lifted his hands, palms up. "A sword could be the murder weapon but Syrovar's sword?" He shook his head. "Not possible."

Fionna sighed. "Perhaps not. But it made for an interesting question."

"I don't care about the damn sword," Ann said, her voice growing taut. "What about Sarolea? If she isn't here, then it means she could still be with the killer."

Fionna closed her eyes and nodded. "I know."

"What are you going to do to find her?"

"There's a lot we're already doing," Fionna said and looked to Kegler. "But there is an order to these things." She turned to Ann. "When we're done here, I'll share what we know with the other investigators on the case and then I'll go back to the beginning...to the *What Cheer*."

"I want to help," Ann said. "Sarolea's my friend. What can I do?"

Fionna thought carefully for a moment. Her eyes flicked to Ann's. "Write down everything you know about Sarolea's ghost arm. The type of energy you sensed when it phased in and out and how it compared to the energy pulse today. I'll fill out the request to add you to my team." Fionna sighed. "Congratulations, Lieutenant. You have your first assignment."

FOURTEEN

SIGNALS

The ball bounced against the balcony's energy shield and ricocheted with a ping. Sean's blade flashed, slicing the orb in two. Ann threw three more from the bucket on the table. The balls hit the shield in quick succession and rebounded in a blur. Sean deflected the first, sending it back toward the shield, sliced through the second and third with a backhanded slash, and then speared the first projectile with a quick thrust an instant after it bounced off the shield.

Sean flicked a wrist to clear the end of the blade. The battered sphere joined a dozen or more orbs that lay in pieces scattered across the balcony tile. The training exercise, no match for the Montressador's skill, came from his early days with the King's Guard. Sean suggested the activity as a distraction after the day's events. Ann agreed but suspected it was just another one of her brother's excuses to get her to man the bucket.

Ann continued throwing balls in random intervals for Sean to cut through. She always experienced a sense of wonder when she stepped across the threshold into her brother's apartment. The Montressador's residence took up most of the top floor of a tower in a busy downtown corridor of the capital city. Large picture windows offered dazzling views above the skyways where the smaller airships cruised. Polished wood and marble and rich fabrics, plush enough to make you swoon, created a level of comfort suitable to the Montressador's office. Ann knew she stood worlds away from the drab, cramped, dormitory housing she used to share with her brother.

The events of Ann's childhood were the last of the shattered memories she recovered after the crash of the *Kairos*. Spending more time with her brother had helped her gather the shards and piece them together. Ann now remembered how when she was twelve, Sean, then a first-year student at the academy, petitioned the courts for custody. The court granted permission with some reservations and Sean, at the age of only nineteen, became Ann's legal guardian. Her brother did his best to provide for them and complete school. A lucky strike with a practice sword during an exhibition match at the academy – a match that Sean lost – earned him an invitation to join the King's Guard. The modest wage had an immediate positive effect on their living situation, but life changed as dramatically as a star turning supernova five years later when Sean was named Montressador.

Ann grabbed three more balls from the bucket

and bounced them off the shield toward Sean's waiting blade. Memories of those years before the King's Guard, the one-bedroom flats and communal bathrooms, filled her head as they often did when Ann visited, but no matter how much she tried she could not remember the tragedy that propelled them to this point. Sean touched on the subject briefly only once since the *Kairos*. At the time, Ann in her grief didn't ask Sean to elaborate. Would the knowledge of how their parents died feel as raw? Ann kept the question to herself like a worry stone in a pocket, holding it during pensive moments, but uncertain as to whether she wanted to know the truth.

"HEY! BUCKET MASTER!"

Ann started and looked up. Sean watched her from a fighting stance, passing the hilt of his sword from one hand to the other with growing impatience. She looked down and saw a ball still in her hand. Ann grinned, cocked an arm, and threw the sphere as hard as she could at Sean's head. He flicked his blade and dispatched the foe with a snicker-snack sound.

Sean spun his sword in a large circle at his side. "So...what are we not talking about now?"

Ann hesitated. But, like so many times before, she kept the question in a pocket. Their parents were dead. Nothing would ever change that.

"I was just wondering...what's going on between you and Fionna?" She reached into the bucket for another sphere, but Sean waved her off.

"That's not the question you were going to ask

me," Sean said, sheathing his sword.

Ann smirked. "Ah, and what topic are *you* not wanting to talk about?"

Sean arched a brow and chuckled. "Okay, fair enough." He unbuckled his sword and belt and handed them to Ann. "We're getting on well," Sean said, leaning against the wall in a hip stretch. "But we're not together."

"I don't understand it," Ann said, shaking her head. "You like her. She likes you. What's the problem?"

Sean grunted and changed sides, stretching the other hip. "Mutual like does not a match make." He grabbed the sword belt from Ann and a beer from the balcony cooler and walked back into the apartment.

Ann followed. The balcony led to a great room with a suite of matching oversized sofas and chairs. A collection of books took up one wall surrounding a comm station and entertainment center. At the room's opposite end, a dining area with a polished table and chairs of inlaid wood enjoyed the twinkling lights of the city through a picture window. Sean hung the sword and belt on the brass stand next to a sofa.

Ann watched her brother, waiting for him to say more. "You never told me what happened with that kiss. Why did Fionna slap you? What did you do?"

Sean fell back full length onto the sofa with a groan and threw an arm over his face. "It's too long of a story. You don't want to hear about that."

Ann blinked, taking a seat. "Yeah, I kind of do."

Sean peeked from underneath an arm and eyed his sister's eager face. After a beat, he rolled his eyes and sighed. "Gather round, children," he drawled in an old man voice. "Grandpa's gonna tell ya a story."

"Wait!" Ann jumped up. She ran to the balcony, grabbed a beer from the cooler, and plopped onto the matching sofa across from her brother. Ann twisted the cap off the bottle and leaned forward, elbows on knees.

Sean chuckled and twisted the cap off his own bottle. "I met Fionna after your accident with the *Kairos*. As you know, everyone thought you were dead, but your body hadn't been found."

Ann pursed her mouth, unimpressed. "Thanks for the reminder. This doesn't sound very romantic."

Sean frowned. "Do you want to hear this or not?" Ann settled back into the sofa and gestured for him to continue. He took a pull from the bottle and began again. "The Ministry of Investigations assigned eight agents to the case. A month after the accident, I filed a No Confidence Order against the Ministry formally stating the Montressador's office did not trust them to investigate properly."

Ann choked on a sip of beer. "You what?"

"It was the fastest way to get their attention," he said with a shrug.

"Couldn't you have tried something a little more diplomatic?"

"Swordsmen, like me, aren't made for diplomacy." Sean grinned. "Anyway, it was a huge embarrassment for the Ministry. Made the news services and everything. I think there might be some higher-ups still mad at me."

"What did the Ministry do?"

"Fionna was one of the investigators already on the case. She was assigned to be the liaison to the Montressador's office. When we first met, she asked me why I didn't have confidence in the Ministry and what did I want the investigation to achieve." Sean's face grew more serious. "I told her the truth. I thought the Ministry was more interested in assigning blame for the accident and not on finding and recovering your body."

Ann nodded, stomach tight. The more she learned about the events surrounding the crash of the *Kairos*, the more she saw how blame was the primary objective.

"During that meeting, I formally asked Fionna to make it her priority to recover your remains. To bring you home. She agreed..." Sean's cheeks colored. "And...well...I guess I got a little emotional." Embarrassment turned to annoyance. "And of course, she was wearing those damn glasses..."

Ann smiled, amused but touched. "You cried?"

Sean eyed his sister. "Blubbered. Or in the very least I blubbed. Not my finest hour."

Ann hid her face behind a sofa pillow and tried not to laugh. Sean flung a pillow at her head. She squealed with laughter as the pillow bounced off a shoulder.

"It's not funny!" Sean's mouth cracked into a

smile. "I couldn't look her in the eye for weeks!"

"Okay..." Ann gasped, trying to catch a breath. "But then I was found alive, so everything should've been fine, right?"

"Well...yes and no." Sean cringed and scratched his beard. "Remember when Fionna reported back to the Ministry about your meeting with Commander Lazar?" Ann nodded. "I thought your memories of Vincent were a personal matter and had no business in her report to the crash investigation committee." Sean gestured with the beer bottle. "I yelled. She yelled back. I forgot she was a Ministry agent first and my liaison second. Technically, her liaison role was over once you were found."

"So, you were right back where you started," Ann said and took a sip.

"Worse. She wouldn't talk to me and hardly ever took off the glasses when I was around."

"I remember Fionna being very angry with you." Ann's mouth curled into a wicked grin. "You know, the entire Republic sees you as this smooth and charming, carefree bachelor when in reality you have as much experience with women as a teenage boy."

"I have plenty of experience!" Sean growled, "It's those ridiculous glasses. Difficult to court a woman who can see what you're feeling before you've had a chance to sort through your feelings for yourself."

"So, what happened with the kiss?"

Sean took another pull from the bottle. "It was the master stroke in my well-thought-out plan."

Ann narrowed her eyes. "You panicked."

Sean muttered, "Like a monkey on fire." Ann snorted a laugh. He gave a rueful grin. "Fionna was going back to the Ministry and with the way things were, I wasn't sure if I would see her again. I didn't know what to do. I couldn't talk to her. So...damn the glasses, full speed ahead...I kissed her."

Ann made a sympathetic face. "That was brave... and kind of stupid..."

Sean nodded. "Gimirri will probably hang those exact words under my museum portrait when I'm dead. At the time, I had few options. Fionna responded to the kiss—quite enthusiastically I might add—and I remember feeling relieved and happy that all I had to do was kiss her."

Ann covered her mouth, eyes wide. "Oh, no..."

"I didn't mean it that way!" Sean hid his face with an arm. "Again, those glasses. They aren't infallible, you know. Fionna interpreted my relief that 'all I had to do was kiss her' to mean I had an overinflated opinion of myself and that I see her as just another sexual conquest."

"You did talk to her, didn't you? Please tell me you straightened it out."

Sean sighed. "I couldn't catch her in time. She left. By the time we crossed paths again, it was too late to explain."

Ann put her bottle down on a side table. "Tell Fionna now! She wasn't wearing the glasses today. I really think if you talked to her..."

"Leave it alone," Sean said with a wave of a

hand. "We're working well together on this case. It's enough for now."

Ann muttered, "Coward."

He opened his mouth to reply, but the comm chimed with an incoming message.

Ann glanced over a shoulder to the comm station. "It's John."

"And my cue to go soak in the tub." Sean stood and stretched. "Goodnight! I'll see you in the morning." He flashed Ann a grin, grabbed his beer and the sword and belt from its stand, and headed to the bedroom.

Ann crossed to the comm station on Sean's desk and tapped the screen. John's worried face appeared.

"Finally!" Relief shot across his features as he swiped the bangs from his eyes. "I couldn't get a clear signal." The image on the screen pixelated. John grumbled and tried to adjust the reception.

"This connection doesn't seem much better," Ann said. "I'll try to boost the signal on my end."

Ann tapped a few keys, and the screen went dark. She looked up perplexed. A cheery beep came through the comm.

Ann chuckled. "Hi, Port!"

John pulled the mini-bot away from the screen. "Out of the way! Go clean something!" Port flicked his wings and buzzed away from the screen.

John's image fuzzed with static but held. Ann sighed. "I think that's as good as the signal's going to get. We may not have much time before we lose connection."

John looked to Ann, face grim. "I got your message. I'm sorry about Sarolea and the crew. Are you all right?"

Ann nodded, her insides turned to ice with the memory. "Yes...but I'm worried. Everyone is on edge. The cadets are practically wetting themselves." She struggled to put a little bravado in her voice partly for John's sake, but more for her own.

"Don't be too hard on them," John said. "They still think danger only happens off-world, not at home. I heard Rectrix closed the Weyl Gate?"

"We're on yellow alert along with a travel ban. All time jumpers are to remain where they are and wait for further instructions. I may be here another couple days."

Without use of the Weyl Gate, traveling to the Colonies from Andarria was only a jump point and a fifteen-hour shuttle ride away, but with the travel ban in place Ann felt every one of the ninety-seven million kilometers between Andarria and the Colonies. From the look on John's face, Ann could tell he was thinking the same thing.

"Hopefully, it won't take any longer than that," John said. "Keep me posted. Has Fionna's request to add you to her team been approved?"

Ann sighed. "Not yet. There's some infighting between the Ministry and the Time Jumpers that's holding things up."

"I'm not surprised," John said with a smirk. "What's the problem this time?"

"Jurisdiction. The *What Cheer* was found outside

of Andarrian space, but the bodies of the crew were found on Andarria." Ann shook her head. "No one is sure who should take the lead."

"That's an old feud. Luckily, it doesn't flare up very often."

"How's everything at home?"

John gave a lopsided grin. "I miss you, but I'm keeping busy..." As he spoke, the signal cut, skewing the picture and dropping the audio. "...projects...Mrs. Beaumont...coming home...might not be back..."

Ann frowned. "John, you're cutting out."

He tried to boost the signal. "Dr. Brainard...Idlewild..."

"What's that? Say again?"

John's inaudible image pixelated and the signal cut to black. Ann tried to re-establish a connection but gave up after a few seconds. Dr. Brainard picking her up in Idlewild wasn't that unusual, but Ann worried what John meant by *projects*. Ann sighed. She shut down the comm for the night and headed for the guest room. Hopefully, the signal would clear by tomorrow.

Ninety-seven million kilometers away at Siren's Cove, John grumbled and pushed back from the comm station in the master bedroom. It was hard to tell when exactly the signal cut out, so he wasn't sure how much Ann actually heard.

He picked up the ion pistol on the desk and checked the power cell before holstering it at his side. He pulled on his long black coat. Port trilled from his roost on the window.

"Sorry, not this time," John said, grabbing the ion rifle leaning against the wall and slinging it across his back. "A.K. is going to be my backup." Port whistled mournfully. John chuckled to himself. If he didn't know better, he'd think the little bot was developing a taste for adventure.

John crossed the bedroom to the brass armillary sphere on a pedestal in the corner and flipped the power switch. The time beacon's lights powered up, emitting a green glow. He entered the navigational coordinates into the control panel at the pedestal's base. The numbers locked on the screen and the sphere's concentric rings began to move slowly along their axis. A blue spiral of light burst from the floor nearby. The radiant coil widened in a matter of seconds into a circle roughly five feet across. John checked his gear one last time. He blew out a breath, took a hop step to clear the gap, jumped into the time portal, and disappeared. The blue portal closed behind him.

FIFTEEN

TOUCH AND GO

As predicted, the travel ban remained in place for the next two days. A geomagnetic storm disrupted communications between Andarria and the Colonies, and Ann was lucky to get a short text message through to Siren's Cove when Commander Rectrix finally lifted the ban and reopened the Weyl Gate. By the time Ann's foot broke through the other side of the portal and landed back on the Colonies, Dr. Brainard's carriage waited for her outside the military prep school in Idlewild.

Equuleus lifted his large copper head and nickered in greeting with a metal-on-metal squeal at Ann's approach. Curls of steam rose from the mechanized horse's nostrils, the furnace in his belly stoked for the drive home. Dr. Brainard gave Ann a hand up next to the driver's seat and they were off with a rattle of metal as Equuleus moved into a smart trot.

The miles rolled under pounding hooves as the doctor caught Ann up on local news. It wasn't long before the peaked roof tops of Llewellyn and the town's blue harbor came into view.

"The Captain wasn't home when I stopped by this morning," Dr. Brainard said, slowing Equuleus' gait as they entered town. "But I'm sure he'll be back by the time we reach Siren's Cove."

Ann looked at the doctor. "Back from where?"

Dr. Brainard mirrored Ann's surprise. "Mrs. Beaumont and I thought maybe you knew? The Captain didn't say except that he was meeting with Agent Max."

Ann frowned. With Sarolea missing, she hadn't had time to worry about what John had been up to. If he was with A.K., it meant Andarrian Intelligence wasn't held to the travel ban, or more likely, chose to ignore it. "John mentioned something about projects the last time we spoke on the comm, but the signal cut out before he could explain."

"From what Mrs. Beaumont said, he made it sound like it was a simple task. I believe he called it, 'a touch and go.'"

Ann arched a brow. "And you believed him?"

The doctor grew pensive and gave Ann a sideways glance. "Well...err...no...He has a habit of glossing over unpleasant details..." Dr. Brainard reined Equuleus into the rutted drive next to the tavern. The metal horse snorted, jetting steam, and the carriage rolled to a stop. The doctor pulled the carriage handbrake and tied the reins. "Perhaps I should come in with you to make sure the Captain doesn't require anything."

Ann grinned and grabbed her satchel. "Good

idea."

She pushed open the door and walked through the sitting room to the kitchen with the doctor. They found Mrs. Beaumont at the counter wrist-deep in bread dough. The cook looked up, face dusted with flour.

"Oh, good! You're home! I thought I heard Equuleus in the drive. Hello, doctor!"

Ann slung her satchel over the back of a kitchen chair. "Is John home yet?"

"No, but he should be back soon," Mrs. Beaumont said with a frown. "At least I think so…" The cook wiped her hands on a dish towel and pulled an antique gold watch from an apron pocket. Ann tensed at the sight of the familiar silver filigree on the watch case. Mrs. Beaumont clicked a button and the watch fanned like nesting spoons into three separate faces. "The Captain said this ridiculous device would tell me when he was coming home, but I'm not sure I'm reading it right." She sighed in frustration and handed the watch to Ann. "What can you make of it?"

Uneasiness settled over Ann as the timepiece rested in her palm. She had shoved the watch into a drawer in the bedroom, but John must have found it and given it to Mrs. Beaumont to hold on to before he left. The timepiece read an infinite number of possibilities from the time beacon in the master bedroom and selected three windows of time with the strongest potential for when John might return, but as the currents of time remained fluid so did his potential arrival. The three watch faces alternately dimmed or brightened based on the strength of probability with the brightest having the greatest potential. John had shown her how to read the watch before leaving on his mission to the black market.

"You can't send for backup every time one of the faces goes dark. It happens all the time," John had said, fanning the watch in his hand.

"Okay," Ann nodded and took the watch. The antique timepiece was surprisingly heavy for its size. She squinted at the three bright faces, their hands spinning wildly. "So how can I tell if you need help?"

"I'm only in trouble if all three watch faces go completely black for more than five minutes." John said. "The watch is set to chime if two faces are black and the third is dim. If that happens, then send a message to A.K. He'll know what to do."

"So, am I right?" Mrs. Beaumont's question pulled Ann back to the present. "Honestly, the middle watch is the only one that makes any sense."

Ann looked at the watch faces. The middle one shone the brightest while its hands ticked steadily, sometimes forward and sometimes back. The hands on the first spun wildly, its face dim. The hands on the third showed no movement at all, its face completely black. Ann's heart pinched. She looked at the kitchen clock on the wall and compared it to the time on the middle watch.

"Yes, that's right," Ann said, handing the watch back to the cook. "John should be home any sec—"

A cascade of violins showered Ann's senses as the

time beacon in the bedroom above activated. She sighed with relief. "There's John now. The beacon just switched on."

A loud crash shook the kitchen ceiling followed by a hoarse yell. Mrs. Beaumont shrieked. Ann ran for the stairs. She threw open the door to the master bedroom. John staggered under the weight of a body slung across his shoulders as he stood next to the beacon, green light fading.

"Help me get him to the bed!" He carried the stranger across the room.

Ann took a step forward and almost froze on the spot. The stranger's face was a mottled purple and swollen to grotesque proportions. The swelling seemed to be getting worse before her eyes. A large welt drew an angry line across the man's features, eyes reduced to slits. His nose disappeared into the flesh that used to be a face. Ann helped John lower the man to the bed. Her heart lurched as she recognized the brown sweep of Agent Max's hair. A.K.'s mouth and lips stretched into a nightmarish grin as he gasped for air. His neck bulged over his shirt collar.

A.K. wheezed, "I'm...supposed to be...*your* backup!"

"Shut up!" John ripped open the agent's shirt and collar.

Ann lifted the agent's chin, tilting his head back, to help open his airway. A.K. sucked air like a drowning man.

Dr. Brainard raced into the bedroom carrying his

medical bag. Mrs. Beaumont's pale face appeared in the doorway. The doctor hollered over a shoulder. "Call emergency services! Tell them to send a transport!" Mrs. Beaumont disappeared, leaving only the sound of footsteps on the stairs.

John stepped back and collapsed in a chair next to the bed.

"What happened?" Dr. Brainard took a quick reading with his medical pad.

"Allergic reaction. The mission went bad," John said, catching a breath and swiping bangs from his eyes. "Had to run for the ship. We fell into a patch of reaper nettles. A.K. took one to the face."

The doctor prepped an injection. A.K. thrashed on the bed in silent laughter and struggled to breathe. "Hold him still!" Dr. Brainard looked to Ann. "The poison acts as a hallucinogen." Ann restrained the agent as the doctor plunged the syringe into the man's thigh.

She glanced at John where he sat in a daze. A vicious welt appeared on the back of his left hand. His fingers swelled.

"Doctor!" Ann jerked her head in John's direction. He eyed John and tossed Ann a syringe. She injected the serum into John's leg and returned to A.K. on the bed.

John looked up perplexed and then down at the back of his hand. "That explains why the walls were melting."

A.K.'s breathing eased even as his face remained horribly swollen. He lay quietly on the bed as Dr.

Brainard fitted him with a mask attached to an oxygen concentrator.

"He's stable, but we need to get him to hospital," Dr. Brainard said.

A.K. looked to John and wheezed through the mask. "The ship...?"

"I took care of it," John said and cracked a smile. "I'm afraid it's going to be a big item on your expense report this month."

A.K. panted out a laugh.

Ann looked at John. "What happened to your ship?"

"Air forces chased us. Took out one of our stabilizers. They were going to board us. I relayed the ship's beacon back to ours and boosted the signal with the ship's power. I set a charge to blow the ship just before we jumped."

Ann's concern turned to amazement as a new thought entered her head. "You cleared the gap while carrying A.K."

"Just barely." John shrugged.

"Just like...old times..." A.K. panted.

John grinned and breathed a sigh of relief. He patted his friend on the shoulder.

"Old times." Dr. Brainard snorted.

Ann looked over a shoulder to the doctor on the other side of the bed.

"Ah, yes. Let's all cheat death and laugh," Dr. Brainard muttered to himself as he repacked his medical bag. "The buffoonery of foolish men."

Ann frowned. John and A.K. hadn't heard the doctor's retort. Ann whispered, "Doctor?"

He met Ann's eye and shook his head, face grim. He snatched his bag from the bed and went downstairs.

Ann cleared the last table as the young couple that occupied it for most of the night finally pushed back their chairs and disappeared through the tavern's front door hand in hand. Before Ann could turn the lock, the bell above the door chimed again and Dr. Brainard slipped inside.

John looked up from behind the bar. "How is he?"

"Agent Max is going to be fine." Dr. Brainard gave a tired smile and took a seat on a barstool. John pulled the stopper from a bottle and poured the doctor a measure of whiskey. "He won't be leaving hospital any time soon. If you'd delayed getting back even by a few more minutes, you'd need a new partner."

"Sounds like I still need a new partner," John said, face grim. He nodded in Ann's direction as she took the barstool next to the doctor. "Is he up for visitors?"

The doctor picked up the tumbler and watched the amber liquid swirl inside. "Give him a day to rest and then I'm sure he'll be happy to see you both."

Ann watched Dr. Brainard sip his drink in silence as John stowed the bottle. The doctor's reticence could be fatigue, or a sign that whatever bothered him earlier continued to gnaw at him.

"Captain!"

Dr. Brainard jumped, almost spilling his drink.

Mrs. Beaumont stormed from the kitchen door and handed John the kitchen's comm pad. The device chimed in urgent tones.

"I've no time to play messenger. Please answer this infernal device before I drown it in the sink." The cook's eyes lit on the doctor. "Nice to see you, doctor. How is Agent Max?"

Dr. Brainard stammered through his surprise at Mrs. Beaumont's abrupt change in tone. "Oh...erm... He's going to make it."

"Very good. I'll leave you to it." Mrs. Beaumont turned on a heel and marched back to the kitchen.

John and Dr. Brainard looked to Ann perplexed. Ann failed to hide a smile. "We're out of copper polish. It always sets her on edge." Mrs. Beaumont's efficiency was well known and so was her impatience when disorder struck.

John gave Ann a serious look as he leaned the comm pad against the tip jar and touched the screen. "Let's do ourselves a favor and buy some more polish in the morning." Ann grinned.

Fionna Knox's image appeared on the comm screen between the static. The agent's bio-vision glasses rested on top of her head, tucking blond bobbed hair behind her ears. Her expression brightened at the sight of familiar faces.

"Wonderful! Everyone I wanted to talk to."

John smiled. "Knox! What can we do for you?"

"Ann, you were right." The signal rolled Fionna's image and then held. "We checked Lieutenant Picquet's medical files. The spacetime distortion frequency created by Sarolea's ghost arm and the monument distortion are almost an exact match. There were only a few markers that were off."

"I knew the energy burst felt familiar," Ann said, leaning on the bar. "What was the difference?"

"Natural versus artificial." Fionna tapped some keys on her side of the screen and two wave patterns scrolled across the bottom of the comm pad. Points glowed where the patterns differed. "Sarolea's ghost arm is caused by a localized, naturally occurring frequency distortion from her time portal accident, but the distortion at the monument was artificially created. More importantly, Kegler found the same frequency distortion on the *What Cheer* and that one was an exact match to the one at the monument."

Dr. Brainard set his glass on the bar. "Forgive me, Agent Knox, but couldn't the distortion on the ship be the residual signal of Lieutenant Picquet's arm? If the frequencies are the same, how can you tell which distortions are natural and which are manmade?"

"It's the difference between listening to a recording of someone singing and listening to the same singer during a live performance," Fionna said. "There are tiny variations in a live performance that can never be completely duplicated even when the same song is being sung by the same performer. The distortion at the monument and the ship were exactly the same. That doesn't happen unless the frequency is artificially generated."

"The killer must have created the distortion to snatch the crew from the *What Cheer* and then again to dump the bodies," John said, tugging the pigtail at the back of his head.

Ann nodded. "But isn't that strange that they are so similar? Is that just a coincidence, or did the killer know about Sarolea's arm? He could've recorded the frequency when it phased, and then duplicated the signal to hijack the crew?"

"It's possible. From what you've told me, everyone knew about Sarolea's arm," John said. "She wasn't exactly shy about showing it around."

"True. And I guess that doesn't really narrow down our suspects." Ann sighed and looked to Fionna on the screen. "I'm guessing you didn't find a time signature?"

Fionna shook her head. "Only the ones of the crew when they were taken from the ship and then again when they reappeared at the monument, so we're dealing with an unknown traveler." Fionna's mouth slipped into a grin. "We did find something else. Captain Galeas, have you ever seen anything that looked like this?"

Fionna tapped more keys and a close-up shot of four blackened and melted metal discs appeared on one side of the screen. Deep cracks in the metal exposed burned-out circuits.

John frowned and leaned in for a closer look. "Where did you get those?"

"My team found them at the top of the monument."

John's eyes flicked to Fionna's on the screen. "What's your security clearance level?"

"High enough that if you have information that directly impacts my case, I need to know." Her eyes shone with curiosity.

"All right. Here's what I can tell you. The discs are navigational anchors for nanobots and are used for interdimensional travel with Splice as the phasing agent."

"Splice?" Fionna frowned. "Time jumpers haven't used it in a hundred years."

"Maybe...but the directional anchors you found are a serious upgrade of old tech," John said, pointing to the discs on the screen.

"No wonder my techs didn't know what the discs were," Fionna said. "Are you sure our suspect is using Splice? Our scans of the victims didn't pick up any embedded tech or phasing agents."

"Splice won't show up in a normal scan," Dr. Brainard said, adjusting his spectacles. "Have your forensic tech check for changes to cellular structures. The phasing agents in the drug cause damage over time. That should confirm it. As far as not finding nanobots, that is a puzzle. Perhaps a glitch in your scanner?"

"Maybe." Fionna frowned. "I'll ask Kegler to scan for nanobots again when he checks for Splice."

"One more thing, Agent Knox. You most likely won't find active nanobots. They draw energy from the body's natural electrical charges. They won't remain active for long after death occurs."

Fionna glanced up at the doctor. "Wait...If nanobots don't survive in a dead host...?"

The doctor lifted a hand. "I would theorize the killer injected the bodies with Splice and freshly charged nanobots right before phasing. The bots that phased the crew members from the *What Cheer* wouldn't have lasted long enough for a second trip."

Ann straightened on her barstool. "That means the killer is going through a lot of nanobots."

"They're easy to acquire and program," Dr. Brainard said. "They're used in medicine all the time. I know some doctors who even replicate their own."

"Can we track the bots back to their source?" Ann looked to John and then to Fionna on the comm screen, excitement growing. "We could use them to find Sarolea and the killer."

Fionna brightened. "Captain?"

"It's possible," John said. "You could build a device that could detect active nanobot swarms, but to find specific bots you'll need to know the command signal the killer is using. The killer would also have to be actively using a swarm to travel in order to detect and track. You might only have a few seconds to lock in on them."

"A nanobot trap. Find the bots, catch the killer," Fionna mused. "I like it, but the only way to know the exact command signal is if we use the same directional anchors designed for the bots. It will be a trick to reverse engineer the fried ones, but we'll give it a try."

"If I'd known two days ago, I might have been able to get a functioning anchor for you."

Ann arched a brow in John's direction. *So that was*

the project he was working on with A.K.

Fionna leaned in as the comm signal flickered again. "Is that still possible?"

John grinned. "The site had an unfortunate industrial accident. There might be more sites. I was helping to track them down and take out their production lines. If I find more, I could try to grab an anchor for you, but no guarantees. I'm shorthanded right now with A.K. injured. Even if I find another site, I need to be assigned a new partner before I can take action."

Fionna frowned. "What happened to Agent Max?"

"A complication on our return trip. He's okay, just not sure how long he'll be out."

"As a senior time jumper, you can request a mission specialist to be a temporary replacement while A.K. recovers," Fionna said. "It would be faster than waiting for a new partner to be permanently assigned to you." John looked to the agent, surprised. Fionna waved him off. "I can't be your partner. I'm a Ministry Agent, not a time jumper...but Ann is."

Ann caught both of their smiles and gulped. "I'm not a mission specialist. I *was* a pilot, but now I'm not even officially on the investigation team yet."

"The approval just came through, and yes you are a specialist," Fionna said. "You sensed the energy pulse at the monument. You can sense and recognize the distortion frequency the killer is using. That's why you're on the team. As the team lead, I can authorize you to assist Captain Galeas for the purpose of obtaining the directional anchor..." Fionna's eyes slid in John's direction. "...assuming he agrees to take you on as a temporary partner."

Anxiety twisted Ann's gut. "But...I haven't been cleared to fly yet." She looked to John suddenly wishing she'd been a little more detailed on the reason for her grounding. When she told Fionna and John about her conversation with Colonel Wick, she'd neglected to share Kel's observations from the flight simulator, not to mention her own recurring doubts about the crash of the *Kairos*. "I thought I had to be able to fly before I could be assigned a time jumping mission."

John lifted a shoulder. "Most time jumpers want both members of a team to be able to fly in case of an emergency, but it really depends on the type of mission and the preferences of the senior team member."

Ann threw John a doubtful look. "After what happened with A.K, I'd have thought you'd know better than to partner with a non-pilot."

"The Captain should know better, but it hasn't stopped him before," Dr. Brainard said.

Ann threw her hands up in frustration. "What if you're injured? I can't fly!"

"Yes, you can," John said, taking Ann's hand. "You *know* how to fly. You're just struggling with the actual flying part."

Dr. Brainard frowned. "I fail to see the comfort in that statement."

"We'll be fine," John said, looking at the doctor. "And depending on where the next site is, we may not have to fly at all."

Ann cringed. Colonel Wick banned her from flying, not from going on other missions. Hopefully, her decision-making problems didn't extend beyond the cockpit.

"Okay." Ann nodded. "If it helps us find Sarolea, then I'm in."

"Great! Then it's settled! Captain, I'll leave it to you to bring Ann up to speed. Keep me informed on your progress." Fionna tapped a key and the screen winked out.

Mrs. Beaumont stepped from the kitchen. "The tea is ready. Will you be joining us, doctor?"

Dr. Brainard stood. "Thank you, but it's been a long day. I should be getting home."

John frowned at the doctor's reluctance. "All right. Well…have a good night then. Thanks for your help with A.K."

Dr. Brainard waved without another word and headed to the door.

Ann hopped off her stool. "I'll see you out."

She closed the tavern door behind them and waited on the stoop while the doctor checked Equuelus' harness. The mechanical horse pawed a hoof between the carriage shafts.

"Is everything all right?" Ann asked.

Dr. Brainard flicked an eye in her direction. "Everything's fine. I'm just tired."

"Why are you angry with John and A.K?"

The doctor pulled on his driving gloves before answering. "Old times." A shade of bitterness colored his tone.

"Doctor?"

"It's nothing." Dr. Brainard exhaled a deep breath and looked up. "I owe you an apology. I overreacted earlier to male bravado. I know that's how Agent Max and the Captain cope with the threats they face. I failed to see the humor at that particular moment knowing my friends had been in danger and that they'll continue to put themselves in harm's way in the future."

Ann's face warmed. She always took for granted that Dr. Brainard would be there to render medical aid but hadn't realized the worry and strain he suffered through until now.

"Where did Mrs. Beaumont get that watch?" Dr. Brainard asked.

Ann looked up, surprised. "John got it from the attic. He must have given it to her to hold on to before he left."

"Have you used it before while he was away?"

"A little..." She shifted on the stoop, uncomfortable by the conversation's change in direction. "On his first mission...I don't know that I'll keep using it."

Dr. Brainard gave her a sympathetic smile.

"I know it was Bonnie's," Ann said, meeting his gaze. "That's not why I don't want it."

"You hated using it."

Ann blinked in wonder. The doctor was full of surprises this evening. "How did you...?"

"Bonnie Galeas used to carry that watch around

all the time when the Captain was gone," he said. "The watch would tell her when to expect him home, but it also changed based on how the mission was going, or if he was in danger. It almost drove her mad. She lived and died with every ticking second."

Ann tried to swallow the lump growing in her throat and picked at a piece of loose paint on the stoop's wooden railing. "There was a moment when John was gone when all the watch faces went dark. It was only for a few seconds. There wasn't any warning. John said the watch would chime before all the faces went black, but it didn't. It was horrible. I couldn't..." Ann took a breath to steady herself. "After John came home, I put the watch away."

Dr. Brainard rested a hand on her shoulder. "Did you tell him how it made you feel?"

"No..." Ann quickly blinked back the tears before they could fall. "I don't want him to think it's because the watch was Bonnie's."

"You need to tell him. He won't think any less of you if you're honest." He turned toward the carriage. "I wish Bonnie had listened to me when I encouraged her to do the same."

Ann watched him climb up into the carriage. "You miss her."

Dr. Brainard settled into the driver's seat and stared straight ahead, mouth pinched tight. "Yes. Very much. Bonnie was a good friend." He looked down at Ann, forcing a smile. "I will make you the same promise I made to her. I'll render aid whenever you and the Captain need me for any reason. I won't lecture or chastise you...at least not too much...no matter how many risks, or boneheaded decisions you and the Captain might make along the way."

Ann felt the tears spring to her eyes again, this time with affection. "Thank you!"

Dr. Brainard's mouth stretched into a genuine smile. "Good night, Ann."

He clucked to Equuelus and they moved off. Ann listened to the sound of the carriage wheels on the cobblestones before going back inside.

SIXTEEN

THE REVEREND

What an ass.

Sean gazed up at his own portrait and took a bite of steak, sliding the hunk of meat off the wooden skewer in his hand with his teeth and chewing thoughtfully.

The official portrait of the current King's Champion always hung in the Montressador's Keep on the first landing of the grand staircase inside the castle's front hall. The spot was a favorite gathering place for tourists, but foot traffic was light that day. Sean held the staircase to himself, free to cast a critical eye over his younger likeness in quiet contemplation without the curious stares of visitors.

Sean frowned as he took another bite of spicy meat. The same thought went through his head as he looked at his cock-sure expression in the portrait.

An arrogant *ass.*

The image, like so many other official portraits, looked down on the viewer with a haughty air, a red tunic draped across one shoulder and his still-unnamed sword—*Thanks for bringing up irritating subjects, Fionna*—belted to one side. The artist was clearly a graduate of the Paint by Numbers School of Clichés. All that the portrait was missing were some vestal virgins wrapped in gauzy togas, clutching his legs and gazing up in glorious rapture, Sean thought. The portrait's expression reminded Sean of the pretty boys at school, the ones who deserved a kick in the teeth. He wondered vaguely if Fionna viewed him the same way when she looked at him. Sean sighed. If only he could use her bio-vision glasses to see what she was thinking for change, then maybe he wouldn't feel so off balance around her all the time.

"Montressador Chapman."

Sean paused in mid-chew and looked up. His office assistant, Josephine, stood at the top of the next flight of stairs wearing a sensible, dark blue wrap dress that could not hide the generous curves beneath. A mass of dark curls gathered at the back of Jo's head tumbled loosely about her face. Sean started up the steps while he finished chewing and swallowed.

"Will you be returning to your office after lunch for your meeting with the Citizens League or will you be going straight to your meeting at the Ministry?"

Sean recognized their code that a visitor waited for him in the office. Someone he may or may not want to speak to, but someone outside of the normal diplomats and politicians he dealt with. Sean noticed a few visitors milling about on the second floor and took a step closer.

Jo lowered her voice to a confidential tone. "I told the Reverend Brink you were pressed for time today and may need to schedule a meeting with him later in the week."

Sean's brows shot up in surprise. "Did he say why he's here?"

"A social call. Nothing of importance."

"He wants something." Sean's eyes narrowed as he looked down the hallway. "I can make time."

Sean walked down the hall with Jo at his side, the ring of his sword belt muted by the plush carpet underfoot.

"I made the Reverend comfortable in your office," Jo said as they stepped into the Montressador's suite.

Sean closed the ornate wooden door behind them and walked toward his office. "Give me fifteen minutes. If the Reverend is still here, bring me something that requires my immediate attention."

"Montressador...your lunch." Jo smiled and pointed to the skewer of meat still in his hand.

Sean looked down and saw one piece of meat left. He bared his teeth and took a vicious bite, chewing with a vengeance as he wiped his mouth and hands on a napkin.

"Do I look official enough to greet a Reverend?" He gave Jo a teasing look, the meat bulged his cheek as he straightened and buttoned his uniform jacket. He might have the breath of an Imoogi, Sean thought, but he should at least try and look the part. He flicked the skewer into a waste can.

Jo's mouth twitched as she tried to hide a smile behind her official position. "Picture perfect, sir."

Sean entered his office and found the Reverend Jeremiah Brink standing in front of the expansive window overlooking the Wilds surrounding the Montressador's Keep. A circle of bare scalp peeked from beneath thinning white hair at the crown of his head. The reverend's height fell on the shorter side of average. From the back, the man appeared narrow in the shoulder and then became broader and lumpier as the eye traveled downward.

The reverend turned. Sean noticed a lift in Brink's shoulders, a straightening of the spine. A flash of gold between the reverend's fingers caught Sean's eye as the reverend slipped his left hand in a coat pocket before offering his right.

"Montressador Chapman, so good to finally meet you." A smile stretched across his face and bunched his cheeks like milk biscuits. His eyes glittered.

Sean gripped Brink's thick hand and struggled to reconcile the person with the image of the farting and burping reverend on the transport screen from a few weeks ago, but for once he felt no urge to laugh. Sean gestured for the Reverend Brink to take a seat.

"What can I do for you, Reverend?"

Brink wore a suit of midnight blue with a shirt of deep purple that formed a 'V' from the top of his open collar underneath a double chin and extended downward across a protruding stomach to the button on his jacket. With thinning hair and a wide upper lip reminiscent of a frog's mouth, the reverend's face was not what one would expect of a charismatic leader of a few thousand followers. On looks alone, Brink would be lucky to bag a half-dozen disciples...except for one feature. The reverend's amber eyes held his gaze in a way that made Sean's scalp prickle. Sean steeled his nerve and took a seat behind his desk, ignoring the nearby sword stand as a primitive instinct warned him not to remove the weapon in the man's presence.

Brink lowered his bulk into the chair opposite the desk. The wooden chair creaked in protest. "I wanted to thank you." The reverend's lips spread into a humble smile. "I was recently made aware that it was the Montressador's office that called the park conservancy about the vandalism to my recorded message at the transport station."

Sean relaxed into his chair. *So, it was a social call after all.* "It was nothing. I was simply at the right place at the right time, and I asked my assistant to call it in."

"Well, it was taken care of quickly and without further embarrassment, and for that, I am in your debt." Brink paused and looked down at his clasped hands. "In some ways, the incident was fortuitous. I admit I've wanted to meet you in person for some time."

Sean's instincts prickled again. "Oh? And why's that?"

"I'll explain in a moment, but I wanted to first offer my sympathy over the theft of Montressador

Syrovar's sword from the museum. Have there been many leads?"

"Not to my knowledge," Sean said, feeling the reverend's eyes on him again. "The Ministry is handling the investigation."

"I'd like to help if I can." Brink leaned back in the chair and unbuttoned his suit coat. Sean could almost hear the button sigh, relieved from its labor of restraining the reverend's belly. "I've told my followers that if they remember seeing anything suspicious leading up to the theft, they should report it."

Sean nodded, seeing the calculation behind the statement. The Luctari were viewed by most Andarrians as freaks, an undesirable counterculture. If it were known they were actively supporting the Montressador's office by cooperating with the Ministry, it would help to raise the group's image.

Sean returned a polite smile. "Are those followers the protestors that I've seen outside the National Museum?"

A switchblade smile replaced Brink's humble countenance for an instant before returning again to that of a gentle pastor. "Yes..." He chuckled. "But I assure you they were only protesting the museum's glorification of Andarria's time jumping history. Certainly not the Montressador's wing." Brink steepled his fingers together as he looked across the desk. "The Luctari have only the highest respect for the Montressador's line and the golden age before Andarria's fall and enslavement. Surely, you see how the tradition of the Montressadors fell into decline around the same time Andarrians were cursed to serve as time's stewards?"

"The role of the Montressador's office has changed since its beginning, but I wouldn't say it's in decline," Sean said, acutely aware of a stack of reports visible on his desk.

"I admire your loyalty, Montressador. But—and not to diminish the lives of those lost—I can't help but notice how the news of the theft of a national treasure has been removed from the public's eye because of yet another time jumping *tragedy*."

Sean narrowed his eyes. "The deaths of the crew of the *What Cheer* were not a tragedy or an accident. It was murder."

"Yes, *murder*." Brink's face changed, gripped with a strong emotion, as he leaned forward suddenly, a surprising feat for a man of his girth. "I assure you, Montressador, I chose my words carefully. Their deaths were without a doubt murder, but you would not know it from watching the news services. They're the ones who call it a tragedy. To cry murder would be to admit to the Andarrian public that we are the victims of a horrible mistake." Brink spread his hands in a pleading gesture, a growing passion filled his voice. "Why should Andarrians alone enforce the laws of time for all the universe? Our meddling in the affairs of others invites jealousy and violence. The burden we've been forced to carry is too great...too dangerous...too..."

"Reverend, why are you here?" Sean asked. Brink's eyes scorched the air between them. Sean moved his sword hand into position under the desk.

Brink leaned back in the chair. His eyes lost some of their intensity as the humble pastor returned. His left hand slipped casually into a coat pocket. Sean kept his hand on the hilt of his sword. "I grow relationships." The reverend withdrew his hand from the pocket and rolled a gold coin between his index finger and thumb. "Your actions the other night led me to believe perhaps you could be counted among our friends."

"I disagree with the Luctari's views on time jumping, but I support your right to voice your opinions," Sean said. "You should've known my thoughts based on my public comments in support of time jumping."

Brink lifted a shoulder. "Many of our friends can't speak publicly. I wondered if given your office and the fact that your own sister, Anaya, is a time jumper that you might be in the same position. I apologize if my assumptions were wrong."

Sean's sword hand twitched under the desk with the mention of Anaya's name. It was no secret they were family, but her name sounded wrong in the reverend's mouth, sticky and sweet, but like rotten fruit, the pulp hid a dark and fetid center. "I assure you my public and private opinions on time jumping are the same."

Reverend Brink pushed himself out of the chair with a look of disappointment worn more for show, slipping his hand with the gold coin into his coat pocket again. "Ah, well. No matter. We will agree to disagree with no harm done." Brink buttoned his suit jacket and looked at Sean. A new light of hope filled his eyes. "Perhaps you will come to one of our group's public outreach meetings?"

Sean escorted the reverend to the door. "It's unlikely but thank you for the invitation."

Jo looked up from her desk, a quizzical slant to the line of her mouth, as the two men entered the outer office.

"You're always welcomed and if there is ever anything I can do for you, Montressador, please don't hesitate to contact me." The humble gregarious pastor returned as Brink extended a hand. The reverend's hand felt soft, but the grip on Sean's fingers showed a hidden strength.

Jo waited a beat after the door closed behind Reverend Brink before looking to Sean. "What was that all about?"

"The cosmos delivering a punchline," Sean said and blew out the tension gathered in his chest.

Jo gave him a puzzled look.

Worry gnawed Sean's gut. "I did something nice and now I'm being punished. Get Fionna on the comm." He turned on a heel to return to his office.

The comm station on the reception desk chimed. Jo's eyes searched the screen. Her face paled. "Montressador, I have a message from Agent Knox." The tightness in Jo's voice pulled Sean's gaze. "They found another victim."

"A body? Where?"

Jo shook her head and swallowed hard before

answering, a tremor in her throat. "In the Wilds ... outside Montressador's Keep."

Fionna's directions led Sean to a secluded dry stream bed a fifteen-minute walk through dense underbrush from the nearest footpath. A few minutes into the brush and Sean was glad he took the time to ditch his uniform and change into a work shirt and pants before leaving Montressador's Keep, the sword of his office remained ever-present at his side. The smell of death guided him the rest of the way to the perimeter sensors outside the blue medical tent. Sean gagged, covering his nose with the back of a hand. A Ministry agent on guard tried to stop him as he stepped past the sensors, but Fionna waved him through.

She walked toward him and held out a small jar containing clear jelly. "Here. Smear this under your nose."

Sean did as he was told. A garden of peppermint and roses smothered the scent of death. "Thanks," Sean said, inhaling through his nose.

Fionna returned the jar to a pocket. Her t-shirt, canvas pants, and muddy hiking boots looked very much at home in the middle of the woods and, as Sean couldn't help but notice, only enhanced the agent's natural beauty. He quickly smothered the familiar warmth spreading in his chest.

Sean nodded toward the medical tent. "Please tell me it's not Lieutenant Picquet?" Hope never seemed so far away, but he didn't want to be the one to tell

Anaya that Sarolea was dead.

Fionna looked pensive for a moment behind her bio-vision glasses, mouth dipped into a frown. "We're not sure yet. A group of junior rangers on a nature hike found it and called it in."

Fionna's use of the word 'it' gave Sean pause. "I guess the rangers weren't expecting to earn their 'Discover A Crime Scene' badge."

She gave Sean a pointed look, lifted the tent flap, and motioned for him to follow.

Inside the tent, the smell of rotting meat ripped up Sean's garden of roses and planted decaying corpses. His stomach rolled.

"Shit fire."

Instead of bodies, the flood lights showed a glistening gray mound in various states of decay five feet across. Entrails snaked across the tent floor in places where animals had torn at the pile. Black pools of putrescent liquid reflected the lights as flies buzzed and pinged inside metal traps hanging from the tent ceiling. Forensic Tech Roan Kegler, gowned and gloved, hovered with a medical pad shadowed by an assistant.

Fionna's voice interrupted the nightmare. "We estimated there are five separate sets of organs. We'll get positive IDs back at the lab, but we're working on the assumption they belong to the four missing crewmembers from the fountain. If we're right, the fifth victim is Lieutenant Picquet."

"You're still missing a body." Sean looked at Fionna, relieved he could still speak without throwing up on her boots.

The agent nodded. "True. But my instincts tell me it won't be long before it turns up. The killer wants us to see his handiwork. That's why he dumped the other four bodies at the fountain. He's showing off. The question now is what does he have planned for us next?"

"I found it!"

Kegler's excited tone pulled Sean's attention back to the horror in the middle of the tent. The forensic tech handed off his medical pad to his assistant, dropped to his knees, and thrust a gloved hand deep into the middle of the mound. Wet squelching noises came from within as Kegler searched the pile. Sean's throat tightened as a knotted coil of intestine slithered from the top of the mass.

"When I was a kid, I paid a dory at the fair to walk through one of those fake murder houses," Kegler said. A spasm gripped the tech's face, pulling his mouth to one side as he continued to search through the pile. "They blindfolded us and told us to put our hands in a bowl of noodles and said it was brains." He rolled his eyes. "Ridiculous. Any forensic tech will tell you brains feel like chiaje fruit."

The roll in Sean's stomach rocked his head. Beads of cold sweat dotted his brow as the tent's hot damp air clung to his skin. The last thing he needed was to add vomiting and fainting to his list of embarrassing moments with Fionna. Sean gripped the hilt of his sword and counted the flies holding court on the roof of the tent.

"Oh, God."

Sean's eyes darted back to the tech. Kegler had frozen, eyes flat, his arm buried deep in rotting flesh.

Fionna stepped forward. "Kegler?"

A wave of panic crossed the tech's face as he took quick shallow breaths. "I'm up to my shoulder in—"

"I know," Fionna said. "Try humming."

Kegler gave a pained look as another spasm distorted one side of his face, breathing ragged. He hummed a few tuneless notes, continued searching, and then stopped again. Kegler gulped air. "It's not working. I can't—"

"Why does chiaje fruit feel like brains?" Fionna's gentle voice rang soft and clear through the tent.

The panic etched on Kegler's face eased as he considered the question. "Because...it's segmented the same way...two hemispheres...and the fruit sections are curved...not sectioned on a diagonal..." His eyes snapped into focus. "I got it."

Kegler pulled his fist from the mound and stood breathing hard. He held out a blackened metal disk between gloved fingers for Fionna to see.

She leaned forward for a better look. "Same as the others?"

Kegler nodded. "Looks like it."

Sean looked from Kegler's gloved hand to Fionna. "Is that...?"

"It's the directional anchor I told you about," she said. "I'm hoping Captain Galeas and Anaya can find me a working one." Fionna lifted a shoulder. "At least the killer is consistent."

Kegler shook the gore from his glove. "That's all I can do here." He dropped the directional anchor into an evidence bag held open by his gowned assistant. "I'm ready to bag it up. We'll untangle it back at the lab." The assistant nodded and stepped toward some medical supplies stacked in the rear of the tent. Kegler looked over a shoulder at Sean and Fionna, eyes dark. "You probably don't want to stick around for this part. It's going to be awful." The forensic tech's face brightened suddenly. "I made a pun. Offal? Get it?"

Kegler turned back to his work with a nervous laugh. Sean saw that the assistant had returned and stood ready with a large body bag in one hand and a pronged metal rake in the other.

Sean burst from the medical tent breathing hard and walked a few paces away, grateful for the cool air on his face. Fionna's footsteps trailed after him. He bent at the waist and took a few deep breaths before straightening and turning to Fionna.

"What the hell was all that about?"

"The gallows humor?" Fionna arched a brow. "Sorry... You get used to it. I've had a lot of practice."

Sean gestured to the tent. "Kegler! One minute he's fine and the next—"

"I've had a lot of practice with him, too." Sean flashed Fionna a look of alarm. She blushed and looked away before meeting his gaze again and continuing. "Roan's an old friend. He had a breakdown a couple years ago and had to take an extended leave of absence. No one wanted to work with him when he came back, but he's a good tech. Really good."

Sean eyed Fionna for a beat. A twinge of discontentment troubled him. The blush was unusual for the agent. Kegler didn't seem like Fionna's type, but 'old friend' was vague enough it could mean almost anything.

Sean marshaled his thoughts, remembering Kegler's words from their first meeting. "Death makes him chatty."

"Talking helps Roan focus on the details and distracts him from the moment," Fionna said. "Most of the time...and when it doesn't, I can usually talk him through it." She sat on a downed log and looked up at Sean. "Jo said Reverend Brink paid you a visit?"

Sean tested the strength of the log with a foot before taking a seat next to Fionna. He told her about his meeting with the reverend, how Brink asked about leads on the sword investigation, and his instructions to the other Luctari to cooperate with the Ministry.

"And then Brink tried to recruit me or at the very least asked for my support...whatever the hell that meant."

Fionna listened, nodding occasionally, and stared off toward the medical tent. Her blond hair fell forward across her cheeks. When she finally turned toward him, Sean saw the regret in her eyes behind the glasses.

"Syrovar's sword will have to wait. I'm off the case."

Sean's mouth dropped open. "*What?* Why?"

"The ministry is pooling resources to find the time jumper killer," Fionna said. "I've been reassigned along with other agents to work exclusively on the murder investigation."

Sean unpacked a grab bag of feelings in the span of a few seconds. The frustration over not finding the sword coupled with the knowledge he would no longer be able to use the investigation as an excuse to see Fionna was more than disappointment—it was total defeat. The longer the sword stayed missing, the chances of ever finding it became less likely. A murder investigation was certainly more important than a missing sword, but the Reverend Brink's words about how time jumping had taken priority over the Montressadors rang in Sean's ears. He shook off that last pathetic voice. It was silly and selfish to feel that way. Sean's shoulders tensed, remembering Fionna's bio-vision glasses. His face burned knowing she saw every emotion that had passed through his head in the last few seconds. Worst of all, she saw that last sentiment too. *Damn it, Fionna!* Sean shoved his feelings into his mental anxiety closet and slammed the door.

To her credit, Fionna said nothing, only casually moved her glasses to the top of her blond head without so much as a smirk. "Agent Drake is leading the team to investigate the murders."

Oh, great! More good news. "How nice for you to be working with him again," Sean said, a sarcastic twist in his mouth. Agent Evan Drake, Fionna's ass hat of a colleague at the Ministry of Investigations, had a long history of jackassery going back to Sean's days at the academy. Fionna had experienced the unfortunate pleasure of working with Drake when they'd found Anaya on the Colonies after her accident with the *Kairos*. "So does Drake still hate me?"

Fionna grinned. "Passionately."

"Shatter a guy's testicle and you're on his shit list for life." Sean shrugged.

Fionna pressed her lips together to hide a smile and pulled a comm stick from a jacket pocket. She held the stick out to Sean.

"This has all my notes from the sword investigation so far," Fionna said. "It includes the list of names from the night tour when the sword was last spotted and the names of the Luctari who were camped out in front of the museum during the time period when the sword was most likely stolen. I interviewed the tour group and most of the others. There are still a few Luctari my agents haven't been able to get statements from. If Brink is telling the truth that his followers have a certain level of respect for your office, maybe they'll be more cooperative with you."

Sean blinked. "I can't interview them. I'm not an investigator."

"The Montressador's office retains some authority when it comes to the law."

"You're confusing tradition with reality like everyone else does around here," Sean said, frustration mounting. "Feathered quills sure...but this?" He gestured to the comm stick. "Is it even legal for me to have that information?"

Fionna dipped her head. "I admit it's *unorthodox*. The files are copies of all my personal notes and not any official reports – only summaries. Once the killer is caught, I'll be able to pick up where we left off with the sword investigation. In the meantime, I see no reason why you couldn't make casual inquiries with the Luctari on your own. See if you can fill in the missing statements. It wouldn't look weird for you to ask questions given the nature of the theft."

"Fionna..." Sean looked down at the sword at his side, suddenly unable to meet the agent's eye. "We both know I'm a walking museum piece." Sean sighed. "The only reason I was helping at all was as a background consultant on the sword. Public opinion and popularity polls aside...I have no real authority, only tradition."

"Tradition may be enough to help us find what we need." Fionna's voice grew more urgent. "Montressador, if we wait too long the trail will go completely cold and Syrovar's sword will never be found." Fionna took Sean's hand and pressed the comm stick into his palm. "If you uncover anything important, let me know and I'll convince Drake to let me work both cases again."

Sean hesitated, enjoying the touch of Fionna's hand more than he should, and wrapped his fingers around the comm stick. "Fine. I'll see what I can do." He tucked the device in a pocket. "Are your friends at the Ministry going to be okay with this? They aren't my biggest fans since I filed that no-confidence order."

"Let me worry about them." Fionna met his eye. "Be careful around the Luctari. They may have respect for your office, but I think your instincts are right about Brink."

Sean nodded, the memory of his encounter with the reverend an unpleasant distraction from Fionna's violet eyes. "I'll be as careful as Fregoli the Paranoid." Sean stood and offered a hand.

Fionna grasped his fingers and stood. Sean's heart zipped into double time for an instant at the touch of her hand.

A doubtful look crossed Fionna's features. "Wasn't Fregoli murdered by his valet?"

Sean gulped and wrestled with his traitorous emotions. "You're not supposed to remember that part. Montressador Fregoli survived no less than twenty assassination attempts."

Fionna released Sean's hand and eyed him sideways. "It wasn't the first twenty attempts that killed him. It was the last."

SEVENTEEN

DIEVA ROKA

The gritty black tar surface crunched under Ann's boots. The jump landed her on a rooftop in the heart of the city where skyscrapers reflected the morning sun and cast cold shadows across the cityscape. The air was damp with dew.

Ann pushed against the edge of the roof and stood. The building swayed, pulling her head sideways. The roof spun. A flash of a twenty-story drop to the pavement below disappeared into the glare of a sun dog. Ann threw her arms wide and stumbled into empty space. A hand jerked her back to center away from the roof's edge.

"Are you all right?"

Ann rubbed her eyes and looked up. John's fist gripped the fabric of her shirt. She blew out a breath to slow the jackhammering of her heart.

"You weren't kidding about the vertigo," she said. "I thought my head spun all the way around."

"It's the distortion from the time whorl." John released his grip on her shirt. "It will pass. Find a point on the horizon and take a few deep breaths while I take a reading." He checked the timepiece strapped to the inside of his wrist. "We can spare a minute."

Ann hitched up the pack on her back. She stayed clear of the rooftop's edge and found a column of sky and water between two buildings. A white sail on a strip of blue ocean drifted a few miles offshore. The pull of the whorl diminished as Ann watched the boat's progress until only embarrassment twisted her insides. *I'm such a Bender.* The first mission since the accident and she almost fell off a roof seconds after the jump. Sarolea and Kel would laugh for days if they knew. Ann's heart ached. *Not Sarolea. Not anymore.* Sarolea was most likely dead and in the gut pile Fionna found. Ann pushed grief aside. The directional anchors wouldn't help find Sarolea, but maybe they could help catch her killer. Ann glanced in John's direction. She would need to get it together if she wanted John to think of her as a partner and not a liability.

John stood a few feet away, head bowed over a navcomm in one hand and an ion pistol strapped to a hip. The med techs had altered his appearance before the time jump. Clan tattoos in red ink covered one side of John's face and ran down an arm. His formerly black hair now shone like copper in the sunlight. His blue eyes were darkened to a reddish-brown. Ann knew she looked just as different with her matching tattoos and hair twisted into knots across the top of her head. Add to that their rough-spun work clothes, common among Maskelyne traders, and their disguises were complete.

Ann chanced a look to the street below. The inhabitants of Dieva Roka moved with the rhythm of a city waking to a new day. A day that, according to the mission file, had repeated continuously for the last five months.

"Ann! Time!"

John sat with his back against a low wall towards the middle of the rooftop, knees bent, and finished pulling grips over his boots. Ann sat next to him and pulled black trak gloves and boot grips from her pack. She activated the gloves and felt the hum spread from palms to fingertips.

"Be ready to move, but not until I say so," John said, slipping protective goggles over his eyes. "Stay sharp. The mission brief doesn't tell us everything. We may need to improvise."

Improvise. Er...Yeah, about that... "Got it." Ann's heart rate picked up speed as she settled her own goggles across the bridge of her nose, lenses tinting the world a pale blue. She hoped the hours of training would make up for any decisiveness she lacked. The training exercises hadn't given her any trouble. Of course, as Kel had so indelicately pointed out to Colonel Wick, that hadn't made any difference during her fifteen attempts in the flight simulator. Ann checked her pistol's power cell, feeling the familiar prickle edge up her arm, and returned the weapon to a holster.

"When do you need me to start tracking Moondarra?" Her ability to sense power sources would be more reliable than any tracking device as the whorl approached its reset point.

"Not yet. She might still be on the move." John leaned in to show Ann the navcomm screen. A digital map gave a bird's eye view of the surrounding area. "Our best bet is to head north and then see where she's holed up. There are only a few places safe enough to ride out the reset. You'll have a better shot of sensing Moondarra's time beacon if we're closer and once the city loses power."

Ann nodded. Their mark was a well-known racketeer and purveyor of illegal time devices with a talent for hiding in time whorls, pockets of repeating time split off from the main current. A few experienced black marketers like Moondarra had discovered a way to shield themselves from a whorl's reset effect, living inside a pocket for weeks or even months at a time while conducting business. Hiding in whorls came with a great deal of risk. Older pockets created eddying currents of their own like fractals, becoming less predictable. Without protection from the reset, anyone caught in the whorl would become subject to its laws, locked into a pattern they couldn't see and without the power to escape – at least until the whorl was discovered by time jumpers. A high-frequency electromagnetic pulse a few seconds before the reset would explode the pocket and force events back into the main current of time. Anyone left inside a time whorl not already subject to its laws would be killed the moment the pocket exploded.

"What if Moondarra doesn't have directional anchors?" Ann asked.

"A.K's informants are rarely wrong." John returned the navcomm to his pack and tightened the shoulder straps. "And even if they are, Moondarra will have something we can arrest her for. You get her to show us the merchandise and I'll grab her. Fionna might be out of luck, but either way we'll get our target." John checked his timepiece. "All right then." He crooked the grin Ann had fallen in love with and looped an arm through her own. "Hold on tight. This could get interesting. Three…two… one…"

The building rippled as the quake hit. Metal and concrete groaned. Glass shattered. All around them skyscrapers swayed like stalks. Cracks echoed, exploding across the cityscape. Terror galloped through Ann's chest. She ducked her head between her knees and still the quake grew in power, reaching a crescendo as the city bucked and twisted all around her.

The quake died as it began and ended with sounds of panic and sirens rising up from across the city. Dust filled the air, obscuring the once bright sun as if seen through a dirty window.

John leaped to his feet. "Let's go. We only have an hour."

Ann ran across the rooftop after John, the cracked surface fragile under her boots. An explosion split the air. A few blocks away a fireball erupted from the street below. John jumped across a gap to land on the rooftop of the next building. Ann lengthened her stride and cleared the short distance, following close behind.

The pair sprinted across two more rooftops, making their way north. Fires burned across the ruined city. Debris and smoke from burning fuel choked the air. Ann could feel smoke and dust clinging to the back of her throat with every breath. The cries of despair from the Rokans drifted through the sounds of havoc. Ann tried to block their pleading voices from her head as she ran.

John slowed and stopped to catch his breath when he reached the rooftop's far edge at the end of the block. Wide boulevards separated them from the block to the north and to the west with only the tops of pedestrian skybridges a few floors below to offer passage. The skybridge to the north lay partially collapsed in the street, metal support girders twisted like taffy. The bridge to the west fared better, leaning to one side but with the west and east ends still intact.

John checked the timepiece on his wrist. "Aftershock! Take cover!"

Ann crouched next to John just as a strong temblor ripped through the city. The shaking lasted only a few seconds. She heard a roar and glanced over a shoulder in time to see one side of a skyscraper crumble and fall. For an instant, the building's upper floors lay exposed like the inside of a doll's house before dust obscured them. Chunks of concrete rained onto the rooftop where the time beacon dropped them only minutes before, covering the shorter building and the street below. A cloud of debris thicker than smoke billowed through the surrounding streets, overtaking everything in its path. Rokans scattered for cover. One second a man and a young child huddled in a doorway and the next they were gone, swallowed by the thunderhead.

The aftershock cut the rest of the power. Ann sensed the change as if the whispering of musical notes from a great orchestra had cut off in midmeasure. Silence settled over the city. The echo of sirens that screamed for help since the first tremor died away.

John sat back on his heels and wiped the dust from his goggles. He took a couple pulls from a water bottle and spat over the side of the building. He looked at Ann. "Are you ready?" She nodded. "All right then. Just like we practiced."

Ann took a sip of water from her own bottle and sat, head between her knees. She touched an ear, forgetting for an instant her keravnos implant had not made the trip into the time whorl. The device had helped to increase her range of detection since the accident but would be useless against the forces of the whorl. Ann closed her eyes and took a deep breath, pushing all distractions away.

Without power, the city lay cold and dead, a dark void in Ann's mind. Occasionally, a bright note caught her attention, but the power source was too small to be a time beacon. Ann sought the clarion notes of the late model, Varas-made, portable time beacon rumored to be favored by Moondarra. In the days leading up to the mission, Ann had practiced for hours with a similar model under varying conditions until she had come to know the sound of the beacon's call as easily as the opening notes of a favorite song. Ann pushed her senses to the edge, searching. Until...

Her eyes flew open. "I've got it!"

John grabbed the navcomm. "Where?"

"Northwest. It's faint but steady."

"You've got a lock on it?" John checked their position on the map. "Can you track it on the move?"

Ann listened to the beacon's song again, memorizing the direction. Now that she knew where to search, locating the beacon was as easy as turning a key in a lock. "Yes!"

John leaned against the western edge of the rooftop and looked down at the twisted skybridge below.

Ann stood and joined him. "Will it hold?

"We'll find out if we can get to it," John said, fingering the pigtail at the back of his head. "I'd like to stay off the street if possible. I don't want to run the risk of getting trapped at ground level."

Ann looked over the edge at the side of the building. Balconies of wrought iron decorated every other window. "There." Ann pointed to a balcony two floors below. "There's a window ledge beneath us that looks wide enough to stand on. We could use it to drop to the balcony and then the skybridge."

"That should work. I'll go first. Give me a head start and then follow me down." John activated his boot grips and trak gloves and lowered himself over the edge of the roof to the window ledge.

Ann followed hand and foot. The gloves and grips held against the building's decorative façade until her feet found the ledge. Loose plaster crumbled and fell to the pavement. She paused on the window ledge and then dropped the last few feet to the balcony to stand next to John. Iron squealed against brick as Ann's boots struck the balcony floor. The roof of the skybridge lay one floor directly below.

John checked his timepiece and swung a leg over the balcony railing. "Ten minutes until the next aftershock. We'll have to hurry. I don't think we'll want to risk crossing after the bridge takes another —"

Metal cracked. The balcony floor lurched then dropped out from under their feet as a support gave way. John yelled. Ann tumbled sideways as the world upended. The pavement rotated into view like a carnival ride from hell. Ann slammed into the railing with a shoulder, momentum flipping her up and over. Her hands flailed, grasping for anything solid, and wrapped around an iron spindle. The grip of the trak gloves saved her by inches as she hung from the balcony, legs dangling into empty space over the pavement.

"ANN!"

John clung to the other end of the balcony on the outside of the railing. The balcony's remaining support pulled against the brick.

"I'm okay!" Ann's voice shook with the pounding of her heart.

"There's a window ledge behind and below you! You'll have to reach for it!"

Ann's mind spun. *If I move, the balcony might fall and John along with it. If I don't, our combined weight could still cause the remaining support to snap. If I don't...If I do...If I don't...What if...?* The balcony gave another terrifying lurch.

"GO!"

Ann lunged backward and made a grab for the windowsill. Her fingertips gripped the ledge as her body slammed against brick. Behind her, a teeth-grinding squeal and the crash of metal striking pavement shattered the air. Her boot grips found a toehold and she pushed and pulled up into the small, recessed window. Ann gulped air. Fear surged through her veins. She looked down and saw the twisted balcony and a few scattered bricks on the pavement below.

"Okay...new plan..."

Ann looked up toward the sound of John's voice. Her heart leaped to see him crammed backward onto a small ledge one floor above and the next apartment over, trak gloves pressed against either side of the windowsill to hold himself in place.

John panted through the words. "You drop to the skybridge...I'll meet you there."

Ann's heart skittered in her chest as she lowered herself to the skybridge, not from her near-death drop to the pavement, but from the hesitation she'd felt while dangling from the balcony railing. In those seconds, her mind had flicked through the possibilities like a deck of cards until John had yelled at her to move. That moment of indecision had almost cost them both their lives. *What have I gotten us into?*

They continued west across crumbling rooftops and skybridges for another block then turned north, taking shelter from the aftershocks wherever they could. Ann tracked the sound of the beacon while John checked their course on the navcomm. The call of the beacon grew stronger, at times building to a crescendo then falling away. Ann became aware of smaller power sources as they drew closer, Moondarra's merchandise she supposed. One source, a playful sound as flexible as a reed, changed in pitch every time she touched it with her mind then returned to its original melody.

Ann panted as she climbed up a rooftop service ladder. "She's close! One of those buildings ahead."

She reached the last rung and swung a leg over the ledge to stand on the rooftop. John followed, pulling binoculars from his pack as they crossed to the north side. Ann threw a nervous glance over a shoulder toward the ocean. She could still see the surf as it drew patterns of foam along the beach. The aftershocks had become less frequent, but the minutes on John's timepiece continued to tick away.

"If she's planning to ride out the reset, she'll need to activate a shield," John said as he surveyed the next block. "You haven't sensed anything? Only the beacon?"

Ann shook her head. "The beacon and some

smaller devices she must be carrying, but nothing powerful enough to be a shield."

John muttered, "Come on, Moondarra. Where are you hiding?" He adjusted the binocular's focus and then a slow grin spread across his face. "She's on the next roof top. Shorter building with the arched windows." He looked at Ann as he stowed the binoculars. "Time to warm up your accent."

"Are you sure you want me to take the lead?" Nerves twisted Ann's gut. Finding the beacon was straightforward. Bluffing Moondarra into thinking they were a couple of Maskelyne traders was a different thing altogether. "I'm guessing you've done this a few times?"

The Maskelyne home world was plagued with earthquakes and tremors. A few thousand years of living on the edge of calamity had produced a culture with a reputation for extreme calm under pressure. More importantly, Maskelynes were known time travelers. Just the sort of people you would expect to meet with a black marketeer in a time whorl in the middle of an earthquake, which made their disguises perfect. Unless Ann couldn't pull it off.

"Your accent is better," John said as they walked to the train trestle that would take them across to the next building. "You're also more patient than I am. Moondarra would figure me out after three sentences." John gave Ann a reassuring pat on the back. "Stick to the script and you'll be fine."

Ann gulped. *I just hope Moondarra sticks to the script.* Fifteen attempts in the flight simulator played in her memory. This time she'd only have one chance to get it right.

The infamous black marketeer wanted by authorities in five sectors was a stooped grandmotherly figure dressed in black, a rose-colored shawl pinned to frail shoulders with a silver broach. Moondarra with her poofy curled gray hair and crocheted fingerless gloves looked like she would be more at home baking cookies than standing on a rooftop with a front-row seat for the end of the world.

Ann watched as they approached from the opposite end of the roof while the old woman carried carpet bags, one after the other, to her time beacon where she activated the device and dropped her wares into the waiting blue portal. *That explains the time beacon's power surges,* Ann thought. Moondarra was clearly not planning on sticking around for the reset this time.

Ann called out as they drew closer remembering to use the Maskelyne vowels and speech pattern she practiced. "Trader! Are you selling?"

Moondarra gave them a bare glance and continued carrying bags to the beacon. "Always selling, but not staying. Sorry." She heaved a bag into the portal with a grunt and returned to her stash for the next bag. "I never like to stay too long in time whorls." Moondarra glanced pensively at the sky. "Time whorls are regular in their irregularity and therefore should never be trusted."

John stopped a few paces behind Ann, according to Maskelyne custom. Ann continued her approach then stopped and spoke over a shoulder in Maskelyne to him in one of their preplanned exchanges. He grunted a reply.

"We will make delay profitable if you have what we're looking for," Ann said, turning back to Moondarra.

The marketeer wavered. Fingers twitched, the lure of one more quick sale too tempting. Ann could practically see the glint of coins in the old woman's eyes.

Moondarra smiled as she dragged a scarred leather suitcase toward the beacon, the bottom of the case scraped against the gritty rooftop. "Most of my stock is already back on my ship. What is it you seek, young Maskelyne?"

"This and that." Another mild tremor rippled under their feet. Ann paid the shaking no attention and shrugged. "Chronoculars. Shifters. Anchors. Mostly anchors."

"Directional anchors?" Moondarra looked up, eyes bright. "You're in luck. I have a good supply."

The marketeer gathered her skirt in one hand, activated the beacon, and shoved the suitcase toward the portal with a foot. Ann winced as the case teetered on the edge of the shining blue oval and fell inside, disappearing from sight. Moondarra's remaining stockpile of bags had shrunk considerably since they first spotted her on the rooftop.

"But the anchors are useless without Splice," Moondarra said. "I have significant stores on my ship. Come with me and we can discuss the price."

"We have Splice," Ann said, forcing her eyes to meet Moondarra's. "We need only anchors. Do you have them here?" Ann bit her tongue. *Too fast.*

"An *impatient* Maskelyne?" Moondarra gave a curious squint then looked past Ann to the ocean. "Well, I can't say as I blame you. Time is growing short. The ocean has left the shore and so should we."

Ann followed Moondarra's gaze. The surf had receded a mile back from the shoreline. A wall of white breakers formed on the horizon. Ann's stomach clenched. Going with Moondarra to a new location would give them another opportunity to capture the marketeer and get the directional devices. But they'd also be off the map and in Moondarra's home territory. A dangerous choice, but possibly a better option than staying inside the whorl. Ann looked to John. His eyes widened with caution.

If we go...If we stay...

Ann shook her head to keep her thoughts from spinning. "I...er..." John's expression turned to alarm. *Stick to the script or improvise?* Sweat beaded under her shirt.

John cleared his throat and muttered just loud enough for Ann to hear. "Dai Dai."

The Maskelyne word for stay. Ann closed her eyes for a beat and blew out a deep breath. *Relax.* She turned back to Moondarra. "Do you have any anchors here?"

The marketeer eyed Ann as she dragged another heavy case forward, panting with exertion. "A bag or two...I keep my best merchandise on the ship...all top grade. Look, if you're anxious to leave, help me stow these cases."

Ann counted the remaining bags. Only six. With every case pushed into the portal, the chances of the marketeer having the anchors diminished.

"We will purchase the anchors you have here," Ann said, nerves ratcheting another turn. "Name your price."

Moondarra ignored Ann and continued to drag the case toward the portal. The sound of metal against the rooftop scraped Ann's insides. "Surely, you need more than a handful. I have whole crates of anchors on my—"

"STOP!" Ann's hand flashed to her sidearm.

Moondarra froze. John muttered a curse that may or may not have been Maskylene and shifted position.

Ann stalked forward and stared down at the old woman, one hand still on the pistol at her side. "Show us the anchors. Now."

Moondarra watched Ann from the corner of an eye. A thin smile deepened the wrinkles in her cheeks. "As you wish."

The old woman raised her hands and walked toward the waiting pile of bags. She gestured to a blue carpet bag sandwiched between two metal cases.

"The few anchors I have with me are in here." The marketeer picked up the bag by its black handles and tossed it toward Ann's feet. "Have a look, Maskelyne. A thousand galactic credits will buy you the lot."

Ann kept one eye on Moondarra and leaned over to open the bag. As her fingers brushed the handles, her senses pricked to an energy source inside. The reed song she had followed for the past several blocks danced in her head. *The anchors?* Ann's only contact with the metal discs had been after they'd been burned out. Could this be what the anchors sounded like when they were still operational?

"Go on then. What are you waiting for? The tide certainly isn't." The old woman snapped. "Pay me so I can leave this place."

Ann pulled open the carpet bag and drew in a breath. A dozen or more directional anchors covered the bottom of the case. The reed song whistled deep within and underneath the anchors.

BANG!

A blinding flash burned through Ann's retinas, searing the back of her skull. Daggers of ice ripped through her senses. Ann yelled, covered her face with an arm to block the pain, staggered backward, and fell. The back of her head cracked against the rooftop and sent another wave of pain crashing behind her eyes. Through the ringing in her ears, Ann heard the sound of laser fire and then a hum that made her skin tingle as a cloak of power unfurled overhead. Moondarra had activated the reset shield.

Ann blinked to clear her vision and fumbled for her pistol, fingers numb. A sharp-heeled boot pressed down on her wrist as a hand yanked the pistol from her grasp. Ann squinted. Moondarra's sneering face came into focus as the after image from the blast faded. The barrel of Ann's own pistol pointed at her head.

Moondarra cackled in triumph, reached into the blue carpet bag, and pulled out a star-shaped device the size of her knobby fist. The star's center glowed blood red.

"A handy little toy. It alerts me when a Vego is nearby and is using electroperception. It goes off when the Vego is in range." Moondarra clicked a button on the star's backside. The center changed from red to blue. "Given the odds that a Vego is also most likely an Andarrian time jumper I'm fairly confident I just foiled your plans to arrest me."

Despair swallowed Ann whole. How many times had her senses touched the device, giving Moondarra plenty of warning of their approach? She had walked them right into a trap. Ann flicked her eyes past Moondarra to the domed energy shield that now surrounded them. She could see John's image outside the dome, blurred like a water painting, as he searched for a way inside. Beyond the rooftop, the first wall of water had reached the shore, crashing over the shorter buildings. A torrent rushed through the streets below.

Moondarra kept the pistol trained on Ann as she took a seat on a large metal case a few feet away. The old woman winced as she laid the weapon on the case next to her and gave Ann a hard look when she moved to sit up. "Don't get any ideas. I can still shoot you from here."

The marketeer removed her shawl, repinning

the silver broach to the collar of her blouse. She frowned at the smoking hole in the shawl's delicate fabric and tossed it aside.

Ann felt a flicker of satisfaction to see the wicked burn on Moondarra's arm. John must have fired off a shot before the shield closed.

"We'll stick around long enough to watch your partner through the reset shield," Moondarra said as she tied up the wound with a floral scarf. "He'll either be killed from falling debris or get stuck in the reset. It's too late to push you outside of my shield. I'll wait for the whorl to reset then shoot you before I go back to my ship. Bumping off two time jumpers so easily has made for a very profitable day."

Ann gulped the fear building in the back of her throat. The shield would be useless when the other team exploded the whorl. Shot by her own pistol or killed in the resulting time shift, she would be just as dead. Ann hoped John would abort the mission and time jump out, but in her heart, she knew he would never leave her behind. She scrambled her brains for a plan.

Ann pulled herself up to a sitting position against a steamer trunk, keeping a cautious eye on Moondarra's pistol hand. "You're right," she said with a bitter laugh, dropping the Maskelyne accent. "You caught us. We're time jumpers and the plan was to arrest you." Ann sighed. "But now I guess we'll just wait for the whorl to explode."

Moondarra scoffed and watched John's image outside the dome. "Save your stories, Time Jumper."

"There's another team planning to blow up the whorl, but we can sit here in your bubble if you'd like." Ann closed her eyes and rested her head against the steamer trunk. "Not that it will do any good."

"Please. Like I haven't heard this one before." Moondarra chuckled. "Your friends are just outside?" She fanned her face with one hand in mock distress. "My goodness, I'm in trouble. Whatever shall I do?"

Ann gave the old woman a sideways look. "How long have you been hiding in this whorl? How long is a whorl safe before time jumpers blow it up?" Moondarra scowled. "You were already planning to leave. You know it's not safe to stay here forever. I'm only telling you this because I don't want to die."

The star device in Moondarra's lap flared from blue to yellow.

Ann smirked. "Huh...I guess the other team has a Vego too."

Moondarra lunged and drove a fist into Ann's face. The speed and power of the old woman's attack took Ann by surprise. "Tell them to call it off!"

"I can't." Ann wiped a trickle of blood from her busted lip with the back of a hand. "There's no way to contact the other team through the whorl effect. You should know that."

Moondarra watched John's image, frantic outside the dome. Her eyes widened as the truth in Ann's words fit together. The old woman jumped to her feet. "I can't use my beacon with the reset shield in place. If I lower the shield, your partner will attack me."

"You could turn yourself in." Moondarra threw her a sour look. Ann shrugged. "Then you better move fast."

Moondarra hesitated. She looked at the remaining cases she still had to transport and then back toward the water crashing through the closest buildings. Chunks of concrete bounced off the reset shield in low echoes. Outside, John ducked and dodged raining debris.

Moondarra scowled, pulled on the backpack containing her beacon, and grabbed a large carpet bag. She touched the silver broach at the hollow of her throat, dropping the shield.

The sounds of destruction and rushing water exploded over the rooftop. Ann leaped to her feet and sprang for her pistol just as Moondarra activated her beacon. A blue portal yawned open, and she hopped inside. The last thing to drop out of sight was the old woman's raised middle finger.

Ann looked to John. Terror seized her by the throat.

"RUN!"

John sprinted forward as a wall of concrete toppled toward the rooftop. He dove toward Ann. The slab crashed behind him, buckling the roof and leaving a gaping hole.

Ann holstered her weapon and helped John to his feet. An eerie silence filled the air. John swiped the bangs from his eyes and looked at the sky. The blue had darkened to a purple hue.

"Bloody hell. Time's up!"

Ann grabbed the carpet bag with the anchors as John activated their beacon. The pair hopped into their portal and disappeared just as a column of lightning struck the heart of the city.

EIGHTEEN

FALL OUT

The jump crash-landed Ann on her stomach like a high dive gone wrong, Moondarra's carpet bag clutched to her chest. John slammed into Ann's back a second later, knocking the wind from her lungs. He quickly rolled to one side. Ann stifled a groan and moved to sit up. Not the most graceful jump, but not surprising given their clumsy exit from the time whorl. Green light from the time beacon faded, leaving the glare of the metal platform's spotlight.

The snap and whine of power cells charging to full strength came from the shadows.

"Stand down!" John yanked the protective goggles from his face and climbed to his feet. "The target got away!"

Three helmeted guards standing just outside the spotlight's glare holstered their weapons and returned to their stations in the beacon control room.

Ann shaded her eyes and stood. Her arms cradled the carpet bag containing the directional anchors. The jump from the time whorl had returned them to headquarters in Palladium Beta where their mission began.

John stepped off the platform, stormed past the technicians and banks of monitor screens, and pushed his way through a set of sliding doors.

Ann tossed the carpet bag to the closest guard. "Take this to Agent Fionna Knox at the Ministry of Investigations. She needs it right away." She ignored the nervous glances from the technicians and hurried after John into the time jumper's ready room.

John kicked a stool as he passed the conference table and sent it careening into a corner. He leaned against the opposite wall, head bowed, his face a knot of frustration underneath the red clan tattoos. The silence between them felt like an eternity.

"We were after Moondarra," John said after a beat. "The anchors were secondary. Moondarra now knows we're watching her and will be even more skittish in the future."

Anxiety plucked Ann's nerves. She lifted her goggles to rest on the top of her head. "How much trouble are we in?"

"Don't worry about it." John shook his head. "I can take the heat for it."

"So...when do we go after Moondarra again?"

"Moondarra's *my* problem," John snapped. He took an aggravated swipe through his hair. "You work for Fionna. She'll let you know what she needs you to do."

Failure sunk Ann's spirits. The triumph of obtaining the directional anchors now seemed foolish.

Moondarra had been the mission target. Her return to time jumping had been a mistake. *I should've stuck with the flight simulator.* Ann touched a panel on the wall, and a rack of Maskelyne firearms slid from the recessed compartment. She unbuckled the pistol on her hip. Her mouth tightened as she read her name plate on the weapon's rack. *Lt. A. Chapman, Mission Specialist.* Ann scoffed as she returned her pistol to its designated slot. A specialist wouldn't have failed to achieve the primary mission objective. *Not even close.*

John retrieved the stool and dropped it back into the empty space next to the table. He blew out a sigh and unbuckled his sidearm.

"I'm sorry." John rested a hand on her shoulder as he walked past. "I didn't mean to blow up like that." He stowed his pistol in the weapon's rack next to Ann's. "If I get more intel about Moondarra or if I need an extra pair of hands before A.K.'s back, we'll head out again. Until then, we wait."

The opposite door slid open, and two med techs entered. John pulled off his shirt, exposing the Maskelyne tattoo that ran the length of his muscled arm.

"Get this bloody stuff off me," John said as he climbed into the med tech's station chair.

The techs worked quickly, stripping Ann and John of their Maskelyne features, and tended to their cuts and scrapes. Ann winced under the hands of the med tech, but the guilt of failure, of losing Moondarra, stung more than the ointment the tech dabbed on her busted lip.

The med techs declared them fit to travel and left. Ann opened a wall compartment in the changing area and found her blue fatigues just as she'd left them. Across the aisle, John pulled on his colonist clothing for his return trip to Siren's Cove.

"One other thing…" John slammed the wall panel shut and finished tucking in his shirt. "When Moondarra pushed us to go to her ship, we never discussed that in training. A.K. and I have worked together for so long we don't have to discuss every possibility beforehand. We just know how the other works. I forgot that. That's on me. I'm sorry I put you in that position."

Ann glanced over a shoulder. "It's okay. We got through it." She zipped up her fatigues and took a seat on the changing bench. "How would you and A.K. have handled it?"

John sat on the opposite bench and leaned forward, arms resting on his knees. "Definitely not go with her. A.K. might have negotiated a neutral meeting point." His eyes crinkled with concern. "You had me worried when you hesitated…" Ann swallowed hard. "…then later when you went for your pistol. You didn't do anything wrong. I might've done something similar with our clock running out." John frowned and tugged his pigtail. "Just caught me off guard, that's all."

Ann gripped the edge of the bench and struggled to meet John's eye. Doubt whispered in her ear. *What if…?* "I wanted to talk to you about that…when I froze..."

"It's all right." John shrugged a shoulder. "Like I said, we never talked about that possibility. That's not your fault." John crooked a grin. "You earn points for talking Moondarra into lowering the shield. How'd you do it?"

Ann's insides squirmed as she told John about her conversation with Moondarra.

"So, all I really did was tell the truth. That we were there to arrest her and there was another team about to blow up the whorl. And then I triggered the sensor again so she would believe me about the demolition team."

John nodded, a glimmer of admiration in his eye. "Nice job. We should mention that sensor of hers in our mission report. I've never heard of a device that can detect Vegos." John stood and reached for his boots. "She probably thought your senses were shot from the attack. Moondarra has always been paranoid, that's why she's so—"

"Kel thinks I freeze up under pressure."

John stopped and stared at Ann.

She exhaled a deep breath and the words tumbled out. "Colonel Wick agreed. That's the real reason why he grounded me. Not the panic attacks. I should've told you, but I didn't because it never happened outside the flight simulator before."

John frowned. "What are you talking about?"

Ann's voice shook as her pulse picked up speed. "I froze on the balcony. I froze with Moondarra." John's eyes grew wide as he listened. "I didn't just hesitate.

I couldn't make a decision—"

John held up a hand. "Stop."

"—it was like my mind was stuck on shuffle and I almost got us—"

"STOP TALKING!"

Ann snapped her mouth shut.

John pointed a finger. Fear burned in his eyes. "Don't say any more or I'll have to put it in our mission report!"

Her eyes locked with John's. Fear had drained the color from his face and tightened his mouth into a grim line. The breath hitched in Ann's chest as the full weight of the consequences of her confession crashed down.

The sound of a door sliding open broke the silence. Ann quickly composed herself just as a driver for the Ministry of Investigations stepped into the room.

"Lieutenant Anaya Chapman?" The driver asked. She nodded. "Agent Fionna Knox sent me. You're needed at the Ministry."

"I need a minute," Ann said. The driver nodded and stepped out to wait in the other room.

She stood and looked at John, but the words dried up in her mouth.

"My God, Ann..." John swiped a hand through his hair.

The worry in his eyes told her everything she needed to know. *How could I have been so stupid?* It was her fault the mission failed, and now because of her confession, he'd have no choice but to enter it into the mission report or risk being charged with falsifying an official record.

She swallowed hard and tried to fight the panic building in her chest. "John, I—"

He reached for her suddenly, pulling her tightly into his arms, and whispered urgently in her ear. "Don't say another word. We can't talk about this now. Not here."

Ann's voice shook. "The report—I want to do the right thing."

"I'll take care of it." John stepped back and met her eye.

Ann's eyes widened. The determination on his face made her pulse race. The thought of what he might write in the mission report – *what he might say to protect her* – choked the words in her throat.

"You need to go," John said and nodded to the door. "We'll talk later."

The Ministry of Investigations dispensed justice in large doses on the top floors of their arched tower in Palladium Beta. Ann remembered her time at the Ministry—although not fondly—from her testimony in one of the upper chambers in front of the crash investigation committee. The great seal inside the chamber read, "Let Justice Be Done Even If the Heavens Fall." The heavens had almost fallen for Ann during the *Kairos* investigation, so there was always some trepidation whenever she entered the Ministry to meet with Agent Fionna Knox.

Ann walked through the network of hives of the

Ministry's lower floors until she reached the command center that housed the time jumper murder investigation team.

The large round room was organized like a honeycomb with dedicated workstations grouped by occupation. Technicians and specialists worked together on the outer edges while investigators claimed the center. Above them, large digital screens curved around the room, showing the timeline of events, pictures of the victims, and the current assignments of investigators and specialists in the field. The screens updated with new information as agents reported their findings, making it so anyone in the room could track the investigation's progress in real-time.

Ann spotted Fionna's blond bobbed hair in a tech work area on the opposite side of the room. As she passed a glass-enclosed conference area in the center, she saw several agents gathered in front of a comm screen with a live feed from the hangar that housed the *What Cheer*. Ann tensed as she eyed the tall thin man conversing with the agent on the screen.

Agent Evan Drake, the lead investigator for the time jumper murders, was working with Fionna when she found Ann at Siren's Cove. The senior agent was all too eager to haul Ann in front of the crash investigation committee, taking pleasure in her predicament. Drake's longstanding grudge against Ann's brother for an ill-timed swing during a gladius practice bout at school probably had something to do with his cold and malicious attitude toward her, although Sean assured Ann that Agent Drake was a full-blown ass even when he still had both of his testicles.

Ann found Fionna conferring with two techs at a workstation. The round directional anchors from Moondarra's carpet bag were spread out on the table like betting tokens.

"Did we get enough?" Ann asked as she approached.

Fionna looked up and smiled. Her yellow bio-vision glasses rested on top of her head. "Plenty. We shouldn't have any trouble making our nanobot tracker." She picked up one of the anchors from a charging station and handed it to Ann. "I wanted you to hear what they sound like before we take them apart."

Ann sensed the steady rhythm from the anchor as it rested on her palm, an odd wooden sound. The hollow note scratched a pattern of long, short, short, long, short like a wooden stick drawn back and forth along a skeleton's vertebrae. The sound made her skin prickle.

She shuddered and pulled her senses back. "They're strange enough. I won't have any trouble recognizing them if I run into one again." Ann handed the anchor back to Fionna.

"I have something else for you." Fionna returned the anchor to the charging station. She glanced to the techs who grinned with interest. "We wanted to test a theory." She picked up a metal canister, the size of a loaf of bread, and handed it to Ann. "Can you sense what's inside?"

Ann raised an eyebrow in suspicion then focused on the canister. A faint power source rippled through the container. Soft chimes sounded in her head.

She looked to Fionna. "The canister has a power cell..."

Fionna nodded. "The power cell is charging what's inside. Anything else?"

Ann stretched out her senses again, peeling back the sound of chimes, to search for any energies underneath. After a moment, she shook her head and handed the canister back to the agent. "Sorry. If there's something in there, it's too faint for me to sense."

Fionna passed the canister to the techs. "Okay, I guess I owe you guys lunch." The techs grinned and went back to work. Fionna looked at Ann. "There are nanobots inside." Ann blinked in surprise. "Do you think you could sense them if you wore your keravnos implant?"

Ann shook her head. "The implant was only meant to restore my natural range. If it were possible, I should've been able to detect the nanobots since I'm this close. They must be too small for me to sense."

"Well, it was a good try and good information all the same." Fionna picked up a digital pad from the table, made a note with a stylus, and tapped the screen.

A tri-chord tone sounded from the ceiling. Ann looked up. A specialist screen with her picture scrolled with new information. Under skills, the screen now read she could sense the anchors and the corresponding time distortion but could not detect nanobots. Other details on the screen mentioned Ann's most recent assignment to Dieva Roka to obtain the directional anchors. Ann winced, anxiety tightened her insides as her thoughts raced back to the conversation with John in the ready room and the mission report he was probably already writing.

Ann caught a glimpse of concern on Fionna's face and quickly changed the subject. "Where did you get the nanobots?"

"Would you believe from the *What Cheer's* wastewater tanks?"

Ann blanched. "How…?"

"There's another team checking into how the killer got access," Fionna said, tucking the stylus behind her ear. "The nanobots originally came from the ship's water filtration system. The filters were replaced with a device that released Splice and nanobots into the tanks. Once the crew was infected, all the killer had to do was use the command signal to call the nanobots home."

"The water tanks are checked for contaminants before every mission." Ann sat on the desk, one leg dangling. "How did security miss it?"

"The scans only checked the tanks, not the filtration system," Fionna said, leaning against the desk. "We think the filters weren't activated until after the ship was on its way to its first delivery. But that's not even the worst part." Fionna met Ann's eye. "The nanobots we found have the ability to maintain a shield and stay undetected as long as they have a charge. We can't detect them through a normal scan until after their power runs out and they lose their shield. When we found the uncharged nanobots in the wastewater tanks, we double-checked the organs from the gut pile and the bodies of the crew from the fountain."

Ann's mouth tightened. "You found more nanobots."

"The nanobots hadn't shown up in the two previous scans. It makes sense we would detect the nanobots in the wastewater tanks first since they were the oldest and would be the first to lose their charge."

A terrible thought entered Ann's head as she saw where the agent's words led her. "Since nanobots use the body's natural electrical charge to function, could people be infected with nanobots and we wouldn't be able to tell?"

Fionna nodded, face grim. "Yes. We're not making the information public, so we don't cause a panic. The techs are working on the problem. I'm hoping our nanobot tracker will let us track them through their shield. We need to be able to detect the nanobots and purge them from anyone who may be infected. The nanobots aren't dangerous but if a person is carrying bots and then is exposed to Splice, they could become the killer's next victim."

"Agent Knox."

Ann turned and saw Agent Drake walking toward them. His dark suit coat was as black as his hair. A white pocket square tucked into a breast pocket. Red capillaries ran lines across the bridge of his nose. Drake's cold eyes swept past the two women to the anchors on the worktable.

"I see you have the directional anchors," Drake said, nodding to the discs spread across the desk. "How soon will your nanobot tracker be functional?"

"The techs are working on it now," Fionna said. "Hopefully, only a couple days."

"Good. I want to know as soon as it's ready." He looked at Fionna and sneered. "While a clever idea, I don't want to have to wait for another death in order to catch the killer. What other leads are you pursuing?"

"Kegler's finishing his examination of the gut pile, and an AIR Unit is cataloging items from the ship. We're hoping we'll find something to lead us to where the killer worked on the victims as well as the recovery of Lieutenant Picquet's body."

Drake arched a brow and looked down his nose at Agent Knox. "You don't know that Picquet is dead yet."

"True, but it's a reasonable assumption," Fionna said. "The gut pile has five separate sets of organs, and we have four disemboweled and confirmed dead crew members with one still missing. Four plus one is five, Agent Drake. I wouldn't be much of an investigator if I ignored the obvious."

Drake's scowl deepened. "Has it occurred to you, Knox, that the reason why we haven't found Picquet is that she's working with the killer?" Ann bristled at the accusation. "The time distortion the killer's using is a match for Picquet's ghost arm. We also now know from searching her cabin on the *What Cheer* that she was in flagrant violation of ship's protocol by keeping unauthorized personal items on a time jumper cargo vessel. The killer could've used Picquet to gain access to the ship."

Ann's eyes widened, remembering Sarolea's duffle bag of cast-off items. "Her collection?" She laughed. "A bag full of random stuff may be unauthorized, but it's hardly proof of any link from Picquet to the killer, and the distortion from her ghost arm is circumstantial evidence at best."

Agent Drake shifted his gaze to Ann and snapped, "And neither does it bolster your assumption that she's a victim." Drake looked back to Fionna. "I've told you before I want you to focus on finding suspects and the killer's lair. Finding Picquet is secondary. Our primary goal is to prevent more corpses from turning up."

Ann hopped off the table and squared off in front of Drake. "Finding Sarolea—dead or alive—will help lead us to the killer."

Agent Drake's face twisted with contempt. "Lieutenant Chapman, I'm glad to see you listed as a specialist instead of one of the missing. Must be nice to have contacts in high places to land such a plum assignment."

Ann returned his scorn. "And it's nice to see you again, Agent Drake." Her mouth curled into a smirk. "My brother sends his best."

Drake scowled again and turned back to Fionna. "I want updates, Knox. Report in as soon as you have something, not just when you find it convenient to share your information."

Ann crossed her arms in disgust and watched the senior agent as he moved to another workstation.

"Drake's a good investigator, just severely lacking in charm," Fionna said. "You're lucky you were already assigned to my team before Agent Drake was put in charge."

Ann scoffed. "I might not have volunteered."

"Yes, you would've," Fionna quipped. Ann glanced at the agent. "You're here for Sarolea. It wouldn't have mattered to you who was in charge."

Ann grunted in agreement. She knew Fionna was right.

"I have one more thing before you go," Fionna said, motioning for Ann to follow.

Fionna led her to a nearby work area. Members of an Artifact Identification and Retrieval (AIR) Unit circulated between large evidence tables spread with odds and ends. Lieutenant Kel Stravage stood at a table cataloging objects with a handheld scanner and placing them in designated sections.

Kel looked up and flicked Ann a half-smile. "Hey, Rewind."

Ann grinned. If she had to have a nickname, she

guessed she could live with that one.

"We're tagging the crew's personal items," Fionna said, gesturing to the table where Kel worked. "We want to eliminate anything that we know belonged to the crew. I've asked Lieutenant Stravage to help us sort through Lieutenant Picquet's things." Fionna sighed. "As Drake already mentioned, Sarolea was using her quarters on the *What Cheer* as storage for personal items."

Ann looked at the piles on Kel's table, surprised at how much was there. Sarolea's stash was bigger than she realized. She'd never believe her friend was involved with the killer and yet her gut twisted in grudging admission that Drake might have a solid foundation for his suspicions. Ann looked to Fionna. "How do you want me to sort?"

Fionna gestured to Kel and stepped away to talk to another agent.

"Known personal items versus stash," Kel said, dividing the table into sections with a slash of a hand. He tossed Ann a second scanner. "Scan it. Catalog it. Tag it. Anything weird gets a red tag."

Ann looked at the scanner's control screen and back to Kel. "Define weird."

"Anything with heat damage or a residual time distortion. We're trying to determine if the killer used an anchor to access the ship. You can help me with Sarolea's duffle bags."

Ann looked under the table. "How many did she have?"

"Seven." Kel glanced up and caught Ann pulling a

face. "Shut up, or I'll put you on refuse cans."

Ann smirked and bent over to unzip the nearest duffle. A shadow of grief passed over her as the bag's contents came into view. To anyone else, the duffle bag would have looked like a bag of junk, but Ann knew the quirky collection belonged to Sarolea. Possessions that would be sorted into evidence, collect dust in storage, and then disposed of never to be seen again, just like Sarolea. A porcelain figure caught Ann's eye. The sadness lifted as a smile spread across her face.

Ann stood grinning and looked at Kel. "Is this what you do all day in AIR Command?"

Kel slid his eyes in Ann's direction. She held the pink bobblehead cat to her cheek and tapped the figurine's head to make it wobble. The cat let out a tiny meow in response. Ann pouted and blinked sad eyes at Kel.

He continued to scan without so much as a muscle twitch. "I haven't assigned anyone to the ship's toilet tanks yet. Are you volunteering?"

"No, sir." Ann activated the scanner and passed it over the bobblehead with exaggerated officialness. "Scanning one pink cat." Kel flicked a half-smile.

Ann heard a chuckle and turned to see Agent Knox watching them.

"I'll be back to check on you later." Fionna turned to leave, almost running into Kegler as he burst into the work area. The forensic tech's eyes lit upon Fionna, the side of his face gripped by a spasm.

Fionna frowned. "Roan?"

"It's not her!"

"What? Who?"

"The gut pile...the organs!" Kegler struggled to catch his breath. "Four sets matched the crew...but the fifth set... They're not Picquet's!" Ann's heart lurched. "I ran the DNA through the database hoping to get a match." He handed his medical pad to Knox.

The color drained from the agent's face. "Oh, my God..."

Ann looked from Fionna to Kegler. "What is it?"

"I wanted to let you know before I—" Kegler fought off another spasm.

Fionna nodded and handed back the medical pad. "Send it."

Kegler tapped the screen. A tone sounded from the ceiling as the victim screen changed. The image of Commander Vesto Garin, former head of Time Jumper Command, joined the pictures of the crew from the *What Cheer*. Another tone sounded as the screen with the timeline of events updated. The room grew silent as heads turned to the screens. Tones continued to sound until at last, all the screens updated. A moment of silence and then a burst of activity followed as agents and technicians rushed to their comm stations to read the details of Kegler's report.

Agent Drake found Fionna from across the room. "Go. I'll update Commander Rectrix.

Fionna motioned to Ann to follow and walked to the door. "You're with me."

Ann traded looks with Kel. He jerked his head toward Fionna. She returned the scanner to the table and raced to catch up with Agent Knox.

"Where are we going?"

"We follow the lead," Fionna said, never breaking stride. "There's still a body and a crime scene to find. We need to retrace Garin's steps. We'll get in touch with his assistant." Fionna exhaled. "But first we notify his family."

NINETEEN
THE LUCTARI

The Reverend Jeremiah Brink lifted the leather-bound book in one hand and stepped to the edge of the stage, the warm breeze fluttering the gilded pages. He turned to the audience gathered on blankets on the grassy slope, cleared his throat, and read aloud.

"The gods saw fit to put a heavy weight upon their backs." His thick fingers skimmed the page. "If the burden could be made great enough, the load might temper the beast. The people repented and bowed under the yoke. They cried out to the universe and all of creation, 'Cursed are we and we will serve until the gods see fit to release us from our labors.'"

The reverend returned the book to the stand a few paces behind him. He looked down, shoulders rounded. "Cursed. That's what we are. Nothing more than a beast of burden." He turned toward the audience hands in his pockets. "I only have one question…" Brink looked up and surveyed the assembled. "…for how much longer?"

The audience murmured and fidgeted on their

blankets.

Sean Chapman crossed his arms and watched Brink's performance with growing unease. His seat on the low stone wall at the edge of the outdoor theater was close enough to keep an eye on the reverend without seeming to be part of the audience and had the added benefit of hiding his sword from passersby, but the thought of the public seeing him at the rally still worried Sean. It was impossible to travel incognito wearing a blade on one's hip, but that didn't stop him from trying. Against Jo's advice, he'd changed from his uniform into his favorite work shirt and trousers before leaving Montressador's Keep. The sword of his office would be all the authority he would need.

Brink raised his voice and stood straighter as he faced the audience. "How much longer are we to be the beast, oppressed by every other advanced race in the universe? We are the dirt under their feet and all because we are cursed." The reverend pointed to the heavens, punctuating the words. "Not *chosen*. Not *blessed*. Not *raised up* by the hand of God. We were cast down and CURSED!"

The faithful gathered in front of the stage grew more animated as Brink spoke. Sean adjusted his sword belt and wondered how much longer the sermon would last.

To the far left, Sean could see the tents of the Luctari encampment in the noonday sun. Behind him, the sweeping manicured lawn stretched to the National Museum, and in the distance, the towers of the capital city surrounded the green expanse of the park like rows of glittering teeth.

Luctari dancers and musicians entertained at the fringes of the modest crowd and invited curious on-lookers, office workers on their midday break and others passing through the park, to stop and watch the show. Sean turned back to the stage as the reverend's sermon continued to whip the crowd.

"We were cursed to do the impossible – to be the stewards of time." Brink dabbed his glistening brow with a handkerchief and returned it to a pocket. He opened his arms in a pleading gesture. "For centuries, Andarrians have bled and died. We FULFILLED our obligation! We PAID for our sins with Andarrian blood and so again I ask you....WHEN WILL THE GODS RELEASE US FROM OUR LABORS?"

The crowd responded, a few of the faithful chanting, "When? When? When?" Brink held up a hand to quiet them.

"Friends, my message to you today is one of good news. Our labors are at an end. If the gods won't release us, then we'll break our shackles. We will no longer be a cursed beast toiling in the dirt. We will rise up and take our place with the other races of the universe without the burden of stewardship. We've done our duty. It's *time* for someone else to carry the load!"

The Luctari leaped to their feet and cheered. Sean frowned, surprised by the reaction from the crowd. The Luctari he could understand but even the few non-Luctari watching were applauding, although

265

less enthusiastically. For Andarrians to relinquish any tradition was unusual, but to abandon time jumping? It could set fire to the fabric of Andarrian society itself.

A celebration followed as musicians took the stage and dancers threaded through the crowd. The reverend mingled with his flock. Brink looked up and saw Sean waiting by the stone wall. The reverend smiled and made his way through the faithful toward him. Sean cringed and stood, resting a hand on the hilt of his sword. He hoped Fionna was right and the awkwardness of the next hour or so would bring results.

The shimmer of bells pulled Sean's attention away from the reverend. A Luctari woman wearing silver bangles–and little else–danced nearby, bells quivering from her short skirt. The sway of her hips held the power to alter the gravitational pull of planets.

Sean's eyes skimmed curves a man could take days to explore. The woman saw him watching and danced closer, carried by the rhythm of the drums.

Smokey eyes locked onto Sean's, and the woman twirled in front of him only a breath away. Her arms mirrored the movement of her hips. Sean returned her smile. A deeper hunger stirred, the woman's body a feast before him.

"She is lovely." Reverend Brink's voice sounded in Sean's ear.

"Yes..." Sean replied, never taking his eyes from the dancer, captivated by the secrets cradled in her bandeau top.

The woman turned and danced only for the reverend. A beast uncoiled inside Sean's gut and lashed its tail, vexed by the loss of the woman's attention.

"You may sample her if you wish," Brink said as the woman's arms entwined around his neck, bells shimmered. "Felicity doesn't charge for her delights. She gives freely of herself because she's Luctari. She's chosen a path of pleasure."

The reverend slipped an arm around the dancer's waist. Felicity pressed her lithe form against Brink's belly, his thick lips and sweaty milk-biscuit face inches from her own. She kissed Brink on the mouth, and he uttered a grunt of contentment as her hand wandered across his chest.

The image of Brink's sweaty palm on the woman's hip strangled Sean's desire. Felicity released the reverend and moved toward Sean. Her arms reached out to pull him into an embrace, but Sean gently held the woman at bay by her shoulders.

"I don't indulge in samples, thanks," Sean said with a smile.

Brink dismissed the woman with a pat on her bottom. "You aim too high, my dear. He is not Luctari...yet."

Felicity gave Sean a smile that smoldered with intent and danced away. The beast in Sean's gut whined once, tucked its tail, and went back to sleep.

Sean flashed Brink a warning look. "*You* aim too high, Reverend."

Brink chuckled. "Lower your blade, Montressador. I'm only jesting with you. You can't blame me for trying."

Reverend Brink motioned for Sean to walk with him toward the Luctari encampment. Sean frowned and matched the shorter man's stride.

"I found the Luctari you're looking for. I'm not surprised the investigators had trouble collecting statements." Brink chuckled at an inside joke. "We've prepared a tent for you to interview them. The group has agreed to talk to you, but special provisions had to be made to ensure their cooperation."

"I only have a few questions," Sean said. "Hopefully, you didn't go through too much trouble."

"No trouble." Brink's smile bunched his milk-biscuit cheeks. "It was the least I could do to thank you for reporting the vandalism to my message at the transport shelter. I'm happy to return the favor."

Sean walked with Brink through the camp. The Luctari went about their business, cooking over small fires or hanging laundry from lines strung between tents. Groups of Luctari were everywhere. Sean watched as they passed Luctari sitting in the grass blowing soap bubbles. Another group lay on blankets asleep in the open, while still others played instruments or passed the time with dice games. The smells of cooking, sweat, and garbage wafted between the tents.

Sean looked between two tents and saw a group of Luctari sitting in a circle deep in conversation with some office workers from the rally. A bare-chested man wearing a chicken mask stood a few paces

away from the group and looked up as Montressador Chapman and Reverend Brink walked by. The
eyes of the mask followed Sean as he passed. One
side of the chicken's beak lifted in a snarl, showing
a row of cracked and gritted teeth. Sean tightened
the grip on the hilt of his sword. Fionna had made
light of her encounter with a Luctari man wearing a
chicken mask, never mentioning how menacing the
mask appeared. Was it possible there was another,
less threatening man in a chicken mask? *At least
this guy's wearing pants,* Sean thought as he returned
the stare until the man in the mask looked away,
stepped behind the edge of the tent, and disappeared.

Brink led Sean to a tent larger than the others.
A Luctari man wearing a donkey mask stood outside the tent's entrance. Like the man in the chicken
mask, the donkey's cartoonish face was pulled back
into a frightening grin, buck teeth jutted forward
as if in mid-bite. The eyes of the mask narrowed in
anger and the ears shot upward, twisting like cork-
screws. Sean took note of the Donkey Man's stance
and athletic build. The men in the animal masks
were most likely Luctari security.

As they drew closer, Sean heard moans and whimpers coming from inside the tent. Before he could
question the wisdom of entering, the Donkey Man
stepped to one side and the Reverend Brink lifted the
tent flap and walked through. Sean gave the Donkey
Man a cursory glance and followed.

Sean drew up short after passing over the threshold. It was the second time in so many days he'd walked into a tent only to be faced with an unpleasant surprise. His brain struggled to process what he saw. A jumble of limbs and naked flesh lay on the cushions strewn on the floor. Sean swallowed hard and flushed as the image sorted itself into sense.

The Luctari lay together in a mass orgy. Every hand, every mouth, every inch of flesh was occupied with giving or receiving pleasure, and despite the unnaturalness of the scene, Sean felt a stirring of deeper urges at the sight of so many naked bodies. He shook off the feeling and tried to focus his mind on the questions he prepared.

"All right, my children," Brink said to the group, completely undisturbed by the sex scrum in front of him. "It's time for you to rest and refresh yourselves. Montressador Chapman is here to speak to you. You may return to your play shortly."

The reverend signaled to a man at the back of the tent and more Luctari appeared carrying trays of food and drink and placed them on low tables near the cushions. Sean watched amazed as the mass of limbs separated and he counted seven naked Luctari. An eighth member reclined still fully clothed on one side of the pile of cushions as if in a stupor. The Luctari turned with languid movements to the trays, helped themselves to the food, and began to eat.

Brink looked at Sean. "You'll want to keep the interview short. The food will only distract them for a little while. I will stay. My presence might buy you some more time, but I can't guarantee for how long."

Sean nodded but said nothing. Brink looked at him and smiled.

"You're uncomfortable?"

Sean shot Brink a look that confirmed the reverend's suspicions.

Brink returned a sad but sympathetic expression. "A pity. All is permissible with the Luctari."

The smell of earth and burning sweetgrass tickled Sean's nose. Lamps hung from tent poles and cast a warm glow over the Luctari's bare skin. The fourth man who sat a little apart from the others stared into the corner, his face a blank slate.

Sean tried to focus on the Luctari's faces as they ate, drank, and lounged on the pillows. Nerves pinged inside him like grasshoppers jumping in a field. *What the hell am I doing? I'm not an investigator.* Sean took a deep breath. "I'm told you were in camp —"

"—the night the tour—"

"—came to see Syrovar's sword." A blond man with a chiseled torso completed a doe-eyed woman's sentence.

"The sword...sword...sword..." The young man sitting in a stupor echoed the last word without emotion.

The doe-eyed woman leaned over, a grape between her teeth, and gently pressed her mouth to the catatonic man's lips. The young man took the fruit into his mouth and chewed, eyes never wavering from their blank stare.

"I explained why you wanted to speak with them," the reverend said, leaning toward Sean.

"That should make things easier." Sean shifted awkwardly and turned back to the group. "I just have a few questions."

A man with a shaved head spoke first. "The others asked us questions."

"They tried," said a long-legged beauty with a heart-shaped face.

"They left," replied the woman's red-headed companion as he sucked a berry from her belly button.

A giggle flowed through the group like wind chimes.

Sean puffed an agitated sigh. *This is going to be fun. Thanks, Fionna.* Sean checked his resolve and began again. "Where were you the night of the tour?"

The Luctari continued speaking in their strange chorus. What one Luctari began, another finished until the syncopated rhythm filled the tent.

"The sun is so bright."

"It burns."

"The moon has a lover's caress." A woman with dark hair drew fingertips across the arm of the person next to her.

"We hid in the bushes—"

"—outside the museum entrance—"

"The palace...palace...palace..."

The doe-eyed woman held a cup of wine to her companion's lips. "—to make love under the stars."

"The stars spin—"

"—and the galaxies—"

"—are so beautiful." The man with a shaved head whispered the words into the ear of the closest playmate and a moan swelled the choir.

"Have you ever—"

"—made love—"

"—under the moon—"

"—in the grass?"

"The grass is so cool—"

"—on our skin."

Sighs fluttered.

Sean ignored the question and adjusted his sword belt. "Did you see the night tour arrive?"

"Yes." The answer echoed from every mouth.

Sean tried to keep up as the chorus began again.

"The scholars."

"The teacher."

"The worker."

"The friend."

"The watcher."

"The lovers." A woman with large breasts stroked the curve of her thigh, prompting another round of sighs.

"The tourists."

"The mother."

"The child."

"The watcher."

"They all entered."

"We saw them—"

"—in the palace...palace...palace..."

The doe-eyed woman pressed another grape to the young man's lips.

Sean rubbed his temple with a pained expression. "Did you see them all leave?"

"Yes."

"The scholars."

"The teacher."

"The worker."

"The friend."

"The watcher...watcher...watcher..."

Sean held up a hand, cutting off the choir in mid-measure. *The swordsman is trapped in the sex tent... tent...tent. Great. Now* I'm *doing it.* Clearly, he would have to compare the group's statements to the tour list. "Three days later the sword was reported missing..."

The man with the chiseled torso waved a cup of wine. "We saw the woman—"

"—with blond hair."

"We saw the technicians—"

"—with their cases."

"We saw you—"

"—crossing the wide lawn."

Sean narrowed his eyes. *Creepy.*

"We saw you leave the museum."

"You looked back—"

"—when the blond woman—"

"—walked away—"

"—longing in your eyes." Another moan swelled and faded.

Sean flushed under his beard. The Luctari must have seen him when he said goodbye to Fionna at the museum side door. He cleared his throat and pressed forward with the next question.

"How can you be sure who or what you saw if you were all...*occupied*?"

"The drug they take enhances their senses," Reverend Brink said, helping himself to a peach. "Their powers of observation are quite keen." Brink sunk his teeth into the fruit's pink and yellow flesh.

The dark-haired woman nibbled a slice of cheese. "This is true."

"All our senses—"

"—make our play—"

"—divine."

Sean smirked. *That certainly explained a lot.* "Did you see anyone or anything strange around the museum between the night of the tour and the night the investigators were at the museum?"

"We see—"

"—many things—"

"—ordinary and strange—"

"—while we play—"

"—in the bushes—"

"—in the grass—"

"—under the trees—"

"—in the palace."

"The moon."

"The stars."

"The galaxies."

"The watcher in the palace...palace...palace..."

Sean hesitated and looked closer at the young man. *Wait...Was that a complete sentence?* "The watcher?" Sean turned back toward the group. "The others you mention – the students, the teacher, the tourists…" Sean shook his head to break free of the choir's rhythm. "Those I understand but who is the watcher? And what does your friend mean when he says, 'the palace?' Is he talking about the museum?"

Silence.

After a moment, the doe-eyed woman responded. "We don't know."

"Ira sees—"

"—and experiences—"

"—things we do not."

Sean cocked a brow. "I don't understand. Wasn't Ira with you? Isn't he part of your *play group*?"

"Ira's part of the group," Brink said. "They're inseparable, but he never participates physically in their play. I'm told Ira is so taken by the drug that he enjoys the games mentally. As far as what he means by 'the palace'…" The reverend shrugged. "Your guess is as good as mine." Brink took another juicy bite of peach.

Sean took a step toward Ira and sat on his heels to look the man in the eye. "Who is 'the watcher?'"

"I saw him in the palace."

"Was he on the night tour to see the sword?"

"The sword…sword…sword…"

"There are many who come to the rallies who are not Luctari," Brink said and returned the half-eaten peach to one of the low tables, wiping the juice off his hands with a pocket square. "We call them Watchers. It's possible the person on the tour was someone Ira recognized from a rally."

Sean nodded over a shoulder to the reverend then looked at Ira. "Is that why you call him the Watcher? What did he look like?"

Ira stared straight ahead, his dark brown mass of hair and clothes unkempt, but judging by the line of dirt just under his collar someone had taken a wash rag to the young man's face and neck. Sean could also smell what the incense couldn't hide. He wrinkled his nose against Ira's body odors and looked into the young man's face, searching for any sign of intelligence in the wide pale blue eyes.

Ira's pupils flickered. Sean frowned and leaned closer. Was it possible the young man's eyes had grown a shade paler?

A red beetle the size of Sean's pinkie scuttled across Ira's forehead and back into his hairline. Sean yelped, fell onto his ass, and scrambled backward.

Brink offered a hand. "I'm sorry, Montressador. I should have warned you. I'm afraid infestations are common among our brethren who sleep outside." The reverend helped pull Sean to his feet.

Sean stood, breathing hard. He looked down at Ira. The young man continued to stare straight ahead, oblivious to the commotion in front of him.

The Luctari finished eating. The dark-haired woman added a few drops from a vial to a cup of wine, took a sip, and passed the wine to her companions. Pulses quickened, bodies writhed, as hands began to wander.

The reverend turned to Sean. "Are you finished with your interview, Montressador?"

Sean nodded and brushed the dirt from his trousers. "For now."

"Thank you, my children," Brink said to the Luctari. "You may return to your play."

The long-legged beauty raised the cup to Sean. "Won't you stay—"

"—and join our game?"

"There is always—"

"—room—"

"—for one more."

Sean winced and waved away the offered cup. "No, thank you. Your game is too *complicated* for me."

The woman smiled and returned the cup to the table. The Luctari rolled back toward one another in a ripple of sighs. The ultimate group hug.

"I hope the interview was useful," Brink said after they left the tent. The sounds of moans and whimpers coming from inside the tent behind them surged to an embarrassing crescendo.

"I didn't learn much." Sean blew out a sigh. "I'm curious about this watcher." He shook his head. "It could be nothing…"

"Or it could be something." Brink tapped a knuckle to his chin. "I will ask my followers about any non-Luctari who regularly attend our rallies." Brink stretched out his hand to Sean. "If I uncover anything useful or if Ira gives more information, I'll send word to your office."

TWENTY

SWORDPLAY

Sean trudged across the park back toward Montressador's Keep, relieved to put some distance between himself and the Reverend Brink. Without the reverend's influence, the chances of finding the right Luctari and talking to them would have been slim but he didn't have to like it. Associating with Brink always left Sean feeling used, like the young woman whose hip Brink groped with his sweaty hand. He shuddered at the image, set fire to it in his mind, buried it in a hole under a mountain of dirt, and then set fire to the dirt for good measure as he crossed the tree line into the Wilds surrounding the Keep.

The winding footpath cut through the uneven terrain as ancient trees dappled sunlight and obscured the view of the surrounding city and muted the drone of airships. Leaves whispered above. The path led across a wooden bridge over a slow-moving creek. Only the scuff of Sean's boots on the dirt path and the soft ring of his sword belt broke the stillness. The serenity of the forest lifted the tension from Sean's shoulders and his thoughts returned to the interview with the Luctari. Was Ira's mumblings about 'the Watcher' the residue of a mind gone to rot or had the young man actually seen something? Sean kicked a stone from the path into the under-brush. Fionna's notes on the night tour might have answers. He grumbled to himself and quickened his pace. At the very least, he could check the notes, re-port back to Fionna, and cross the whole damn in-vestigator business off his chore list.

Montressador's Keep stood on a hillock deep in the Wilds of the park. During the golden age of the Andarrian monarchy, the stone castle garrisoned an elite force of one hundred and fifty guards, but now it stood as a monument to tradition. Sean entered the Keep through an old servant's passage hidden in the castle's southern wall, the blackened battle-ments above showed where Montressador Impero the Red repelled an invading force for three days be-fore falling under the enemy's blade.

Sean's hands brushed the rough-hewn stone blocks as he climbed the winding stairwell, foot-steps echoing through the dim passage where Im-pero died. Sean breathed in the cold damp. Long white scratches on the stone walls showed where the swords struck during the close-quarter fighting. Impero's last words to his men were said to be, *It was fate. I will protect your flank.* Sean shivered. The clash of steel and the shouts and screams from the men seemed to infuse the air of the narrow passage. He climbed the last few steps and slipped through the door into the castle's carpeted second-floor hallway.

"THERE HE IS!"

A chorus of shrieks loud enough to shatter glass and crack stone pierced Sean's ears. He spun. His hand flashed to the hilt of his sword as he came face to face with...

...an afternoon tour group.

Josephine stood when Montressador Chapman walked into the office suite a few minutes later.

"Jo, I thought we agreed we're going to keep the tours on the first floor," Sean said with a scowl, shutting the door behind him. "I just spent the last ten minutes posing for pictures with a pack of pre-teen girls."

Jo pursed her red lips. "I'm sorry, Montressador. The tour was the special request you approved last week." Sean gave his office assistant a blank look. Jo arched one slim dark brow from under her mass of curls. "For Minister Greffenius' granddaughter's birthday?"

Sean grunted. He'd forgotten. If it was for Minister Greffenius, then he couldn't complain. The old time jumper had proven to be a loyal supporter of the Montressador's office on more than one occasion. "Remind me next time. I almost relieved them of their heads."

"That would've been unfortunate," Jo said, a wry twist to her mouth. "We're out of accidental beheading forms."

Sean smirked. "I'll be in my office."

"No, you won't." Jo stepped from behind her desk and retrieved Sean's uniform jacket from the arm of a guest chair. "I'm afraid you're needed outside."

"Why? What's the problem?" He took the jacket and pulled it on.

"There are some hecklers by the East Gate. Captain Wahler asked if you would make an appearance when you returned."

Sean sighed and fastened the silver buttons. It wasn't uncommon, especially in the warmer months, for a few jackasses to show up every now and then to heckle the guards.

"All right. I'll go out and do my bit but clear my calendar for the rest of the afternoon. I have work to do."

The East Gate opened to a small, treelined courtyard underneath the castle walls, a favorite spot for tourists to watch the changing of the guard. A velvet rope separated the guard's walk from the rest of the courtyard. Sean found his Captain of the Guard just inside the arch of the East Gate in the guardhouse.

"The hecklers haven't crossed the rope. They just shout insults. I wouldn't have called you except it's one of our newer recruits. Thought you could boost his morale."

Captain Wahler, a tall, thick-set man in his late twenties, spoke with the easy rhythm of a farmer from the provinces. Some people thought Wahler was unintelligent because of his slow drawl. *Some people are rather stupid that way,* Sean thought.

Sean nodded. "Which guard?"

"Connor. He's on the far corner."

Sean tugged the bottom of his jacket. "I'm ready."

Captain Wahler stepped from the shadow of the arch and announced, "GUARDS! PREPARE FOR IN-SPECTION!"

Sean moved down the guard walk, pausing a moment to inspect the first guard before continuing to the second standing at the corner. Tall and lanky, Connor had the bristle haircut of a new recruit. The close-cropped sides of his brown hair were just visible underneath the edge of his dragon-hide helmet.

The tourists crowded the velvet rope, eager to see the show. Connor drew his sword and presented it in regimental style.

Sean inspected the length of the blade, his back to the crowd, and muttered, "Connor. How goes the watch?"

The guard's eyes flicked to Sean's, surprised by the breach in protocol. Connor licked his lips, nervous. "Fine, Sir."

From his thin build, Sean had expected Connor to be in his late teens like most new recruits, but the sharp planes on the guard's face suggested he was older, closer to his mid-twenties.

Sean continued to examine the sword, every motion practiced and deliberate as he turned the blade in his hands. He raised the tip of the blade to his shoulder and met the guard's eye. "Ignore the assholes. Remember, they're only good for one thing. Spewing shit."

Connor blinked in surprise. The corner of his

mouth twitched, flashing a half smile, and dimpled his cheek before regaining his disciplined composure.

Sean slashed the blade downward and returned the hilt to Connor with a final flourish. "Carry on."

Connor sheathed the weapon, threw a crisp salute, and returned to his guard stance, facing the crowd.

An object whistled past Sean's shoulder and struck Connor on the brim of his dragon hide helmet. Sean spun, hand on his hilt.

The startled guard drew his sword, pointing it at the stunned crowd. "STEP BACK FROM THE ROPE!"

Sean's eyes darted to Connor. The guard's face dripped with red juice, spoiling the front of his immaculate uniform. A squashed fliver fruit lay on the cobblestones at his feet.

Laughter and jeers came from behind the line of tourists crowded against the rope.

Connor sheathed his sword and resumed his post, breathing hard. More laughter and hoots came from the back of the crowd. The guard's lips pressed into a thin white line as the red juice trickled down the side of his face into his collar.

A flame sparked inside Sean, igniting a black rage that burned under his skin. Sean gripped the hilt of his blade. *Impero the Red, Montressadors Jabiru, Fregoli, Syrovar – none of them would have stood for this. Feathered quills, ceremonial batons, empty honors, tour groups, and worst of all they trained you, made you into a skilled swordsman, and gave you a blade for your hip that they never intended or expected you to ever use.*

The whisper of steel echoed off stone as Sean drew his sword. He took three steps to reach the red velvet rope. The sword spun, slicing through the divider in an upward arc. The crowd backed away, eyes wide and faces slack with shock, as Sean strode past.

A man in a ragged sleeveless shirt stood under a tree a few paces behind the crowd, a fliver fruit gripped in one hand ready to throw, his head turned the other way. Sean lunged. The tip of his sword flashed, piercing the fruit in the man's hand and flicking it away. The man turned in surprise a second before Sean's left hook smashed into his jaw.

Sean pushed the man up against the tree, arm pressed to his throat. "YOU FILTHY BASTARD! I SHOULD OPEN YOUR GUTS RIGHT HERE!"

Movement caught the corner of Sean's eye. He released the man and stepped back, sword raised, and stared down the barrel of an ion pistol. Light flashed from the barrel, the bolt hitting Sean in the chest.

Pain ripped through his body. Muscles snapped. Lungs on fire. Air rushed in his ears as he fell backward, slamming into the ground. His sword slipped from his fingers, a ring of steel as the blade struck the cobblestones. Darkness pressed in. The world slipped sideways, wrapped in muffled screams and running feet.

A guard from the walk loomed over him and yelled for assistance. The words tumbled from Connor's mouth, muted by the thundering in Sean's head. The sun reflected on the scales of the guard's dragon hide helmet and cast rainbows in the fading light.

Sean's thoughts turned to Impero the Red. He muttered the words as blackness fell.

"It was just fruit..."

Sean woke with a jolt, heart and head pounding. Lying on his back, he looked up at the cross beams of his office ceiling. He reached for the sword at his hip and felt a momentary panic when he found the sheath empty, but then saw the blade resting in the sword stand within arm's reach. More relief flooded in as Jo stepped into view.

"What happened?" A vague memory of being carried up the grand staircase to his office flicked through Sean's brain. He tried to sit up, thought better of it, and sunk back onto the couch cushion.

"You were shot. I called the doctor." The tension in Jo's voice threatened to crack her professional image.

"The Keep is on full lockdown." Captain Wahler's voice came from across the room. "I have two guards stationed in the outer office."

Sean tried to sit up again and this time made it halfway. He leaned back against the arm of the couch, breathing hard with the effort. "Cancel the doctor. I'm fine."

Jo eyed Montressador Chapman, mouth pursed in disapproval, and tapped the screen of the data pad in her hand. "Yes, Sir."

Sean turned to Captain Wahler. "When's the last time Montressador's Keep was on lockdown?"

Wahler stood at ease, helmet tucked under an arm. "It's been more than a hundred years." Sean gave the Captain of the Guard a pained look. Wahler stood a little straighter. "It was a good run, Sir."

Sean exhaled a deep breath. *Something else to add to my legacy.* "We'll have to change the sign in the break room. What about the guy who shot me?"

"The shooter and the man who threw the fruit at Connor got away when the crowd scattered," Wahler said.

Sean rubbed his head and ran through the events in his mind. The ion pistol only stunned him. Surprising, given he was shot at point-blank range.

"How am I still alive?" Sean looked down at his uniform jacket and fingered a burn hole in the fabric directly over his heart. His fingers brushed unfamiliar ridges sewn into the lining of the jacket. Sean frowned and looked at Jo, pointing to the ribs of the dielectric vest visible under the burn hole. "What's this?"

"A precautionary safety measure."

Sean raised his voice to a more commanding volume. "On who's order?"

Jo stiffened. "Someone who has an interest in keeping you alive."

It wasn't like Jo to be so cryptic. *Probably Andarrian Intelligence,* Sean thought. *Sneaky bastards.* " Wahler, did you know about this?"

"No, Sir."

Sean turned back to his assistant. "When?"

"A few months ago."

"Why wasn't I told about it?"

"It was believed you would resist wearing the jacket if you knew," Jo said, finally relenting. "The jacket was made with the lightest protection possible, so you wouldn't notice the weight change. You're lucky the man who shot you used such a small-caliber pistol. Shall I have the jacket repaired or should I order a new jacket without the vest?"

Sean ground his teeth, irritated by Jo's deception, irritated at himself for losing his temper with the hecklers, and irritated that his office assistant was right. He probably wouldn't have worn the jacket if he'd known about the vest. It would seem that he wasn't immune to foolish pride and misguided tradition.

Sean grumbled, stripped off the jacket, and tossed it to Jo. "Fix the jacket and the vest but keep it our secret. And up the gauge. That stung." Sean rubbed his chest. "It feels like I still have electrical current arcing between my nipples."

"Yes, Sir." Jo bit back a smile as she folded the jacket over an arm. The digital pad in her other hand beeped. She glanced at the screen. "A representative from the Park Conservancy is waiting outside and wishes to speak to you about your attack on the tourist. He would like a statement."

"I attacked the divider rope and a jackass who was harassing my guards," Sean said. "I frightened the tourists. Big difference."

"Montressador, there's also a news service crew at the front gate," Captain Wahler said. "There's a rumor going around that says you might be dead."

Sean sighed and stood, head swimming for an instant. "I guess we've stayed in hiding long enough. Lift the lockdown and escort the conservancy rep inside." He reached for his sword. "Jo, put out a statement. There'll be no horse-drawn caskets today." He returned the sword to its sheath.

Jo opened the door to the outer office. Captain Wahler dismissed the two guards on duty then turned back to Montressador Chapman, face tight with concern.

"Montressador, given what's happened I don't think you should leave the Keep without an escort anymore."

Sean dismissed the suggestion with a wave of a hand. "We've had hecklers before…"

"But the others never did anything more than yell insults," Wahler said. "The attack with the fruit didn't happen until you joined the guards on the walk."

Sean eyed his Captain of the Guard. "You're worried about fruit?"

"I'm worried they wanted to draw you out into the open." Wahler leveled his eyes. "They wanted to make you so mad you would cross the rope to confront them."

Sean snorted. "I didn't even know I was going to do that. How would they?"

"With respect, Sir. Whenever you've lost your

temper before, it's been when you've been defending someone else."

Wahler's observation struck Sean speechless. He started to splutter an objection and looked to Jo.

"It's one of your finer qualities, Sir," Jo said with a gentle smile.

Sean grumbled in defeat. "If they wanted me dead, they brought the wrong caliber pistol."

Wahler thought a moment before answering. "The hecklers didn't know you were wearing a vest. A small pistol is easy to obtain and conceal. At close range, a well-aimed shot could've killed you and would've looked like an unfortunate accident."

"Except the hecklers had no way of knowing I was even inside the Keep," Sean said. "Are you saying they took a chance and got lucky?"

"Reverend Brink knew where you were a good hour before the attack," Jo said. "He also knew you would most likely come back to the Keep when you were finished with the interviews."

A chill crept up Sean's spine. Fionna's warning about the reverend came back to him. "But why would Brink want me dead? To listen to him talk, the Luctari want to end time jumping and return to the golden age of kings and castles. Seems counterproductive to kill me, don't you think?"

Wahler shrugged and settled his helmet back on his brow. "Maybe. I just know what I see. You've been asking a lot of questions about Syrovar and her sword. Maybe someone doesn't like the questions you're asking?"

TWENTY-ONE
FOR THOSE IN MISERY

Ann fidgeted in the passenger seat as the shuttle-craft descended through the clouds, wind currents buffeting against the craft's hull. She typed replies to John's text messages on her data link pad.

John: Are you okay? Where are you?

Ann: Yes. With Fionna. Heading to Outer Banks. Garin's dead.

John: I heard.

Ann: We need to talk about the mission report.

John: Already took care of it.

Ann exhaled slowly and tried to push out the fear and panic swirling in her chest. She'd hoped to talk to John in person before he submitted their report on Dieva Roka, but the old-fashioned detective work, as Fionna called it, had taken a few days and delayed her return to the Colonies.

John: Don't worry about it. We'll talk soon. In person.

Ann: When?

John: Soon. I'll be out of range for a little while. Might not be able to respond right away. Send updates anyway.

    Ann: When will you be back?

    John: Not sure. Gotta go. Love you.

    <End signal>

Ann rested her head against the seat. Whatever John had done, whatever risks he'd taken with his career for her sake, he'd already gone and done it, and now there was nothing she could do to undo it.

She looked out the shuttle window. The craft had broken through the cloud cover. Acres of green wilderness stretched out in all directions below. Her eyes followed a muddy two-track as it wound through the forest over a sawtooth ridge to a house on a rocky seashore. Commander Garin's family homestead was not what Ann expected. The residence, a two-hour shuttle flight from the capital city, was not a stately home or a quaint cottage by the sea, but rather a thoroughly modern structure that looked like it had been plucked from the top of a penthouse tower from Palladium Beta. Built on straight lines, the home was stacked like a child's building blocks. Large windows gleamed between three levels of flat roofs in a palette of dark reds and grays that blended into the landscape. Warm light burned from the windows under heavy clouds.

The shuttle rocked sideways, smacking Ann's forehead against the window.

"Ow!"

Forensic Tech Roan Kegler hollered from the back seat, "Contusion at three o'clock!"

Fionna looked up from her data link pad at Ann.

"Are you all right?"

"I'm fine." Ann cringed and rubbed her head.

Willimon Reed, Commander Garin's personal assistant, glanced over a brown tweed shoulder from the shuttle's cockpit. "I'm terribly sorry about that, Lieutenant," Reed said as he pushed the yoke of the shuttle forward to begin their final descent. "I should have warned you. It can be a rough ride with the updrafts from the ridge this time of year."

Ann noticed no words of concern came from Agent Drake who sat in the cockpit next to Reed. The senior agent had insisted on accompanying them to Commander Garin's home, saying he couldn't wait for Fionna to get around to sending her reports.

With help from Garin's family and his assistant, Fionna and Ann had retraced the commander's steps from the moment he left Time Jumper Headquarters to his apartment in the capital city to finally his home on the Outer Banks, a chain of islands north of Palladium Beta.

Garin was dead. The grisly find in the gut pile proved it, but Garin's body could still hold clues if found. And while the possibility of Sarolea still being alive offered Ann hope, it also added weight to Agent Drake's theory that her friend was somehow involved with the killer. Ann's thoughts twisted around her grief. *Sarolea, where are you?*

The small craft bucked the air currents and touched down a few minutes later in a green field a short walk to the house, maneuvering thrusters flattened the tall grass surrounding the landing pad.

Ann stepped down from the shuttle's running boards and adjusted the pistol strapped to her hip. Her canvas pants and long-sleeve denim shirt kept out the chill of the sea air that threatened to creep under her collar and played with the wisps of hair that escaped from her braid.

The rest of the passengers spilled from the shuttle doors and followed a path of stepstones to the home's front porch. Kegler and his assistant brought up the rear carrying their forensic equipment.

"Please wipe your feet," Reed said as he entered the code to unlock the front door, then froze. The lines on his face deepened and took on a grim cast. "Not that it matters anymore I suppose. It's not like the Commander will scold." Reed finished entering the code and the click and slide of a deadbolt rang from the lock.

Fionna settled her bio-vision glasses across the bridge of her nose and placed a hand on the older man's shoulder. "It still matters. We'll be extra-careful. Please wait outside with the forensic team while we make sure the house is clear."

Reed gave a grateful smile and stepped aside to allow Fionna to pass. Ann and Agent Drake followed close behind.

A quick sweep showed the house was completely empty of inhabitants. Ann stretched out her senses and searched for any sign of the directional anchors the killer might have left behind. Except for a hidden ion pistol in a drawer, the house offered nothing of interest from Ann's perspective. The only recent activity seemed to be the pile of gifts left on the front hallway table.

"Knox!" Drake called from the other end of the house.

Ann and Fionna hurried to the commander's study. Agent Drake gestured to a side table next to a wing chair. A white gift box with a gold crest and bow lay open on its side. A bottle of Andarrian whiskey and a glass kept company with the molded remains of a half-eaten steak on a dinner plate.

The whistle from the tech's scanner scratched through Ann's senses as Kegler peered through the remaining whiskey in the bottle. Ann shifted with impatience. The discovery suggested Commander Garin was abducted in the middle of dinner, a scene eerily similar to what investigators found on the *What Cheer*.

Kegler adjusted the scanner's controls. The whistle shot into an even higher octave. Ann cringed. She tried to block out the sound of the scanner clawing at the insides of her skull and turned her attention to the commander's study.

Books and awards lined shelves on blue walls while pictures decorated tabletops and showed a life well spent. A large picture in a scalloped frame dominated a group of smaller family photos. Ann looked closer. A much younger Commander Garin with hair, much to Ann's amazement, stood beaming next to a woman surrounded by a large brood of children. It was impossible to tell whether the woman in the picture was Mrs.-Garin-number-one or Mrs.-Garin-number-two. Five sons and two daughters gathered around the commander and his wife, all happily smiling except for the youngest. The boy had the same wild curls as his mother. Mrs. Garin's hand gripped the boy's shoulder as if he might bolt from the picture frame at any moment, her dimpled smile radiating motherly patience. Ann grinned, remembering a few photo sessions of her own she would have preferred to skip.

Kegler finished his examination of the whiskey bottle and clicked off the scanner. Ann sighed with relief as the whistle faded from her head.

The forensic tech set the bottle on the end table and looked at Fionna. "The whiskey contains Splice just like the water tanks on the *What Cheer*. The cork shows signs of tampering. My guess is the killer inserted a micro-needle through the cork to deliver the drug. You can probably guess the rest." Kegler held up fingers as he counted off. "One, the chronocular confirms the time distortion matches the signal the killer is using. Two, the time signature is Garin's." The tech paused as he returned the scanner to its carrying case. "But I'm not detecting nanobots in the whiskey."

Fionna's eyes darted to Kegler's. "What?"

Kegler fought off a mild spasm beginning to tug the corner of his mouth. "I should be able to detect dead nanobots in the whisky along with the Splice given what we know about how long nanobots can carry a charge outside a host. I can't. The only explanation is Garin must have already been infected with nanobots before to drinking the whiskey." A chill passed over Ann. "All the killer needed to do was expose him to enough Splice and activate the nanobots retrieval signal. Sip. Boom. Gone." Kegler snapped his fingers.

Ann traded looks with Fionna across the room. The agent's words came back to her about how people could be infected with nanobots and never know it. Ann gulped the anxiety building in the back of her throat.

Fionna returned her focus to Kegler. "What about a timeline? Any guesses as to when the abduction occurred?"

"Based on the bacteria growth on the dinner plate, I would guess within forty-eight hours of Garin's retirement announcement."

"That's around the same time the crew from the *What Cheer* was abducted," Ann said.

Kegler lifted a shoulder in a half shrug. "The killer had a lot going on. The decomposition of the gut pile shows Garin was killed first by a couple days."

Fionna gestured to the bottle on the table. "There was only one glass?"

Kegler nodded. "He was drinking alone from what I can see."

Fionna leaned back against the commander's desk and jotted a note in her data pad. "Do a standard chronocular sweep of the rest of the house. Look for any signs of a house guest. I want to confirm the commander was here alone. Also, check the water filtration system for tampering. The killer might have delivered the nanobots the same way as the *What Cheer*."

Kegler sighed, shoulders drooping, and gave Fionna a quick salute. He mumbled to his assistant as they left the room, "I hate standard sweeps. It's so boring without a body."

Ann picked up the gift box from the table and peered at the gold foil crest. "This whiskey goes for two-hundred dories a bottle on the Colonies. Anyone buying it would probably be remembered by who-ever sold it."

"Nice to see serving drunks has taught you a few useful things," Drake muttered, lounging in the wing chair behind Ann.

A jagged insult formed in Ann's mouth, but she swallowed it when she caught a warning look from Fionna.

"The sender must have known the commander well to give a gift like that," Fionna said. "Drake, did you see a card?"

The senior agent rested his head against the back of the chair and with a bored expression, waved his hand. "If only our job was so simple. In addition to being a murderer, the killer did not concern himself with the niceties of leaving a gift card."

Fionna smirked and turned to Garin's assistant standing in front of one of the large bookcases. "Mr. Reed, are you keeping a list of who sent retirement gifts?"

"If it came through our office, I should have it

right here." Reed scrolled through his data pad, his mouth dipping into a frown. "It's not on my list as a recorded gift, but I can check with the delivery service in the village." He tucked the data pad under an arm. "Lieutenant Chapman is right. The sender has impeccable taste. The whiskey is certainly a gift the commander would appreciate. I'm not surprised he chose to open it over the others."

Ann moved to put the gift box back on the table and saw something flutter inside. She pulled out a slip of folded paper and read the note aloud, "'*For those in misery, perhaps better things will follow...*'" Ann frowned as she looked at the neat, blue script. "A strange quote for a retirement gift."

Reed looked quizzical. "May I?" Ann handed over the paper. He glanced at the writing, his face instantly brightening in surprise. "This is Commander Garin's handwriting."

Fionna straightened. "You're certain?"

"Agent Knox, I've stared at the commander's handwriting for seven years. I can recognize his script as easily as my own."

Drake leaned forward in the wing chair, a look of incredulity on his face. "Are you saying the person who sent the whiskey also sent Garin's quote back to him from something the commander wrote?"

"It would appear that way, Agent Drake, but I don't know to whom the commander would have written," Reed said. "Vesto Garin was a very private man. His written correspondence was only to family or to close friends."

Fionna wrote furiously in her data pad. "Can you think of any other place where he might have written this quote? A journal or a note to a colleague?"

Reed looked out the window, eyes narrowed in thought. "Commander Garin liked to include a quote in the rejection letters he sent to time jumper applicants, parting words to help ease the sting. This sounds like a quote the commander might have inserted, but we always used an auto signer for the quotes and his signature." Reed handed the paper to Fionna. "This quote is without a doubt written in the commander's own hand."

Ann tilted her head in thought. "Mr. Reed, could the Commander have added a handwritten note to a letter without you knowing about it?"

"I suppose it's possible but I'm not sure why. The rejection letters are routine correspondence."

Fionna examined the paper before sealing it in an evidence bag. "How many rejection letters did the commander send out each year?"

"Since I joined the commander's staff, we've averaged close to seven thousand," Reed said.

"I can see why Garin used the auto signer," Ann muttered.

"I must also tell you, Lieutenant," Reed's face flushed as he shifted the data pad from under his arm and stared at his boots. "The quote is not as inappropriate for Commander Garin's retirement as you might think."

Ann frowned. "What do you mean?"

Reed's face hardened, wrestling for a moment

with indecision, before drawing a deep breath and meeting Ann's eye. "Two months ago, Commander Garin was diagnosed with Kraepelin's disease."

Ann blinked as a thought clicked in her mind. "Is that why Garin retired? Because of the diagnosis?"

Reed nodded and gave a sad smile. "The commander had been showing signs of dementia for about six months. At first, I thought it was simply age-related, but his condition kept getting worse. The usual treatments didn't work. Commander Garin was a proud man. He wanted to retire before the symptoms became obvious. The entire transition plan was pulled together in only a few weeks."

"So, whoever knew about the diagnosis could also have sent the whiskey and the note," Ann said, catching Fionna's eye. "Who else knew about the commander's condition?"

"Officially, only his family, immediate staff, and Admiral Dhow, but you know how these things go." Reed shrugged. "Anyone on the admiral's staff could have overheard a conversation. Commander Rectrix was informed when she was offered the interim position."

"A secret everyone knew about." Drake scoffed. "Typical for time jumpers."

Ann ignored Drake's remark and focused on Reed. "Was there anyone who might have been happy about his retirement? Anyone he didn't get along with who would be glad he was leaving?"

Reed shifted uncomfortably and tugged at the cuffs of his tweed jacket. "I don't know about happy.

If you have a long enough career there will always be some people who grow weary of your presence."

Fionna watched the older man through her bio-vision glasses and gave a coaxing smile. "That's true and the commander had a reputation for getting things done. I'm guessing his tenacity didn't always sit well with everyone?"

Reed's mouth tightened as his face flushed a deeper shade of red. "I don't want to give you the wrong idea, Agent Knox. Commander Garin didn't have enemies if that's what you're wondering. He had colleagues that he sometimes disagreed with but that was part of the job." Fionna returned his gaze and waited without comment. Reed sighed, surrendering to the question. "Commander Garin noticed about a year ago what he thought was an in-crease in time jumper mortality and accident rates. He wanted it looked into and became rather insist-ent about it."

"Kraepelin's patients are easily fixated on ideas," Drake said, barely looking in the other man's direc-tion. "It's impossible to reason with them or steer them away from a line of thinking once they've grabbed onto it no matter how illogical their claim."

"That's true, Agent Drake, but this was long be-fore the commander exhibited any symptoms of the disease and the mortality reports did seem to show an upward tick in the long term over the past five years," Reed said. "Nothing that would have been ob-vious unless you dug into the numbers. Commander Garin started pressing higher-ups for additional training, better equipment, more intel, and risk analysis…" Reed waved a hand as he rattled off the list. "He encountered resistance."

"People don't like to spend money when they disagree on a solution," Ann said.

"Or when the problem doesn't actually exist," Drake countered.

Ann shot Drake a dark look before turning back to Reed. "Did Commander Garin get into a lot of arguments about it?"

"No, it never became contentious," Reed said. "It was simply a difference of opinion, but by then some of Commander Garin's earliest symptoms began to show and he focused on other things. I suppose some were glad he dropped the matter. I don't know if anyone will take up the cause now that the commander is gone."

Fionna watched Reed through her bio-vision glasses another moment then pushed back from the desk. "Thank you for your time, Mr. Reed. I would like a copy of the commander's calendar showing anyone he met with from the last six months. If you think of anything else that might be helpful, please contact me."

"We'll also need a list of everyone he personally corresponded with and any letters he received," Agent Drake said. "If possible, I'd also like a list of everyone Commander Garin sent rejection letters to from the past three years." Drake stood and straightened his jacket.

"You have my full cooperation…" Reed said. Uncertainty colored his words as he squared his shoulders. "...and I'm happy to coordinate with the rest of the staff, but I must warn you the list of rejection letters could be substantial. Upward of twenty-thousand names if I were to guess."

"It's a place to start," Drake said.

Fionna made a note in her data pad. "Would it also be possible to get a copy of those mortality reports you mentioned?"

Reed arched a brow in surprise. "Yes...I believe that could be arranged. The reports are not public information, but under the circumstances, I can file a request on your behalf."

Drake stepped forward. "Will you excuse us for a moment, Mr. Reed? I need to speak with my colleagues."

"Of course, Agent Drake," Reed said with a smile. "I'll contact the office to make arrangements for the information you requested."

Drake turned on Fionna as soon as Reed disappeared into the hall. "Mortality reports? That's a rather wide net you're casting, Knox."

"It was the last thing that Garin was working on," Ann said. "It's possible he ruffled some feathers before he retired."

Drake locked eyes on Ann. "Where's the connection to the *What Cheer*? The crew wasn't murdered because of a lack of training or equipment."

"We won't know until we look," Ann said, beginning to seethe. Her hand resting on the pistol at her hip twitched, energy from the weapon's power cell danced across her fingertips.

"We don't have a motive for any of this," Fionna said. "I'll keep kicking over rocks until I find one. I'm not ready to rule anything out yet."

Drake sneered, turning to Fionna. "You want a motive? Garin had retired. He was no longer creating opposition in the office. The killer then went out of his way to abduct Garin and leave a message with the gift. This was *personal*—not policy. It's possible the name we're looking for is buried in that list of twenty-thousand rejection letters. That list and the quote are our strongest leads yet, and you want to divide our efforts?"

Energy from the pistol's power cell edged up Ann's arm and prickled her skin. "If Garin's murder was *personal*, then there's no connection to the *What Cheer*."

Drake took a step toward Ann and opened his mouth to return fire.

"ENOUGH!"

Ann snapped her head in Fionna's direction. The agent's eyes flashed behind the gold lenses of her glasses, a look Ann had only seen from the agent twice before. Sean could have that effect on people. Ann stepped back and chewed on her anger. The prickling of her skin subsided as the energies from the pistol dispersed.

"The killer may have had two separate motives," Fionna said. "The abductions from the *What Cheer* took time to plan. Garin's retirement came as a surprise. The killer could have acted on impulse. It takes a lot less time to spike a bottle of whiskey than to sabotage the water filters on a cargo ship."

Ann checked her anger. Fionna was right of course, but it didn't make Drake any less of an ass.

"Right now, our biggest problem is when and where Commander Garin came in contact with nanobots. If the killer could get to Garin, then anyone could be at risk." Fionna turned to Drake. "I'll ask the techs to investigate while I follow up on the whiskey bottle and the Commander's personal correspondence." Fionna looked to Ann. "Lieutenant, I want you to review the mortality reports. You'll probably have a better understanding of the lingo anyway. Tell me right away if anything jumps out."

Drake turned his dark glare to Fionna. "I want to know how much time she's spending on those reports. If I think it's a waste of resources—"

"—I agree. Lieutenant Chapman's talents are better suited to the field. The reports won't be ready right away. I'll reassign her as needed."

Drake scowled one last time and headed for the door.

Fionna watched the other agent leave then wheeled on Ann. "You need to be more careful. He's baiting you."

Ann shrugged and leaned against the arm of a chair. "He's never liked me because he hates my brother. You know that."

"I don't know *why* he's doing it. I just sense he'd like to remove you from my team." Fionna frowned. "Drake's the lead agent. I can't protect you if he charges you with insubordination."

"Fine, I'll behave." Ann sighed and crossed her arms. "But what's Drake's problem with the mortality reports? We should at least review them to rule out a possible motive."

"I agree but Drake wants a suspect. Simple solutions. The mortality reports, if they lead anywhere, make things more difficult."

"So, he doesn't care about more victims or finding Sarolea? He just wants to make his job easier?"

"I didn't say that." Fionna looked over a shoulder and stepped closer. "Drake is *complicated*. I can't always interpret his motives. I can sense he wants to close this case as quickly as possible and avoid having more victims. We all do. Stay out of his way and stop taking his bait." Ann rolled her eyes and gave a reluctant nod. The agent's serene smile returned. "I appreciate your support, but I can handle him on my own."

The data pad under Fionna's arm beeped. She glanced at the screen. "We're needed at the Ministry. Our nanobot tracker is ready," Fionna said and moved to the doorway.

Ann followed the agent into the hall. "Where do you think Garin picked up the nanobots?"

"I don't know. After we found the sabotage to the *What Cheers'* water tanks, the techs did a sweep of the water filtration system at headquarters as a precaution. Everything came back clean."

"So, whoever did this got close enough to Garin to expose him directly," Ann said.

"It's possible...but we don't even know when he was exposed let alone the method." Fionna lifted her bio-vision glasses, resting them on her blond head.

Ann felt the pull of despair. "You don't think Sarolea had anything to do with this, do you?"

Fionna shook her head. "There's nothing that points to Sarolea as a suspect except for her continued absence. That's not enough, but Drake may be right about one thing." Fionna slowed her step to meet Ann's gaze. "The killer could be one of our own."

TWENTY-TWO

DOUBT

Back at the Ministry, Ann and Fionna followed Agent Drake through the doors of the busy command center, the large digital screens overhead already updated with Fionna's notes from their visit to Commander Garin's homestead.

"So...Commander Lazar's wedding is in a few days," Fionna said after Kegler and his assistant headed off to the forensics labs. "Your brother told me you and Captain Galeas are going?"

Ann glanced to Fionna, surprised by the sudden change in subject. "Yes. I almost forgot. I guess I should find something to wear."

"More importantly..." Fionna whispered to Ann as they walked past a row of cubicles, "Have you forgiven John yet?"

"What?" Ann met the agent's eyes through the glint of yellow lenses. Fionna arched a brow at Ann's reaction and smiled. Ann began to understand why Sean hated Fionna's bio-vision glasses so much. "That's not fair," Ann said, pointing to the agent's lenses.

"I didn't need my glasses to know something's wrong." Fionna shrugged. "You've hardly mentioned John since your mission to Dieva Roka."

Ann sidestepped a team of techs exiting a workstation and snapped, "I've been busy helping you with this case."

"True, but before when you talked about John, I could see something in your face and now..." The agent narrowed her eyes. Ann pretended to focus her attention on following Agent Drake through the crowded central ring of the command center. Fionna blinked. "Ah, so I had the back end of things. You're not sure you've forgiven..." Fionna's face twisted with confusion and then surprise. "... yourself?"

Ann's thoughts spiraled through all the things she'd tried to block out of her mind the past few days —the mission report, that moment of panic when she froze on the balcony and with Moondarra, the fear and worry on John's face. Would he really jeopardize his career to protect her? *What if...?*

Fionna frowned, teasing turned to concern. "Anaya, what's going on?"

Ann swallowed her doubt. "There are some things I need to work out...but not right now."

Fionna pressed her lips together as her eyes searched Ann's face.

"Agent Knox..."

The crowd parted a fraction and Ann saw Kel waiting by the central glass-enclosed conference room, a black box under one arm.

Agent Drake reached Kel first. "What is it, Stravage?"

Kel's eyes darted to Fionna then back to Drake. "My team finished going over the items from the *What Cheer*."

Drake let out an irritated sigh. "*And?*"

A flicker of unease passed over Kel's features. Ann's nerves tightened.

Kel met Ann's eye briefly before turning to Drake, shoulders stiffened. "We found something…"

The glass doors of the conference room sealed behind Ann, shutting out the sounds of the command center. Agents and technicians could still be seen through the room's glass walls and appeared to move in silence in the busy workstations beyond. She took a seat at the table next to Fionna.

"I've been stuck for hours on a shuttle and now we're late for a meeting with the nanobot techs, Stravage," Drake said as he pulled out a seat. "Make it quick."

Kel nodded and placed the black box he carried at the head of the conference table. He touched the table's control panel and the glass walls of the conference room darkened, obscuring the view of the command center outside.

Fionna arched a brow. "Are restrictions necessary?"

Kel nodded as he opened the box. "I think you'll agree when you hear what I found."

Ann leaned forward. A silver necklace lay on the black cushion inside the box. A gap in the row of medallions hanging from the chain looked like a missing tooth. A nagging thought prodded. *Where have I seen this before?* Ann looked at Kel. "Is there a medallion missing?"

Kel nodded. "We think it was a directional anchor. The necklace shows signs of a residual spacetime distortion." Kel pointed to the pendants on either side of the gap. "You can also see scorch marks from heat damage here and here. I believe the killer used the directional anchor to gain access to the ship's water filtration system prior to the crew leaving port and then disposed of the necklace in a refuse chute. All the killer had to do was get someone to smuggle the necklace on board."

Fionna made a note in her data pad. "You're certain the killer had inside help?"

Kel gave a reluctant nod. "Yes."

Drake leaned across the table, eyes dark. "Lieutenant Stravage, in which refuse chute did you find the necklace?"

Kel's mouth tightened. "Lieutenant Sarolea Picquet's quarters."

Ann's heart lurched. *Could it be true?*

Agent Drake turned to Fionna, his face an inch thick with arrogance. "Do you still think Picquet is a victim?"

Fionna ignored the question. "Lieutenant Stravage, are you sure the necklace belonged to Picquet?"

"Yes." Kel's face twisted in a sudden flood of emotion, his voice cracked. "Because I'm the one who handed it to her."

Ann's mouth dropped open. "Kel?"

"Explain." Drake barked out the order. His hand hovered over the table's control panel. "Quickly, before I call security."

Kel took a deep breath to steady himself. "It was about a month ago." The knot of emotion on his face loosened as he told the story. "I met a Luctari woman. I would watch her dance and then we'd meet after and..." Kel swallowed hard, his face blazed red.

Fionna nodded encouragement. "We get the picture, Lieutenant."

Kel gathered his resolve and began again. "She asked to see Saro...I mean...Lieutenant Picquet's stump from her ghost arm. I told her she would need to give something in trade. She agreed so I took her to see the lieutenant. The last time I saw this necklace it wasn't missing any medallions and Lieutenant Picquet had just zipped it into her duffle bag."

The breath hitched in Ann's chest as the mystery of the necklace fell into place. "Kel, is this the same dancing girl I saw you watching a few weeks ago?"

He nodded. "Her name's Felicity."

Fionna turned to Ann. "You knew about this?"

"No, but I remember seeing Felicity in the park. She wears a necklace similar to this one," Ann said pointing to the box.

"Anaya didn't know anything about it," Kel said. "She wasn't at headquarters that day."

Fionna jotted another note in her data pad. "And Lieutenant Picquet didn't know Felicity before you introduced them?"

"No. They'd never spoken before."

"That you know of." Agent Drake sneered from across the table.

"I'm certain," Kel said, fighting another knot of emotion. "If they had met before, I would've been able to tell."

"You were set up, Lieutenant," Drake said, with a self-satisfied smirk that made Ann want to shatter his other testicle. "You admit you were involved with the woman. Your judgment was already compromised. Picquet and this woman could have been working together and using you to cover their tracks."

"I don't believe it," Ann said. "I know Sarolea. She would never—"

"And Lieutenant Stravage wasn't known for being a complete fool and yet here we are," Drake said.

"Agent Drake," Fionna said, looking up from her data pad. "If Lieutenant Picquet was involved, why would she need Felicity to hand off the necklace? She could've put it in her duffle bag at any time and walked onto the *What Cheer*."

"Use your imagination, Knox," Drake said, rolling his eyes. "Obviously, Piquet and the killer couldn't be seen together. The dancing girl was a go-between and Lieutenant Stravage gave them the perfect opportunity."

Ann tried to keep the anger from her voice as she clenched her fists under the table. "Or maybe Sarolea was set up just like Kel."

"If only Lieutenant Picquet were here so we could ask her," Drake said, sarcasm dripping from his crooked mouth. He turned to Kel. "Stravage, you're off the case. I'm also taking you into custody. I can't take the risk you might tell the Luctari woman we're looking for her."

Drake reached for the table's control panel and pressed a pair of buttons. The glass walls of the conference room cleared, making the room visible from the outside again. From across the command center, Ann saw two guards step into view and make their way to the conference room doors.

Ann turned to Fionna. "Kel made a mistake, but he didn't do anything wrong! You can't let Drake do this!"

"Careful, Lieutenant..." Drake's black eyes narrowed.

Ann slammed her hand flat on the table and locked eyes with the senior agent. "*You* should be more careful! You're not *investigating*. You're only focusing on the facts that match your *theory!*"

Drake stood and calmly straightened his suit jacket. "Agent Knox, the behavior of your mission specialist reflects poorly on your leadership."

Fionna's face tightened, her gaze a mixture of anger and rebuke as she pushed her chair back to take her feet. "Lieutenant Chapman, you're out of line."

Ann stiffened. Regret crept across her insides like frost. Fionna had warned her about Drake.

"I agree with Agent Drake." Fionna turned to Kel.

"Lieutenant Stravage, you're a person of interest, which means I have to treat you like I would anyone else. The best thing for you to do is cooperate and tell me everything you know about the Luctari woman."

Drake's lip curled. "Thank you, Knox. I appreciate your support even though I'm afraid it doesn't make up for Lieutenant Chapman's insubordination, not to mention the appalling lack of judgment by Lieutenant Stravage." He took his data pad from a jacket pocket and tapped some keys.

"It was a mistake." Kel's voice held a tremor Ann had never heard from her friend before. "I didn't know what the necklace was."

"Intentional or not," Drake said. "You're responsible for passing the directional anchor to Lieutenant Piquet. The ensuing security breach resulted in the murder of four crew members."

Kel looked like he might be sick.

"These lapses from your team are inexcusable," Drake said, turning to Fionna. "I'm taking over as lead for your team and demoting your investigator status to secondary." Ann's insides clenched. "You will submit your reports directly to me. You and your individual team members will follow my instructions moving forward."

Ann looked to Fionna. *What have I done?* Fionna paled behind her glasses.

"Your team is now *my* team, Agent Knox. Is that clear?"

"Yes, sir." Fionna's voice rang with defeat.

The conference room glass doors slid open. Drake

motioned to the guards as they stepped inside.

"Agent Knox, see if you and Lieutenant Chapman can find this dancing girl and bring her in. *I* will meet with the technicians about your nanobot tracker."

"Felicity is usually in the park this time of day," Kel said. "I would meet her by the outdoor theater near the museum."

"Thank you, Stravage. You can tell me more when I take your official statement." Drake said, motioning for Kel to take a seat.

Fionna moved toward the door.

Ann stood, gripped Kel's shoulder, and whispered, "You never told us about Felicity. Why didn't you say something?"

Kel glanced up from the table. "How would that have gone over? A time jumper and a Luctari? People would have said I was sleeping with the enemy." His face returned to despair. "I guess in this case I actually was."

"Lieutenant Chapman, you have your orders." Drake gave an impatient motion toward the door as he took a seat. "I have work to do."

Ann gave a final glance to Kel, face grim, and followed Fionna through the conference room doors, the glass walls darkened behind her.

Fionna walked through the command center's central ring, dodging agents and technicians who stopped to stare up at the display screens. Heads turned to watch as she passed. Fionna held her head high, back straight, but walked with a quickness in her step. Ann refused to look at the screens over-head, not wanting to see her friend's disgrace, and focused on following the agent's blond bobbed head as she retreated through the crowd.

Ann raced through the network of offices finally catching up when she burst through the doors of the Ministry's garage. Rows of gleaming black and silver hovercars lined both sides of the bay in levels three stories high.

"Fionna!" Ann stopped to catch her breath. "I'm sorry!" Her voice echoed through the garage.

Fionna stopped at a control panel and entered a security code. A lift hummed and moved down a row of cars, selected a vehicle from the stack, and lowered it to the floor of the bay. The hovercar flashed its lights and glided forward.

"I warned you, Lieutenant." The agent's voice was calm but carried an edge sharp enough to cut stone.

"I know...I don't know why I..." Ann swallowed hard. She did know why but guessed Fionna didn't want to revisit her struggles in the flight simulator or hear about hesitation on the rooftops of Dieva Roka at that precise moment.

Fionna stared straight ahead. "Let's focus on the work." She stepped forward and lifted a hand as the vehicle approached.

The sleek hovercar rounded a perfect U-turn, its black windows reflecting the overhead lights, and stopped with the driver's door inches from Fionna's outstretched hand. Her fingertips touched the han-dle and the car door opened.

The agent threw a frosty glare over the roof of the car. "Get in."

Fionna kept a tight grip on the steering wheel and her eyes forward for the ride through the capital city, her face unreadable through the yellow tint of her lenses. Ann watched the scenery and the late afternoon traffic. The silence crawled over her skin. A half-hour later, the car slowed and glided to a stop by a walkway at the edge of the park. Flags marking the Luctari encampment flapped in the breeze a short distance away.

Fionna tapped out a sequence on her data pad and shoved the device into a jacket pocket. She then opened a panel on the dash and pulled out a paper notebook and ink pen before exiting the car. Ann kept pace with Fionna as they left the walkway and struck out across the grass.

"I put a request in to Drake for security footage of the park to see if we can get an image of Felicity to run through the Ministry's database," Fionna said. "That should keep him happy for a while. Unfortunately, I've noticed the Luctari tend to stay in areas of the park where there are fewer security cams."

Ann watched her friend, glad to see that some of the tension had left her face during the ride from the Ministry, but the agent's chilled expression suggested caution.

"A coincidence, I'm sure," Ann said with a note of sarcasm, hoping to defrost the air between them.

Fionna gave Ann a blank look without comment and continued walking toward the camp. Ann cringed. *I suppose I deserve that,* she thought.

"Stay on alert," Fionna said. "We've had reports of Luctari carrying weapons in the camp."

The Luctari milling around watched the pair as they entered camp and then went about their chores. Children wearing brightly colored smocks and short pants darted between tents or helped prepare the evening meal over communal campfires.

Ann and Fionna were only a few paces past the first cluster of tents when a man wearing a goat mask, black cargo pants, and a short-sleeve shirt blocked their path, arms crossed. Thick forearms formed an impenetrable wall between intruders and the rest of the camp.

Ann's muscles tensed. She'd heard about the strange animal masks worn by Luctari security, and the man's goat mask appeared no less menacing. Horns sprouted from the top of the goat's head and curled backward, coming full circle until the points ended level with the side of the mask's face. Yellow bloodshot eyes and a grimacing goat mouth looked down on the visitors. Ann focused her senses. A quick search for energy weapons showed the Goat Man wasn't carrying an ion pistol. It didn't mean the guard was unarmed, but the thought of the pistol on her own hip gave Ann some comfort.

Fionna, unmoved by the Goat Man's appearance, stopped a few feet in front of the guard and gave a peaceful smile. "We're here to see the Reverend. Is he available?"

"Is that Fionna Knox I hear?"

A fat man in a sky-blue suit stepped into view from a nearby tent.

"Yes, I'm available." The reverend's cheeks bunched into a smile. "Nice to see you again, Agent Knox." The man's amber eyes found Ann. "You have a partner with you today. I don't believe we've met. I'm Jeremiah Brink."

Ann eyed the reverend. Every doughy inch of him was exactly as Sean described. In his bright blue suit, he looked like a balloon that had lost its string.

Fionna gestured to Ann and made introductions. "This is Lieutenant Anaya Chapman."

"*Anaya* Chapman?" A shade passed over Brink's face before his smile returned. The man extended a thick-fingered hand. The touch of the reverend's hand in hers made Ann's insides squirm. "I'm acquainted with your brother, the Montressador."

Ann's discomfort grew. "Yes, he mentioned you had met."

"How nice." Brink grinned in earnest, but Ann thought she caught a glint of something false in his pearly smile. "Please give him my regards." Brink turned to Fionna. "What can I do for you today, Agent Knox?"

"We have some questions for one of your followers," Fionna said. "A dancing girl named Felicity. Is she in camp today?"

Brink thought a moment and tapped a knuckle to his double chin, making his neck fat wobble. "It's possible." He looked up sideways at the Goat Man. The guard lifted one broad shoulder in a half shrug.

The reverend looked back to Fionna. "The faithful are free to come and go as they please, but we could stop by the tent where Felicity usually stays when she's in fellowship with us. I'm happy to walk you through camp. We'll look together."

"Thank you, Reverend. That would be very helpful."

Brink made a sweeping gesture with one arm and motioned for Fionna to join him. The agent exchanged looks with Ann before stepping to the reverend's side.

Fionna and Brink made small talk as they strolled ahead with the reverend doing most of the talking. Ann walked behind only half listening to Brink's chatter as she took in her surroundings. The tents grew closer together in this section of the camp. Plenty of places for Felicity to hide and not much room to run if the situation turned into a foot race. Ann gave a nervous look over a shoulder to the Goat Man a few paces behind her. The guard responded by cracking his knuckles against the open palm of his opposite hand. Ann cringed and faced forward again. The fingers of her pistol hand tingled as they brushed past the weapon's power cell. Ann breathed through the tension. *Take it easy, Lieutenant.*

The back of Ann's neck prickled as her senses caught a familiar wooden sound scratching out a hollow rhythm.

Long, short, short, long, short.

Ann slowed her step as she sharpened her senses, searching for the energy source. The prickles spread from her neck, crept across her shoulders and down her arms as the rhythm repeated. The sound came from energies emanating from a nearby tent. Ann's eyes widened.

Directional anchors.

Ann took a step toward the tent entrance.

A hand like a meat hook clamped down on her shoulder and jerked her backward into a wall of muscle. A thick forearm encircled Ann's neck, choking the cry for help in her throat. Fionna and Brink continued walking down the row of tents.

Ann threw an elbow into the Goat Man's sternum. The guard grunted and tightened his grip. She reached for her pistol, but before Ann could draw the weapon the Goat grabbed her hand, crushing her fingers against the pistol grip. The bones in her hand screamed as the guard continued to squeeze.

Ann groaned in pain. A surge of energy from the pistol's power cell danced across her palm. She focused her will, drawing in more energy until the arcs edged up past her elbow. She let loose with a back kick to the guard's knee. The guard's kneecap cracked under the sole of her boot. The Goat hollered, staggered backward, and released her hand. Ann dropped her weight, ducking under the man's arm. She turned and delivered a blow with the heel of her hand into the guard's chest. The energy gathered under her skin released on contact.

The force of the shock hit the Goat Man like a galactic shuttle. His body snapped, arms outstretched. He flew backward and landed in the dirt. Shouts rang out as Fionna came running, weapon drawn.

"I'm terribly sorry, Agent Knox!" Reverend Brink puffed behind the agent, face blank with shock. I don't know what came over him!"

Fionna ignored him and looked to Ann. "What happened?"

Ann sucked air, hands on knees, and pointed to the tent. "Directional anchors!"

Fionna jerked her head. "Go!"

Ann ducked inside the tent. A lantern hung from the center pole and cast a yellow light over a sleeping form under a cover of ratty blankets on the floor. The wooden scratching of the directional anchors came from a pile of belongings in the far corner.

Ann drew her pistol, wincing as her bruised fingers found the safety, and whipped back the covers.

A young man looked over a bare shoulder and rubbed the sleep from his eyes.

"Hey! What are you...?" His eyes widened at the sight of Ann's pistol and raised his hands. "Whoa! Whoa! Take it easy!"

"Don't move!" Ann gripped her pistol tighter, wincing again from her sore fingers.

Fionna entered the tent, weapon in hand. "I'll keep an eye on him." Ann stepped aside. The agent looked down at the man lying under the covers. "Stand up and keep your hands where I can see them."

The young man climbed to his feet. Ann and Fionna traded looks as the man stared down at the dancer's gold bandeau top stretched tight across his hairy chest. A matching short skirt clung to his hips.

"Whoa..." The young man smirked and ran a hand through his sandy blond hair. "I guess things got a little crazy last night."

Fionna blew out a sigh. "What's your name?"

"My friends call me Weed." Fionna raised an eyebrow. The man stammered, "You can call me Weed, too. I guess everyone calls me that." Weed shivered and hoisted the skirt higher on his hips then quickly lowered it a fraction when he saw the startled looks on the women's faces. "Sorry. Um...Could I have a blanket? I'm cold."

Fionna narrowed her eyes. "No. If you're cold you'll cooperate and then we'll be out of here faster." She looked to Ann. "Lieutenant, any luck?"

Ann holstered her pistol and searched the pile of belongings. Within seconds, she found a half dozen directional anchors buried in the bottom of a leather knapsack. Ann looked at Weed and held up the bag. "Is this yours?"

"No."

Ann's brows shot up in surprise. "This is your tent, isn't it?"

"Pffft!" Weed pulled a face. "No, I just sleep here."

Fionna watched Weed through her yellow bio-vision glasses. She looked at Ann, nodded her head, and holstered her pistol.

Ann sighed and pressed on. "Okay, so if it's not your stuff, then whose is it?"

With Fionna's pistol out of sight, Weed relaxed his stance, almost losing the grip on his skirt. He jerked a thumb toward a vapor stick on a low table next to his bed. "You mind?"

Ann rolled her eyes. "Fine."

Weed took a drag from the cylinder and closed his eyes. He blew out vapor and turned sleepy, red-rimmed eyes to Ann. "All that stuff over there," Weed said, waving his hand in the direction of the pile. "That's Felicity's. She said I could borrow it until she got back."

"Where did she go?"

"Pfft! Do I look like I know?" Weed ran a hand through his disheveled hair. "I don't even know what day it is." He coughed and put the vapor stick to his lips. "She said she had to take off for a while."

Ann glanced to Fionna and back to Weed. "Did she say why?"

Weed scratched his belly and muttered around the vapor stick in his mouth. "She didn't say. I didn't ask. It's not like anyone does roll call around here." Weed shivered again and snatched the cylinder from his lips. "Great, now I gotta pee! Are we done?"

"Not yet." Fionna's peaceful smile returned as she pulled her data pad from her jacket pocket. "I think Agent Drake might want to talk to you."

Ann watched as ministry agents loaded Weed and the hobbling Goat Man into a ministry transport vehicle. Other agents carried Felicity's few belongings from the tent.

Reverend Brink fidgeted between Ann and Fionna. "Lieutenant Chapman, please accept my apologies for the miscommunication with my guard. Security has instructions not to allow outsiders inside the tents without an escort. I hope my guard didn't hurt your hand too badly."

Ann flexed her bruised fingers and did her best to keep the pain from reading on her face. "Next time I have a miscommunication with your guard he'll lose more than his kneecap." Ann kept her tone neutral without a trace of humor or malice.

Brink contemplated the threat level of Ann's statement then turned to Fionna. "Agent Knox, I don't want this unfortunate incident to damage our relationship with the Ministry."

"That depends on how you cooperate moving forward, Reverend," Fionna said. Ann noticed with some amusement the agent had returned her data pad to a jacket pocket and now scribbled her notes by hand in her paper notebook. "Your guard is being charged with assault. We're taking Weed to the Ministry for further questioning. He said he last spoke to Felicity at a midnight rally, but he wasn't sure how long ago that was."

Brink let out a sigh that felt overly dramatic from Ann's point of view. "Brother Weed never knows how long he's been asleep when he wakes up. The rally was last night."

Fionna checked her notes. "We talked to your other guards. No one has seen Felicity since last night and no one knows where she went. Did Felicity have any family nearby? Any friends outside of camp she might stay with?"

"I don't know. I'm afraid I don't really concern myself with where my followers go when they're not in camp."

"I'll need the names of everyone Felicity associated with in camp," Fionna said. "The Ministry is confiscating her belongings and the directional anchors we found in the tent. Any idea where she got them?"

Brink shook his head and wrung his hands. "I wish I knew. I fear Felicity may have strayed from the faith. From what you've told me about those directional anchors, just possessing them is forbidden by the tenets of our faith."

Ann eyed the reverend. "I thought the Luctari only objected to time jumping? The directional anchors only fold spacetime—not redirect it."

"The end result is the same. Nature's laws are turned inside out," Brink said. "All the more reason for the Republic to give up this ridiculous notion of being the stewards of time. We've seen the toll on Andarrian lives for hundreds of years and now a serial killer walks among us. Nature will not be mocked, Lieutenant. We reap what we sow."

Ann's eyes widened. "You think the killer was sent to punish time jumpers?"

Brink dismissed her with a wave of his hand. "I was speaking metaphorically. But in a way...yes. Evil always befalls evildoers. The Luctari know this and we look forward to a day of reckoning."

Fionna looked up from her notepad, stunned by the reverend's admission. "Do you realize that you just put every one of your followers on my suspect list?"

"The Luctari believe in non-violent resistance to time jumping," Brink said. "I'm confident that whoever the killer is, he or she is not Luctari."

Ann smirked. "Then how do you explain Felicity's involvement?"

"I can't," Brink said, narrowing his gaze in Ann's direction. "It's possible she's left the faith or was deceived and taken advantage of by the killer. The Luctari will either excommunicate her or bring her back into fellowship and see she's disciplined."

"The *Ministry* will deal with Felicity when we find her," Fionna said, clipping her pen to the notepad. "Contact me immediately if you hear from her. Goodnight, Reverend."

The lamps of the Luctari encampment flickered to life in the growing twilight behind them as Ann and Fionna walked back to the hovercar at the edge of the park.

Ann looked to Fionna. "So, is Brink telling the truth? Does he really not know where Felicity is?"

"He doesn't know and he really does want to find her." Fionna frowned. "But not for the same reasons we do."

"Is it because he's worried she's left the Luctari for good?"

"No, he seems more concerned about how her involvement will affect the image of the group," Fionna said. "I think Brink would almost prefer it if Felicity left the Luctari because then he could say she was no longer one of them. He wants to find her for a different reason. He's not telling us something, but I don't know what."

The hovercar sensed the agent's approach and powered up its running lights. Fionna activated the driver's door and slid behind the wheel.

Ann climbed into the passenger seat. "Did it feel like Brink knew we were coming?"

"Your friend the Goat Man certainly appeared in a hurry. It's possible someone tipped them off." Fionna glanced in Ann's direction and saw the look on her face. "But I don't think it was Lieutenant Stravage if that's what you're worried about."

"That's what Drake will think."

"So maybe we don't tell Agent Drake about that part."

Ann threw Fionna a questioning look.

"We gave Drake Weed and the Goat to question," Fionna said. "That should keep him busy for a while. We need to find Felicity before Brink does." She threw the hovercar into reverse then put it in park again, drumming her fingers on the steering wheel deep in thought. "The Luctari come and go from the camp all the time. Most of them have places where they hole up outside the park. Did you notice anything about Felicity's stuff we found? Anything that might tell us where she went?"

Ann thought for a moment, remembering the bags of clothes she searched through when looking for the directional anchors. "There wasn't much there. Only a few days-worth of dancing outfits." An idea sparked in Ann's head. "She needs new clothes. That's why she left them. She would be too recognizable dressed as a Luctari."

Fionna looked at Ann. "You're a time jumper. What else besides clothes would you need to blend in?"

"Money. Food. Weapons. Transportation." Ann listed off the possibilities she and John had discussed when they made a plan to capture Moondarra. "New identification in case you're stopped by the authorities."

Fionna's mouth spread into a peaceful smile, the first one she'd given Ann since they left the Ministry.

Ann returned a grin. "There are plenty of shops and residential buildings around here. Someone might have spotted her."

"Not to mention a few side businesses with sketchy reputations," Fionna added, throwing the hovercar in reverse. "We have time to kill while we wait for the cam footage from the park." Fionna traded her peaceful smile for a fierce grin as she eased the car into the stream of traffic. "Let's go hunting."

TWENTY-THREE
PICK UP AND DELIVERY

The Flokete Nebula spread across the black sky like a pink and green ink blot, pushing the other stars to the opposite pole and casting an eerie twilight over the arid plain below. John stood at the bottom of the entrance ramp to the cargo hold of his ship. He leaned against a metal strut and watched the night sky, listening for the sound of engines over the whisper of the ventilator mask strapped across the lower half of his face.

The oxygen-rich mixture of the mask supplemented the moon's thin atmosphere and made John's thoughts dance like a boxer in a ring, inevitably drifting back to Ann as they so often did of late. His worry for her flared again. The mission report for Dieva Roka had put the immediate concern to rest but it didn't solve the underlying problem. He needed to talk to her—preferably in person and not in disjointed half-sentence texting through the data link pad—but Ann's duties with Agent Knox and his responsibilities had kept that from happening. John blew out a sigh and wrestled his thoughts back to the task at hand.

John scanned the scrub brush and short grass just outside of the glow of his ship's running lights. *The Eyes in the Dark.* The back of his neck prickled. John stretched a shoulder and went back to watching the sky.

A sonic boom and the roar of engines split open the sky as a smuggler's runabout dropped out of warp. John shielded his eyes and squinted in the glare of the ship's searchlight. The runabout circled, its light sweeping the sand and scrub brush of the desert floor. The small craft touched down a few yards away, kicking up a spray of sand and blowing John's long black coat behind him.

The searchlight cut. Engines dropped to a whine. The runabout's forward hatch yawned, spilling interior light, as a figure moved cautiously down the ramp. A shadow stretched across the sand toward John and then the short, round Grandk merchant from the black-market fun fair stepped into view.

"I got a delivery for Disko. That you?"

John made a face under the mask. "Yeah." The old nickname came with its own baggage, but it made more sense than giving the merchant his real name.

"Take off the ventilator," Chabot said. "I wanna see your face."

John pulled a strap on one side of his face and let the mask hang free. The Grandk merchant peered at him through the glow of the ship's running lights. John counted the seconds. The barren atmosphere stole his strength with every breath. Chabot finally nodded approval. John snapped the side of the ventilator back into place and sucked air. He noticed the Grandk didn't wear a breathing device. *Oxygenated little bastard.*

Chabot rubbed a thumb over his fingertips. "You got the money?"

John grabbed two canvas bags from the top of the cargo ramp and lifted them so Chabot could see.

Chabot's pink face broke into a wide grin. He called over a shoulder. "BRING 'EM OUT!"

Two Grandk crewmen appeared at the top of the ramp carrying a large metal case between anti-gravity clamps. Chabot walked toward a patch of sand midway between the two ships. The crewmen sidestepped down the ramp and hurried forward, dodging scrub brush, dropped the case where Chabot pointed then turned and darted back up the ramp. John met the Grandk in the middle, carrying the canvas bags.

Chabot hooked a thumb into his wide leather belt. "Let's see it."

"Fifty thousand," John said, pulling open the bags. "And another fifty for the rush job."

"Beautiful," Chabot said and nodded to his crewman.

John opened the metal case and did a quick scan of its contents. Satisfied, he eyed the crewmen as they dropped off another case and hurried back up the ramp.

"I need the cases in the cargo hold," John said, jerking a thumb over a shoulder.

"Sorry, pal. We deliver. You load." Chabot reached to pick up one of the bags. "If you wanted better service, you should have sprung for the gold package."

John pulled a pistol from under his coat and leveled it at the Grandk's head. Chabot froze.

"I think that extra fifty qualifies me for the gold package. Don't you?"

Chabot studied the glint on the laser pistol's barrel then hollered over a shoulder to his crew. "HEY, YOU PROKS! LOAD 'EM UP AND MAKE IT FAST!" He looked back at John. Not an ounce of concern weighed on the merchant's face. "You happy now?"

John holstered the weapon and let his coat sweep forward. "Bloody ecstatic."

The Grandk crew worked double-time loading John's ship. It wasn't long before they trundled forward carrying the last of the ten cases.

John did a quick scan of the scrub brush surrounding the two ships. The prickle on the back of his neck began a slow march down his spine. John blew out a slow breath. *Any second now.*

"Thanks for these," Chabot said, shouldering the two bags of money. "Call me when you need another delivery."

John nodded and turned to watch as the Grandk crewmen exited the cargo ramp and headed back to their ship.

Chabot raised a fist and hollered to his crew. "WE'RE OUT!"

The green blast from a laser rifle slammed between John's shoulder blades. The pain tore a yell from his throat as the force knocked him to the ground. Energy from the blast dispersed over the dialectic vest under John's shirt. His limbs jerked in wild spasms.

Chabot spun at the sound of the blast, eyes round with fear. Laser fire pierced the air from all directions. The Grandk and his crew ducked and tried to make a run for their ship but dropped one by one under the hail of laser bolts.

Silence.

John panted to catch his breath, his limbs numb. He strained his eyes to see past the edge of light into the scrub brush beyond.

A clump of tall grass moved. Then another. A dozen figures wearing camouflage suits and carrying rifles stood. Andarrian Intelligence's elite tactical team, *The Eyes in the Dark,* stepped from the shadows. John closed his eyes and grinned under his ventilator mask.

Red tile.
Black tile.
Red tile.
Black tile.

John watched the floor tiles slip down the hallway past his boots as the two guards dragged him backward across the floor. It was difficult to see with one eye covered, but John knew what he looked like. Clothes torn and spattered with blood. Dark purple bruises rising from exposed skin. The dried blood on his face itched like a hive of hiekka flies. John caught the smell of burnt flesh and ozone reminiscent of laser fire and started to count the number of times he'd been dragged down a hallway in such a state over the years.

Focus. You've got a job to do, idiot.

One of the guards muttered, "Almost there."

John let his head droop to his chest in response.

A few more paces and the guards stopped. John heard the sound of a key grinding in a lock and the squeal of a door hinge. The guards dragged John into a small dim room, dropped him in a corner, and left, slamming the door. John groaned and pushed himself into a sitting position, his face against the wall.

Chabot sat curled in the opposite corner. John couldn't see the Grandk's face, but he could hear the man breathing. Shallow. Uneven. Fearful.

A minute passed and then he heard Chabot shift on the hard tile floor.

"What'd they want?"

John opened his good eye to peer at the little man. The merchant looked like he'd been dragged a mile through sand and brush.

"They're looking for someone." John grimaced. His breath came out in rasps. He coughed, spat on the floor, and wiped his mouth with the back of a bloody hand. "Showed me pictures. I told them I didn't know who they were."

"The people in the pictures. What'd they look like?"

"Nothing special." John let a little fear creep into his words. "Look... I can't take another beating...and

I'm guessing it would take a lot less to kill you." He turned to Chabot and saw the Grandk stiffen. Horror blanched the merchant's features as he looked at the raw meat that was once the other side of John's face —the eye swollen shut in a field of purple flesh. Skin and muscle torn open in strips from the hairline to the jaw. "If you know anything, you should tell them. Maybe we'll get out of here alive."

A key twisted the lock, and the squeal of hinges announced a new arrival as Agent A.K. Max walked into the room followed by the two guards. A faded red slash diagonally across the intelligence man's face was all that remained of his encounter with the reaper nettles. A.K. looked at John and delivered a vicious kick into his side. John grunted and bit back a moan ripe with real pain.

The agent gave a satisfied smirk and turned his attention to Chabot. "How's your eyesight? Your crew and your friend over there weren't much help to us."

"He's not my friend!" The merchant's words raced with panic. "I...I just make deliveries. Where's my crew?"

A.K. sat on his heels to look the Grandk in the eye. A cold smile played on the agent's lips.

"You already have my money," Chabot said. "Keep it. I can get you more. Whatever you want!"

"For now, I just need a favor," A.K. said. "It's real easy. I need you to look at some pictures for us. Tell us who and what you see. Think you can do that?"

Chabot nodded until John thought the Grandk's head would fall off. "Yeah, sure! I...I want to help!"

A.K. looked over a shoulder at the two guards. "He wants to help. How nice." The agent stood and motioned to the guards. They grabbed Chabot by the arms and dragged him from the room.

John winced as a med tech peeled the silicone prosthetic of swollen flesh and blood from the side of his face in a single sheet of rubbery gore. He blinked his eye and rubbed his cheek, glad to be free of the meat patch. The med tech laid the prosthetic on a surgical tray then turned her attention to cleaning some very real lacerations on John's forehead just as A.K. entered the room.

"Ow!" John flinched under the hands of the med tech. He looked at the intelligence agent. "You know, not all of this blood is fake. Your takedown crew played a little rough. And what was that last kick for?" He gestured to a second med tech who was busy scanning the bruise already rising from his side.

A.K. shrugged and took a seat in a med tech chair across from John. "It looked like Chabot needed one more nudge."

John grunted. "Your nudge almost broke a rib."

"Almost is not broken." A.K. grinned. "The good news is it worked. Chabot gave us a whole list of new names to go with the faces. And the best one…" He pulled a data pad from a jacket pocket and handed it to John. "He named his Splice supplier. Your hunch paid off."

John looked at the picture on the screen of a man

leaving a tent and recognized the curly-haired youth he saw sitting next to Hengen Vanamo and Little Sister in the black-market beer tent. He smirked with satisfaction.

"Chabot said our friend in the picture goes by the name Torch," A.K. said. "I'm assuming that's an alias. An unimaginative one. We're checking in to it."

John handed the data pad back to A.K. "Send whatever you find out to Agent Knox at the Ministry of Investigations. Her suspect is using Splice to abduct victims."

A.K. nodded and stowed the data pad in his jacket. "How did your mission go with Lieutenant Chapman?"

"You read the report?"

"Yeah. Moondarra got away." A.K. swiveled in the med tech chair. "But I wanted to hear about what you *didn't* put in your report."

John shrugged and kept his expression neutral. "Nothing else to tell. Moondarra got away. We'll get her next time."

A.K. nodded. "How'd Ann do?"

"Not bad for our first time out."

"Good to hear. Most new teams need time to gel." A.K. swiveled his chair back to center and stood. "Nice work today. Your payment is already in your account." He reached into a jacket pocket and pulled out a crumpled paper bag. "And here's the little extra I promised. Safe travels."

Back at Siren's Cove John's boots struck the master

bedroom floor as green light from the time beacon faded into nothing. Mrs. Beaumont caught him as he walked down the stairs into the sitting room.

"Oh, good. You're back." The cook glanced at the gold watch in her hand and shook her head, still puzzled by the three watch faces, and tucked the device in an apron pocket. "Captain, I need to talk to you about this favor you needed."

"Here's that fancy oil you wanted." He handed Mrs. Beaumont the crumpled bag as he walked past into the kitchen. "There a problem?"

"Well...yes. A big problem." Mrs. Beaumont followed him into the kitchen. She opened the bag and pulled out a bottle of Dojinian white truffle oil. The cook admired the bottle and set it on the counter before turning back to John. "That suit of yours. I'm not sure alterations will improve it. Did you know there's a laser pistol burn on one arm?"

John grabbed a plate of ham and cheese from the cooler and two slices of bread from the cutting board. He frowned in thought as he stacked meat and cheese. "I forgot about that. Gee Orona shot me while we were playing cards. Thought I was cheating." John grinned. "I was. Lucky for me, she was always a lousy shot when drunk." He shook his head. "No matter. The suit was only a backup plan in case I couldn't make it back in time to buy a new one." He took a bite of sandwich.

"Backup plan?" The cook's face twisted around an irritating thought. "Your *backup* plan was a twelve-year-old suit?" She snorted and crossed her arms.

"If your planning skills are no better than that, it's a wonder you survived all your galivanting around with those freighter pirates. Why don't you wear your uniform to the wedding?"

John glowered over his sandwich and finished chewing. "Because I know Sean and Commander Lazar will be in uniform and I don't want to look like I'm posing for a recruitment poster when I stand next to them." He shrugged a shoulder. "I'm back now. I'll buy a new suit." He took another bite of sandwich.

Mrs. Beaumont smirked. "Men and their vanity. Have it your way." She turned on her heel with a wave of her hand. "You better get on it. The commander's wedding is in two days!"

TWENTY-FOUR

THE WATCHER

The Scholars.
The Teacher.
The Worker.
The Friend.
The Watcher...Watcher...Watcher...

Sean pushed back from the comm screen and rubbed his eyes. Drawing his blade on the hecklers at the East Gate triggered an inquiry from the Park Conservancy and produced vomitus streams of information requests that flooded Jo's office communication channels and clogged their to-do list. Sean wondered if disemboweling the men outright would have required less paperwork—the most convincing argument for legalizing murder he'd ever heard. Even more irritating, the inquiry had also kept him from reviewing Fionna's sword investigation notes. Until now...

Twenty background checks, files full of corresponding documents, and seventy-two hours of security footage later, Sean was ready to eat his own blade. He'd spent most of the evening in his office at

Montressador's Keep trying to find some connection to the Luctari's statement, but nothing in the agent's notes offered any hints as to who the Watcher might be.

Sean leaned into the glow of the comm screen and watched the flickering image of the empty museum gallery as the comm fast-forwarded through security footage. The comm was programmed to freeze the image when motion was detected on the screen. He began the evening by watching footage from the night tour before moving on to the more mundane sections.

The night tour had been uneventful just as Fionna described except for the student who leaned awkwardly over one of the exhibit pedestals. The student was immediately reprimanded by the tour guide. The exhibit, Sean noted, was a bronze statue of Montressador Syrovar standing on the rocky banks of the Goulburn. The peaceful scene was meant to depict the moment before Syrovar crossed the river to commit bloody acts and seal her dark place in history. The incident between the tour guide and the student, however, lasted no more than a second and was hardly worth the footnote in Fionna's files.

Sean tapped the resume key. He yawned as he watched Gimirri make his rounds followed by a parade of day tour groups. Occasionally, a nose-picking security guard strolled through the screen. Sean sighed as the image sped on. Syrovar's gallery didn't get many visitors. Maybe the Luctari's ramblings were just that and nothing more?

A soft knock on the office door drew his attention. Jo stepped into the room carrying Sean's black dress uniform.

"Your uniform is back from the tailor." Jo hung the jacket and trousers on a convenient peg and took out a garment brush. "The dielectric vest is sewn into the jacket's lining. You'll notice the weight change, but it won't restrict your movement. I also spoke to Mr. Gimirri. He said you can stop by the day of the wedding and the museum's restoration team will polish your sword. Don't forget. You'll want to give yourself enough time to get to the wedding."

Sean grunted as he glanced over the comm at his uniform. Covered in medals and braids, the jacket looked like a diarrhetic bird shat silver all over it. The comm screen froze and showed a pack of school-children flooding the gallery. Sean tapped the resume key. "Are you expecting a lot of shooting at Commander Lazar's wedding?"

Jo swept away a few stray threads with a quick touch of the brush. "Just don't stand next to the bride."

Sean snorted. Apparently, Marina's reputation proceeded her. Poor Vincent. If he hadn't backed out of the marriage by now, Sean doubted he ever would.

Jo finished brushing the jacket and stepped back to examine her work, hand on her hip.

Sean watched the screen as the school kids filed out of the gallery. "Have you thought any more about my invitation?"

"Yes." Jo picked a final thread from the jacket then looked over a shoulder. "I will accompany you to Commander Lazar's wedding as your date...assuming our standard agreement is in play?"

"New dress and the day off to get ready. Anything else?" The comm froze again as an inquisitive spider landed on the lens blocking the screen. Sean clicked to another angle and tapped resume.

"Two days off. The second day will be my choice."

"Done. Send me the bill." The screen froze. Sean made a face. The nose picker was back.

Jo tucked the garment brush in a pocket and looked at the thick report on the edge of Sean's desk. "Did you review the Padome's progress report yet?"

Sean grumbled. "A bit optimistic to call it a *progress* report."

The Padome's steward delivered the report that afternoon. The council could not yet offer concrete proof as to why Montressador Syrovar murdered the nobles, but the report did offer several possible theories along with a few outrageous conspiracies and reams of data.

"I thought you asked the council to research the murders because you wanted them to feel useful," Jo said, picking up the report. "Not because you actually cared about the outcome?"

"I care," Sean said, protesting. "It won't help us find the sword, but I guess I still wanted them to find something. A lead. Anything. I don't know." Sean sighed. "I lost hope when I got to the section on plagues and weather patterns."

Jo flipped through pages in the report and rested the curve of a hip on the edge of the Montressador's desk. "They are very thorough. The part on royal infidelity was interesting."

"A queen diddling a duke usually is but hardly unheard of." The image on the comm froze. Sean looked at the screen but saw nothing in the frame. *The damn spider must be back.* He reversed a couple seconds and then resumed the image at normal speed.

Sean's heart jumped. Something—*a shadow?*—slid across the gallery floor and disappeared under one of the exhibit pedestals. He tapped the keys to view the reversed angle. *Probably a mouse.* Sean smirked, imagining the museum curator's reaction to the news of rodents in the gallery.

Jo returned the Padome's report to the desk. "Do you think you'll be much longer? I can stay if you need me to."

There it is again. Sean's heart rate picked up speed. Not a shadow. Not a mouse. He watched the reverse angle again to be sure. An object darted out from under the portrait's floor-length curtain and shot across the gallery floor. Sean checked the date of the footage. It was recorded the night before the sword was reported stolen. Fionna hadn't mentioned in her notes about finding anything at the scene. Whatever it was might still be in the gallery.

"Neither one of us have had dinner...." Jo said. "I could order us something..."

Sean pushed back his chair and stood, eyes glued to the comm screen. "I was just finishing up. I think

I'll stop by the museum on my way home." No sense mentioning anything to Fionna until he knew for sure. Less embarrassing in case he was wrong.

Jo jumped to her feet. "All right. Have a good night, Sir."

"Good night, Jo." Sean glanced at his assistant as she turned and walked to the office door. The hem of her fitted skirt brushed the back of her knees with every step. *Wait a minute.* He snapped his head in Jo's direction as the door closed behind her. *Did she just invite me to dinner?* Sean gulped. Guilt tweaked his insides. *She couldn't have. Not Jo.* Sean shook it off. There was no time to dwell on it. He had to get to the museum.

Sean struck out along the footpath from Montressador's Keep through the Wilds of the park. Gimirri wouldn't be happy with an interruption this late in the evening, but if there was a chance that whatever Sean saw on the comm screen was still in the gallery it would be worth the snide remarks from the museum curator. Sean trotted along the forest path. His sword belt rang in time with the crunch of boots as he took the turn toward the National Museum.

Light from the lamp posts at the edge of the forest glowed like pearls in the gathering mist. Frogs singing in a nearby culvert—the mist a delightful addition to their lovemaking—fell silent at the swordsman's approach then renewed their chorus after the intruder passed. Sean listened to the chirps and croaks, the crunch of boots, and the jangle of his sword belt as he walked and underneath it all... Sean slowed his step.

Crying?

Sean's pulse quickened. A woman wept softly in the darkness.

"Hello? Who's there?"

The wailing stopped then began again. Louder. More urgent.

Sean took a few steps off the path, muscles tensed. One hand rested on the hilt of his sword as he gauged the direction.

"Are you hurt?" Broken sounds of despair came from the culvert.

Sean plunged into the ditch. Water trickled through the mud enough to make his boots squish and sucked at the bottom of his soles with every step. Frogs scattered. The stench of decay filled his nose as he splashed through the puddles. The rushes grew thicker along with the sound of running water.

The lamplight on the path behind him faded as another came into view. Sean pushed through the cattails and cursed under his breath. A woman covered in filth lay bound and gagged among the reeds near a rusted sewer drain. Arms twisted behind her back. Tears streaked her muddy face. The uniform crew patch on her shoulder was barely visible under the mud in the light of the nearby lamp post. Lieutenant Sarolea Picquet lifted her head from the muck. Her eyes widened at the sight of the swordsman. Terror shattered her features as she forced a muffled scream through the gag in her mouth.

"Sarolea?" The woman continued to scream and struggle against her bonds. Sean raised his hands and took a cautious step forward. "It's me! Anaya's brother!"

The terror left Sarolea's eyes as she sunk back into the mud, gasping. Sobs of relief racked her frame.

Sean fell to his knees. The metal brace encasing Sarolea's ghost arm had frozen in place. Electrical wires sprouted from the mechanism like wire brushes. Sean removed the arm brace. His hands shook as he struggled to unbuckle the gag from Sarolea's head and cut the bonds from her wrists and ankles. The disbelief at finding her alive whirled in Sean's head even as anger burned at the sight of a broken tooth and raw flesh where the straps had cut across her skin.

Free of the gag, Sarolea sucked in a breath. She struggled to form the words and they came out of her mouth as raspy as a metal file. "They're dead! They're all dead!" She collapsed against Sean's shoulder. Her body shook with the memory. Sean held tight as Sarolea wept like a child in his arms.

"It's okay. You're safe now." He patted her back and scanned their surroundings.

Water from the culvert continued its slow trickle, spilling through the rusted grate. Echoes splashed from the pipe below. Past the drain, a wooden footbridge suggested they weren't far from a path, but the rushes at the top of the culvert blocked the view of the road. Sean cocked an ear. The frogs had stopped singing. Not surprising given all the noise he'd made tramping through the ditch, but the two had sat quietly for several minutes while Sarolea composed herself and still...no frogs. Sean's instincts prickled.

"We should get out of here." He moved to stand. "Can you walk?"

Sarolea lifted her head from his shoulder. "I...I think so..."

Sean put an arm around Sarolea's waist and helped her stand on shaky legs.

Movement. His eyes flashed to the shadows under the footbridge. The silhouette of a man crouched under the support beams. Sean moved his sword hand into position and stepped between Sarolea and the threat. Captain Wahler's warning about the gunman at the East Gate raced back to him and on its heels the knowledge he had left his uniform jacket, the one with the dielectric vest, at Montressador's Keep. Sean gritted his teeth and pulled his blade a couple inches from its sheath.

A white spotlight from above burned across Sean's retinas. He swore and squeezed his eyes shut.

"PUT YOUR HANDS UP AND STEP AWAY FROM THE WOMAN!" The voice came from somewhere beyond the spotlight.

Sarolea buried her face into the back of Sean's shirt. He did as the voice commanded and took a cautious peek between his fingers as he raised his hands. The man under the bridge was gone.

Sean growled in irritation. "All right! You caught me!" He jerked his face away from the glare.

"WOULD YOU GET THAT DAMN LIGHT OUT OF MY FACE?"

The spotlight wattage dimmed. Sean blinked to clear his vision and two gunmen on either side of the culvert, rifles drawn, came into focus. A third man stepped from the reeds, a fully charged ion pistol pointed at Sean's head. Sean relaxed when he recognized the field jacket worn by Ministry of Investigations agents.

Great. Assholes with guns.

Agent Trigger Finger barked out the order again. "I told you to step away from the woman!"

Sarolea clung tighter to Sean's back.

He whispered over a shoulder, "It's okay. I'm not going anywhere." Sean turned to the agent, careful to keep his hands in plain sight. "I'm Montressador Sean Chapman." He did his best to project authority or at least as much authority as one can while standing in a ditch and covered in mud. "This is Lieutenant Sarolea Picquet." Surprised blanched the agent's face. "She needs a medical transport. Do you think you can handle that, Trigger?"

Armed Ministry agents escorted them from the culvert to a team of rapid response vehicles waiting near the bridge on the road above. Agent Trigger Finger took Sarolea to a support vehicle to wait for medical transport while Sean, followed by another agent, walked behind.

As the group drew closer, Senior Agent Evan Drake wearing his customary sneer and funeral black stepped from a Ministry car. For the first time in memory, Sean was glad to see his old rival. Drake, despite his personality flaws, could cut through procedures and get Sarolea the help she needed.

"Agent Drake." Sean nodded in greeting.

"Montressador Chapman." The agent barely acknowledged him then sneered as he passed. "You look and smell like something that came out of a goose's ass."

Sean smirked. *Nice to see you too, jackass.* He started to reply but instead sniffed his shirt and pulled a face. Drake was right about one thing. The smell from the ditch now covered him from head to toe.

Sean fell into step behind Drake and walked to where Sarolea sat in the passenger seat of a support vehicle attended to by another agent.

"He killed my friends." She took a swig from a water bottle and clutched a blanket around her shoulders. Her short, matted hair framed her round face. "He had a sword."

Sean drew in a breath and stepped closer. The agent asking questions glanced from Sarolea to the sword resting on Sean's hip.

She caught the agent looking and snapped, "Don't be an idiot! Montressador Chapman *found* me. The killer is someone else." The water bottle trembled in her hands.

The agent sensed he was quickly losing control of the interview and looked to Agent Drake for help.

The senior agent sighed and pulled a data pad from a jacket pocket. "What did the sword look like?"

Sarolea's face paled. "It was a sword. It had a pointy end and a handle."

Sean stepped closer and leaned against the car door frame. "Sarolea...I'm sorry. We wouldn't ask you if it wasn't important. Can you remember anything about the sword?"

She pressed her lips together. The muscles in her jaw tensed as she wrestled with dark memories. "There were gold leaves on the hilt."

Sean traded looks with Drake. The senior agent turned back to Sarolea. "You're certain?"

Tears flooded her eyes. "Yes." Sarolea wrapped the blanket tighter around her shoulders and shivered. "Don't ask me again."

Sean took a few steps back from the car and motioned for Drake to follow. "That sounds like Syrovar's sword. The grape leaf design on the guard is hard to miss."

Drake nodded and updated the data pad. His lip curled. "Too bad. I would have loved an excuse to confiscate that blade of yours as evidence."

Sean returned the agent's glare and rested a hand on the hilt of his sword. "Any time you think you can take it from me..."

Another ministry vehicle arrived followed by a medical transport. Before the car reached a complete stop, Ann darted from the passenger door and ran to Sarolea followed by Fionna. Ann consoled her friend then stepped back to make room for the med techs.

"You forget." Drake's eyes narrowed. "I bested you once, Montressador. Are you asking for a rematch?"

"Sure." Sean flashed a wicked grin. "What do *you* have to lose?"

The agent's face reddened, eyes black with fury, but said nothing more.

Ann joined Fionna and walked toward Drake. The women looked surprised to see Sean standing with the senior agent and even more surprised to see him covered in mud. Sean knew the exact moment they were close enough to smell the stench wafting from his clothes. The odor hit them like they'd walked into a pane of glass.

"Montressador Chapman...?" Agent Knox coughed and tried not to wrinkle her nose.

Sean sighed. "It's okay. I know I smell..."

"You *and* Sarolea," Ann said, hand to her nose. "Like a sewer."

Sean shot his sister a dark look.

Fionna gave an apologetic smile and took a step back to a more breathable distance. "So, *you* found Lieutenant Picquet? We saw the report come over the comm."

Sean quickly explained how he found Sarolea while walking to the museum from Montressador's Keep.

"And..." Sean said, looking to Fionna. "The killer has Syrovar's sword." Fionna's pale brows arched in surprise under her bio-vision glasses. "Sarolea saw it. She said it had gold leaves on the hilt." Sean shook his head. "It has to be the same sword."

Drake ticked a note in his data pad. "I can believe you just happened to be walking by when you heard

Lieutenant Picquet crying in the culvert, Montressador, but why were you going to the museum this time of night?"

Sean shrugged. He didn't think Fionna wanted Drake to know he had access to her case notes, but the senior agent was busy looking at his data pad, so he chanced a meaningful look in Fionna's direction. "I was following up on some *paperwork.*"

Comprehension flicked across Fionna's face. She turned to watch the med techs with Sarolea. "Nice to see our nanobot tracker worked."

"The tracking system needs fine-tuning to narrow down the search area, else we would have gotten to Picquet sooner," Drake said. "But yes. It worked. The tracker picked up the nanobot swarm within a few minutes of her phasing."

Fionna eyed the senior agent. "Did the techs find the directional anchor?"

"Not yet." Drake smirked in Sean's direction. "There's a lot of mud down there to search through."

Sean sighed and rolled his eyes. *Yes, I'm disgusting. I'm an affront to other living things. I get it.*

Ann looked at her brother. "Did Sarolea say why the killer let her go?"

"No. I don't think she's ready to talk about it."

Drake looked up from his data pad. "Knox, any luck finding the Luctari dancer?"

"Lieutenant Chapman and I are searching the area surrounding the park," Fionna said. "No solid leads yet."

Sean's ears perked up. "What dancer?"

"She's in the park a lot," Ann said. "Dark hair. Curvy. Clingy outfits. Wears a lot of silver bangles—"

Sean blinked. "Felicity?"

Drake's and Fionna's eyes shot to Sean in surprise. Ann gave her brother a knowing look, arms crossed.

Sean flushed under his beard. "Reverend Brink threw her at me as a bribe." He saw the look on his sister's face and whispered under his breath, "*I didn't!*" Ann continued to shoot him doubtful looks. Sean gave up and turned back to Fionna. "Why are you looking for her?"

"Felicity planted a necklace containing a directional anchor in Lieutenant Picquet's duffle bag," Fionna said. "Lieutenant Stravage may have inadvertently helped."

"Stravage is facing a conspiracy charge," Drake interjected. "The extent of his involvement has yet to be determined."

Fionna sighed. "That's how the killer gained access to the *What Cheer*."

"You could save Fionna and me a lot of trouble and our sore feet if you know where Felicity is," Ann said.

"Sorry, I wish I could help." Sean shrugged and adjusted his sword belt. "I met her a few days ago at a rally in the outdoor theater. That was the last I saw of her."

The med techs helped Sarolea to the transport and got ready to leave.

Drake returned his data pad to an inside pocket. "Knox, I want you and Lieutenant Chapman to keep looking for the Luctari woman. I'll interview Picquet."

"You should take Lieutenant Chapman with you," Fionna said. Sean saw Anaya shoot the agent a look of apprehension. "Picquet's been through a lot. It might be easier if a friend leads the questioning."

Drake frowned. "How will you find Felicity?"

"Montressador Chapman knows what she looks like," Fionna said, nodding in Sean's direction. "He can help me look for her."

Drake nodded. "Fine. Lieutenant Chapman, let's go." The senior agent headed toward the transport with Ann at his heels.

Fionna called after them. "Agent Drake, does this mean Lieutenant Picquet is off the suspect list?"

Drake opened the door to the transport and narrowed his eyes at Agent Knox. "For now. Find Felicity. She's our only link to the killer."

Ann hopped into the transport next to Drake and drove off.

Fionna took a small jar from a jacket pocket and smeared clear jelly under her nose. Sean grinned. The agent took a step closer, eyes bright with curiosity. "So, what did you find out?"

The museum curator's resentful expression never changed as he waited for Montressador Chapman to sign the scroll.

"I'm not accustomed to letting Ministry agents in the museum at this time of night, Montressador, but you seem to be making a habit of it." Gimirri huffed in his blue cassock. The edge of a striped dressing gown hung a finger length below the hem of his formal museum robes.

"We wouldn't be here if it wasn't important, Gimirri." Sean scrawled his signature and handed the scroll along with the feathered quill back to the curator.

Sean had brought Fionna up to speed on his interview with the Luctari and his discovery on the security footage on the way to the National Museum. Gimirri was less than pleased to have his evening interrupted but had given them access to Syrovar's gallery without argument and with only a few snippy remarks.

"We're sorry to disturb you," Fionna said. "This shouldn't take long."

"I would hope not, Agent Knox." The curator threw one more disapproving look at Sean's muddy pants and boots and eyed the trail of flecked, dried mud left on the polished gallery floor. "You know where to find me." Gimirri left the gallery closing the brass doors behind him.

Fionna opened her data link pad and tapped the screen. "So where in the security footage did you see it?"

"The night before the sword was reported missing. Between two and three in the morning," Sean said. "It shot out from under the portrait's curtain and crossed the floor here." He pointed out the trajectory along the floor. "It's quick. I almost missed it even with help from the comm."

A moment of silence passed as Fionna searched the security footage. "I think I found it."

Sean leaned over Fionna's shoulder and watched the screen. Once again, the shadow on the data pad screen sped across the gallery floor and disappeared.

"There!" Sean pointed to the screen. "Did you see it?"

"Yes!" Fionna backed up the footage, eyes narrowed, as she watched the scene play in reverse and forward again.

"Don't tell me that's my imagination."

"It looks like a directional anchor." Fionna looked up from the screen and studied the gallery floor in front of Syrovar's portrait. "It ended up over there under that display pedestal."

Sean traced the object's path across the gallery, dropped to his knees, and swept a hand under and around the pedestal. "Nothing." Sean sighed. "Not even dust."

"My techs didn't find anything when they searched the gallery," Fionna said. "It's possible the cleaning crew swept it up and didn't realize what it was."

"Then it's gone," Sean growled and climbed to his feet. "I was really hoping we'd find something, or at least something more exciting than just a directional anchor." He shook his head. "I'm sorry I wasted your time."

Fionna gave a sympathetic smile and tucked the data pad under an arm. "You didn't. Little clues are still helpful. They're not all as dramatic as finding a missing person bound and gagged in a ditch."

Sean gave the agent an arched look and adjusted his sword belt. "How is finding, or in our case *not* finding, a directional anchor helpful? Sarolea described Syrovar's sword. Even if we found an anchor in the gallery it would only tell us what we already know—that the thief is also the killer."

"You're not thinking like an investigator," Fionna said. "We've learned a lot more than you think."

Sean threw up his hands in defeat. "Fine. Enlighten me."

Fionna crossed the gallery to the floor-to-ceiling curtain covering Syrovar's portrait and empty sword brackets and pulled it to one side. "I think what we saw *was* a directional anchor, dropped or kicked when the thief returned to steal the sword. The thief must have planted the anchor behind the curtain – days maybe a week before the theft," the agent said, examining the edge of the portrait's frame and the plaque above the sword brackets. "Any longer than that and someone might have found the anchor and removed it." Fionna judged the distance between the curtain and the empty sword brackets. "If that's true, then we know how the thief got into the museum. He appeared behind the curtain, grabbed the sword, and used another directional anchor to phase out again. That's why the thief never appeared in any of the security footage. The entire theft took no more than fifteen seconds."

"So now we know what to look for on the security footage and the timeframe we need to look." Sean relaxed his stance as he followed the agent's line of thought. "Anyone who stood that close to the portrait had an opportunity to plant the anchor."

Fionna took a step back and looked up at Syrovar's portrait, arms crossed, with one hand tucked under her chin. "A directional anchor might also be the answer to something that's nagged me from the beginning." Sean shot the agent a quizzical look. "During our initial sweep of the gallery, the chronocular picked up *two* spacetime distortions."

"I remember. You said one was faint and the other was much stronger."

"The stronger signal was by the portrait," Fionna said, gesturing to Syrovar's picture. "We searched for the source but couldn't find it. The second signal was roughly where I think your mysterious shadow may have stopped. A directional anchor could explain both signals."

"You think the anchor had enough remaining charge to be the source of the second time distortion?"

Fionna looked over a shoulder to Sean. "Seems logical enough. Without finding a directional anchor at the scene it's all theory, but I think it's a pretty good one."

Sean rested a hand on the hilt of his sword as he thought. "If it was the killer's directional anchor, then those spacetime distortions should match the same signals you found on the *What Cheer*."

"And the time jumper monument and Commander Garin's house." Fionna grinned.

Sean's brows twitched as he realized where the agent had been leading him all along.

"And that's how we prove the thief used a directional anchor even if we can't find it and then the rest of our theory makes sense," Fionna said.

"But we still don't have a motive or how Commander Garin's murder fits in to all of this."

"One thing at a time." Fionna pulled the curtain back into place, covering Syrovar's portrait. "Now that we know the thief and the killer are the same person it might start to sort some things into sense. I'll include your interview with the Luctari and Ira's statement about the Watcher when I combine my notes with the murder investigation. We'll see if anything clicks."

"So..." Sean cleared his throat and shifted his stance, slightly humbled by the schooling Fionna had given him. "Back to Felicity. You still need me to help you find her?"

Fionna looked at the timepiece on her wrist. "It's late. You're covered in mud. And I need a drink."

Sean's mouth slipped into an easy grin. "Is that an invitation to join you for a drink, Agent Knox?"

Fionna looked at Sean, a coy glint in her eye. "If you mean go back to your place and I have a beer while you wash the mud off...then yes."

Sean blinked. His face burned hot under his beard.

Fionna flashed a clever smile. "We can't look for someone if they can smell you coming from a mile away, Montressador. I can combine my sword theft and murder investigation notes while you get cleaned up. Let's go."

TWENTY-FIVE

DRAGON HAIR

Sean walked from his bedroom into the front room carrying his sword belt and rubbing a towel over his damp hair. Fionna sat at the dining table bent over her data link pad, a stylus in one hand. The agent's bio-vision glasses rested on top of her head and swept blond hair behind her ears. The city's night skyline created a starry backdrop through the picture windows. Fionna pressed a beer bottle to her lips and took a sip.

The push and pull of emotions in Sean's chest began again, but this time Fionna's bio-vision glasses rested safely on the top of her head, so he let the drama play out for a little longer. The glow of the screen turned the agent's violet eyes blue. The curve of her bottom lip reminded him again of the kiss—a stupid, reckless move on his part.

Sean sighed. He dropped the towel on the kitchen counter, ran a hand through his damp hair, and grabbed a beer from the cooler. "Careful. If you stare too long at that screen, it will steal your soul."

Fionna gave Sean a look that indicated she questioned his sanity as he walked toward her.

"I'm just kidding." Sean grinned and hung his sword belt on a nearby stand. "That's just an old superstition. Everyone knows Ministry Agents don't have souls." He set his beer on the table and took a seat.

"Ha." Fionna's mouth curled. "While you've been making yourself beautiful, I sent in a request to bring Ira in for questioning. Maybe our interviewers can sober him up enough to get a description of the Watcher out of him."

"Good luck." Sean twisted open his beer. "There may not be much left of his mind even when he's sober."

"I also got a message from Drake." Fionna tapped the screen with the stylus. "He wants me to sort through the list of names from Garin's rejection letters."

Sean took a pull from the bottle. "Any luck?"

"I only just started, but I was able to eliminate one hundred and thirty-two names."

"How did you do that?"

"I didn't." Fionna tapped the screen. "Death did it for me." Her eyes flicked to Sean. "Don't worry. They all died from known causes." She leaned back with a sigh and took another sip of beer. "Only twenty-one thousand, seven hundred and eight names to go."

Sean rested one arm on the table. "Sounds like you're looking for a dragon hair."

Fionna narrowed her eyes. "I didn't think dragons had hair?"

"They don't." He flashed a wicked grin. "At least not any you can get at easily. Quests for dragon hairs either frustrate the searcher or piss off the dragon. Is your list worth the trouble?"

"It's a lead but this list is only from the last three years," Fionna said, tapping the stylus on the table. "Garin's career lasted decades. Plenty of time to make enemies much more powerful than twenty-year-olds with bruised egos." A sly grin spread across her mouth. "If I went back about fifteen years, I might even see the name of a certain senior agent that we've all come to know and love."

Sean's eyes widened from behind his beer bottle as he took a sip. He spluttered beer and came up laughing. "You're kidding!"

"It's old news," Fionna said, chuckling and waving him off. "There are rumors at the Ministry that Drake applied to be a time jumper shortly after he graduated from the academy. When he was rejected, he joined the Ministry. A lot of our agents come to the Ministry that way. If getting a rejection letter from Garin makes you a potential murderer, then a third of my colleagues should be on the suspect list."

"I'm still curious to know why he was rejected," Sean said, wiping spilled beer from a trouser leg with his hand. "Was it his less than sparkling personality or his emotional constipation?"

Fionna leaned back in her chair and stretched her arms over her head in a graceful arc. Sean forced himself to read the label of his beer bottle as the fabric of the agent's blouse pulled tightly across her chest.

"That's a mystery we'll probably never figure out," she said through a yawn. Fionna dropped her arms and leaned forward again in her chair, resting her chin in one hand as she stared at the screen. "The stories I've heard never talk about the why, and after fifteen years, I doubt it matters anymore."

Sean nodded and met Fionna's eye. "So, what about these more recent rejects? Do we know much about them?" He took another sip of beer.

"A fair amount." The agent shrugged. "Test scores. Reasons for the rejection. Where they're living now."

Sean thought a moment and scratched his beard. "Anaya told me that a lot of candidates wash out after their psych evaluation. You could focus on those?"

Fionna tapped the screen. She nodded with approval at the results and took a sip. "A lot of crazy people want to be time jumpers. We're down to sixteen thousand, two hundred and eighty-one names."

"I've met a lot of time jumpers." Sean waved his bottle of beer. "They're *all* crazy."

Fionna's mouth twitched and she tapped the screen again. She frowned in disappointment. "Still no dragon hair." Sean raised an eyebrow. She gestured to the screen. "I compared the names with our database of known Luctari members. Nothing. I wouldn't expect a Luctari to apply to be a time jumper, but it was worth a shot."

Uneasiness settled in Sean's gut. "You think the Luctari are involved?"

Fionna set her bio-vision glasses on the table and rubbed her temples. She rested her chin on her hands, elbows on the table, and looked at the screen. "My mind keeps going back to them. The Luctari fit the profile of the person we're looking for. They don't like time jumpers, and our sword thief could have stolen Syrovar's sword as a symbol of political change like the Padome suggested, but they don't seem the type to use directional anchors. At least they shouldn't, given their beliefs."

Sean leaned back in his chair, crossed one leg over the other at the ankle, and rested the beer bottle on a knee. "You should talk to my Captain of the Guard." He quickly told Fionna about the hecklers at Montressador's Keep. "Captain Wahler thinks my scuffle at the East Gate was a setup. Brink knew where I was in plenty of time before the attack and that I would most likely head back to Montressador's Keep after the interviews."

Fionna frowned. "But that doesn't make sense. Why would Brink want you dead? The Luctari want Andarrians to give up time jumping and go back to how things were before."

"I know. That's what I told Wahler."

Fionna stared out the window at the night skyline, eyes narrowed in thought. Sean could almost see the gears turning in the agent's head. After a moment, she turned back to look at him. "What would have happened if you'd been killed?"

Sean snorted a laugh. "A dramatic ending to an otherwise uneventful career?" He shrugged. "The museum would get a new sword for their collection and they'd swap out my portrait on the grand staircase at Montressador's Keep."

"Seriously, what would have happened? How would the public react?"

Sean sipped his beer. "People would be upset...at least I hope they would be. A state funeral. An investigation. Months of the news services running sensational headlines." He framed imaginary quotes in the air and used his best dramatic announcer voice. "Who will be the next Montressador?"

"Public focus would shift away from time jumping," Fionna said. "If Brink wants a revival, your death would give it to him."

Sean frowned. "But he also loses his hammer. He's been using the time jumper murders as another reason why the Republic should give it up. Besides, if you're right, Brink's really grabbing the dragon by the balls. An investigation of that size would use every agent at the Ministry and Andarrian Intelligence. If the trail led back to the Luctari, it could destroy the entire movement. Would Brink really want to take that big of a risk?"

Fionna considered the question. "An investigation like that would pull agents off every other case. Even possibly the time jumper murders." She tapped her stylus on the table. "I guess it depends on what Brink hopes to gain."

Fionna's data pad beeped with an incoming message. Her expression turned to surprise as she read the screen. "It's from Agent Max."

"What's he want?"

"He sent me the name of a Splice dealer." Fionna scrolled through the information. "Otis Mingo. Goes by the name Torch." Fionna tapped the screen. Her eyes widened with her smile. "Do you want to go for a ride?"

The old warehouse district clung to the edge of the capital city like a stain on a rug. The glare of the hovercar's headlights swept through the empty yards of abandoned structures and caught eyes in the shadows that blinked and scurried back to their hidey holes.

Fionna steered the car through the broken gates into the yard and parked on the crumbling pavement between two buildings. Sean hopped out of the car and followed the agent to the trunk. The smell of garbage on the night breeze mixed with the rot of dead animals until he thought a corpse had shit its pants.

Sean shivered from more than just the cool air as he looked up at the empty windows and gripped the hilt of his sword. "Looks like the neighbors moved out."

"We're being watched." Fionna grabbed a satchel bag from the trunk. She pulled out two palm-sized spotlights and handed one to Sean. She checked the power cell in the pistol on her hip as she scanned the windows through the tint of her yellow glasses. "We shouldn't have any trouble unless we accidentally stumble into some place that's already been claimed by someone else." Fionna slipped the strap of the satchel over a shoulder.

"That's what I'm afraid of," Sean said as he flicked on his palm light. "Have you been here before?"

"I've been in the general area, but not for a while." Fionna closed the trunk and headed across the yard to a double set of warehouse doors. Sean trailed after the agent with his palm light.

One door hung lopsided on its hinges while the other lay flat in the threshold. Fionna stepped carefully through the doorway and shone her light inside.

The beam from the palm light swept across the warehouse floor. The floor rippled then churned in a frenzy as hundreds of brown rats fled into the shadows. The sound of their claws scratching echoed from the walls to the ceiling.

Sean stifled a yelp and muttered a curse.

Fionna looked over a shoulder. "Don't worry. They're just rats. They won't bother us as long as we keep our lights on."

Sean muttered more obscenities and flicked his light back and forth as he followed Fionna to the base of the metal stairs.

The stairs led to a third-floor walkup. A cracked keypad hung on the wall next to a metal door. Without power to the keypad and no handle on the outside, the door offered no options for entry.

Fionna tucked her palm light in a pocket and pounded on the door with a fist. "Otis Mingo!" The echo from the door reverberated through the empty warehouse.

Sean eyed the agent. "You sure he's home?"

Fionna listened and pounded again. "Otis, open up! Ministry of Investigations!"

Sean smirked. "Oh, sure. That will make him open up."

Fionna listened for a beat then reached into her satchel and pulled out an anti-grav clamp. She attached the device to the door and activated the anti-gravity field. Sean watched as she gripped the clamp and lifted the door with one hand until the gap was large enough to duck underneath. Light from inside shone into the corridor.

"Isn't this breaking and entering?" Sean grinned, switched off his palm light, and tucked it into his belt.

Fionna gave a peaceful smile. "We didn't break anything. We simply entered in pursuit of a person of interest." She ducked under the door.

The smell of the corpse hit Sean's nose as he moved under the door and stepped inside the apartment. He drew his blade. Fear, primitive and raw, pumped his blood faster.

Fionna gripped the pistol in her hand. "My god..."

The corpse lay on a large table on its back. A bucket on the floor, sticky with blood, was positioned directly below the stump of the neck. The torso glistened, the skin a mottled green under the glare of the overhead lights. The stomach bulged like a mound of bread dough. A trail of primitive stitches made from what looked like baling wire strained against the dark incision that ran from below the man's bellybutton to his sternum, giving a clue as to where the head might have ended up. A storage container of intestines under the table provided a feast for flies.

Fionna motioned to Sean to search the apartment. He moved cautiously around one side of the table as Fionna took the other side of the room.

The apartment branched off into multiple adjoining rooms. Everywhere he looked, there were signs of a struggle. Personal belongings lay scattered and broken. A rack of lithium batteries blinked on a shelving unit on the opposite wall. Black cables snaked across the floor toward the bank of batteries and up through the ceiling to the roof, most likely to a solar panel array, Sean thought, which would explain why the building didn't have power, but the apartment did.

Past a wall of cabinets, an unmade bed filled a corner next to a makeshift closet with a curtain hanging in the doorway. Sean moved to inspect the cabinets when his ears pricked to a sound behind him. His sword spun. The tip of the blade flashed through the closet curtain as a stifled shriek pierced the air. The edge of the blade struck the doorjamb leaving a slash in the wood. The fabric of the curtain parted and dropped to the floor.

"Montressador!" Fionna darted from the opposite side of the room, pistol ready.

Sean held up a hand. He gripped the hilt of his sword at his side and peered into the dark corner of the closet. A pair of battered bilge-water-brown canvas shoes scooted backward into the shadows.

"Come out! I already saw you."

Labored breathing came from the closet followed by movement from the shadows as a skinny teenage girl with shocking pink hair stepped into view. The girl wore baggy denim trousers, rolled at the cuffs, topped with a white t-shirt. An oversized green jacket hung to the back of her knees. Her brown eyes, wide with fear, darted to the corpse on the table across the room and then quickly looked away.

Fionna watched the girl for a moment through her glasses then holstered her weapon. Sean followed the agent's lead and sheathed his blade. Fionna pulled a chair from a desk area and turned it, so it faced away from the corpse and motioned to the girl.

"Sit down."

Sean studied the girl's features as she took a seat. "I know you." Fionna glanced to Sean. "You were at the transport shelter the night Reverend Brink's message was hacked."

The girl nodded and stared at her hands in her lap.

Fionna went to the kitchen and returned with a glass of water. "What's your name?"

The girl drank the glass dry, wiping her mouth with the back of a hand before answering. "Dia." Her voice croaked, and she cleared her throat. "My name is Dia." She narrowed her eyes in suspicion.

Sean sat on the bed across from the girl and looked at her skinny frame and sunken eyes. He thought a moment. "Are you hungry?"

Sean sat next to Dia on the steps outside Torch's apartment. Spotlights clamped to the metal railing left a trail for Ministry agents as they moved between the crime scene and the rest of the warehouse. Sean took a bite of the steak sandwich that Kegler, the forensic tech, had brought. He'd asked the tech to bring food but hadn't specified exactly what he should bring. *Leave it to Kegler to bring steak sandwiches to a gruesome crime scene*, Sean thought. Surprisingly, Dia hadn't seemed to mind. Sean watched the girl, impressed with her speed and enthusiasm as she plowed through her own sandwich. The food had done wonders for Dia's mood and put some color back into her cheeks.

Dia reveled in the last few saucy bites of steak. She popped the final morsel into her mouth and closed her eyes, absorbing all the flavors as she chewed. Finished, the girl leaned back against the steps with a sigh. She wiped her mouth with a napkin, crumpled it up, and tossed it over the railing to the warehouse floor below.

"Thanks for the sandwich." The girl stood and headed down the steps.

Sean looked up, perplexed, his sandwich halfway to his mouth. "Wait. You can't leave yet."

"Watch me." Dia continued her pace down the stairs.

"We still need to ask you some questions." Sean reluctantly left his sandwich on the step and jumped to his feet, almost bumping into Kegler's assistant on his way up the stairs. "What were you doing in there? How do you know that guy?"

"I was hiding. Torch is..." Dia shook her head. "...*was* my supplier."

Sean caught up and placed a hand on the girl's shoulder as she turned the landing. "Slow down!"

Dia spun. "Hands off!" She batted his hand away. Fists ready. Tattoos in black ink across her knuckles spelled out 'Ouch' on one fist and 'Pow!' on the other.

Sean read the threat—literally—and took a step back, hands raised in a calming gesture. "Just stick around a few more minutes until Agent Knox can talk to you, okay?"

"Am I being detained?" The girl stared a hole through him.

Sean blinked, uncertain. "Uh...no...?"

Dia broke into a gap-tooth grin and continued down the steps. "Catch you later, Sir Loin of Beef."

Sean grumbled and raced after the girl. "Yes! Yes, you are being detained." She was almost to the bottom of the stairs. "You can't leave!"

"Too late." Dia tossed a glance over a shoulder. "You already said I could go."

Sean cursed. *Where's Fionna when I need her?* "Oh, come on! I bought you that sandwich."

Dia stopped halfway across the warehouse floor and turned to look back at him. "Oh, so you thought you'd buy the scared girl a sandwich and... what?" She flashed another gap-tooth grin. "We'd be friends? Meat between two slices of bread?" She pressed the back of a hand to her brow in a fake swoon. "My hero!"

Sean gritted his teeth as his patience began to slip. "I thought if I showed you some kindness—"

Dia shot him a look of incredulity. "Kindness?"

"—you might return the favor—"

"You bucking for sainthood now, Blade Boy?"

"— and *talk* to us!" Sean gestured up the stairs. "Don't you want the Ministry to catch the guy who did that to Torch?"

Dia crossed her arms. "I *want* to get as far away from this place as possible."

"I'll help you get to anywhere you wanna go," Sean said, pleading. "But I need you to talk to me first."

Dia arched a brow. "Anywhere?"

Sean grabbed hope with both hands. "Anywhere. As far away as you want. I'll have my office set it up. You have my word." He mentally cringed on that last part. Jo was going to love playing travel agent to a surly teenager. Dia eyed him, teetering on indecision. Sean took one last shot. "I didn't report you and your friends to the park conservancy for vandalism at the transport shelter, did I?"

Dia thought another moment then rolled her eyes and leaned back against a crate, hands in pockets. "Fine. What do you want to know?"

Relief flooded through Sean as he tried to organize his thoughts. "Why were you in Torch's apartment?"

Dia rolled a shoulder and sighed. "I came for a pickup. I sometimes hustle for Torch when I'm low on cash. I sell to the other students. I came in through the back window."

"Okay." Sean nodded, happy to finally be getting somewhere. "Is that when you found the body?"

"No. I heard voices. Torch was talking to another hustler in the pickup room. They were arguing." The girl looked down at her shoes. "It sounded bad. I didn't want to stick around, but I couldn't get back to the window to leave without them seeing me, so I ducked in the closet when they came in the front room."

"What were they arguing about?"

"The other guy was there for a pickup. He was mad because it wasn't as much as he wanted. He kept saying he needed more. Torch said it was all he could give him. He'd have to come back next week. The guy was still mad. He said it was his recipe and the deal was Torch would give him as much as he wanted whenever he asked for it. Torch said the rest was for the Luctari." Dia gave a gesture of amazement. "Like that would make a difference somehow. The guy didn't care."

Sean's pulse ticked faster. "The Luctari?"

"Yeah, the Luctari are big customers. Torch told me Reverend Brink sometimes paid him to make an extra big batch of whatever he wanted to sell off-world for him. Brink always gave Torch a healthy cut. Torch didn't like Brink, but he said Luctari money spent the same as anybody else's so..." The girl shrugged a shoulder.

"Okay, so they argued," Sean said, trying to rein in his excitement. "What happened next?"

Dia looked away. Her throat bobbed in a hard swallow before answering. "He killed Torch. I didn't see it. They started fighting. Crashing into things. I heard stuff getting broken and then just the sound of punching. It got real quiet. When I peeked through the curtain, Torch was on the floor. He wasn't moving." The girl shifted nervously against the crate. "And then the guy goes to the kitchen and he's opening drawers and cabinets. He put Torch on the table. That's when I saw the sword..." Dia shivered with the memory and hugged her shoulders. "I had to wait for him to finish. It took forever. And then he grabbed a bunch of stuff from the pickup room. After he left, I kept thinking he might come back...but I couldn't leave the closet. I couldn't walk past..." Her voice trailed off.

Sean nodded in sympathy. "How long ago was this?"

Dia pressed her lips together, face grim. "Yesterday."

"You stayed in the closet all this time?"

The girl's face twisted in anger. "I just told you I did!"

Sean resisted the urge to snap at the girl. He couldn't blow the last few questions. "Did you get a look at the guy? What did he look like?"

"Besides the sword?" Dia threw her hands up in a hopeless gesture. "Tall. Brown hair. Kind of lanky."

Sean burned the description in his brain. "Did you hear a name?"

"Torch called him Blade." Dia glared at him. "Are

we done? Can I get my ticket to Anywhere now?"

Sean watched the glow of the hovercar's taillights as they left the warehouse yard and disappeared through the front gates. After updating Fionna, he'd asked another Ministry agent to drive Dia home and gave the girl instructions to stop by Montressador's Keep in the morning for her ticket to Anywhere. Sean sighed. He'd better give Jo a heads up. She wasn't going to be thrilled about having to stop by the office on her day off.

Fionna stepped to his side in the open warehouse door as the low hum of the hovercar faded into the distance. "So, Brink was bankrolling Torch to help fund the Luctari? Clever. I wouldn't have guessed that."

Sean nodded and adjusted his sword belt. "It sounds like Torch made a lot of deals. That's how he got the Splice recipe from Blade."

Fionna narrowed her eyes in thought as she stared off into the yard. "Blade made a deal with Torch. He gave Torch the recipe for Splice with the promise he'd get as much as he wanted, whenever he wanted it." She looked back to Sean. The agent's mouth dipped into a frown. "Blade had the recipe. Why couldn't he make it himself?"

"Torch already had a production line." Sean shrugged and rested a hand on the hilt of his sword. "Maybe it was just...easier?"

"That makes sense." Fionna nodded. "Torch was definitely dealing in high volume. Kegler said his product room has everything from A to Z and a lot of stuff we've never even seen before. Blade didn't want a little Splice for his own personal use. He needed a lot."

"Enough to contaminate the water tanks on the *What Cheer*. That's no easy task." Sean's insides clenched with another thought. "If he can pull off something like that..." Sean's eyes darted to Fionna's. Her eyes grew round with comprehension.

Fionna pulled out her data link pad. "If Blade came for another large pickup, it might mean he's planning something else." Her fingers flew across the screen as she spoke. "I'll send an alert to Drake." Her mouth pursed as her typing slowed. "Blade must have really trusted Torch."

Sean chuckled. "And look how it turned out. Torch got a better deal from the Luctari and told Blade to get to the back of the line."

"But Blade didn't know Torch was going to turn on him." Fionna's eyes met his. "He had a recipe. He knew what it could be worth and he took it to Torch. From what Dia told you, Blade didn't sell the recipe. He just had an agreement that Torch would make him Splice whenever he wanted it."

"Blade's not in it for the money," Sean said and leaned against the door frame. "He wants to kill time jumpers."

Fionna finished sending the message and tucked the data pad under an arm. "But once he handed off the recipe there's nothing he could do if Torch didn't hold up his end of the deal."

Sean followed the agent's line of thinking. "Blade took a hell of a risk unless…"

"…unless he didn't think he was." Fionna's excitement grew. "He trusted Torch would keep his promise." She looked at Sean. "What does that sound like to you?"

Sean grinned. "They knew each other from way back. Family or old friends. From school maybe?" He scratched his beard in thought. "How does Felicity fit in?"

"Felicity's the go-between. Drake was right on that point at least," Fionna said. "It's possible Brink was using Felicity to deal with Torch and that's how she met Blade. Blade can't be seen anywhere near his victims and Torch is a warehouse rat. He's not going to get out to do much of anything."

"So, Felicity gets the directional anchors from Blade and drops them wherever he tells her to. She might not have even known what they were for." Sean drummed his fingers on the hilt of his sword. A strange thought entered his head. He eyed the agent. "The student on the night tour. The one who leaned over the exhibit. Can you show me that footage again?"

Fionna cued up the security footage on her data pad. "What are you looking for?"

Sean scanned the screen. "I thought maybe the student was Felicity…" He frowned at the image and shook his head. "It might be her, but I can't get a good look at her face."

"But we know the directional anchor wasn't

planted by the statue. It was by Syrovar's portrait."
Fionna reversed the footage.

Sean watched the screen as the sequence played again. "Stop! Roll it back. Can you slow it down?"

Fionna tapped the screen and the sequence replayed at quarter speed.

Sean pointed to the screen. "Look right there. I thought it was weird how she leaned over the statue. She's not looking at the exhibit, she's looking at something across the room. The guide tells her to step back. Everyone in the gallery turns to look..." Sean drew a line across the screen with his finger. "...everyone except for *that* guy...by the portrait. It's just a split second."

Fionna took in a sharp breath. "He planted the anchor."

"I can't see his face." Sean squinted. "Don't you have a better angle?"

Fionna tapped the screen and sorted through several camera angles of people in the gallery. "They know where the security cameras are. They keep turning their faces or blocking. I'll pull up the pictures from the background searches."

She tapped the screen again and brought up a collection of pictures and scrolled through the album. Sean recognized the photos as people from the night tour.

"Here she is." Fionna clicked on a name and a picture of a plainly dressed, dark-haired woman appeared on the screen.

Disappointment filled Sean. He shook his head.

"That's not Felicity. Similar features..."

"That's not the woman I interviewed." Fionna's voice stretched thin with tension. Sean's eyes darted to the agent. "I interviewed everyone on the night tour. The woman in that picture is not the student who leaned over the display."

Sean's pulse quickened. "Then who is she?"

"I don't know." Fionna tapped the screen and scrolled quickly through a picture gallery. "I recognize everyone on the tour from my interviews except that woman..." Her finger moved across the screen and pointed to a picture of an unsmiling man in a dark blue shirt. "...and this guy."

"They aren't the people in the security footage?"

"No." Fionna pursed her mouth. Worry flickered across her face. She closed her eyes for a beat as the full weight of the discovery sunk in. "When I set up the interviews, I contacted the people on the tour group using the information they provided to the museum when they signed up for the night tour. But the background information...That came from the visual record from the security footage. The comm must have misidentified them and pulled the wrong background."

Sean's mind reeled. "How does *that* happen?"

Fionna sighed. "It's rare...but it happens sometimes." A blush spread across her face. "It's my fault. The comm didn't throw any red flags so I never gave it a second thought, and then Drake took me off the case."

Sean gestured to the screen. "So, we have no idea

who the people in the security footage are?"

Fionna shook her head. "Unless we can find someone who knows them on sight by looking at the security footage, even if they're in disguise, we're in the dark." She tucked the data pad in her jacket pocket. "I need to finish up here and get back to headquarters to sort this out. I'll show the footage to Lieutenant Stravage. He might be able to identify Felicity, but if you couldn't it might be a lost cause."

Sean looked at the uncertainty in the agent's eyes. It wasn't like Fionna to let a setback rattle her. "Do you need me for anything?"

"Thanks." Fionna's peaceful smile returned but failed to erase the worry from her eyes. "But I'm good. I can drop you off at home." She started walking toward the hovercar. You should get some sleep anyway. Isn't Commander Lazar's wedding tomorrow?"

Sean followed Fionna across the yard. "Yeah, but if there's something I can do to help..."

"I have a description of Blade. I'll compare it to Torch's background check to see if we get any matches." Fionna opened the driver's door. "Don't worry. I know where to find you if anything pops up."

Sean sighed as he climbed into the passenger seat. "I'll be watching my best friend make the biggest mistake of his life."

TWENTY-SIX

SAROLEA

Lieutenant Sarolea Piquet lay in bed in a private room in the hospital's trauma unit, her body curled around the comfort pillow at her side. Her short, tangled hair had faded from her signature blue to her natural brown, and the mechanical brace and clock that had monitored her Ghost Arm the past several months was nowhere in sight. From what the doctors had told Ann, the phasing energies that had caused Sarolea's Ghost Arm to disappear had completely dispersed, the one positive side effect from her ordeal, making the brace no longer needed. Sarolea draped her solid, former Ghost Arm, across the bed, pulling the comfort pillow to her chest.

The trauma room was designed to soothe suffering from the worst physical and mental injuries. Ann was doubtful that the room's specialized care would encourage her friend to talk about her ordeal, but much to her surprise Sarolea hadn't required much prompting. Agent Drake asked her to start at the beginning and so she had, taking them back to the *What Cheer* and the night of the crew abduction.

"It was Ensign Thorn's birthday." Sarolea pulled the blanket up toward her chin. "We'd finished our first delivery and were having a party in the galley. Captain Bowditch programmed the food processors with his chocolate cake recipe. He'd been bragging about it for weeks." A faint smile curled Sarolea's mouth. "It was really good. We were all laughing. Everyone was giving Thorn a hard time. Melita's the youngest so…" The pain of the memory hitched in Sarolea's throat.

Ann saw the danger and quickly coaxed her through the thicket. "What happened next?"

Sarolea took a breath and began again. "I was sitting across from Calvin. He took a bite of cake and then he got a weird look on his face."

Agent Drake jotted a note in his data pad in his chair at the foot of the bed. "That's Crewman Calvin Vaux?"

Sarolea nodded. "He said he didn't feel well. And then it was like we all felt it at the same time. There was a bitter taste in my mouth. I tried to stand up. My whole body hurt like something was stabbing me from the inside. I guess I blacked out. I don't remember. When I woke up, I was on the floor." Her eyes darkened with the memory. "But I wasn't on the *What Cheer*. I couldn't move. I couldn't talk. There was a gag in my mouth. We were all there in a line on the floor. Captain Bowditch was next to me."

Ann let the silence fill the space between them before asking the next question. "Can you describe where you were?"

Sarolea pulled the pillow closer. "It was cold. Damp. Not completely dark but it was hard to see. The floor was stone. I heard water running. I think we were underground."

Agent Drake looked up in the middle of writing a note. "Underground? Like a basement?"

"Maybe?" Sarolea frowned in thought. Uncertainty creased the corners of her eyes. "There was an echo. Like when you're in a cave. I don't know for sure if we were. It just felt that way." She closed her eyes and let out a sigh. "It must've been a basement."

Drake continued jotting notes. "So, you were bound and gagged on the floor. For how long?"

Sarolea fidgeted. Ann's senses pricked to a low hum. The comfort pillow had read the change in Sarolea's pulse and respiration and radiated soothing vibrations.

"A few minutes." Sarolea stared across the room, eyes vacant. "I heard footsteps. There was a man. He had a sword."

Drake looked up. "The sword you described before? The one with the gold leaves on the hilt?"

Sarolea pressed her lips together and nodded.

Ann leaned closer and rested a hand on her shoulder. "What did the man look like?"

Sarolea trembled. Her cheeks paled, making the abrasions on her face and the exhaustion in her eyes more prominent. "I don't know. He was wearing a black hood." The hum from the pillow increased. "He didn't say anything. He walked over to Thorn and…" Sarolea's features twisted. Angry tears filled her eyes. "He put a block under Melita's head... and cut off her..." She took a shuddering breath. Panic pinched the words in her throat as she forced herself to speak through gritted teeth. "I tried to yell. I couldn't move. Melita's feet were tied to a rope. He hoisted her up by her ankles. The blood...was everywhere. He did the same thing to Solloway and Vaux. Captain Bowditch was next to me. He looked at me when his head was on the block."

Grief won. Sarolea turned her face to the pillow with tortured sobs.

Ann soothed her friend in her anguish and fought the tears that pricked the corners of her own eyes. She looked to Agent Drake at the foot of the bed and was surprised when he held up a hand in a gesture of patience and sat quietly with the data pad on his lap. When Sarolea had composed herself somewhat, Drake spoke, and again Ann was stunned by the gentleness of his voice.

"Is that when the man let you go?"

"No." Sarolea fitted the words between sobs. "He finished with Bowditch. He was walking toward me." She looked to Ann. "It was my Ghost Arm. I felt it start to phase, but the distortion was different. It was all over me. Not just my arm. And then I was somewhere else."

"We know the killer used directional anchors to abduct the crew," Drake said. "Your arm must have reacted with the nanobots and Splice already in your system. After you phased in the basement, where did you reappear?"

"There were bright colors everywhere. I...I was floating. I couldn't see anything."

Ann nodded and looked at Drake. "That sounds like a spacetime pocket." She turned back to Sarolea. "How long were you there?"

"I don't know. I fell asleep. My arm phased again, and I was in the ditch where your brother found me."

Agent Drake scratched a few more notes in his data pad and stood. "Get some rest, Lieutenant. I might have more questions for you later."

Ann followed Drake into the hallway. "Did it feel like Lieutenant Picquet hesitated when you asked her if she thought she was in a basement?"

Drake continued to tap out an update on his data pad screen. "What else could it be, Lieutenant?"

Ann wavered, remembering the consequences from the last time she challenged the senior agent. "I don't know...I just..."

"Trauma distorts memories and can cause muddled thinking," Drake said, eyes locked on the data pad. "A basement is the most reasonable explanation at this point."

Ann quietly blew out a sigh and released the frustration building in her chest. Drake did have a point. "Sarolea mentioned a stone floor. The buildings in the Historic District are one of the few areas in the capital that I know of that were built using stone and could have basements."

Drake looked up. His black eyes held Ann's gaze. After a moment of thought, the agent nodded. "Yes,

I believe that's correct. Excellent work, Lieutenant."

Ann had expected an argument or in the very least a snide remark, but the compliment left her as astounded as if the agent had offered a marriage proposal.

Drake tapped the screen of his data pad. "I'm sending agents to canvass the area. Stay with Picquet and contact me immediately if she remembers anything else." The agent started off down the hall.

"Agent Drake, the killer will most likely have more directional anchors with him. I could help you search for them."

"You're right where I need you, Lieutenant," Drake spoke over a shoulder, never breaking stride. "If anything changes, I'll send for you. If you don't hear from me by morning, report to Agent Knox."

Morning came with no word from Drake. Ann woke a couple hours before dawn with her neck as stiff as a board from sleeping in the hospital guest chair. She'd wanted to be close by for Sarolea's sake, but medication accomplished what exhaustion couldn't and Sarolea had fallen into a deep sleep soon after Drake left. Ann tried to rub the soreness from her neck as she watched her friend sleep. Sarolea slept curled around the comfort pillow. The pillow's low humming filled the room. Ann sighed. Sarolea was safe, but there was still work to do.

Ann checked her data link pad. She'd sent John an update about Sarolea the night before. He'd replied with a quick text message.

John: I'm back home. Glad Sarolea is safe. Contact me on the comm when you get this.

Ann chewed her lip. John would have to wait until she was back at Sean's place. She wrote a quick note for Sarolea before leaving for the Ministry of Investigations.

Ann found Agent Knox in a workstation in the Ministry's command center staring at two large comm screens, a tech seated to one side. Rows upon rows of pictures filled one screen while the second showed the enlarged photos of six women – all in their early twenties and all with dark hair and eyes.

Fionna lifted a cup of coffee to her lips and took a sip. Her bio-vision glasses rested on top of her head. Fatigue covered the agent's face like eight miles of bad road. A half-dozen nearly identical coffee cups clustered around a waste receptacle chute under the desk.

"Next," Fionna said, speaking to the comm tech.

The tech tapped a sequence of keys, the screen flickered, and six new pictures appeared, replacing the first group. All the women shared similar features – age, weight, hair, skin, and eye color – but differed slightly in appearance like a variation on a theme.

Fionna nodded to Ann as she entered the workstation then turned her attention back to the comm screen. "How's Sarolea? Did you find out anything?"

"Sleeping. She's going to be okay," Ann said and helped herself to a cup of coffee from the workstation's syntho food port. "We didn't learn a lot.

From what Sarolea said, she and the rest of the crew were held captive in a basement of some kind. She remembers the floor was made of stone. Drake's canvassing the historic district now. He told me to report to you." Ann looked to the screens again then back to the agent and frowned. "What's going on?"

"Next," Fionna said, speaking to the comm tech. The tech tapped the keys and a new group of six appeared on the screen. Fionna met Ann's eye. "The comm misidentified two people in the tour group."

Ann's mouth dropped open in disbelief. "What? How does that—?"

Fionna took another sip of coffee and waved her off, impatient. "Dazzle paint. It's camouflage for the facial recognition comm. You can't see it with your own eyes. Suspects paint their faces with reflective geometric patterns that can only be seen under certain types of longwave light. It messes with the comm's ability to recognize faces, so it misidentifies them or simply doesn't see them as being people at all." Fionna squinted at the screen. "The Ministry hasn't been public about this for obvious reasons." She shook her head and muttered, "Next." The comm tech tapped the keys.

"So, you're looking through the entire database?"

Fionna sighed. "Right now, I'm only reviewing the people who match our suspect's description, but for some reason the comm rejected them. After talking with your brother, I'm convinced the student who leaned over the museum display was Felicity. I think I interviewed her in person, but the comm pulled the wrong background information. Next."

Ann sipped her coffee and watched the screen change again, marveling at the number of pictures she estimated the agent had already searched through and how many more she might still need to review. "What if she's not in the database?"

"*Everyone's* in the database," Fionna said, grim. "We'll find her."

"I know what Felicity looks like," Ann said. "Set me up in another comm station. I'll help look."

Fionna shook her head and grumbled. "I need to be the one to identify her since I'm the agent who interviewed her and I'm the one who challenged the results of the background check. I'm almost done anyway." Fionna slid her gaze in Ann's direction. "Go home. Get some sleep. I'll message you when I have something."

***

Ann walked through the door of Sean's penthouse apartment, feeling every inch of the hospital chair she'd slept in the night before. She took a seat at the comm station, checked the timepiece on Sean's desk, and fired up the control panel. It was still early, but she couldn't wait any longer.

The signal locked and a few seconds later John's face filled the comm screen from the kitchen at Siren's Cove, hair tousled as if he'd just rolled out of bed.

"Good morning," he said, and gave her a sleepy smile.

"I just got back." Nerves fluttered in her stomach.

"I hope it's not too early?"

"I was already up," John said, holding up a coffee mug. "I have a few chores I need to finish before I can meet you for the wedding. Are you able to break away from the investigation?" He took a sip.

Ann nodded. "Fionna has us on standby." She inhaled a deep breath, and the butterflies in her stomach took flight. "Please tell me you didn't do anything stupid with the mission report. I don't want you to throw away your career for me." John blinked in surprise. "It's okay. Sean has a secure comm channel. Just one of the perks of the office."

John set his mug down, his expression growing more serious. "I didn't do anything stupid. I wrote my report based on what I knew to be true. Your hesitation didn't cost us the mission. What you told me afterward didn't change that."

"Only because you yelled at me to stop talking and didn't ask me any questions."

John shook his head. "I've thought about it a lot and I stand by what I wrote. The mission failed because of Moondarra's Vego sensor. She knew we were coming because it sensed you were using electroperception. If it wasn't for that one thing, I believe we would've gotten her."

The tension in Ann's chest slowly lifted and she breathed a sigh of relief for John's sake as well as her own.

"Having said that," John ran a hand through his hair and blew out a deep sigh. "You should've told me about your hesitation problem before the mission. When I said you should talk to a counselor, I didn't mean you couldn't talk to me." He met her gaze and his face darkened. "The biggest mistake of my life was when I stopped talking to A.K. after Bonnie died. I should've told him what I was dealing with. He would've gotten me the help I needed, and I wouldn't have wasted years trying to sort it out on my own. I don't want that for you. "

Ann's cheeks burned. "I know. It's not you. I...I just don't have the words sometimes. I guess I'm still sorting through things from the *Kairos*." She sighed. "I'd never hesitated like that outside the flight simulator before. I told you as soon as I could."

John nodded. A smile twitched at the corner of his mouth. "I believe you, but next time don't tell me in the ready room."

Ann threw John a puzzled look.

John took a sip of coffee and leaned forward on the kitchen stool. "A.K. and I tell each other everything before a mission, anything that might distract us or slow us down, but we're always careful about what we say in the ready room. We look out for each other. The people who read the reports don't see what we see. They only know what they read. If they'd read what you said in my report..."

"They would've blamed me." Ann cringed. He nodded.

"When we're on a mission, we're partners. In the ready room, I'm also the senior time jumper. But when we're having a conversation like this one right now..." John's mouth slipped into an easy grin. "...

the same rules don't apply."

Ann smiled and exhaled the last of the butterflies she didn't know she'd been holding back.

"I can't wait to see you in whatever you'll be wearing to the wedding," John said.

Ann rested her chin on her palm and leaned toward the comm screen. "If you meet up with me early enough, I'll give you a preview." A playful smile curled her mouth.

"I'll have to meet you there. I'll be coming through the Weyl gate with only minutes to spare." He cringed. "I still have to buy a suit."

Ann blinked in surprise. "I thought you said you had a suit?"

"I did," John said. "But I forgot it took some damage the last time I wore it." He lifted a shoulder at the question in her eye. "Laser fire burn."

Ann laughed. "I should've known." She looked into his blue eyes and longed for his arms around her. "I miss you."

His mouth crooked the grin she loved. "I promise I'll make it up to you." The huskiness in his voice warmed her down to her toes. "I'll see you soon."

TWENTY-SEVEN
IN THE PALACE

Sean finished buttoning his black dress uniform jacket and looked in the full-length bedroom mirror. He rolled a shoulder and stretched his arms to check the fit. Jo was right. The jacket felt thicker with the dielectric vest sewn into the lining, but he could move just as easily as before. He tried out a few dance moves.

Ann had shown up at his apartment early that morning and interrupted a pleasant dream he'd been having about Fionna and a romantic camping trip (a dream that had taken a weird turn when Forensic Tech Roan Kegler had shown up). She'd given him a quick update on Sarolea's condition and the state of the investigation between yawns and then headed for the guest room. Apparently, Fionna had put them *both* on standby mode until she had more information. As long as they kept their data link pads handy, there was no reason why they couldn't attend Vincent's wedding.

Ann leaned into the bedroom. Her expression changed from surprise to annoyance as she eyed her brother's antics in front of the mirror. "What. Are. You. Doing?"

Sean spun, flashed the mirror a debonair smile, and arched a brow. "I'm just finishing up."

Ann let out an agitated sigh. "I've been ready for ten minutes, our driver will be here any moment, and you're in here messing around. I doubt Vincent is taking this long to get ready and he's the one getting married."

Sean grabbed his sword and belt from the stand by the bed and followed Ann into the main room. Sunlight sparkled the cityscape outside the sitting room picture windows. "Vincent doesn't need as much time to get ready. He's never out of uniform. He probably has a body-sized tattoo of his dress uniform under his clothes in case of an emergency cocktail party."

Ann threw her brother an amused sideways glance. She sat on the arm of one of the oversized couches, legs crossed at the ankles, and checked her lipstick in a pocket mirror. Ann had chosen a simple yet figure-hugging, full-length gown of purple orchid with a plunging halter neckline. Diamond earrings and a pendant added sparkle, while the hem of her skirt swirled about her sandaled feet. A slit past her knee showed the inner layer of the skirt, a lighter shade in complementary pink. Ann wore her hair down for the occasion rather than a formal updo, so her auburn hair tumbled in waves past bare shoulders.

Sean buckled his sword belt as Ann finished with

her lipstick and returned the pocket mirror to her purse. "So, do you think Mirina will wear a traditional wedding dress or something more modern? From what you've said, she likes to make a statement."

"Either way, I'm sure she'll stand out." Sean adjusted his cuffs.

"I'm just trying to get an idea of what she'll be wearing so I know her when I see her."

"Oh, trust me. You'll know her." Sean nodded. "She'll be the one clawing your eyes out when she sees you in that dress." Ann smirked. "And John is going to be picking his eyes up off the floor when he sees you, too." Sean grinned. "I doubt Andarrian fashion makes it to the Colonies very often."

Anaya blushed at the compliment. The data link pad in her purse beeped with an incoming message. She checked the screen. "That's our driver waiting downstairs." She eyed Sean and stood to leave. "Are you ready to go or do you still need to test out a few more dance moves?"

Sean waved his arm toward the door. "Lead the way."

The pair took the tower lift to the main floor and walked to the front entrance. Through the glass doors, Sean saw their driver in formal livery standing at the curb next to a long black hovercar. He adjusted his sword belt. A thin layer of grime covered his palm as he gripped the hilt of his sword. Sean frowned and pulled the blade a few inches from its sheath. Traces of leftover dirt from the culvert speckled the guard, dulling the gold. He even caught a whiff of pond water.

"Shit fire!" Last-minute panic nipped at Sean's heels.

Ann looked over a shoulder as she stepped through the glass doors. The drone of city traffic filled the lobby. "What's wrong?"

The driver slid open the car door and waited for them to climb in. Sean motioned to the driver to return to the front of the car and looked at Ann.

"You're going to have to pick up Jo and head to the wedding without me."

A transport rumbled in the sky lane above them. The sound of its engines reverberated off the sheer sides of the towers on either side of the street.

"*What?*" Anaya shot her brother a look of incredulity as she lifted her skirt and climbed into the backseat.

"I forgot to stop by the museum to get my sword cleaned. I'll grab a mini-cab and meet you there."

Ann glared from the backseat. "You've got to be kidding me."

"I won't be long. By the time you pick up Jo and get to the wedding, I'll be right behind you." Sean whistled and waved to an approaching mini-cab. The driver ignored him, activated the hovercraft's thrusters, and shot past skimming over the slower moving traffic. Horns blared. *Bastard.*

"It's a little late now," Ann said. "Can't it wait?"

"I promised Jo I'd get it cleaned before the wedding. If I don't, she'll never let me hear the end of it."

Sean gestured in desperation. "She wrote it into our agreement so I wouldn't forget!"

Anaya leveled her eyes and smoothed her skirt. "And you forgot anyway."

Sean waved away her irritation. "Just go. Have a drink with John. I'll be there before you need a refill." Sean slid the car door shut. He whistled to another mini-cab as the black hovercar lifted from the curb and joined a sky lane of air traffic.

***

"You're late." Gimirri's eyes traveled the length of his uniform as Sean stopped to catch his breath. "But I'm happy to see you're dressed more the part today. What's the occasion?"

"I'm late for a wedding," Sean said between gasps. The mini-cab had dropped him off at the museum's front entrance, but he still had to run up the steps to the main hall where he met the curator at the visitor's welcome desk.

Gimirri arched a stern brow. "Congratulations."

Sean's eyes darted to the curator. "Not *my* wedding! Commander Lazar's." He was surprised to see his mouth slip into a wry smile.

"I'm only joking." The curator turned toward the administrator's hallway and beckoned for Sean to follow. "You'd have to find a woman who'd have you first."

Sean's mouth twitched as he fell in step next to him. *Touché.*

Gimirri walked, hands clasped behind his back, to the end of the corridor and opened the restoration workshop door. Sean stepped inside and looked around the deserted shop. Equipment and workstations sat idle. The room was so quiet you could hear the hands of the clock on the wall knitting the hour.

Sean blinked. "Where is everyone?" He looked over a shoulder and saw Gimirri had hung his blue cassock on a peg by the door and was busy rolling up the sleeves of his work shirt.

"You were late, so I sent them home," he said. Sean's stomach clenched. "I'm afraid you're stuck with me today." The curator gestured to Sean's sword belt. "Your sword please, Montressador." Sean arched a brow in disbelief. Gimirri sighed with impatience. "Don't look so surprised. I wasn't always the head curator. I apprenticed in a weapons restoration shop."

Sean considered his options. If he was going to make it to Vincent's wedding before the vows, he'd better do as he was told. He unbuckled his belt and handed over his blade. "Sorry I was late. I appreciate the favor."

"No trouble at all, Montressador. You've given me a unique opportunity." Gimirri pulled the sword from its sheath in one smooth whisper of steel. He smiled like a child with a birthday present as the blade rested against his palm. "Let's see now. What has he done to you?" Gimirri walked to a worktable in the back corner of the shop.

Sean followed the curator with a feeling of wonder. He'd never seen this side of the man before.

Gimirri laid the sword in the middle of a worktable and grabbed a rubber apron and gloves from a storage bin underneath.

Sean sat on a stool and drummed his fingers on the table. With nothing better to do, he craned his neck to see the artifacts waiting for repairs at the other workstations.

"Go take a look if you'd like." Gimirri nodded toward the other worktables as he poured cleaning solution into a large rectangular trough. Sean looked at the curator then glanced at his sword on the table. Gimirri's mouth curled into another rare smile. "We don't stand on tradition in the workshop, Montressador. We'd never get any work done." He submerged the sword in the basin then turned his attention to cleaning the leather belt and sheath. "It's all right. The public isn't here to see."

Sean thought for a moment as he watched Gimirri oil and work the leather with a cloth. He took a few steps away from the table. It felt strange to be out of arms reach of his blade. Sean shook off the feeling and took a closer look at the artifacts in the nearby workstations—a tapestry with an unraveling rose garden, a painting with a cracked frame. Sean stopped. Scattered across a table lay the crested helm and armor worn by Montressador Lacuna of Sky during the Battle of Tilia.

"What's wrong with Lacuna's armor?"

Gimirri lifted Sean's blade from the basin. "Some degenerates keep looking under the chain mail skirt and touching the cod plate. The fingerprints tarnish the metal. Since we can't polish just one section of armor, we have to dismantle the display and polish the entire suit."

Sean bit back a comment about cod piece polishing and simply nodded. "You could display the armor without the cod plate."

"We tried that." Gimirri sighed. "People still lift the chain mail to look and then drop trash in the hole."

Sean clamped his mouth shut and swallowed a laugh that he thought would burst through his ears. "That's terrible."

Gimirri worked a brush over the hilt of the sword. "I suppose it's funny, but all it does is create more work for us and damage a priceless piece of history."

Sean nodded, feeling chastised. The curator had a point. He walked to another table piled with books wrapped in clear plastic. Bowls of oil sat inside the plastic with the books.

"What's with the books?"

The curator glanced up from polishing the blade. "Book lice."

Sean jumped back to a safer distance. "*Lice?*"

"Oh, yes. They eat the glue used in the binding."

Sean leaned in again and curled a lip in disgust when he saw the tiny translucent bugs floating in the oil.

Gimirri returned the sword to its sheath. "Since you're in a hurry, I only gave it a quick polish. Bring it back in when you have more time, and my team will do a more detailed cleaning."

Sean admired the shine on the blade before buckling the belt around his hips. "This is much better. Thank you." He glanced over a shoulder toward the books again as he walked with Gimirri to the workshop door. "Do the lice only eat antique books? Not newer books I hope…"

Gimirri exchanged the apron and rubber gloves for his blue cassock. "Unless you have books that are two hundred years old or more, you have nothing to worry about. And these lice only like books, not people."

"That's a relief." All this talk of lice was making Sean's scalp itch. He checked the workshop clock on the wall as they passed. If he hurried, he'd only be fashionably late and avoid Mirina's wrath.

"There used to be a strain of book lice that *would* infect people," Gimirri said as they stepped into the hall and walked to the front entrance. "Nasty things. Big as a man's pinkie. They used to call them Royal Lice because only people rich enough to buy leather books would catch them."

"Hmmm…Seems like a bigger problem than polishing cod pieces." Sean scratched the back of his head.

The curator shot him a knowing look. "Thankfully, that strain is extinct now. They haven't been seen in hundreds of years. We've only had one encounter with Royal Lice. Back when the National Museum moved into the old winter palace."

Sean slowed his step and looked at the curator. "The museum used to be a *palace*?"

Gimirri nodded. "Parts of it. Most people don't

know because the museum has grown up around the original palace footprint."

Sean's heart beat faster as Ira's words came back to him. *I saw him in the palace.* "Which parts?"

Gimirri frowned in thought. "It's hard to say. The galleries have grown so it's almost impossible to tell where the original foundation is anymore, but the interior galleries in the East Wing are most definitely parts of the original residence."

"The East Wing." Sean gulped. "You mean Montressador's Hall?"

"Yes." Gimirri gave a puzzled look. "Syrovar's gallery used to be the original palace library. It was completely infested with Royal Lice when the museum renovated the space to expand the Hall. We have Montressador Goreck's signature giving the museum permission to hire an exterminator." The curator eyed him. "Montressador, are you all right? You look rather pale all of the sudden."

Sean felt like he'd walked into a wall. Sweat poured under his shirt. "How long ago was this?"

"Six hundred years give or take a decade."

Sean's head swam. *The watcher in the palace. The second spacetime distortion.* The image of the red beetle scuttling into Ira's hairline flashed in Sean's memory. He took a breath to steady his nerves. Maybe there was no need to panic just yet.

"Gimirri." Sean gripped the hilt of his sword. "What do Royal Lice look like?"

Sean stumbled down the museum steps in a daze. The glow of the setting sun painted the city skyline in swirls of pink and yellow cream while the sky above held on to the afternoon's pale blue. Nothing had changed since Sean had entered the museum— nothing except the impossible had become probable.

Cox's Conundrum had failed. Two thousand years had passed since the Time Quake and the Awakening. Time travel for Andarrians on their home world had been impossible while Cox had held, but if what Sean suspected was true, Ira had traveled back in time far enough to stand in the library of the winter palace and brought back with him Royal Lice. Sean's mind staggered with the implications.

"Montressador! HEY! Did you still need that ride?"

The driver of the mini-cab called to him from the bottom of the museum steps. Sean had forgotten he'd asked the driver to wait for him. He pulled his thoughts together and climbed into the backseat. " Take me to the Luctari camp."

Fionna answered her data link pad on the third beep. "Knox."

"Fionna. It's me." Sean spoke quickly as park scenery flashed past the mini-cab's window. "Do you still have Ira in custody for questioning?"

"No, we released him this afternoon. The interviewers couldn't get anything useful out of him. Aren't you supposed to be at a wedding?"

"We've got a problem. You need to go to the Luctari camp and find Ira. Check him for lice. Big ones."

"*Lice?* What are you talking about?"

Sean saw the driver's eyes flick in the cab's rear-view mirror. "I can't explain right now. I'll meet you at the camp."

"I can get the Ministry of Health to shut down the whole camp if you—"

"NO!" The driver's eyes narrowed. Sean lowered his voice for whatever good it would do. "Just Ira. Do it now. Keep it quiet. Make up an excuse to take him in. Bring Kegler to help. You'll figure it out."

"Figure *what* out?"

The mini-cab swerved hard. Sean crashed against the passenger door window as the small craft rocked on its side then righted itself like a bathtub toy. Sean's data link pad bounced across the cab's interior and landed on the floor.

The driver laid on the horn and shouted a stream of curses as a figure ran past the front of the mini-cab. Sean lunged for his data link pad.

"Montressador!" Fionna's voice came through the device. "What's going on?"

"Sorry! I dropped my..." Sean glanced through the window. His pulse spiked. A Luctari woman in a dancer's outfit ran into the woods. The mini-cab started to move forward then slammed to a stop as a second figure darted in front of the cab, throwing Sean against the front seat. Sean yelled and swore along with the driver.

The driver shouted and flashed a rude gesture at the second figure. "Get out of the way!"

Sean blinked. His mouth hung open as he watched a man wearing a chicken mask run into the woods after the Luctari woman.

"Fionna, I gotta go. I just saw Felicity. I'll meet you at the camp."

"Wait! Where are—"

Sean ended the call, threw a handful of bills at the driver, and exited the cab.

The driver shouted after him. "You should arrest all of them. Worthless freaks." The mini-cab sped off.

Sean plunged into the underbrush. The Chicken Man dodged through the trees ahead of him, gaining on Felicity with every stride. Sean gritted his teeth and put on a burst of speed. The Chicken Man caught up with Felicity, leaped over a downed log, and slammed the Luctari woman into the ground in a back-breaking tackle. Felicity screamed as the man struck her again and again in a rage.

"Hey!" Sean reached for the hilt of his sword as he ran. "Hey, you!"

The Chicken Man jumped to his feet and spun. Steel flashed. Sean's blade cleared leather and crashed against the Chicken's weapon. He looked at the other man's sword. The golden leaves on the guard of Montressador Syrovar's sword caught against Sean's blade.

The foes separated. Swords raised. Sean eyed the flat stare of the Chicken Man's mask. Felicity moaned at his feet and dragged herself backward, breathing hard. Blood dripped from her nose and mouth. Her eyes, round with fear, darted to Sean's. The Chicken's head jerked to Felicity then back to Sean. The motion of the mask was almost comical despite the snarl on the chicken's beak.

Sean shifted his stance and tightened the grip on his hilt. The weight of the blade balanced perfectly between earth and sky. He kept one eye on the Chicken Man and muttered to Felicity. "Run."

The two swords crashed as the combatants lunged toward each other. Sean pivoted and blocked the Chicken's blade. He pushed the tip of his sword forward in a counter-strike to the Chicken Man's head. The Chicken dodged and turned his blade upward, pushing Sean's sword away. The Chicken attacked again, this time from the opposite side. Sean stepped clear and met the strike. He countered with an attack of his own. The ring of steel filled the glade. The swordsmen circled each other, moving between light and shadow, each trying to gain an advantage in the wooded terrain.

Sean pivoted, dodging the Chicken's blade, and swung high as he passed. His blade parted through the top of the man's mask, slicing through the Chicken's comb. The red rubber of the mask fluttered to the ground. The Chicken Man turned, stunned. He looked at Sean and felt the top of his head with the palm of one hand then looked at his fingers as if checking for blood.

Sean grinned and lifted a shoulder with a shrug. "Whoops?"

The battle resumed. Swords spun and crashed together. Sean's breath came faster, the shirt under his jacket sweated through. He was pleased to see the Chicken Man's shirt was also drenched with sweat. The man's chest heaved with exertion. Sean could hear the man gasping for air underneath the mask.

"How can you breathe through that thing?" Sean pivoted, dodged the Chicken's blade, and followed through with a thrust of his own. "Don't you want to take your mask off?"

The Chicken's sword slid down the length of Sean's blade past the guard. Sean stepped aside just as the tip of the blade nipped his arm, slicing a neat cut through the fabric of the jacket. Sean winced as the blade drew blood.

"Well done!" Sean's sword flashed in a diagonal, cutting deep across the Chicken's thigh. *Heh. Chicken. Thigh.* "But you're still learning."

The force of the Chicken Man's attacks lessened. The man puffed like a steam engine underneath the rubber mask. Sean took control, blocking and countering at will. He pressed forward, pushing his opponent toward a bare patch of ground riddled with tree roots, hoping to gain an advantage on the uneven terrain. The Chicken Man spotted the trap and spun to one side, but Sean's sword was faster. The edge of the blade sliced upward through the rubber mask where the beak met the chicken's head. The man screamed as the rubber parted and the chicken's beak fell to the ground. The man covered his face with a hand. Blood seeped through his fingers. When the man removed his hand, the lower half of his face was covered in blood. He was missing the tip of his nose. The mask still covered the man's eyes and forehead.

That face...Where have I seen it? Sean pointed his sword at his opponent, breathing hard. "Yield!"

The Chicken Man raised his sword with a hoarse yell and attacked with renewed fury. The swords clashed again and again. Sean countered every strike and pushed forward.

"Yield!"

The Chicken wheezed and struggled to block.

"Yield!"

Sean pushed the Chicken Man's blade aside.

"Yield or I *will* kill you!"

Sean unleashed a devastating series of blows pushing the Chicken backward. The blades met again with a mighty crash that shattered Syrovar's sword at the midpoint and threw the Chicken to the ground still holding the hilt.

Sean pointed his blade at his foe and stepped closer. "You're done. Drop your sword and come with me."

The Chicken Man pointed the remains of Syrovar's sword at Sean and fumbled with the grip. Sean sighed and lowered his blade a fraction.

"Come on. Give it up. You can't fight with—"

A shot ripped through the air. A force hit Sean in the shoulder. Momentum spun him, knocking him backward to the ground. Sean gasped. Raw, burning pain deep within his shoulder throbbed, his arm numb. The smell of gunpowder and burning flesh filled his nose. Sean released the hilt of his sword and touched the wound on his shoulder. Blood painted his fingertips and pooled under his shirt as he remembered the description of Syrovar's sword he had given to Fionna at the museum. *One-shot brass barreled pistol mounted on the right ricasso. The trigger located below the clamshell languet.*

"Damn." Sean grimaced against the pain. He wheezed out a laugh at the absurdity. "You brought a gun...to a sword fight." His lungs protested and he coughed so hard sparkles filled the corners of his eyes.

The Chicken Man stood over Sean, still holding the hilt of Syrovar's broken sword. Smoke drifted from the barrel of the pistol hidden in the hilt. The remains of the rubber chicken mask shifted. Light through the trees spotlighted where the mask had been cut away by Sean's blade.

My God. Sean gasped as he looked up at the man's face. *The guard from Montressador's Keep.*

The edges of Sean's vision darkened. His breathing deepened as he struggled to remain conscious. Sean looked past Connor's face. He stared at the treetops against the blue sky tinged with pink. His heartbeats slowed as blue faded to black.

TWENTY-EIGHT

THE WEDDING

Ann checked the time on her data link pad and sent Sean another message.

Where the hell are you?

She'd stood in the foyer of Hautwesel Hall tapping out messages for thirty minutes without a single reply. Another group of wedding guests arrived and streamed past into the grand hall. Ann's mouth twisted in irritation as she fired off a final series of messages.

You.

Are.

Such.

An.

Ass.

Ann shoved the device back into her purse after the last ping and turned to Josephine with a sigh. "I'm sorry, Jo. I don't know where that idiot brother of mine could be. He said he would be right behind us. We might as well go in."

Jo smiled and shrugged bare shoulders. "It's all right, Anaya. It was an agreement, not a date. I still

SPLICE

got a new dress out of the deal." She smoothed manicured hands over the curve of her hips. The hourglass silhouette of her midnight blue gown had drawn appreciative looks from male—and a few female—guests since they arrived. "And to be honest at times like this I've learned…" Jo's words trailed off as her eyes focused past Ann.

She followed Jo's gaze hoping to see her brother and instead saw a distinguished, broad-shouldered gentleman wearing a dark gray suit enter the foyer. Ann arched a brow. *My…my…* Like many of the other guests, the cut of the man's suit and his confident manner as he surveyed the room hinted at a social standing well above most other capital city residents. She had to give Mirina credit. Her guest list *was* impressive. Ann had watched many prominent members of the capital city elite enter the hall, including politicians, military brass, and even several foreign ambassadors.

The man's face brightened in recognition when he saw Jo standing by the entrance to the grand hall. Jo blushed and returned the man's smile along with a discrete wave. She looked to Ann. A mischievous glint sparkled in her eyes underneath dark curls. "As I was saying…I've learned at times like this, there's always a backup plan. Please excuse me."

Jo crossed the foyer with fluid grace and greeted the man in the gray suit. The man kissed Jo's hand. Ann smirked, impressed. Jo's ongoing arrangement with Sean to fill in as needed as his date to formal functions had certainly resulted in some *interesting* side benefits for the office assistant.

Ann left the foyer and crossed into the grand hall. Rows of chairs created an aisle in front of the palatial marble staircase. Guests mingled. A few had already claimed their seats, but John was nowhere in sight.

"Anaya!"

Ann looked over a shoulder and smiled as she saw Vincent walking toward her. As usual, the commander wore his blue dress uniform, but this time he also wore a traditional groom's stole in gold draped around his shoulders.

"I'm so glad you came," Vincent said, pulling Ann into a hug. "I wish we could have gotten together before now. I haven't met John and you haven't met Mirina yet."

"It's great to see you." Ann looked into Vincent's beaming face. "I'm looking forward to meeting Mirina." A slight exaggeration on Ann's part, but her guilt was softened when Vincent's smile brightened another degree.

"I'll introduce you at dinner. She wants to make a grand entrance." Vincent looked around. His eyes crinkled with concern. "Where's Sean?"

Ann bit her tongue to keep from cringing. "He's on his way. I was looking for John if you want to meet him?" Anything to distract Vincent from the fact that his best friend hadn't arrived yet.

An attendant across the room beckoned. Vincent waved back and looked to Ann as he retreated across the hall. "I need to go, but you might try the drawing room." He pointed to a set of doors. "A few guests are waiting in there." Vincent grinned over a shoulder. "When Sean gets here, the six of us should share a bottle of wine."

Ann smiled and turned with a wave. "That would be wonderful!" If *he ever gets here*, she thought.

More than a few guests had found the gilded oasis of the drawing room. Ann could barely see past the milling crowd. An ice sculpture filled the center of the room surrounded by large serving bowls of frothy pink wedding punch. White-gloved attendants circulated with silver trays of drinks and canapés. Ann chose a glass of punch from a passing waiter to sip as she wandered.

Several well-dressed gentlemen gathered at the bar caught Ann's attention. One man picked up his glass and turned to watch the rest of the room. Ann's heart leaped in surprise. The classic lines of John's black suit and blue vest came straight from the shops in downtown Palladium Beta. The familiar stiff pigtail at the back of his head was the only thing that hinted he was from the Colonies.

John took a sip of whiskey. Ann saw his eyes widen and he almost spilled his drink when he saw her walking towards him. Her heart did another flip as John grinned and watched her as she crossed the room.

"Imagine finding you at the bar," Ann said as she slid into the open space next to him.

"Some habits never die," John said, turning toward her.

"Nice suit."

John opened one side of his jacket to show the vest. "Do you like it?"

Ann smiled. The blue vest underneath brought out the color of his eyes. She sipped her punch. "It will do."

John's eyes skimmed her silhouette. He leaned forward and whispered in her ear. "How long do we need to stay?"

A shiver of delight ran down Ann's spine. She rolled a hip as she turned to lean against the bar. "Wedding etiquette says it's usually a good idea for guests to stay at least until after the vows are done."

John flashed another roguish grin over the top of his glass. "Then I'll wait." He took a sip. His eyes turned more serious. "Any more news on Sarolea?"

Ann blew out a sigh. "She's going to be all right. Sleep is the best thing for her. Drake's still scouting out basements in the historic district last I heard." The same nagging thought dogged her memory of the interview. Ann frowned and set her glass on the bar.

John gave her a questioning look. "Something wrong?"

She shook her head. "Just a feeling I can't shake."

"In my experience, I've found those feelings to be the most useful." John set his empty glass on the bar and motioned to the bartender. "What's it telling you?"

Ann took a sip of punch and pursed her mouth. "The way Sarolea first described the basement. She didn't call it a basement. Drake was the one who called it that first. She only said that it felt like they were underground."

"So, Drake led her to it." John picked up the fresh drink the bartender had set down.

Ann nodded. "Sarolea agreed with him, but I don't think she really *believed* it was a basement. When I asked Drake about it, he said that a basement was the only thing that made sense and that trauma causes muddled thinking."

"He has a point." John swirled the amber liquid in his glass. "But it does sound like Drake was the one that planted that idea in her head."

Ann thought for a moment. "An echo. Sarolea said there was an echo. Like a cave."

John fingered his pigtail. "An echo means whatever it is it's a fairly large space..." He shook his head and shrugged. "I suppose it could just be a large basement."

Ann smirked. "A masterful analysis. Are you sure you want to give away such wise council for free?"

John grinned and clinked his glass against hers. "If it's free, then you can't complain if I'm wrong."

Chimes sounded telling guests it was time to take their seats. Ann and John finished their drinks and joined the other guests moving toward the grand hall. Ann waved to Jo sitting with her gentleman friend. She looked around and frowned as they took their seats. Still no Sean.

John took her hand and leaned in. "Where's your brother?"

She worried her lip. It was the question of the evening. "He's running very late."

The lights in the hall dimmed and the groom's processional music began. Vincent, looking resplendent in blue and gold, took his place at the bottom of the stairs and waited, looking back down the aisle a bit nervously Ann thought. She smiled as she saw Vincent release a deep breath and covertly tug at the bottom of his jacket.

The music stopped. The lights went out completely and were replaced by a single spotlight on a figure at the top of the staircase. Vincent turned. The guests let out a collective gasp then murmured approval as the bride's music began.

John muttered, *"What in the bloody hell is that?"*

Ann elbowed John in the side and looked again. Her mouth fell open.

The bride hadn't chosen a modern or even a traditional wedding dress, but rather a gown that harkened back to the days of the monarchy. In a word, the dress was enormous. Yards of gold fabric wrapped tightly to form the bodice and then bloomed into a full ball gown skirt that almost filled the entire space between the railings of the staircase. Mirina carried a bouquet of white orchids that gleamed in the spotlight. Her hair was piled high on her head in curls the size of teacakes. In a smaller venue, the bouffant would have encountered resistance from the ceiling. But the bride's most striking feature by far was the train that flowed from her shoulders and followed in her wake. Mirina beamed a smile as wide as her skirt as she stepped slowly down the staircase. The train of her dress grew longer with every step along with the guests' and the groom's amazement. When she finally stood next to Vincent, the train stretched all the way back up to the top of the grand staircase in a continuous river of gold.

The guests broke into applause, unusual for such a formal occasion. A man seated behind Ann burst out, "Stunning! An absolute triumph!"

Ann exchanged amused glances with John. He leaned over as he clapped and whispered, "I don't know about stunning, but the groom does look stunned."

Ann chuckled. Vincent did look more than a bit shell-shocked by the spectacle.

They exchanged vows and the happy couple was presented to the guests as husband and wife. In the end, the bride was released from her train, attendants flung open the doors to the ballroom, and the bridal couple escorted their guests into dinner.

Instead of joining the queue, John grabbed Ann's hand and steered her back through the drawing room onto a balcony overlooking the gardens. Lights burned from the windows of Hautwesel Hall, but the hedgerows and garden paths stretched into the shadows. The sunset was only a memory on the horizon and the moon had not yet reached her peak. He slipped an arm around her waist, pulled her into an embrace, and kissed her till Ann thought her sandals would melt from her feet.

John whispered in her ear. "Do you think we've

stayed long enough we could make our exit now?"

Temptation pulled Ann, but then she remembered that Sean had already missed the wedding. If they didn't show up for dinner, Vincent would feel as if all his friends had abandoned him.

"We can't." Ann sighed as John left a trail of kisses from her neck to her shoulder. "Not yet. We haven't congratulated the happy couple."

"Wedding etiquette again?"

"Yes." Ann felt her resolve begin to buckle as John's hand slid across her hip.

"They won't miss us for a few minutes." His fingers explored the top of the slit in her dress. He muttered, "Weddings were easier when I was a freighter pirate."

Ann chuckled then bit her lip as his hand reached the back of her thigh. "You went to a lot of weddings?"

"Only one. We stole all the gifts and kidnapped the bride." John pressed his lips to hers again.

An energy pulse crashed Ann's senses. She winced and rubbed a temple.

John took a step back. His face darkened. "What's wrong?"

"Spacetime distortion." It wasn't as loud as when she wore the keravnos implant, but it was still loud enough.

"Where?"

Ann blinked and tried to focus. "It's close...it's..." Fear prickled the back of her scalp. "The ballroom."

John and Ann ran from the balcony through the

drawing room to the grand hall.

"It's the same energy pulse I sensed at the time jumper's monument," Ann said, her sandals clicking on the tile floor.

"When the bodies of the crew appeared?"

Ann nodded. "But the killer also used directional anchors to gain access to the museum when he stole the sword. He could be inside with the guests." The lively strains of a grand waltz drifted into the hall. Whatever was happening inside the ballroom, there were no outward signs there was anything wrong.

John reached into his jacket and pulled an ion pistol from a back holster.

Ann gave him a look as they stopped on either side of the ballroom doors. "You brought a pistol to a wedding?"

"You didn't?" John blinked. "Is this more wedding etiquette I should know about?" He flipped the safety and charged the pistol's power cell to full strength.

Ann gestured to the silhouette of her dress, one hand on a hip. "Where would I put it?"

John smirked, pulled a second pistol from an ankle holster, and handed it over.

Ann winced as a second energy pulse blared in her head. The sounds of the orchestra trickled to a stop. She locked eyes with John. "A second energy pulse."

John's face brightened in surprise. "Any way to tell if the pulse was incoming or outgoing?"

"No." Ann charged her pistol's power cell. "But our nanobot tracker should be able to track any movements."

John nodded. "Ready?"

"Yeah." Ann tightened her grip on the pistol and felt the charge of the power cell hum under her fingers. She held the pistol behind her purse as best she could.

John narrowed his eyes. "If you feel yourself hesitating again..."

She gulped and nodded. "I'm fine."

John opened the door to the ballroom, and they slipped inside. The packed room buzzed with wedding guests, some standing while others huddled at their tables talking excitedly. Couples on the dance floor looked toward the orchestra, confusion written on their faces.

Ann looked around past groups of people. "I can't see anything."

"I don't like this," John said, shielding his pistol under his jacket. "Let's spread out. See what we can find." He looked around at the excited guests. He returned the weapon to its holster but kept his hand on the pistol's grip. "They're spooked about something."

Ann kept her pistol close to her body, shielded by her purse, and pushed into the crowd. A group of musicians gathered in the orchestra's string section made frantic gestures, their backs to the dance floor. Ann moved closer. A page of sheet music slipped from a music stand and fluttered to the floor, joining more pages scattered across the stage. A cellist moved to pick up the music and the knot of musicians parted. Ann stopped and stared. The first violin's chair sat empty. On the floor, a discarded violin lay upside down on the stage next to a glass of ice water. Ann's pulse rocketed. *The water tanks.*

A crescendo blasted through her head as another energy pulse ripped through the ballroom. A woman in a floral dress near the dance floor screamed. The air around her shimmered. Guests watched horror-struck as the woman's body folded, snapped backward, and disappeared through a rip in the air.

Terror whipped the crowd with chaos at his heels. The room exploded as guests screamed and stampeded. Tables overturned. Plates and centerpieces shattered on the floor. Ann looked for John and was knocked down by the panicked crowd. She grabbed the edge of a table and pulled herself up in time to see him fall under the heels of fleeing guests.

"John!"

Ann's mind flicked through the options. *Can I get to him in time? What if...?* Her thoughts spun. She closed her eyes, lifted her pistol, and fired two laser blasts into the ceiling, hitting the crystal chandelier. Sparks and glass showered the ballroom. Guests fled from her like ripples on a pond. Ann helped John to his feet, and they dove for cover between an empty serving table and the wall.

"Are you all right?"

John swept his bangs from his eyes and nodded. "Thanks for that."

"The killer is taking more victims." Ann winced as three more crescendos took a trio of guests in quick succession. "I've got to get a message to Fionna." She fumbled for the data link pad in her purse.

John looked over the table at the carnage. "We need to get everyone out of the ballroom."

"It won't matter where they run." Another crescendo rocked Ann's head. She watched as a man lying on the floor tried to escape being trampled but was pulled sideways into the distortion. "They were already exposed to nanobots and Splice."

"But at least the rest of us won't get trampled to death." John stepped from behind the table and fired four shots in quick succession, taking the hinges off the closest set of doors.

The doors burst open and fell to the floor. Guests streamed through. Ann took aim and fired toward the doors at the opposite end of the ballroom, clearing a second exit.

Guests fled, shoving tables and chairs out of their way in their panic. An ice sculpture tipped and crashed in an explosion of icy shards. More screams filled the ballroom as fleeing guests slipped on chunks of ice and fell as they ran toward the exits. Ann saw Mirina, wide-eyed at the head table, frozen in fear as wedding guests continued to disappear. Vincent grabbed her arm and pulled her through the crowd toward one of the large stained-glass windows overlooking the gardens. He picked up a chair to break the glass and helped Mirina step through. Another guest tried to follow but was buffeted by the surge of the crowd. A crescendo trumpeted in Ann's head and the man was pulled through the distortion in the floor and disappeared.

A luckless waiter slipped on some ice and caught his balance on the edge of John and Ann's table. A second of relief filled his face as he made eye contact with them. Ann heard the crescendo of an energy pulse. The waiter's face took on a strange expression right before he was sucked backward into the distortion.

Ann caught a glimpse of Jo as she ran for the exit. Another crescendo and a woman following Jo screamed and was pulled upward through a distortion.

The ballroom emptied of the remaining guests. Screams and the sound of running feet followed. Ann and John stepped from behind the table.

"I sent a message to Fionna." Ann looked at the data link pad in her hand. "With that many people phasing, the nanobot tracker should have picked up the signals."

A peculiar sensation covered Ann like the fluttering wings of a moth. A metal taste flooded her mouth, souring her stomach. Ann fumbled the data link pad and pistol and they fell to the floor.

She swallowed hard. "John?"

The fluttery sensation on her skin increased. The air shimmered. She tried to catch her breath.

"Ann, are you—" John reached for her hand.

The crescendo blasted through Ann's head. Pain sliced through her insides as her body folded. A force jerked her backward, squeezing her through a black tunnel. The light from the ballroom receded to a pinprick and winked out.

TWENTY-NINE

TAKEN

John's hand hung stupidly in the air, reaching out into empty space where Ann had stood only a split second before. The bright flash that accompanied her disappearance still burned in his eyes. John's mind flexed, struggling with what he had just witnessed. Fear's icy fingers played timpani along his spine.

No. No no no...

The crack of wood hitting the floor echoed through the ballroom like a shot. John spun, dropped to one knee, and aimed his pistol.

A wedding guest had crawled out from under a table and stumbled into a wooden chair, knocking it over backward. The man's forward motion pulled the tablecloth after him as the place settings followed, shattering on the floor one after another in a trail of destruction. He finally shed the tablecloth, regained his footing, and sprinted from the wreckage of the ballroom.

John ground his teeth, pushing the fear from his

mind. Ann was gone. Taken by the killer. He couldn't waste time gawping. He had to find her. John holstered his weapon and reached for the data pad and pistol Ann had dropped. A quick scan of the device's screen showed the last message Ann had sent and Fionna's reply.

Fionna: Already on the way. Be there soon.

John pocketed the device and returned Ann's pistol to his ankle holster. He would meet Fionna at the hall's front entrance. He turned toward the closest ballroom exit.

The sparkle of a large diamond ring hurtling toward his face caught John's attention a second before a fist slammed into his eye.

"YOU SON OF A BITCH!"

John staggered and blinked, struggling to bring the wall of gold taffeta in front of him into focus.

Ambassador Mirina Canopus glared at him with all the fires of hell burning in her eyes. The bride's towering hairdo had fallen, spilling curls down her back and shoulders. One sleeve of her gown was torn open from the shoulder to the elbow. Eye makeup ran down her cheeks in rivulets of black. Only a trace of pink lipstick remained on her lips. The rest had smeared to one side of her mouth.

Commander Vincent Lazar and two stewards wearing Hautwesel Hall's customary black and yellow livery flanked the enraged bride and looked on in stunned horror. Lazar's wedding attire had fared better than his wife's dress, although he was missing his groom's sash and one sleeve of his uniform jacket looked as if he'd dragged it through his dinner plate. A glob of mashed potatoes and a stray green bean still clung to the cuff.

Mirina sharpened her gaze and pointed at John. "Arrest this man!"

John rubbed his bruised eye, still feeling the sting of the bride's fist. He'd have a proper shiner within an hour. "Ambassador...?"

The stewards traded nervous glances. Lazar, recovered from his shock, placed a tentative hand on his wife's arm. "Mirina, I think there's been a misundersta—"

The ambassador wheeled on her new husband. "I saw him, Vincent! He shot the chandelier! HE'S responsible for all THIS!" She gestured to the broken chairs and tables and general destruction strewed about the ballroom. The aroma of roast beef in red wine still drifted through the air. She turned her anger back to John. "Arrest him! Arrest him NOW or give me your pistol so I can blast his feckless head off his shoulders!"

Lazar cringed, a painful expression that John suspected would soon become the commander's standard response to all his wife's demands, and shifted uncomfortably. "It wasn't his fault, darling. The guests were already panicked. I saw them disappearing."

John tried to bite down on his anger, but he didn't have time for diplomacy. He returned the ambassador's glare. The heat from his anger grew as he growled out the words, "Your guests were panicking because the time jumper killer was abducting them using SPLICE!" Mirina's eyes grew round with surprise, but the new information did little to ease the rage simmering on her face. "If Ann and I hadn't shot the hinges off the exit doors, your guests would have trampled themselves to DEATH!"

Lazar's expression changed to surprised recognition as his eyes darted to John. "You're Captain Galeas." He looked around the ballroom. "Where's Anaya?"

"Gone!" Fear tightened John's inside's before being smothered again by his rising anger. "She was taken like all the others. Agent Knox is on her way."

"Why would the killer take my wedding guests?" Mirina demanded, hands on her slender hips. "What does my wedding have to do with time jumpers?"

"I don't know." John shrugged out of his suit jacket, tossed it over the back of a lone dining chair, and started rolling up his sleeves. "You had a lot of important people on your guest list. The killer might be trying to make some kind of a political statement, but that doesn't matter right now. We need to figure out who was taken. Maybe that will tell us something."

A muffled shout came from the hall outside.

John hollered toward the open doorway, "In the ballroom!"

Agent Fionna Knox stepped through a second later followed by a crew of technicians carrying equipment. Her bio-vision glasses rested on the top of her blond head.

"I want every distortion mapped," Fionna said to a tech walking next to her as she strode past the shattered remains of an ice sculpture. Her boots crunched on the icy shards. "Keep scanning for more with the nanobot tracker. See if you can get a read on where they were taken." The tech nodded and hurried toward where the other techs were setting up a command post. Fionna nodded to Commander Lazar and Ambassador Canopus when she reached the group then turned to John. "We started getting hits on the nanobot tracker a few minutes before I got Anaya's message." She pulled her data pad from an inside jacket pocket and looked around. "Where is she?"

"Taken," John said. Fionna's violet eyes crinkled with concern. "The last one as far as I know." He gave Fionna a quick summary of events.

Fionna gave a grim nod and entered the information into her data pad. "The tracker picked up a total of two hundred and thirty-seven separate distortions."

Mirina stared at Fionna in disbelief. "That's a third of the guest list."

"Not all of them were guests," John said. "We saw a waiter get taken."

"One of the musicians too, I think," Commander Lazar added.

"My techs are scanning for secondary distortions." Fionna's fingers flew over the data pad's screen. "If our tracker can pick up when they rematerialize, we'll know where the killer's taken them."

She looked to Mirina. "I need you and Commander Lazar to gather up all the remaining staff and guests and make a list of the missing."

"All of the guests checked in as they arrived." A steely resolve tightened the bride's mouth and drained away the last of her anger. "I can get you a copy of the list." She nodded to the closest steward who hurried away.

A new fear twisted John's gut. "Sean never arrived that I know of. Ann said he was running late."

Grief flicked through Fionna's eyes as she looked up from her data pad. "The Montressador's been shot."

John's head reeled. Lazar muttered a curse.

Mirina appeared to sag under the weight of her taffeta for an instant. "Is he all right?"

Fionna pressed her lips into a thin white line. John braced himself, fearing the worst. "He was alive when they took him to the hospital. That's all I know." She looked down at her data pad and regained a more professional tone as she read from the screen. "He was found in the Wilds near the museum about forty minutes ago. A Luctari woman we've been looking for turned herself in and reported the shooting to the park authorities."

John took an agitated swipe through his hair, remembering the updates Ann had sent him. "Felicity."

Fionna nodded. "Agent Drake's interviewing her now."

Lazar threw his arm toward the rest of the ballroom. "Could it be related to all this?"

"That's what Drake's trying to find out," Fionna said. "Felicity's been a person of interest in the time jumper killings for some time." She tapped the screen on her data pad. "I need to know what everyone was drinking tonight."

Mirina threw the agent a puzzled look. "It was a wedding. Wine, of course."

"Whiskey. Neat." John answered and was surprised to hear Commander Lazar's voice echo his own.

"What about Anaya?"

John shook his head, trying to remember. "Something pink. Frothy."

"Wedding punch." Mirina sighed with exasperation. She looked to Fionna and spread her hands. "Why? What does it matter?"

The steward returned with a data stick and handed it to Fionna.

"The killer has used both water and alcohol as a delivery method for the nanobots and Splice." Fionna downloaded the information from the data stick.

Lazar's eyes widened. "The punch is made with shaved ice."

Fionna flagged down a passing tech. "Check the water tanks. If it's in the water, it'll be in the ice." The tech hurried toward the kitchen. Fionna looked to Mirina and handed back the data stick. "Thank you, Ambassador. I'm sorry for—"

A warning bell pealed from the makeshift command post. All heads turned to the tech waving frantically in their direction.

"Agent Knox! We have incoming distortions!"

John hurried with Fionna to the tech seated at the console.

Fionna scanned the screen. "Where?"

"They should be visible on the tracker now," the tech said, tapping keys.

John peered at the three-dimensional map of the capital city as ten bright pin pricks of light rippled across the screen in singles and pairs.

John traded looks with Fionna. Her knitted expression mirrored his own confusion.

"What's he doing?" Fionna rested a hand on the console, leaning over the map. "Why would the killer take them only to have them reappear all over the city?"

John's eyes darted across the screen, mind racing. There was no discernable pattern. No grouping in one area or even a single district. The dots of light looked as if they had been carelessly scattered like a handful of pebbles strewn across the map. The Financial District. The Historic District. The Waterfront and Warehouse Districts. *What's the connection?*

The breath hitched in John's throat as the shock of adrenaline exploded through his veins. *The most dangerous part of being a time jumper was reappearing and not knowing where you might be, and in a city the size of Palladium Beta with its towering structures, crowded skyways, water connections, and electrical grids...*

"Fionna," John tried to swallow. His mouth had turned as dry as dust. "He's not going to kill them by his own hand this time." He pointed to the dots on the screen. "He's going to let the directional anchors do it. They'll be killed the moment they reappear, and they could reappear anywhere." John locked eyes with the agent. *"Anywhere he could get an anchor to fit."*

Fionna's back stiffened. The horror of his words came to light in her eyes.

John gulped the fear rising in the back of his throat. "If there's any chance of saving them...*of saving Ann*...we've got to get to her as soon as she reappears and hope we can get there in time."

Fionna spun back toward the tech. "Relay the tracker information directly to my data pad. Notify all the other Ministry teams. We need to flood the city with first responders and alert teams in real-time. Recruit everyone you can." Fionna nodded in John's direction as she turned and headed for the door. "Captain, you're with me."

The pin pricks of white light on the navigational screen bathed the hovercar's interior in a bluish-white glow as they sped through downtown Palladium Beta. In the time since they'd left Hautwesel Hall, the number of dots on the screen had tripled from ten to thirty.

"Only send coordinates for victims matching Lieutenant Chapman's description," John shouted through the comm and braced himself in the passenger seat as Fionna accelerated the hovercar into a curved on-ramp like a battle cruiser jumping into warp. "That last one was a forty-year-old male!"

"I'm sorry, Captain." The dispatcher's voice that came through the control panel sounded young but carried an edge of cool efficiency. "We're doing our best. The state of some of the victims and where they've been found—" Alarms sounded in the background and the dispatcher swore under his breath. John traded looks with Fionna in the driver's seat. "We'll notify you again when we have something. Dispatch out."

John ground his teeth in frustration. Each new dot that appeared on the screen sent a punch to his gut. Teams were already reporting mangled bodies all over the city. Victims impaled on posts, crushed by light rail trains, shattered bodies on pavement after falling to their deaths from impossible heights. The images would haunt him later in his dreams, but for now, he could only feel relief when the victim's description was relayed over the comm. *Not Ann. Not that one.*

The map changed again, and three new dots appeared.

"Entertainment District!" John pointed to the dot a few blocks west of their position. "We're the closest team."

Fionna eyed the screen, nodded, and took the car into a hard-left turn.

John returned his focus to the passenger console and the screen where Agent Drake's sullen face waited impatiently. "Drake. Say that again."

"Felicity identified the killer. His name is Jessup Connor. He was working in the Royal Guard at Montressador's Keep. Montressador Chapman must have figured it out and that's why Connor shot him."

Fionna frowned from the driver's seat. "He never said anything about Connor." She squeezed the hovercar between two large transports and slipped out the other side as smooth as glass. Her eyes flicked back to Drake on the passenger comm screen. "What else did Felicity tell you?"

"She knows where Connor's hiding," Drake said. Smug satisfaction curled one side of his mouth. "She told me Connor thinks we'll be too busy rescuing wedding guests to bother with him. I'm taking a squad. We'll catch him by surprise and have him in lockup before midnight. Keep tracking down wedding guests. We'll reconnect later." The screen winked out before either could reply.

John gripped the arm rests with his fingers. *Jessup Connor.* The name meant nothing to him. He didn't care who the killer was. There would be plenty of time to kill Connor later if... John pushed the thought from his mind.

Fionna edged the hovercar through the crowded Entertainment District, setting down on the curb in front of a nightclub. A knot of people had already gathered. *A bad sign.* A gawker in front of the crowd reeled back through the onlookers and puked on the walkway.

John exited the car and followed Fionna. He muscled his way through the crowd and stopped short. He swallowed hard to keep the gorge from rising in the back of his throat.

The crowd had gathered around a gap between two buildings – a space no bigger than the width of one of Mrs. Beaumont's saucepans. The light from the nightclub's sign revealed the bloody mass of flesh and bone inside.

The body had been squeezed into the space as if crushed by a hydraulic press and hung suspended between the two buildings a few inches from the ground, arms pinned to its sides. Blood sheeted from a single bare foot as it dangled in midair, barely brushing the blackened directional anchor on the ground beneath it. Long auburn hair covered the victim's face and the remains of a purple silk dress.

John clenched his hands at his sides. His heart beat faster. *A purple dress.* His head swam. Lights from the flashing club sign blurred his vision. *Ann wore a purple dress.*

Fionna donned a medical glove and reached into the narrow gap up to her shoulder. She lifted the woman's hair from her face. The woman's crushed jaw canted at a forty-five-degree angle. Blood dripped from the corner of her ruined mouth, staining the delicate fabric of the bodice and blurring the floral pattern into a solid shade of purple. One brown eye stared without seeing.

John swayed with weary relief. He looked at Fionna and shook his head. "It's not her."

Fionna blew out a sigh and pulled out her data link pad. "I'll tell dispatch to send a recovery team."

Guilt prickled his conscience as he felt the stare of the corpse. The unnamed woman was the victim of a merciless killer and deserved better. *They all did.* John turned back to the crowd. "Step back! Make some room!"

John slid into the hovercar's passenger side just as more alerts sounded from the comm. A second team arrived and helped secure the scene for the recovery team.

He closed his eyes and rested his head back against the seat. He heard Fionna open the driver's door and climb in.

"It's going to be a long night," Fionna said, starting the hovercar engines.

THIRTY

INSIDE OUT

The kettle-drum of motors hammered Ann's senses in time with the sound in her ears while the smell of burning fuel and hot metal scorched her lungs. A bitter taste as sharp as metal shavings lingered on the back of her tongue. Her body ached. Her arms and legs felt as if they'd been torn away and hastily reattached. Ann peered from lidded eyes and the blackness lifted a shade at a time.

A maze of pipes ran in all directions and pulsed with a whooshing sound with the machinery above. The pipes, the machines, and the drumming of the motors pressed in. Ann tried to roll to one side in the tight space and met resistance from a pipe a few inches above her back. She fought a surge of panic. She slowed her breathing and focused her thoughts on the stone floor. The memory of the ballroom came back to her. *The black tunnel. The sensation of being squeezed through a garden hose. How long ago was that?*

Ann lifted her head as much as space would allow

and wriggled forward on her elbows. She shuddered to think what would have happened had she rematerialized in a smaller space. She squeezed past machinery and pipes, grunting with the effort, until she stood on shaky legs.

The cavernous room was filled with ancient industrial water pumps in rows ten feet high. Dials glowed from control panels like eyes in the dim light. Pipes connected the machinery then disappeared through stone walls. Nearby, a set of stairs led to a catwalk and a metal door. Ann took a step toward the stairs and the whooshing from the pipes and the pounding of the machinery stopped.

Ann froze. Dread rushed in with the silence. Her heart pounded in her head and then a familiar rhythm scraped her senses.

Long, short, short, long, short.

Adrenaline burned the remaining fog from her brain. *Directional anchors.* Hundreds of them. The anchors scratched out the same pattern from the opposite end of the room where a single light glowed from behind a row of pumps. Water dripped and echoed off stone.

Sarolea's basement?

Ann wrestled with fear. She looked toward the stairs. She needed to get aboveground. Find her bearings. Get help. But she needed to be sure. She had to see for herself. Ann took a step down a row of machinery and heard the click of her heel on the stone floor. She quickly removed her sandals, buckled the straps together, and slung them over a shoulder before moving forward on stealthy feet.

She was halfway down the aisle when the sudden pounding of the pumps of the machines starting up again almost made her jump out of her skin. Ann peered cautiously around the end of the row of machinery. Light poured from an alcove. She hesitated then stepped around the corner.

Boards balanced on stone blocks created a makeshift workstation with a lamp, comm screen, and a nanobot replicator. A large worktable pressed against the opposite wall while shelves and drawers stuffed to overflowing with books and papers filled the rest of the space. On the floor under the table, someone had tossed bloody gauze toward a trash bin and missed. An unzipped sleeping bag lay on a low cot.

Ann turned her attention back to the desk. A storage bin filled with directional anchors took up one corner. Next to the bin, a metal rack held rows of glass vials with numbers written on the stoppers. A map pinned to the wall above showed the streets and boroughs of the capital city. The same numbers as the vials appeared across the map written in red ink. Ann's pulse quickened. Here was all the evidence she needed.

Ann unpinned the map from the wall. She started to pull vials from the rack, but then a sudden thought twitched. She chose one vial and set it aside. For the remaining bottles, Ann pulled the stoppers and, working quickly, poured the liquid inside back and forth from one vial to the next until all the bottles were contaminated. The killer would get a nasty surprise if he tried to escape before Ann could get back with reinforcements. She returned the tainted vials to the rack, rolled the folded map around the remaining vial, and slipped from the workstation.

Ann moved silently between the machinery back toward the stairs. The pounding from the motors cut out again, but this time she was ready. She paused her step and listened to the echo of water dripping before moving on. The cold stone under her bare feet sent a chill up her spine. The outline of the stairs was barely visible at the end of the aisle. Ann took another step forward. Her ears pricked to the sound of a boot scrape against stone. Someone moved behind the pumps. She held her breath and stepped back into a fighter's stance.

A black shape charged from around a corner. Ann grabbed the sandals from her shoulder and swung hard. The thick heels cracked against the attacker's skull. The figure slammed into Ann and knocked her to the ground. The impact rattled her bones and punched the air from her lungs. Hands grappled. Hot breath wheezed in her face. Ann threw a fist and connected with the man's jaw. The man grunted and struggled to regain his advantage. Ann followed with a knee strike, rolled left, and threw an elbow into her attacker's face. The crack of her elbow and the yell that followed told her she'd hit home. She grabbed the map and vial from the floor and sprinted for the stairs.

Footsteps pounded behind as Ann's bare feet

slapped cold stone. She reached the bottom of the stairs and lunged for the handrail. A blow cracked across her shoulders and ripped a scream from her throat. The force of the blow sent a shock of pain down the length of her spine. The clang of metal sounded as an object struck the stone floor. Ann stumbled. Her knee slammed into the bottom step, tearing open a gash to her shin. The map and vial slipped from her fingers. Glass shattered. Ann lay against the steps gasping for air, unable to move. She moaned, clenching her teeth against the pain. Tears rolled down her face. Her back and knee throbbed in an agony of fire.

Behind her, footsteps slowed and then the dark shape of a man became visible in the half-light. The man stooped and picked up the pipe wrench he had thrown. The cold scrape of metal against stone echoed from the walls. Ann's heart hammered in her chest as the man turned toward her. Fear screamed in her head like a siren. She squeezed her eyes shut just before the man's fist smashed into the side of her skull.

Long, short, short, long, short.

Ann awoke stretched across a table with a head thick with sludge. She tried to swallow to steady the roll in her stomach, but her tongue pressed against an object that forced her mouth open. The gag's straps dug into the back of her head. Cold numbed her back and legs. She tried to move, but restraints held her to the table. Fear rose above the pain in her head as clarity came back to her. She looked down and saw the blinking lights of a medical cuff wrapped around an arm. *My God, what has he done to me?*

The sound of drawers and cabinets rapidly opening and closing pulled her attention. In the glow of the desk lamp, Ann could see her captor bent over the workstation, his back towards her, rummaging through drawers with impatient hands. On the wall above the desk, the map of the city hung as before. The man turned and searched through another drawer. Ann drew in a sharp breath. The tip of his nose had been sliced away, leaving a glistening, bloody hole. Cartilage shone white in the fresh wound.

The man looked up and met Ann's eye. His brown hair was shaved short. A plain work shirt rolled to the elbows and rough-spun trousers covered the lanky build of a teenager, but the hardness in his face told his age to be a few summers past twenty. He took a breath as if to steady himself before moving to another drawer at the opposite end of the table just past Ann's feet.

"You'll have to forgive me. I'm not as prepared as I'd like to be." A slight shuffle in his step drew Ann's eye to the bloody bandage wrapped around his thigh. "I knew I dropped one of my anchors but didn't realize I'd dropped it so close to home." The anger in his voice thrummed just below the surface like a cable ready to snap.

He pulled a pair of scissors from the drawer. Ann

choked on the fear building in the back of her throat. The man glanced at the scissors in his hand and his mouth twisted into a grin that dimpled his cheek. "Oh, these aren't for you, Lieutenant Chapman. They're for your dress. I have to cut it." The man started at the hem and slowly cut in a straight line up the front of her dress. "The others were wearing those crew uniforms with the zippers in the front. Very handy."

The scissors reached her bodice and jammed. The man struggled, opening and closing the blades, but the fabric refused to cut. In a burst of rage, he threw the scissors across the room, gripped the folds of the fabric with both hands, and ripped the dress up the center to the neckline. Ann lay exposed and trembling.

The man clenched his fists, breathing hard. Eyes burned black with hatred as they swept over her curves, naked except for her black brassiere and panties. Ann's face burned.

The man exhaled and the rage sunk back beneath the surface. He pulled a surgical tray forward. Instruments laid out in neat rows reflected the light. "I'm going to have to improvise a bit." His frown pushed his bottom lip into a pout as he fingered the grip of a handsaw. "Thanks to your brother, I don't have my sword anymore." The man leaned forward and pointed to the dark hole in his face where his nose used to be. "The Montressador gave me this, but I paid him back a portion when I left him in the Wilds. I'm going to pay you the other half. I'm sure he's bled out by now."

Ann's heart froze. Grief tore through her. *No. Please, not Sean...* Memories filled her head of the crewmembers from the *What Cheer* lying gutted in a medical tent, and now Sean's body lay somewhere in the Wilds. Ann moaned in anguish.

Her captor's mouth slipped into another grin at the sight of her tears. "Sorry...no sword for you. We'll just have to muddle through this together."

Ann shouted obscenities through the gag in her mouth. She would tear the flesh from his bones if she could only break free. Her head swam. The room spun out of focus as she fought to pull air into her lungs. Ann let her head fall back, gasping. The cold in her legs and lower back had crept to her chest. Icy fingers played across her ribs and arms. Everything below her waist was numb, ghosted out of existence. She panted a few shallow breaths, and the room came back into focus.

The man stared down at her, showing no concern for her rage or tears. He tapped the medical cuff strapped to her arm and turned to the tray of instruments. "I was five-years old when my father died. My stepfather taught me the rules of time jumping. Rules that meant my father—my real father—would never be saved." Anger twisted his features as he arranged the instruments on the tray. "And then my mother died, and my asshole stepfather who could have gone back in time to save her did nothing. *Rules.*" He spat the word like poison from his mouth. "He was a hypocrite. Time jumpers break the biggest rule of all, and nature is turned inside out. Just as you will be soon."

The man selected a scalpel from the tray and drew it across Ann's stomach. She gasped as the blade cut deep, the numbing cold a barrier to the sting of the blade. Blood oozed down her side and pooled under her hand. Ann shivered. She closed her eyes and prayed oblivion would pull her under before her killer cradled her intestines in his hands.

"Brother Connor."

A familiar voice came from the shadows. Ann's eyes flew open. Her captor held the razor edge of the scalpel to her throat. The pressure of the blade caused a trickle of blood to roll down the side of her neck.

Connor's gaze swept the shadows. "Who's there?"

"A friend."

Ann's eyes grew round as Agent Drake stepped into the light. Drake held up a gold coin and tossed it. Connor caught the coin in one hand and examined it between bloody fingers. Satisfied, he lifted the scalpel from her neck. Ann trembled with relief.

Drake cast a quick glance in her direction and turned to Connor. "The Reverend sent me. You've done well, Brother. Your faithfulness has brought the Luctari closer to our redemption."

Ann's mind lurched. *A Ministry agent working with the Luctari?* The hope she felt a moment ago shattered.

Connor frowned. "Why are you here?" Suspicion colored his words.

"It's too dangerous for you to stay in the city. You need to leave."

"The time jumpers are *here*." Anger worked Connor's jaw. "I need to hunt them *here*."

"You hunted the crew of the *What Cheer*, you can hunt time jumpers anywhere," the agent said as he pulled a letter from an inside coat pocket. Connor opened his mouth to argue, but Drake pressed. "You're too important to us. The Luctari will carry on with your work here in the city. The Reverend has a different task for you. He sent me to give you this."

Connor ripped the letter from Drake's outstretched hand. His eyes devoured the words on the page.

Drake caught Ann's gaze and gestured for patience with a flick of a hand.

Ann's eyes widened. *He's faking?* Hope sparked within her. With every ounce of effort, she lifted a finger from the table and pointed to the desk.

Connor read the letter, his face skeptical, but then glowed with pride. "Brink says he's going to make me a prophet."

Drake's eyes followed to where Ann pointed and turned to study the map above the desk. "On the Day of Redemption, you'll stand next to the Reverend himself." The agent unpinned the map from the wall and selected a few vials from the rack. He turned and met Ann's eye briefly before handing the folded map and vials to Connor. "The Ministry is getting close. You need to leave. Now."

Connor hesitated and glanced at the comm and

nanobot replicator on the desk. "My equipment..."

"Will be brought to you."

Connor gestured to Ann. "And her?"

"I'll take care of it." Drake's eyes narrowed. "Brother, it's time."

Connor took a quick glance at the map, chose a vial, and slipped the remaining vials into a pocket. Ann watched as Connor popped the stopper with a thumb and downed the liquid in two gulps.

Drake smiled and took a slow step back. "Safe travels, Brother. We'll meet again on the other side."

Connor clenched his fists and jaw as the Splice began to take effect. A shade of doubt then pain crisscrossed his features. He locked eyes with Drake. The crescendo from a time distortion crashed Ann's senses. Multiple discordant notes blared, growing in intensity until she thought her head would burst. Connor's face twisted in agony. Fear lit his eyes. The scream from his mouth turned into a gurgle as his body ripped apart, pulled into a half dozen space-time distortions. The sound of a bedsheet tearing in half echoed as blood and gore rained onto the stone floor where Connor once stood.

Ann squeezed her eyes shut. The sound of Connor's scream played in her head.

"I'm sorry you had to see that."

Ann looked up with grateful eyes as Drake tapped the medical cuff on her arm.

Icy fingers spread across her ribs to her throat. Ann tried to take a breath. The numbness in her chest tightened. She looked at the agent with panicked eyes. Drake's face blurred in the fading light. Darkness feathered her vision.

The slam of a metal door echoed from far away followed by the sound of running feet.

"MINISTRY OF INVESTIGATIONS! GET ON THE GROUND! NOW!"

Fionna…

Ann felt Drake's fingers on the medical cuff again. The cold faded from her chest. Air slammed into her lungs.

Drake shouted, "Down here! We need a medical transport!"

Ann drifted between light and dark. Hands fumbled the straps on the back of her head. Fionna's face shone above her.

"Oh my God! Ann! Hang on! We've got you!"

Her thoughts spun.

John's face at the end of a tunnel.

Sean's body lying in the Wilds.

Oblivion rushed in.

THIRTY-ONE

SHADOWS

Mumbled words slid past Ann's ears in half whispers as she drifted in the hazy black. The air thrummed. Connor's face pressed in like a thunderhead, the dark hole above his mouth red with blood. Steel flashed in his hand and a blade sunk deep into her belly, slicing her from hip to hip. She screamed her throat raw. Connor ripped the wound wider, thrust his hands inside, and pulled.

Ann awoke to a pillow buzzing against her cheek. The soothing blue walls of a hospital trauma room and the scent of lavender on the sheets dispelled the nightmare. She breathed in the dusky scent and gripped the pillow tighter. The touch of Connor's hands on her body faded. The comfort pillow vibrated three more short bursts and then fell silent.

She rolled to her back and winced at the pull of a bandage across her stomach. Ann cupped a hand over the dressing. The slash from Connor's knife was tender, but not painful thanks to whatever pain meds she was sure pumped through her veins. Ann sighed. She felt like a doll that had all its stuffing pulled out.

A deep snore rattled the room. Ann looked to the other side of the bed and her heart nearly burst with joy. Sean slept in a guest chair, head tilted back, mouth open. His hair stuck out in all directions like he'd battled a whirlwind and lost. A blue brace cradled his left arm and shoulder. The hem of Sean's hospital gown barely reached his knees, and in his slumber, his bare legs had splayed apart at an angle that would have given a start to any visitors entering the room. His sword and belt rested in his lap. Tears filled Ann's eyes. The breath hitched in her throat. Never had she seen a more wonderful sight.

Sean stirred. He rubbed his face then focused sleepy eyes on Ann. His mouth slipped into an easy grin as he moved to the edge of the bed.

"Hey, roomie. I was wondering when you'd finally wake up." His eyes softened at the sight of her tears. "Hey...easy now...it's all right."

The flood opened as Sean pulled her into an embrace. Ann buried her face in her brother's chest and sobbed.

Ann sat at the edge of the fishpond and sprinkled food pellets into the water. Brightly colored fish darted through the murk. Dark mouths broke the surface of the water to feed.

She leaned back with a sigh. "How much longer am I supposed to do this?" A med tech had led her down the steps through the hospital gardens to the pond, handed her a pellet can with scant instruc-

SARA JUDSON BROWN

tions, and left.

Sarolea looked up from her spot from across the pond and chucked another pellet into the water. Fins splashed. "Until the fish food is gone." Her mouth twitched at the look on Ann's face. "It's supposed to be soothing. Part of the therapy."

Ann grumbled and shook more pellets from the can. Soothing felt a lot like boring. The languid pace of hospital life the last few days had left her restless to the point of irritation. She readied another handful of pellets then hesitated as a wicked thought entered her head. She tossed the handful and then upended the can, dumping the remaining food pellets into the pond. The water erupted as swarms of fish surged.

Sarolea shrugged and emptied her own pellet can. Water boiled with orange and yellow fins. Fish leaped from the water, landing on the walking path next to the pond. Sarolea and Ann shrieked and raced to scoop up the fish and toss them back into the water just as John and Fionna stepped from around a hedgerow.

John narrowed his eyes at the chaos and grinned as he set a wicker basket on the table. "I thought feeding fish was supposed to be relaxing?"

Ann collapsed into a chair, breathless with laughter, arms across her stomach. "It was...and then it got boring."

"And then Anaya made it less boring." Sarolea laughed as she juggled another slippery fish and tossed it back into the pond.

Fionna took a seat at the table. "Well, if you're done feeding fish, we can eat." She gestured to the basket. "I think Mrs. Beaumont packed half of the pantry of Siren's Cove in there."

A shade passed over Sarolea's face as she wiped her hands on her pants. "I should get going."

Ann frowned in disappointment. "Stay and eat with us."

"I can't...I..." Sarolea fidgeted then glanced toward Fionna. "Look, I know why Agent Knox is here."

"Sarolea—"

"You're going to talk about *him*...and I...I just can't."

"It's all right, Lieutenant." Fionna smiled in sympathy. "I understand."

"Take a sandwich with you at least," John said as he reached into the basket and tossed her a package wrapped in brown paper.

Sarolea caught the sandwich one-handed, flashed an apologetic smile to Ann, and disappeared down a garden path.

Ann watched her friend leave. Sarolea hadn't spoken about what had happened to the crew of the *What Cheer* since the interview with Agent Drake. In so many ways, Sarolea was the same person Ann had always known and yet Connor had taken so much from her. *From both of us.*

John took a seat next to Ann, twisted the cap off a bottle of lemonade, and poured a round.

Ann unwrapped a sandwich and stared hard at Fionna before taking a bite. "I'm not Sarolea." She muttered around a mouthful of meat and cheese. "I want to know who he was. I want to know everything."

John traded looks with Fionna and put his sandwich down. "Jessup Connor." He growled through the name, not bothering to hide his anger. "He was Commander Garin's stepson."

The sandwich in Ann's mouth turned to gravel. She suppressed a shudder and squeezed her eyes shut. She would carry that name inside her long after her scar faded. Images from the nightmare returned. Ann felt John take her hand under the table. The strength in his grip steadied her and then her own strength rose to meet his. The black memories faded. Ann opened her eyes. She hadn't flown apart. Everything was as before.

Ann took a sip of lemonade before she spoke and was relieved when her voice didn't shake. "Connor told me his stepfather was a time jumper. He was mad Garin wouldn't break the rules to save his mother when she died."

Fionna nodded. "Odessa Garin traveled off-world and was killed in a shuttle accident eight years ago. I checked with Garin's family. The commander and Connor haven't had much of a relationship since. I looked at the rejection letter list again and Connor's name was on the list from two years ago. Garin must have written the personal note on his rejection letter but didn't tell his staff."

Ann narrowed her eyes in thought. "Connor must have thought he could do what Garin wouldn't.

He wanted to become a time jumper to save his mother."

"Luckily, his psych eval saw through him," John said, wiping his mouth on a napkin.

Fionna looked thoughtful as she studied her glass on the table. "We think Connor got involved with the Luctari after his rejection letter. He took Reverend Brink's teaching and used it to justify hunting and murdering time jumpers. He stole Syrovar's sword because he saw himself as an avenging angel of sorts. He'd already planned to abduct and murder the crew of the *What Cheer* when he sent the bottle of whiskey with the quote to Garin."

"Brink has denied any personal knowledge of Connor," John said. "Claims he was not Luctari. At most, he admits that a few of his followers told him a Watcher matching Connor's description was spotted at some of the Luctari's public rallies." John took another bite of his sandwich.

Ann scoffed. "And we trust Brink? Sean told me Connor was wearing a chicken mask when they fought in the woods. That means he was acting as Luctari security."

Fionna nodded and blew out a sigh. "Circumstantial. I interviewed Brink myself and didn't sense any deception from him. Brink claims anyone could have bought and worn a mask. He's not wrong on that point. We don't have any definitive link to the Luctari."

"What about Felicity?" Ann looked across the table. "We know she helped plant the directional anchors and the necklace."

"Felicity said that Brink knew nothing about it." Fionna shrugged. "Connor developed the Splice recipe, convinced his friend Otis Mingo to manufacture it, and talked her into planting the directional anchors. She also showed us evidence in his lair that proves he sabotaged the water tanks with nanobots at Hautwesel Hall before a large time jumper gala about six months ago. Very exclusive guest list. Lots of time jumpers and ministry brass. I confirmed with Garin's staff that he attended, which explains how he was exposed to the nanobots. It was bad luck that Mirina had a lot of the same people on her guest list. Connor added Splice to the Hall's water tanks right before the wedding. The *What Cheer* was sabotaged about a month before the crew disappeared."

Ann straightened in her chair. "But I haven't been to Hautwesel Hall in over a year. I was only exposed to Splice at the wedding. How did I get infected with nanobots?"

"The water bottle you brought home," John said. "You told me you got it from Sarolea. I asked Dr. Brainard to test it. It had nanobots embedded inside the bottle's lining. All you had to do was drink from it."

"I'm guessing the water bottle was an early attempt to abduct one of the crew members," Fionna said. "Sarolea kept the bottle in her stash too long, so Connor came up with the more ambitious plan of sabotaging the water tanks and abducting the crew all at once."

Ann's arms and legs suddenly crawled with the sensation of tiny feet marching across her skin. She fought the urge to scratch. "The nanobots...are they still...?"

Fionna gave her a reassuring smile. "Kegler and Dr. Brainard figured out a way to detect and flush them out. Everyone who was infected is now in the clear, but the Ministry has quietly asked the medical community to keep an eye out just in case we missed anyone."

Ann sighed with relief and picked up her sandwich. "What happened to the other wedding guests? Are they all right?"

"You were one of the lucky ones," John said. A shadow passed over his face that Ann had not seen for some time. John muttered, "The Ministry hasn't been able to locate all the victims' remains yet."

A twist of cold tightened Ann's gut. She winced as she remembered her own experience and how close she'd come to being embedded in the pump station machinery. "Sean told me about Ira and the lice. Is it true? Is Cox's Conundrum down?"

John swallowed a slug of lemonade before answering. "Andarrian Intelligence checked into it. Cox isn't down but something weird did happen." John poured himself some more lemonade and topped off the other two glasses. "I spoke to A.K. The higher-ups added this new form of Splice to their list of contraband. We were already going after the directional anchors so it will be easy enough to add to our watch list."

"Here's hoping the hiccup with Cox was just a fluke," Fionna took another bite and chewed thoughtfully for a moment and swallowed. "There's one more thing we need to discuss. I haven't even reported it to my superiors at the Ministry yet." Fionna's eyes flicked to Ann and then to John. "I wanted to wait and talk to you both together. I had a chance to review Garin's mortality reports. I think he was on to something."

John's cheek bulged as he muttered around a bite of sandwich. "What mortality reports?"

"Commander Garin was worried there'd been an increase in time jumper deaths over the last five years," Ann said. "He thought it was a lack of training or equipment."

"Except it wasn't." Fionna put her sandwich down and wiped her hands. "Before Commander Garin retired, he started quietly looking into a few of the mission fatalities. He labeled many of the deaths suspicious." Fionna looked at Ann. "Your accident with the *Kairos* was one of them."

Ann's blood ran cold. *What if...?* Her eyes widened as she stared back at Fionna. "Sabotage."

John gulped down a bite of sandwich and raised his eyebrows in surprise.

"I've had this horrible feeling for months." Ann's voice shook. She took a sip of lemonade, her mouth suddenly as dry as dust. "I had a thought right before everything went wrong with the *Kairos*. 'What if...?' But I couldn't put my finger on what it was." She drew in a shuddering breath. "What if it was sabotage? That's what I was thinking right before the accident, but I didn't have time to try and figure it out. I was too busy trying not to die."

John looked at her, his face grim. "You never told me."

A pang of guilt struck Ann in her chest, remembering their earlier conversation. "I did tell you. I think it was what was causing my anxiety about flying again."

"Your panic attacks in the simulator?" Fionna asked.

Ann nodded. "It was part of it. I can see that now." She looked back to John. "I would've told you more, but I couldn't put it into words."

John eyes wavered. He nodded and blew out a breath, gripping her hand under the table.

Fionna nodded. "Garin couldn't prove it but based on his notes he suspected sabotage too, but the *Kairos* wasn't the only one he was looking into. By my count, he flagged twenty incidents."

"But you're talking a wide-scale conspiracy," John said. "The number of people that would need to be involved on the inside—"

"That's why I haven't reported it yet. I'm not sure who Garin shared his notes with at Special Forces."

Professor Huxley's warning came back to Ann. "Could this be connected to what Huxley told me about with my First Law violation review?"

Fionna looked to Ann. "I don't know. When you were found alive, the committee seemed eager enough to blame you for the accident. If you were dead or serving time in a penal colony, either way, you wouldn't be a time jumper anymore. Someone could still be trying to remove you." The agent sighed and looked at them from across the table. "This is too big for the Ministry to investigate alone. I'm not sure we've ever investigated an entire division before. Things could turn political real fast. The Ministry has the original mortality reports, but not Garin's personal notes." Fionna reached into a pocket and turned to John. "Captain, would you be willing to hold on to a copy for a little while? Just until I do some digging and then take them to Agent Max if I run into interference?" She held out a black data stick.

John blinked in surprise then a sly grin spread across his face. "Agent Knox, are you withholding evidence from your own division?"

Ann studied the agent, remembering her paper notebook. "I've seen her do it before. With Agent Drake."

"I'm not withholding evidence," Fionna said. Light danced in her eyes that betrayed the peaceful smile curling the corners of her mouth. "It's just a tactical delay."

"You would've made a good intelligence agent," John said as he pocketed the data stick.

Thoughts tumbled through Ann's head as she looked at Fionna. "How much do you trust Agent Drake?"

Fionna shrugged. "Setting aside his personality flaws, I trust him as much as I would any agent.

Why?"

The ghost of Connor's knife cut across Ann's skin. She pushed the feeling aside and took a deep breath. "There was a moment when I was on Connor's table. I couldn't tell if Drake was lying to Connor or lying to me. And then after Connor was killed. Drake didn't do anything to help me right away."

John's hand found hers under the table again. "You'd lost a lot of blood...maybe you're remembering things wrong?"

Ann shook her head. "Drake did something to the medical cuff on my arm. I couldn't breathe. It wasn't until you and the other agents showed up that Drake fixed it so I could breathe again. I heard him yell for a medical transport. I don't remember what happened next."

Fionna looked at Ann, eyes full of compassion. "Drake mentioned in his report that due to his inexperience with the medical cuff he may have dialed it the wrong way at first. He corrected it as soon as he realized what he did."

"He didn't take off my gag. He didn't try to stop the bleeding." Ann swallowed to keep her voice from shaking.

John blinked in surprise. "Ann, Drake had already removed your gag and was packing your wounds when we came around the corner." He frowned and spread his hands in disbelief. "I know you have good reason to not like the man, but—"

"I'm talking about before you got there," Ann said, shooting John a dark look. "He didn't do any of those things until after he knew the other agents had arrived." She turned to Fionna. "You said yourself Drake's complicated. That you can't always read his intentions."

"I also told you that I could sense Drake wanted to solve the case quickly and avoid having more victims."

"All right." Ann crossed her arms and leaned on the table. "Then how did Drake get to Connor first and why was he alone?"

"We had our hands full with abduction victims," Fionna said, nodding to John. "Drake interviewed Felicity. She told him that Connor shot your brother and that he was hiding in the old water pumping stations under the National Mall. Drake split up his team to cover more ground faster. It was luck that he got to you first."

"But the way he talked to Connor," Ann looked at Fionna and then to John. *Why couldn't they see it?* "It was like he was one of the Luctari. Drake gave Connor a coin as proof that Brink sent him."

"It was all an act. I've had to do it myself. You did it with Moondarra." John crumpled his sandwich paper into a ball and tossed it back into the picnic basket. "Felicity gave Drake the coin and told him to use it. She said it was a way for Luctari members to recognize each other when they weren't in camp."

Ann looked back to Fionna. "But why would Felicity turn herself in? Why would she want to help Drake unless he was already working for the Luctari?"

"Because she's pregnant," Fionna said.

Ann drew back in surprise.

"Felicity wanted out," Fionna said. "For her baby's sake. And because your brother saved her life—in a rather dramatic fashion from what I hear. Connor beat her up pretty badly when she tried to leave him. She wanted to get back at him." Fionna gave a hopeless shrug at the look of disbelief on Ann's face. "It's the only explanation I have. Felicity admits to being involved with the sword theft, but she says it wasn't until later when she found out about the murders. When she realized what Connor was planning for the wedding, she tried to leave. Connor would have killed her if your brother hadn't stopped him. She also gave a statement that Lieutenant Stravage didn't know anything about what the necklace was and that she used him to plant it with Lieutenant Picquet."

Ann blinked. "So, Drake never pressed charges against Kel?"

"All charges were dropped. Only a side note in Stravage's permanent record which shows Drake can be reasonable when he wants to be." Fionna checked the timepiece on her wrist. "I need to go. I'm meeting with your brother at the Padome's quarters."

"I heard a rumor that there's big news expected from the Padome any day now," John said as he stood to pack up the picnic basket. "Is it true?"

"You've been spending too much time with Intelligence officers, Captain Galeas," Fionna said with a smile as she gathered her things. "I'll be in touch."

She followed the path back through the hospital grounds, disappearing behind a hedge row.

Ann tore pieces of bread from the remains of her sandwich and tossed them into the fishpond. She watched the fish nibble at the floating crust. Everything Fionna had said about Agent Drake had seemed reasonable and yet Ann couldn't shake the feeling she was wrong. The touch of John's hand on her shoulder made her jump.

"Hey, I was talking to you." John's eyes crinkled with concern. "I'm staying at your brother's tonight. We'll head home tomorrow as soon as Colonel Wick clears you to travel."

Ann nodded and looked back toward the fishpond. "It'll be good to go home."

John took a seat on the bench and tossed a piece of crust into the water. "How are you holding up?"

"I'm fine."

Ann heard John sigh and turned to find him looking at her. The pain and worry etched across his face were as clear as the noonday sun.

John swept the bangs from his forehead. A shadow passed over his features again, lingering in his eyes. "After you were taken...more than two hundred people were missing...and then they started reappearing. Reports of bodies came from all over the city." He exhaled a deep breath. "I looked for you in every mangled corpse. There's only been one other time in my life when I felt that helpless." John rested his elbows on his knees and stared at the fishpond. "So, if you asked me how *I'm* doing I'd say I'm not fine. I'm a little shaky."

Ann slid across the bench to sit next to him, taking his hand in hers. John put an arm around her and pulled her tight to his side.

"I'm sorry." Ann rested her head against his shoulder and whispered, "I'm not falling apart...but I know I'm not fine. I feel..." She struggled for the right words. "...strange. Like Connor managed to turn me inside out after all. I don't know how to make that feeling go away."

John lifted Ann's chin and looked into her eyes. "Keep talking about it. Don't bury it. And then one day you start to feel better than fine."

Ann nodded, remembering Dr. Brainard's advice. "While we're being honest...I wanted to talk to you about Bonnie's pocket watch. I don't like it." John's brows shot up in surprise. He opened his mouth to reply. "And it's not because it was Bonnie's. I just can't look at those hands tick back and forth and wonder how your mission is going. If you're not coming home, I don't want to find out from a blank watch face."

"All right then." John tugged his pigtail in thought. "Mrs. Beaumont can hold on to the watch for us. She'll need to use it anyway if we're both gone." He finished packing the basket and set it next to his feet. "When you're feeling stronger...A.K. wants to talk to you about something."

Ann gave John a quizzical look.

He tugged at the pigtail at the back of his head. "A.K.'s decided to take a step back from fieldwork to a more supervisory role. He needs to assign me a new permanent partner. The job is yours if you—"

"Yes."

He gave her a hard look. "Are you sure? I'll understand if you don't." His mouth slipped into a grin. "A.K. will tell you I can be a bastard to work with sometimes."

"I know all about you being a bastard." Ann smirked and cast John a sideways glance and was rewarded with his chuckle. "I still want the job." Doubt crept in as soon as the words had left her mouth. *I need to be honest with him.* "But I'm not ready. Not yet. And I don't know when I will be. I still can't fly, I haven't been fully reinstated yet, and I'm not sure if or when I'll freeze up again."

"Did you freeze up at the wedding?"

"Not exactly," Ann said. "Maybe a little when the crowd knocked you down. I snapped out of it faster that time."

"That's progress," John said, nodding encouragement. "We'll work on it. You have plenty of time. A.K. waited ten years for me." He stood and picked up the basket.

Ann took John's arm as they walked the garden path back to the hospital. "But what if you're assigned a mission before I'm ready?"

"If I need a partner, they'll assign me a substitute," John said. "And there's always Port."

Ann frowned. "I don't like the idea of you working with a substitute."

His mouth slipped into another easy grin. "Then

we've got some work to do."

THIRTY-TWO

MONTRESSADOR LIVONIA SYROVAR, THE DOGE OF ERNA

Bright lights from news drones filled Syrovar's gallery. The drones buzzed and jostled for position in the crowded airspace, each trying to get the best angle to record the interview. A scrum of news service reporters below shouted questions at the Padome and jotted notes on their data link pads.

Sean watched from the opposite end of the gallery near a refreshment table, content to be in the background and let the Padome have their moment. Sabadell took it all in stride while the other members of the council, Sean noted, seemed a little dazed in the glare of the lights. He tugged at the collar of his dress uniform jacket. The arm brace he wore since being discharged from the hospital cut into the side of his neck. Thankfully, the bullet Connor fired hadn't hit his sword arm or caused any permanent damage to his shoulder. Except for a persistent ache, that the doctors assured him would fade over time, and not being able to rest his left hand on the hilt of his sword, which he was in the habit of doing, his recovery had been uneventful.

Gimirri stepped to Sean's side. His blue cassock looked freshly pressed for the occasion. "Congratulations, Montressador. This is quite an achievement."

"The Padome were the ones who figured it out," Sean said, nodding in the council's direction. "I had no idea they even solved the mystery until I read their final report while I was still in the hospital."

"Perhaps, but you were the one who set everything in motion. You asked the right question."

Sean started to respond with a half-shrug and pulled a face when pain gripped his shoulder like the twist of a knife. Immediately, the snap of a camera lens sounded from above. He looked up in time to see a news drone that had been circulating above the gallery fly off. Sean scowled. *Great.*

He turned his attention back to Gimirri. "All I said was that I wanted to know why Syrovar committed the murders. I asked Sabadell if the council could do it. I wasn't sure if they could."

Gimirri studied him from the corner of an eye. "Sometimes people surprise you."

With the group photos done, the Padome stepped aside to allow the museum maintenance crew to take down the curtain that once covered Syrovar's portrait. The news drones recorded the moment the curtain dropped to the floor and the maintenance crew unbolted the metal curtain rod from the wall.

A female reporter wearing a teal blue suit pushed

to the front of the group. "Sabadell, what would you say was the big break that helped you solve Syrovar's mystery?"

The old man's thin gray mustache stretched with his smile. "I would have to say it was Helda's and Lydian's discovery of the midwife's letter."

Reporters and drones converged on the two council members. Lydian swallowed and blinked in the glare of the drones' lights. "The letter was a deathbed confession fifty years after Montressador Syrovar's execution. The woman claimed that during an outbreak of Gall Fever midwives in Erna practiced infant swapping."

"Infant swapping?" A man with an owl-like face spoke. "Is that what I think it is?"

Lydian opened his mouth to reply but Helda was faster.

"An unfortunate but not uncommon practice for the time period. If an infant born to a wealthy family died, the midwife would be paid to bring a replacement child and pay off the baby's mother." Helda sighed. "Sadly, there's never a shortage of illegitimate or unwanted children."

A reporter's voice rang from the middle of the pool. "But how does Syrovar's parentage connect to the murders of the noblemen?"

Helda leaned forward to address the questioner, but Lydian snapped, "I was getting to that!"

Sabadell cleared his throat and gave Lydian a warning look.

Lydian relaxed his shoulders and bolted a patient

smile on his face before turning back to the reporters. "The woman said in the letter that she apprenticed to a midwife named Midge Odo who told her to take an infant girl to the Syrovar's home. The letter claimed that Lord Gilyard Syrovar and Lady Odette's true daughter had died from Gall Fever at six months of age and that the infant taken to the Syrovars that night was the illegitimate daughter of King Haakon."

The pool of reporters erupted with a fresh round of questions. Drones circled, snapping pictures.

Gimirri leaned toward Sean as they watched from across the room. "It really is remarkable after all this time. Syrovar was the daughter of the king."

"The DNA tests proved it," Sean said. "Syrovar might have been the *only* legitimate heir thanks to the queen working her way through members of the court, but it makes sense now why King Haakon appointed her straight to the Montressador's office and not to the Royal Guard. He was preparing to name Syrovar his heir."

The woman in the teal suit shouted over her colleagues, "But that still doesn't answer the question why Syrovar killed the noblemen!"

Gregor held up a hand trying to draw the attention of the crowd, his bald head reflecting the glare of the spotlights. "We were at a dead end until Aural tracked down a piece of the robe Syrovar wore to her execution." Gregor pulled the smaller man to the front. "After her beheading, the robe was cut into scraps and sold as mementos."

"W-we...we thought they were all lost," Aural stammered. He blinked behind his thick lenses. "But I was able to locate one in a private collection. The fabric had traces of blood. For the first time, we were able to extract a sample for testing."

The reporters shouted another series of questions. Sabadell waved for silence. "Your attention please! Coloma analyzed the sample. She can share with you what we found."

Coloma nodded thanks to Sabadell, took a deep breath, and turned to the group. "Syrovar's blood at the time of her death contained high doses of a hallucinogen found in a mushroom commonly known as the Red Priest. The mushrooms were plentiful in the region during the rainy season. In small doses, they cause paranoia and make the subject easily suggestible. In higher doses, they cause hallucinations and manic episodes. We believe Syrovar was poisoned by enemies of the King, tricked into killing the nobles, and then given large doses while in prison to keep her in a manic state. It would explain Syrovar's erratic behavior during her trial. It's all outlined in our report."

A voice called from the back of the group. "Sabadell, is it the council's conclusion then that Syrovar was a victim of Court politics?"

Sabadell nodded. "King Haakon's enemies killed his most ardent supporters, removed his Montressador and heir, and except for digging up a few mushrooms, never even got their hands dirty."

Sean watched as the reporters continued to shout

follow-up questions, then turned back to the refreshment table and helped himself to a breadstick.

Gimirri picked up a buffet plate and served himself some sliced fruit. "Did you know the mushrooms that poisoned Syrovar were the same ones that Montressador Fregoli the Paranoid used? He wrote in his journal he intentionally consumed small amounts of Red Priest to achieve a state of hyperawareness."

"Clever." Sean crunched the end of his breadstick. "Maybe I should give that a try?"

"I wouldn't recommend it. The poison caused a painful infection in Fregoli's testicles. He was impotent the last few years of his life."

Sean coughed on the dry bread and pivoted to a change of subject. "So...I guess you'll be busy updating Syrovar's exhibit?"

"Extremely. Taking the curtain down is only the first step," Gimirri said, picking through the fruit on his plate with a fork until finding an orange slice. "We'll be redoing the entire gallery to show a timeline of events from the Padome's report. The museum is also planning to commission a new portrait for Syrovar. The current picture no longer seems appropriate."

Sean nodded in agreement. "I'm sorry about Syrovar's sword. Can you repair it?"

"No," the museum curator sighed. "But it would be wrong to try. It was broken in battle. The sword is part of Syrovar's legacy...and now yours. Her sword will be displayed as-is and with a plaque that tells its story and of your heroism."

Sean stared at Gimirri, momentarily speechless.

The curator smiled and handed his empty plate to a passing waiter. "We have a legacy display planned for you as well. The museum has obtained the bullet that was extracted from your shoulder. You are the only Montressador to survive being shot by both a laser pistol and a ball and powder firearm."

Sean arched a brow as he considered Gimirri's words. "It hadn't occurred to me that not dying from random acts of stupidity was considered a noteworthy achievement."

"We were also given the remains of the chicken mask that Connor wore during your sword fight," Gimirri said, a wry twist in his mouth. Sean gave the curator a sour look. "Good day, Montressador." Gimirri chuckled and crossed the room where a reporter approached him.

Sean's mood lifted when he saw Fionna step through the gallery doors, smile, and walk toward him.

"So have you thought of a name for your sword yet?" Fionna's bio-vision glasses rested on top of her blond bobbed head.

Sean scoffed and finished his breadstick. "No."

"I thought you said that most Montressadors named their sword after a major event in their career?" Fionna gestured to the gaggle of reporters still hounding the Padome with questions. "This is pretty major."

Sean tugged at his arm brace. "My blade had nothing to do with any of this except for breaking Syrovar's sword which wasn't particularly useful."

"Not true." Fionna grabbed a buffet plate and filled it with a few morsels. "If you hadn't challenged Connor and rescued Felicity, she never would have reported him to the Ministry. You also injured him when you sliced off the end of his nose. Made it much easier for Drake and Ann to identify him and confirm Felicity's story." She turned and munched a carrot stick. "Speaking of useful...I wanted to make you an offer." She held the buffet plate out to him.

Sean pinched an olive from the plate and popped it into his mouth with a smile. "Is it of a *personal* nature?"

Fionna's smile widened. "I would like to make your consultant role a permanent one...as one of my investigators. I promise it won't interfere with your duties as Montressador."

Sean tilted his head back and laughed. He heard the snap of a camera lens and was irritated to see the damn news drone fly off again. He looked to Fionna. Her smile was as peaceful as a monk's. Sean blinked. "You're serious?"

"You have good instincts. You were very helpful with this case."

Sean shook his head in disbelief. "You want to give a junior investigator badge to the guy whose only legacy is a chicken mask and stopping bullets with his body?"

"You interviewed the Luctari and spotted the directional anchor on the security footage. You also figured out the connection with Ira," Fionna said, picking up another carrot stick. "Kegler ran a toxicology test on Ira when we brought him in for questioning. It turns out, he and his friends were taking Splice. A *lot* of Splice," she quickly added with a pointed look before Sean could utter the sarcastic comment he'd been formulating. "In Ira's case, it created a localized distortion that caused him to phase." She took a bite of carrot and offered Sean her buffet plate again.

He took a slice of cheese from Fionna's plate and considered the new information. "But if that's true how was Ira able to travel without using an anchor?"

Fionna cringed. "We're still trying to figure that out. I still think the residual charge from the discarded anchor under the pedestal might have had something to do with it. Technically, Ira didn't travel anywhere – he just phased so that he was simultaneously present on multiple planes of existence."

"A neat trick," Sean said, polishing off another slice of cheese. His eyes widened as the information in his brain clicked. "Like Sarolea's Ghost Arm?"

Fionna nodded and finished chewing a bite of carrot. "Ira was ingesting ten times the amount of Splice compared to what the others were taking combined. Anything's possible." She looked at him, a glint in her eyes. "But you're asking questions and that's the first thing I like to see with my investigators."

"I'm still a swordsman," Sean said, gesturing impatiently to the blade on his hip. "Not an investigator. It would make more sense for me to be a museum security guard. I'd have a better chance of blending in with the exhibits."

"You're thinking about this all wrong." Fionna pressed. "Like I said before, the Montressador's office retains some authority when it comes to the law. Did you know Montressador Jabiru the Mute assisted local law enforcement with the apprehension of a horse thief in the port city of Garff? I looked it up."

"That was nine hundred years ago," Sean said. "You're going out on a limb and you're going to hang me right next to that horse thief."

Fionna's expression grew more serious. "Montressador, I need investigators I can trust. When I report what I found out in Garin's personal notes, everything is going to change." She leaned in and whispered, "There's something else going on, and the Ministry is going to need all the help it can get." Fionna patted his arm and turned to leave. "Think about it."

Sean watched Fionna as she crossed the room. Her touch on his arm sent his emotions into orbit for a second before he could ground himself again. He was glad the agent hadn't been wearing her biovision glasses.

The group standing in front of Syrovar's portrait had finally moved off. Sean moved closer and admired Livonia Syrovar's image. He wondered how different the new portrait would be.

Sean looked down at the hilt of his sword and muttered the name, "Livonia…?" trying the name on for size. He looked back up at the portrait. His mouth slanted in a thoughtful grin.

"Maybe."

ABOUT THE AUTHOR

Sara Judson Brown

Sara Judson Brown lives near St. Cloud, Minnesota, (yes, it is as cold here as you imagine) with her husband, two children, and her dog. She worked as a freelance writer for several years slinging copy for magazines, blogs, corporate communications, and marketing clients, but it wasn't until 2009 when she decided to start writing her own stories.

When she's not writing about freighter pirates and time jumpers, she likes to spend time with her family or hang out at the St. Cloud Public Library. Sara is a graduate of Drake University in Des Moines, Iowa. Her debut novel SIREN'S COVE from her Perigalacticon Series published in January 2021.
Connect Online:
www.facebook.com/SaraJudsonBrown
sarajudsonbrownauthor.wordpress.com

BOOKS IN THIS SERIES

THE PERIGALACTICON SERIES

The Perigalacticon Series is a sci-fi/fantasy adventure set in the Andarrian universe and its territory the Colonies. Andarria is separated from the rest of the universe by an ancient time quake – some say divine judgment - and cursed to serve as the stewards of time. The Colonies is a top ten tourist destination with a thriving intergalactic trade. The series focuses on the adventures of a recurring cast of characters featuring time jumpers, pirates, and space travel.

Siren's Cove (Book 1)

Splice (Book 2)